TREMBLING SURRENDER

As she handed Simon his wine, he looked full into her eyes, set the untasted wine down, and ran a questing finger up her arm as he pushed the lace aside.

Carlotta tried to pull away but his touch held her as it traced warmth up to her shoulder. He put the other hand on her neck and tilted her head to his, then the questing lips came down on hers. They touched, moved, at first in gentleness. Then he swept her to him, her slenderness molded to his strength, his arms firm about her body...

Carlotta was suddenly afraid of what she was feeling with this stranger and she tried to pull back, but he held her easily, his mouth still questing and hard on hers.

This Triumphant Fire

Anne Carsley

AVON
PUBLISHERS OF BARD, CAMELOT, DISCUS AND FLARE BOOKS

THIS TRIUMPHANT FIRE is an original publication of Avon
Books. This work has never before appeared in book form.

AVON BOOKS
A division of
The Hearst Corporation
959 Eighth Avenue
New York, New York 10019

First Avon Printing, April, 1982

AVON TRADEMARK REG. U. S. PAT. OFF. AND IN
OTHER COUNTRIES, MARCA REGISTRADA, HECHO EN
U. S. A.

Printed in the U. S. A.

WFH 10 9 8 7 6 5 4 3 2 1

To William Charles who has caused the light to shine.

Mizpah.

CHAPTER ONE

The Dark Way

CARLOTTA was catapulted into wakefulness, her sobs muffled, her throat dry as she struggled to draw air into her lungs. She sat upright, damp nightgown clinging to her shivering body. The taste of blood was on her lips, and she wiped her hand across them in a swift gesture. The cloak hanging at the end of her bed seemed to hide the face of her nightmare. She fought to regain her calm, speaking the old formula of reality out loud.

"I am safe here at Barthorne House, England. It is November 6, 1804. The Revolution in France is over and we are at war with Napoleon. I have to get up and work in a few hours."

It was no use. The fragmented horror swept over her again as always. There was never any sound but she knew the marchers were there, their pikes already bloodied, as they sought her. She crouched, watching the slowly reddening sky and waiting. Then they circled her, coming to stand just beyond the circle of lifting light that showed smeared faces. Her arms and legs were weighted so that she could not move. Footsteps began approaching and the watchers parted for him. His face was in darkness; when it was revealed she would begin to die.

Carlotta knew she would not sleep again, but to think this way was unbearable. She was thankful for this little room, airless and cramped though it was, which had once held both Aunt Rosa and herself. Now it was hers alone, since her foster aunt had died over eight months ago. That loss was still deep, though she could not have wanted life prolonged in such pain.

She turned on the narrow bed and tried to put her thirst out of her mind. The day that would soon dawn would certainly be just as hard as the ones before it. They had all been the same since the daughter of the house, Lady Leticia Edmond, and her elderly husband, Sir Reginald, had arrived from Bath with a party of friends. Barthorne was one of the lesser country houses of Lord James Kilburton, her father, who was one of the King's advisors. The small household had been thrown into a frenzy by the demands made, and every member was pressed into double service. Carlotta had washed, scrubbed, turned spits,

1

and even mended some of the dresses of the visitors, a task she did badly. It was long past midnight every night when she climbed to the attic room and barely dawn when she was expected downstairs again.

A rustle in the corridor outside brought her upright again. The thought that it was probably a rat rather than an intruder was not comforting. The flames of her nightmare flickered in her mind again, and recitation of the formula did not help. She rose and paced around the room in the hope that action would help. It did not. She dreaded the idea of the journey down all those endless stairs to the bucket in the kitchen but there was really nothing else to be done. The discomfort was definitely preferable to remaining here, thinking about the past, wondering about the future, and knowing that she would finally be sleepy just when it was time to rise. Never had she been so parched; her lips were cracked and tender, her tongue a lump against her dry teeth. In the days when there were those who loved her, a cup of water stood on the table beside her bed and a candle burned all night. Unexpected tears flooded her eyes and she wiped them angrily away. She could hear Master Arnold's dry old voice saying, "To pity yourself is the most useless of feelings." The child she had been then knew it for truth; the woman did not forget.

Cautiously she opened the door, which creaked loudly in spite of her effort to prevent it, and inched out toward the stairs, which were narrow and dark at this top-level where only the lesser servants were quartered. Her bare feet made no sound on the cold stone as she felt her way down. She went this way many times a day and was surefooted in the darkness. The thin robe was no ease against the chill that remained here summer and winter, but any positive action was better than being prey to the thoughts and dreams that besieged her now as they so often did.

Finally she rounded a curve in the stairs and came to a doorway that led into the darkness of the kitchen, which was readied for the preparation of the day's meals, with pots stacked close at hand and a fire freshly laid. Water stood in buckets to one side, meat and herbs to the other. Carlotta lifted the dipper and drank eagerly, relishing each swallow and, for the first time, becoming conscious of the cold that seemed to rise around her.

She put the dipper aside and wrapped both arms around her slender body in an effort to ward off the chill. Then she heard

2

the whispering, so faint as to be part of the movements of the old house. Curiosity stirred, for she knew that none of the servants should be here at this hour and even the young boy whose duty it was to tend the fire would still be sleeping. Her lips quirked downward as she thought that possibly she had stumbled upon an assignation of some sort, one of the maids and a footman or even several of the villagers taking this chance to see the lord's house and engage in a quick dalliance. Household help had been recruited from there in this time of need, she knew. On the other hand, it might be a pair of thieves taking advantage of this opportunity to make off with plunder from the sleeping nobility, all of whom had drunk deeply.

Carlotta tiptoed across the wide length of the kitchen, past the stacked supplies, through the partially open door that lead to several storerooms, and, as the whispers lifted and became more distinct, halted beside one that was seldom used because of the extreme chill that clung there night and day. The door was ajar, and the barest light of a sheltered candle shone out. She edged closer and pressed herself against the damp stone, oblivious of the shivers that racked her.

There was a long sigh, and then a female voice said softly but quite distinctly, "Surely it must work soon. Is he immune, do you think?"

Deeper tones murmured something unintelligible to the listening girl, and she heard the rustle of clothes as the speakers moved together. Lovers, not thieves. Properly, she should retreat, but curiosity held her rooted. Knowledge was a useful thing.

The woman said, "I cannot bear his life another day; he has leeched from mine long enough."

The man spoke more loudly now, the undertone of dominance showing in his voice. "We must both be patient only a little longer. The potion is insidious but certain. It will be as I promised, and meanwhile we have this."

There was a long silence punctuated by quick breaths and then the sigh came again, followed by the woman's soft laughter. "Freedom, how good it will be!" Venom touched the words.

This was spoken in a near normal tone, and Carlotta felt the shivers rise to her hair and slide down her arms. There was no mistaking that voice, for it had been raised in imperious demands and orders for the past few days. It belonged to Lady Leticia Edmond, and Carlotta could not doubt that she plotted with her lover against her husband.

3

It all fit, the girl thought as she clung to the wall. Only yesterday there had been talk in the kitchen of how Sir Reginald, portly and rubicund, a passionate hunter despite his age, had been forced to forgo that pleasure for the day due to stomach spasms. It seemed that these were not uncommon for him and he had been put to bed, given watered wine, honey, and bread sops. Her Ladyship had been most angry when this was not immediately forthcoming, and the housekeeper had borne the brunt of it. Sir Reginald had roared, demanding to know how a man could live on such a diet. Now it seemed that he was not expected to do so.

Soft moans were coming from the room now, and Carlotta knew that there would be little plotting for the next minutes. She must make her escape and then plan what to do. She moved away from the wall as carefully as she could, determined to make no sound, but she reckoned without the effect of the cold, which had seeped into her very bones. Her bare feet and legs were stiff; the very care she took made her stumble and she fell to her knees.

The sound that resulted was very slight, a momentary bump and a quick breath as Carlotta regained her lost balance, but the response from the room was swift.

The man's voice called out sharply, "Who is there?" The candle was lifted and Carlotta saw the faint light it cast as his steps sounded on the stone. She spared a second to wonder at his temerity; he must be one whose authority would not be questioned in any section of the house. "What are you doing out there?" Now he was closer but still cautious.

She knew that she could not take the time to hide, even though she knew this area well from her times of working here. Instinct told her that she was in great danger. Sweat beaded her forehead, for it seemed that the world of her nightmare was closing in for the second time in one night. She slipped swiftly behind the nearest door and used it as a screen to slide to the next one. Fortunately the door to the stairs was open; she could see it yawning in the darkness beyond.

He was in the corridor now, the flicker of the candle coming closer. Carlotta shrank against the door, making herself as small as she could in the shadows. There was a movement of skirts and a hiss behind him and he whirled with an exclamation. The girl heard his steps as he retraced them to speak to Lady Leticia in an angry monotone. Carlotta took her chance,

4

the only one she might have, and scuttled across the space toward the stairs with all the speed of the hunted.

"Look, there she goes!" The shrill voice of Lady Leticia came, although she instantly muted it. The man was running now in response, and he did not waste breath to call out.

Carlotta dashed through the door and up the dark stairs, using both hands to guide her. She had reason to be grateful for all the time she had spent going up and down them, for she knew the curves and inclines they took as one neared the highest floor. Doors branched off into other corridors, and it was unlikely that a thorough search could be mounted before morning. Her breath came in shallow gasps and the blood drummed in her ears, but she did not stop until she had reached the steepest flight of all.

She listened as hard as she could but there was no sound in all the darkness above and below her. When her breathing slowed, she slipped up the remaining stairs, pulled the door open, and looked out at the emptiness of the hall. It was but a few steps to the welcome safety of her room, where she dropped onto the rickety bed in an exhaustion so intense that she reeled with it.

Try as she might, she could not relax. All that she had heard continued to ring in her ears. There was no turning back from it; she had heard murder plotted, no other interpretation of the words presented itself. The determination to catch the eavesdropper had been apparent. She could only thank fortune that she had escaped unscathed and unseen except as a swift running figure melting into darkness. Sighing, Carlotta turned over on her stomach and buried her face in the pillow. Sympathy welled in her for Sir Reginald, whom she did not know and had never seen, but what could be done against the will of the powerful?

There was a hammering at the door and Carlotta started up in shock. Her head ached and her whole body felt stiff. It was full light in the room now, and she knew that somehow, impossible as it seemed, she had fallen asleep. She swung her feet to the floor and called hastily, "Yes, what is it?"

The door swung wide and one of the young girls recently recruited from the village entered. She could not have been more than ten or eleven; the wide white apron and cap she wore dwarfed her, but she was full of self-importance at the message she had to deliver.

"Mistress, I am bidden to tell you that Madam the housekeeper must see you immediately. It is urgent."

5

Carlotta felt the chill of fear. What could it be? There had been no way to identify her in the dark, of that she was well nigh certain. Her voice was rough, her mouth dry as she asked, "Did she say why?"

"No. Only that you must hurry." The girl backed out and Carlotta saw the awe in the large eyes at these workings of those who served the nobility.

"What hour is it?" She knew that it was late, there was that feel to the air, and she wondered again that she could have slept so long or at all.

"Nine and after." The child threw that over her shoulder as she ran for the stairs, and Carlotta knew that she had been told not to dawdle.

Nine and she had been due in the kitchen at six! No wonder she was sought! She jumped up quickly and pulled the old brown dress of yesterday over her head, adjusted a less than white cap over her hair, which was more red than brown in the pale light of the room, and washed her face in the icy water left over from the wash of the previous day.

Minutes later she stood in the presence of Mistress Alice Holmby, called Madam by all the servants, who had come to fear and respect her redoubtable eye and sharp tongue. The anteroom to her apartment, where she viewed the nervous Carlotta, was chill and sparsely appointed, much like the person of the lady herself.

"I overslept, I cannot think how." Carlotta had meant to offer other explanations but found her voice trapped in her throat at the assessing look in Madam's eye.

"It does not matter, there are other concerns now." She peered closely at the girl, and Carlotta lifted her chin in the pride that was an integral part of her person. "You are well versed in the printed word, I am told, and have a pleasant voice for reading when you are not out of breath."

Carlotta stared in surprise and, in spite of the fear that had not ceased since her nightmare, she half smiled. "Yes, Madam, Mistress Rosa's dead brother, my foster uncle, taught me well in English and Latin."

Madam stared in her turn at the small pointed face so transformed by the smile, which seemed to travel to the curious amber eyes and upward to the curving dark brows. "And you have wielded broom and mop and duster since poor Rosa died, her wits quite gone from the pain. I knew her when she was nurse to her late Ladyship, Lady Kilburton, so long ago. Am-

bitious, she was. Wanted more for you than service, I warrant."
The musing voice ceased, and she watched Carlotta for a long
moment.

Carlotta forgot the fears she had experienced as she cried,
"It is so! I wrote a letter to Lord Kilburton after Mistress Rosa
died and thanked him for his hospitality, asking if he knew any
post I might fill as a scholar's assistant or researcher, even a
tutor. Has he decided to act upon it? It has been so long!" She
could even forget that this woman had spoken realistically to
her in the days of her sorrow, saying that hard work cured
much and that lodging was not free to those who had no call
on the family.

Madam was unsmiling, "My Lord has had more on his mind
than the foolishness of one small girl. Have you forgotten that
England is at war?" She sniffed and gave Carlotta a hard look.

Carlotta felt her spirits droop. Likely he had never even
received her letter. Well, she would not spend her life as a
servant, nor subservient to others, that much was certain. "I
have not forgotten. Will you tell me why I was summoned?"
Amber eyes challenged faded blue ones and the housekeeper's
were the first to fall.

"Sir Reginald's stomach is worse, but he will have none of
the village doctor and insists on his own being fetched from
London. Lady Leticia is most upset, I can tell you, and he is
fretful as well as bored." Madam frowned as she realized that
all this might be immediately spread about the servant's quarters. "You will hold your tongue. No idle chatter."

Carlotta felt a pang but pushed it aside. Surely the man's
own physician would be able to help him if he were indeed
being poisoned. "I do not chatter, I assure you." She had not
fit in this household, since she was neither servant, for all that
she worked as did they, nor of the gentry, and had, as a result
been isolated. It took forebearance not to inquire what there
was to chatter about.

"Sir Reginald is bored and must be amused. Lady Leticia
is quite exhausted and must rest. She has commanded that
someone be furnished to read to him or converse quietly if he
wishes it; the person must have learning yet be discreet and
demure. The matter was left in my hands, and so I thought of
you."

Carlotta bent her head. "I shall try to be satisfactory." The
strangeness of it was frightening. If she were cautious, here
might be a chance for the future. Who knew but that an old

man, ill and senile, might give commands that would free one who pleased him from the round of drudgery that life had become? In all kindness, she thought, there might be a way to warn him without giving herself away. The volatile side of her nature surged up and a flush mounted to her pale cheeks.

Madam did not see for she was turning toward the side door and clapping her hands for the little maidservant on duty there. "Go, bring the dark green cap and gown and those slippers we put away last week." She rounded to Carlotta who stood calmly now. "You certainly cannot go dressed as you are. Circumspection is expected."

"Aye, lady."

"There is one other thing. His Lordship spent much time in France before the revolution and likes to speak of it. I imagine it is too much to suppose you understand any of that gibberish?"

Carlotta's eyes flickered as the irony drove home. "The tongue was once as my own." Chills lifted on her flesh then, and she seemed to see the shadowed face of her nightmare drawing ever closer.

CHAPTER TWO

Suspicion's Mask

TIME passed slowly for Carlotta as she sat in the anteroom of Madam's apartments and waited for her summons to the bedside of Sir Reginald. She was newly dressed in the clothes hurriedly produced, but the fit was not good and a sash was, of necessity, wound around the waist of the dress. Carlotta was small and fine-boned, her breasts well developed, but clothes had never fit her well, even in the days when Aunt Rosa had tried to sew for her. Now her attire was neat and she was clean: that was enough, as Madam had pronounced.

There were no books here, nothing to busy her except her own thoughts, and the girl found them turning back to a happier time, a time she tried to school herself not to remember, for the pain was too great when she compared her memories to the life she now led.

The world of the present faded as she saw again the little village of Tofton set between the rolling hills of the countryside and near to a great wood which was said to stretch for miles. It was there that the scholar Arnold Harmon and his sister, Rosa, a spinster, had lived for years with Arnold's foster daughter, the girl Carlotta. It seemed in memory that that time was always sunlit, filled with household tasks, books, quiet conversation, discussion of the philosophers, work among the flowers and vegetables of the garden, study of the languages of the ancients, even the learning of the rudiments of medicines and the tending of wounds. Then Master Arnold had died peacefully while at his books, Mistress Rosa had fallen ill of the disease of the bone that was eventually to take her mind and kill her, and a wealthy merchant in the next town had exercised his option to buy their cottage and the small plot of land around it. There had been no place to turn except to the noble family with whom Mistress Rosa had once been in service. After what seemed months of living on sufferance with an old pupil of Master Arnold's in the village, the message had come bidding them to go to one of the country houses of the Kilburton family, Barthorne. The two were absorbed into the sparse household, which was visited at most once a year by the members of the Lord's family. Welcome there was not; tolerance, grudgingly given, there was. Carlotta tended the woman who had been as her mother and, when she died in pain beyond speaking, the girl worked where she was bidden and spent much of her time in the library, where the voices of the past could be invoked and the present forgotten.

The door opened to admit the little maidservant who had helped her dress earlier. There was a frightened look on her face and she seemed in a great rush. Carlotta stood up, thankful enough to let the past go and to become immersed in the realities of the present.

"You must come now! His Lordship is newly wakened and calls for amusement and refreshment."

"And which am I to be?" It was the sort of remark that did not endear Carlotta to the others of the household. Hastily, she added, "I am ready to attend him."

"Hurry!" The girl was already half out the door, and Carlotta wondered once more what sort of ogre Sir Reginald must be to produce this reaction in the servants. They seemed to spring to work in the presence of Lady Leticia who, in Carlotta's own estimation, was petulant and given to small cruelties.

They went out into the main portion of the house, which was furnished with elegance grown shabby over the years. Once opulent carpets now were faded, the brilliant colors dimmed to dullness. But heavy chairs and chests gleamed with polish, and paintings were newly cleaned in honor of the current residents. Tapestries covered stone walls that still dripped with the chill of early winter, and candles by the scores lit the dim rooms. Barthorne dated in large part from the reign of Henry VII, though descendants of the first Lord Kilburton had added sections and made improvements.

They went up a winding staircase, along a corridor hung with paintings of ancestors, many of which seemed inter-changeable, and paused before a heavy door which swung instantly open as they approached. The manservant who looked out was white-haired and severe in appearance, but the look he gave them was one of relief.

"His Lordship awaits."

Carlotta felt a little chill of fear which she thrust sternly back, as one hand went up to twitch nervously at the too large cap which seemed to list forward with every move she made.

"Is the wench here yet? Why am I being made to wait for

the pleasure of a servant? Charles, see to it that she is brought immediately! Damn, if my eyes would only hold out I could read myself! Damn, I say!"

The bellow was that of no sick man; it was full-throated and stentorian, the rage of an active man confined inside by a fluke of circumstance and determined to exact full penalty from those who seemed to defy him.

The man, Charles, gave Carlotta an assessing look and called, "She is only just arrived, your Lordship." He gave Carlotta a little push. "Go in, girl. Go on."

She straightened her shoulders, moved around him, and entered through the wide oak doors. The room seemed huge at first glance. Books lined the wall on one side, candles shimmered against the gray day and a leaping fire crackled in the fireplace. The huge bed was placed so that the occupant could see both the fire and the outdoor panorama of neglected gardens and wind-tossed trees. Several low couches upholstered in violet silk stood about, and two delicate caned and ornamented chairs had been pushed against the wall. A heavy, dark chair piled with cushions was placed near the richly carved bed.

But it was Sir Reginald who held Carlotta's attention so that she stared rudely. He was a massive man in his late sixties, that she had known from the servants, but she was surprised to see that his face was red, either with drinking or fury, and white hair stood in an aureole around it. There were dark pouches under piercing black eyes, and his cheeks were sunken. Carlotta had nursed Aunt Rosa long enough to know pain when she saw it. Her sharp eyes did not miss the beads of sweat on his forehead or the shaking of the heavily veined hands.

"What are you staring at, girl? God, this has to be the most forsaken of all Leticia's properties, and the servants are just as bad. Boney ought to have the lot! He'd soon think twice about fighting England. But what would the likes of you know about that, eh?" He reached for the cup by his hand and drained it with one gulp, then gave a loud belch.

Carlotta's swift tongue triumphed over the realization that something was indeed happening to this man. "I rather think, sir, that all England is acquainted with Napoleon Bonaparte and his ambitions. This backwater, as some call it, is still our country."

Sir Reginald sat upright on the many pillows piled behind him and peered at her, his expression suddenly savage and watchful. His face twitched with the effort and his thick shoulders moved convulsively.

"You are pert for a servant."

Carlotta saw the watchful look and regretted her momentary sauciness. "I beg your Lordship's pardon. I am sent to read to you if that is your pleasure."

He snorted. "I am beyond boredom, that was the only reason I thought of it. My eyes . . ." He hesitated and lifted one hand to them. "They blur. I do not know how long I can manage to listen to someone stumble over the masters of the language, however."

The wind gusted against the panes of the windows, bringing showers of raindrops, and beyond the bare trees bent before it. The air seemed to darken in spite of the well-stoked fire.

She ignored his last words and said. "What is your pleasure that I read?"

His laughter was harsh in the room, and Carlotta knew that it was with an old pain that had nothing to do with this time or place. "Get the book there on the end of the bed and read until I tell you to stop."

She picked up the sturdy leather volume, moved her sensuous fingers over the illuminated binding, settled herself in the chair, and bent to the Latin with the sense of having gone back to the lessons of her youth with Master Arnold.

The pungent phrases and savage observations of the Roman satirist, Juvenal, lifted above the slap of the rain and the soft hiss of the fire. Sir Reginald watched her sharply before relaxing against his pillows, his fists clenched. Carlotta had no idea how long she read, but she was conscious of his eyes on her and her discomfort grew even as she forced her voice to remain calm.

"Stop." The word came harshly, followed by a cough as he drank once more of the cup that had been refilled by the watchful servant who stood just inside the door.

Carlotta paused and lifted her curious amber eyes to his. One finger marked the page where she ceased.

"You are of France."

If he had slapped her across the face Carlotta could not have been more shaken. For a moment she could say nothing, and her mouth was as dry as after her nightmare.

"Do not deny it, my ear is keen." He was sitting erect now, and there was malevolence in his face.

Carlotta felt a rush of fury and a hope that the poison would

12

instantly work. "I have no intention of denying it. England has welcomed many who fled from the Revolution and the resulting terror. I was not aware that it was a crime to be of that country. Has Parliament passed a new law?"

There was silence in the room as her words hung between them, and she had visions of being cast out of the household, sent away without any sort of reference or remuneration. Then the measured words of the sick man came to her as if from a distance, and she seemed to hear the mutter of the mob as it sought her.

"Girl, girl, what is it? Take hold of yourself. You're as white as these sheets ought to be." This last was a snort.

Carlotta giggled as the present came rushing back. "Forgive my sharp tongue, my Lord, I cannot think what makes me speak so." Sheets and Frenchmen all in one breath! What manner of man was this? Laughter often came to her at moments of stress and it was so now; this made people look at her strangely and wonder, not always silently, if she were in her right wits.

"The physician. Where can he be?" The question was not addressed to Carlotta but rather to the room itself. The high, wheezing voice carried to the servant who had remained discreetly away, and his anxious face loomed now almost at her elbow.

"My Lord, it will not be long. Shall I summon her Ladyship?"

"God forbid!" Sir Reginald coughed until it seemed that his lungs would tear loose. He put a hand over his mouth, and the back of it seemed to pulse with purple veins. "I need diversion, and the written word does not give me solace. You, girl, how came you to this land? Divert me, tell me. If the tale grows boring you shall read to me again."

Carlotta grew white, her eyes huge under the wide cap. "There is nothing to tell, sir. I came here as a very young child and was cared for by a schoolmaster and his sister, who was once nurse to the mother of her present Ladyship. I owe much to England and my allegiance is wholly for this country."

"I did not think you a spy," he said tartly before the coughing overcame him again. The servant proffered the contents of the cup which was replenished from a larger jug on the table. Sir Reginald drank and was easier almost at once. He peered at her and continued, "Who were your parents? What of them?

How came you to the schoolmaster? Your hands are delicate, your face fine of bone. I might almost suspect breeding."

"My Lord, I have not spoken of these matters for many years." Carlotta was standing erect now, determined to remain silent, conscious as never before of all-pervading fear. His command to speak of the past threatened to give the nightmares voice and daily reality after all the times of pushing them away. She was not aware that her voice trembled.

Sir Reginald snapped at the servant, "Fetch claret and leave it at the door. Yon concoction is vile, prescribed though it is."

The man scurried away, and Carlotta sank into the chair, aware of the weakness in her legs. Sir Reginald ran both hands through his hair, thus making it stand up even more, as he said, "I did not mean to frighten you, girl. I forget sometimes that I am not as I used to be. What is your name again?"

"Carlotta, sir."

"That is neither French nor English. How came you by it?"

She looked at him, and this time he saw the shadows there. He spoke as if to himself, "I have seen men in battle sustain savage wounds, walk away, and recall little of it later. So it seems with you." He shifted in the bed and it creaked under his weight. "Fetch the Chaucer and read to me of the Knight."

Carlotta was only too thankful to do so, glad that his whim seemed to have passed. When the claret was brought, she poured him a tankardful and read until his snores were resonant in the room and she could slip away.

That night the nightmares came four times, and she was forced to stuff a corner of the bedclothes in her mouth lest unwelcome queries come.

In the next few days she was summoned to read to Sir Reginald regularly and grew more at ease with him. They talked at random of literature and the weather, then she would listen while he embarked on long, rambling tales about the excellent advice he had given King George in the past and would again if he were asked. The wheezing would set in if he talked for very long, but the liquid he drank from the jug which always stood at his bedside seemed to soothe him. Once she tasted a little of the mixture after he dozed off. The heavy, cloying taste nauseated her even as it raised a warning in her memory. Somewhere she had encountered a thing very like this, but the meaning eluded her. The odor clung to her fingers and she wondered that Sir Reginald, surely a fastidious man, should be able to tolerate it. Likely he was thankful enough for the surcease it gave him. She looked at him as he lay listlessly on the pillows, his swollen eyelids drooping down and his cheeks unhealthily red, and wished that she could warn him of what was being planned. Her conscience smote her once again.

"I should have died years ago. I am reduced to a hulk." The tired voice that greeted Carlotta in the late afternoon of the rainy next day was totally unlike that of the bold man who had tried to badger her that first time. His face was round and bloated and his puffy blue-veined hands lay across his chest as if they had no life of their own.

She could think of no words of comfort, nothing to say, but inane chatter rose to her lips. "Rain makes me sad sometimes. Doubtless it is that way with you today or on days when it seems the summer will never come again."

His pale lips lifted in a half smile. "Tell me of summer, Carlotta."

Put that way, it was easy to speak of the past and the village and those who had loved her as their own. She was unaware of the warmth and texture of her voice as she evoked memory; the light came into Sir Reginald's eyes and his breathing grew less heavy. She did see his stirring interest and wondered again at the power of the mind that could see so easily into the past. Perhaps he might yet fight off the poison. He sighed heavily and the rain hammered down outside.

Carlotta said, "I remember that early summer when we worked in the garden. . . ." Her words drifted on in pleasant patterns, but behind them the memories rose and she let them come. Her mind was far back in her childhood now, in warm gray walls, hearing shared laughter and knowing tenderness from shapes not quite seen, as a voice called her name, "Carlotta," in soft accents. Then there was spattering blood, cries of anger, swinging blades, and her own terrible fear. It seemed that she walked long in a mist punctuated by the sounds of quarreling and cursing. Sometimes she ran with other shapes and spoke to them in words that were answered, but mostly she was alone in a cold and fearful world of gray that shimmered with blood. Then the clearest sensation was that of burning and shaking, then waking to the faces of strangers.

She came from her reverie to the sound of her name being urgently called, "Carlotta! Carlotta!" Sir Reginald was trying to sit up and wheezing with the effort. His eyes were anxious, and she saw the real concern in them.

"My Lord! What are you doing to so excite yourself? Her

Ladyship has given strict orders that you are to rest quietly!" The servant was looking in the door, his face agitated as he saw himself blamed for whatever might transpire. He started to enter but jerked back as the tankard slammed past his head.

"Get out! I am still master here!" Sir Reginald still had amazing strength for his condition, but his hands shook as he stretched one out to the girl. "Carlotta, are you all right?"

She shook her head in a dazed fashion, but the fog seemed to rise around her and she could hear the cries of long ago as she whispered, "Yes, of course. I cannot think. Forgive me."

The watching servant closed the door softly and smirked to himself as he thought of the tale he would have to tell in the kitchen that night.

CHAPTER THREE

Across the Styx

"WHAT did you see in that waking dream?" The hoarse old voice held a note of command, but behind it Carlotta heard the call of one human being to another and her own need met his.

"My nightmare. It returns that way at times. Uncle Arnold, Master Arnold as I was told to speak of him here, since familiar forms of address are not suitable in a proper household, used to call it 'the terror that flies by night.' We used to talk about it and it was never so bad or frightening." Carlotta had been speaking almost to herself but now she roused to concern for the sick man. "But I forget myself, Sir Reginald! Are you feeling worse?"

He was still sitting up against his pillows, red spots flaming in his puffy face as he sipped more of the medicine that had been placed on the table beside him. He waved his hand and made a small boy's face. "Nonsense, girl, I'm better for all this. Now tell me about this dream of yours. And about France, in your own tongue, that lovely language that I have missed these years."

Carlotta made bold to say, "Why not let me fetch you some good wine? That medicine does not always seem to agree with you."

"No, no, Lady Leticia herself sees to my medicine. She'd know in a minute if I didn't take it. Now, oblige an old man as I have asked."

Carlotta longed for the release that words would bring, for it was as though a boil had been topped and it had been long since she had spoken. She remembered how she, Uncle Arnold, and Aunt Rosa sat together in the little bedroom where candles blazed, the fire glowed on the hearth, and fear was banished. Quickly now, as then, she told of the substance of the nightmare, adding, "It is always unvarying and so very real!"

Sir Reginald spoke as to himself. "Aye, a nightmare of our times, yet produced in the purest terms of freedom and justice. You and many others were the victims."

Carlotta could still hear the old voices blending with each

other as they told her the story of which she never tired. She said, "In the spring of 1794, just when the Terror was at its height and Robespierre ruled undisputed, my uncle received an urgent plea for help from one of his former students who was in hiding in Boulogne. In spite of the war and travel difficulties, my uncle and aunt made the difficult journey only to find the world gone mad with blood and the young man long dead. Both of them spoke fluent French, but apparently they were less than discreet and were forced to leave more quickly than they had planned the inn which had been set as the meeting place. Their coach had been left at another place, wisely so, as it turned out."

She stopped and they listened to the rain as it tumbled out of the gray sky. Sir Reginald's wheezing breathing was the only other sound.

Carlotta listened to herself speak the smoothly cadenced French that had not passed her lips in a long time and saw the half smile on her listener's face as he shifted under the load of coverings on the bed. The story came more easily now that she was past the nightmare. She drew an unsteady breath and took up the threads again.

"Small bands of children roamed the streets seeking food and money during these times. I understand it was common practice. One such band set on my aunt and uncle who had only one hired soldier for escort. They were soon routed by his stout stick, but one lay insensible and moaning at his feet."

Sir Reginald smiled and her heart was shaken by the warmth of it. "You, Carlotta."

"Aye. Seven or eight years old at the most, lice-ridden, emaciated, possessed of a remarkable vocabulary of street curses. They took me up, spoke of a grandchild and the pox, gave the remnants of their gold where needful, and so returned to England."

"Had you no memory, then? Why are you called Carlotta rather than Charlotte? Were inquiries instituted?" He drank once more of the medicine, and she saw that the blue faded a little from around his nostrils.

"They said I had brain fever for a very long time, that I cried out my first name, Carlotta, and would have no other. It was assumed to have been a pet name or a derivation of another. It is all that I have of mine own and I will never alter it."

Sir Reginald's eyes narrowed, and he seemed to be examining her face minutely. She turned her eyes away, knowing nothing to mark about the scrutiny, and finished the story.

"It was thought that my parents were victims of the Revolution, and my uncle always said that if a way could be found to save life at a time when so much blood was being shed, it must be undertaken. We hoped that, when times grew stable, we might travel to France and there seek information concerning my family. That was never possible for the war continued, there was no money, and then the illness came."

Sir Reginald's head was slowly turning back and forth, his nostrils were spread wide with the hunger for air. Carlotta went fearfully to his side and bent over him. His eyes looked directly into hers, and she saw the shock there.

"The look, you have it . . . knew I had seen . . ." The words ended on a choked cry as he fought for breath.

"Sir, you must be quiet. Please." Her actions were those of instinct as she pushed up the pillows behind him and pulled the elaborately frilled nightshirt open to expose his throat. His hands beat at her and one of them caught the side of her head, sending the cap askew. She jerked it off and leaned close as a low gurgling sound began. He tried to speak again but could not, though his eyes bulged with the effort. They were fixed now not on her face but on the auburn hair that fell over her shoulders. One hand lifted toward her and fell back.

The hard rattling sound started and Carlotta knew it for what it was. Just so had Aunt Rosa sounded in the last hours of her pain. She dared not leave him, and there was nothing in the way of medication except that concoction, which invariably made him worse. She looked down and saw that his face was growing dusky, his struggles weaker.

The whisper trailed off even as she heard it. "Dark lady, Carlotta." The rattle was louder now.

She jumped up and ran to the door, which she jerked open so hard that it bounced back against the wall. Her screams rang down the hall, and her own breath seemed caught in her ribs. "Come quickly, anyone! Help! Help! The master is dying!"

The house was understaffed even now with the guests and new servants so hurriedly added. No one would willingly stay near a sickroom, especially on so dark and gloomy a day. There was no flurry of movement, no response of any sort to her cries, and she had no power left for more.

Behind her the room was very still. She turned to look at Sir Reginald and saw that he lay, chest exposed, hands bent

19

into claws, half in and half out of bed. She could not move from the door but clung to it for support. It would be impossible for her to approach the bed and verify for certain what she already knew.

She heard the sound of running feet and a woman's high, excited voice. Carlotta forced herself to move and once she did so, found the urge to run almost impossible to contain. It was that swift movement of the hunted that Lady Leticia recognized in the brief instant that she stood in the door. Others ran to the bed. Carlotta's eyes shimmered with tears, but she could not speak as quick triumph and then malevolence rose in the woman's face before she began to wail in ritual agony for her dead husband.

Orders flew rapidly in the next few minutes from the older of the two men who had come with Lady Leticia and the frightened manservant. Carlotta had only a brief impression of him as soberly clad, dark hair, beginning to gray, and keen eyes that missed little. Only when they rested on Lady Leticia did they soften. He spoke suddenly and the sound of her name spun Carlotta around.

"Your name is Carlotta? Have her Ladyship's personal maid called at once. Say nothing of what has happened here on pain of dismissal. I will speak to you later and you are to hold yourself in readiness for it." His glance did not miss her shaking hands and the wild tumble of hair about her shoulders as the line of his mouth grew severe.

Authority sat heavily on him as he put a firm hand on Lady Leticia's shoulder. By now Carlotta's one idea was to escape this chamber of death and be alone for a few minutes. She said, "Aye, sir, I will do as you have bidden."

"See that you hasten." He turned his back and began to speak softly to the widow. The other man, younger and pale blond, edged closer and whispered something, but she jerked back and began to weep all the harder. Neither man had the voice Carlotta had heard only that one morning; that morning that seemed a thousand years ago now instead of scarcely more than a week.

She made her way on trembling legs to the hallway and gave the order to the first footman she saw. Her voice was high and hysterical but the urgency of the mission was unmistakable and the usually supercilious man went dashing to find the required maid from whom he would later get all the details.

Carlotta went to a nearby rack, took up the first cloak she

saw, a heavy blue one with an attached hood, and tossed it over her shoulders. Then she went blindly out a side door and into the pouring rain. Her thin shoes were soaked in a matter of seconds but it did not matter for she was in the winter freshness, away from the airless, damp house. She began to walk as she always did when upset, rapidly, with a loose, swinging stride.

She soon came to what had once been the parkland in the days when this had been one of the regularly visited homes of the lord. The garden had boasted a formal elegance then, but now trees, shrubs, and vines ran riot over paths that could barely be traced. The world was brown-gray with cold and rain. One trail led off to the right and she took it blindly. She might have been a wounded animal going to ground as she pushed deeper into the thicket and almost lost her balance over a stone faun which had once been part of an ornamental fountain.

Her toes were wet and icy; the blow hurt out of all proportion. She sank down on the ground, under the partial shelter of some thick vines which were so grown together that they were one thick mat. Then she let the tears come. They were long bottled up and soon she was gulping with them in a way she had not done since the death of Uncle Arnold. Death had been a blessed relief for Aunt Rosa.

She invoked the past once more and was conscious of the relief that talking about it to Sir Reginald had given her. What had that strange look of recognition been? Did she resemble some ancestor or someone in his past experience? She knew that she wept for him now as well as for herself and wished that she might have tried to save his life, fruitless though such an effort would have been.

A low roll of thunder came from the east and she looked up to see that the sky seemed much darker even through the streaming rain. Her hair dripped down her back and the heavy cloak was now sodden. Weariness pulled at her body; she would have no trouble sleeping this night. Slowly she rose and began to walk back toward the house, which loomed massively against the clouds.

She entered one of the doors at the back and started along the narrow corridors that would eventually lead to the stairs and her room. A tall man in nondescript clothes stepped from the shadows to bar her way. She did not remember having seen him about the house before. Now she started to go around him only to find his arm held in front of her.

"You are the woman called Carlotta?"

"I am she. Why do you ask?" She had begun to shiver in the dank passage as fear was added to cold.

"You have been sought for the past hour and more. Men are posted in the entrances to fetch you to her Ladyship. Come along now."

She started to protest, then saw from the way his brows drew together over glittering eyes that he would like for her to resist. "Naturally, I am ready to obey, but I cannot appear before her dressed in this manner."

"Instantly." He reached for her arm, but she shrugged away and walked ahead of him, her slippers squishing with every step.

Lady Leticia was reclining in bed, her maids on both sides of her holding smelling salts and restorative sips of wine in readiness. Her golden hair was loose and flowed over her shoulders. Her bedgown and the hangings about the bed were the same brilliant blue as her eyes. Carlotta thought that she resembled a sea-tossed flower. She herself felt nervous and hulking as she stood waiting to be noticed. The minister from the village stood in the shadows, Bible in hand. The dark, older gentleman who had been with Lady Leticia earlier was now standing in front of the roaring fire. His face was grim as he turned to Carlotta.

"Where have you been? Were you not bidden to remain close at hand?"

"The air is close in the house. I felt the need for freshness." She wanted to move toward the fire but dared not.

"In such weather?" He frowned as he brushed one hand across his brow.

Lady Leticia's voice was at variance with her beauty, it was always harsh and commanding. Now she cried, "Jesu, Edward, get to it! Find out what the wench knows. She was certainly the last person to be alone with him."

The gentleman answered her, but his words caused Carlotta to tremble violently. "What motive would there have been, Leticia? I quite understand your grief but we must be cautious."

She began to cry and he bent over her soothingly. Carlotta crossed to the fire and stood so close that her dress began to steam. Did they know that Sir Reginald died of poison or did they only suspect? She knew that Lady Leticia would try to remove any specter of blame from herself, but how could Carlotta be blamed? She forced herself to be calm.

The man called Edward turned back to Carlotta and said, "You must tell us all that happened from the time you were first summoned to read to Sir Reginald this day." His eyes locked on hers as she lifted her head. "You must not fear to tell the truth."

"My husband is dead and not by natural means. Edward, dear cousin, you are blinded to truth; it comes of belonging to the legal profession, scoundrels all! Tell her, or must I bear that, too?"

He swung round, glared at her, then said, "Carlotta, I am obliged to tell you that the medication in Sir Reginald's cup was a deadly and secret poison known to produce a condition very like a paroxysm of the heart. Did you knowingly administer this to him?"

Carlotta spoke clearly, trying to still the shake in her voice, conscious of the covert gaze that Lady Leticia turned on her. Edward never took his eyes from the girl's face.

Her voice was low and steady as she said, "I have spoken truly, sir. He asked for drink and I did give him that which I saw the manservant give him earlier and on other occasions as well."

"He denies it."

"Then he lies." She blurted out the words before she could stop them and did not miss the quick tilt of Lady Leticia's golden head. "What reason would I have?" She looked directly at the noblewoman who began to weep bitterly.

"Get her out of here. She shall be punished, I swear it! Get the lying slut out of here!" The last words were a shriek.

Edward motioned to the maids who began to soothe and pat. He took Carlotta by one hand and jerked her into the draughty hall. The man who had escorted her there stood impassively beside the door. Even though the heavy oak barred some sounds, they could still hear the cries of the widow.

He said, "The physician will soon arrive from London and, upon examination of the body, can tell us the cause of death. He was ill, that is very true, but this death is so sudden." There were dark pouches under his eyes, and the lines seemed graven on his face. "If you took anything, a jewel or a trinket, in the agitation of the moment, it would be best to tell me now."

Carlotta lifted her head and looked him full in the face. "There is nothing to confess. Things happened as I said."

She saw the zeal in his face as he said, "Then you need fear nothing; those of low birth are not hounded in this realm. My cousin sorrows for her husband and speaks savagely in her pain. It is her way. If you have lied to me, girl, it will go harshly with you."

Carlotta bit back sharp words; they would do her no good now, and meekness would serve her well. "I am innocent of any wrong, I swear it."

"John, come here." He called to the nondescript man who had moved discreetly away. "Take her to the north chamber and post a guard. She will remain there until the physician's findings are known."

"Aye, Master Frobish." He came to stand at Carlotta's side.

Edward Frobish started back into the bedchamber, then turned and said, "This measure is for your own protection, girl, while the evidence is gathered."

Carlotta's lips lifted slightly in an ironic smile. She did not doubt that some things belonging to Sir Reginald would be found to have vanished. The penalty for thievery was death. The lawyer might be concerned with justice, but his feeling for his cousin was evident. She had no illusions about the place in which she found herself; she stood alone. She should thank this earnest man, she knew, but she could not bring herself to speak.

A fresh burst of sobbing came from the room just then, and he rushed in. John pulled at Carlotta's arm so that she was off balance and grinned down at her.

"You were foolish to come back. Did you want more than you had already taken?"

Carlotta stared into the flat eyes and knew that it had begun.

CHAPTER FOUR

Wild to Live

CARLOTTA paced up and down in the tiny room, which contained no more than the bare necessities. A faint light filtered through a glassed-in slit far above her head, but she could hear nothing from the rest of the house. She had tossed her wet clothes to one side and now wore a coarse old robe and one of the blankets from the bed but she still felt cold. Her head swam with theories and fancies but she could not plan. Terror enveloped her as she thought of the noose that surely awaited her. "Such a convenient scapegoat!" The frost from her voice hung in the air.

A minute sound caught her attention suddenly and her eyes went to the door, where the knob was being manipulated slowly as the key was removed from the lock. She lay down as quickly as she could and pretended to be asleep but continued to watch through her dark lashes. Her body was taut, all her senses alive to this new threat.

The door was pushed slowly open and a man slid through the opening. His every move was one of stealth. He stood for a second, seeming to assess the situation before him, and she saw that he was tall and slender with very dark hair and a small beard. She could not distinguish his features but, from the few movements he made, she deemed him to be young.

One instant he was touching a hand to his beard and in the next that same hand was over her mouth, the other clasping her throat. She bit down as hard as she could but he wore leather gloves and she could not reach his fingers. She fought savagely but the pressure increased on her throat and the world swung darkly before her.

In the vortex she heard him whisper, "Keep that up and I'll kill you on the spot. Quiet and you will live a little longer."

Then Carlotta knew that she was well and truly lost, for it was the voice of Lady Leticia's lover; there was no mistaking that tone of casual dominance. She ceased fighting and lay still. He had come to kill her, that much was certain. Still, she would bargain for a bit more of life and watch for a chance.

"Good. Your advantage is your first concern, I see." His voice had a trill of excited laughter in it. His grip loosened a trifle and she drew deep breaths of air.

"Who?" It was all she could manage at the moment.

He laughed out loud now, the sound ghostly in the room. His cheekbones were high, his eyes some metallic color, as he leaned over her face and savored her fear.

"You ought to know. You heard us on that day and I suppose you have chattered about it by now to everyone in typical village fashion."

"No, oh, no." She whispered the denial.

"But you knew me when I came in. You knew for certain as soon as I spoke." He squeezed her flesh and smiled.

His voice had been almost teasing, but with deadly purpose behind it. Carlotta began to tremble in his grasp and tears rolled down the sides of her face to his fingers. He pulled back a little to study her and she whispered, "I know nothing of the ways of the great. I want only to live. Sir, please do not kill me."

His glance was quizzical as he drew her to a sitting position. "I can tell you do. But so do Leticia and I, you see. Did you really say nothing?"

"Is the truth not apparent? I swear it."

He laughed again and she knew that he enjoyed this. "Leticia knew you by the way you moved in the kitchens and then in Reginald's bedroom. We were so careful, and then you had to come along. We really meant to draw out his death a bit more, for the sake of realism, you know. The new poison was quite concentrated and he received too much. Regrettable."

Carlotta suddenly twisted toward the edge of the bed and heaved. He lunged toward her and they tumbled to the floor. He was up in an instant and tossed her backward so that she fell against the rickety stool.

"I'll scream!" She knew the words were foolish from the moment she uttered them. Who would hear or care that she stood only inches from death?

The young man laughed in real amusement. "Do so and you will not live to draw another breath. The guard is drugged and will not wake for hours." His hand reached out to touch her face in a curiously gentle gesture. "Ah, no, little curious servant girl, that very curiosity you sought to satisfy will destroy you now."

"Suspicion will fall upon Lady Leticia! She is beautiful and young, he was old and ill. What more reason than that she should take a lover? You cannot have been so careful all the time." Anything, any words to keep him talking so that she might buy time for herself!

The gloved forefinger flicked at her chin and rose to trace the curve of her mouth. He mused, "You really ought to know my name, I suppose, since there is no closer relationship than that of victim and killer. I am Michael Lanwardine, an old name in the North, but we have been penniless for years and I forced to live as best I might. Leticia would have none of me without money and we have had no choice. Her father chose Sir Reginald for her and we began to plot from that day."

Carlotta saw that he really wanted her to understand, but she further knew that he was ruthless. Guile touched her words as she said, "Why add another murder to your list? Let me live and I will go from this place into another city. You will never hear of me again."

"So slender and helpless, a small thing in fear." The dark eyes burned into hers and his mouth quirked up. "The word of a woman is as meaningless as her sighs of love. Your conscience overcame you in the night, you could bear your sin no longer and sought relief by hanging yourself from yon beam. Several pieces of rather good jewelry and some gold will be found in a hiding place near the wood from whence you came. Neat, I think." He reached for the cloak and began to hack strips from it with his dagger.

"No!"

He rose and started toward her. "Come here, little one. You could be fair, even in your old robe you are comely. Who can blame a woman for being curious? It is her nature. I promise you that you will feel little pain."

He might have been trying to persuade her to engage in dalliance or a stolen kiss, thought Carlotta hysterically. She dodged back and threw the stool in his path. He jumped over it and bent toward her as she shivered in the corner, one arm over her eyes, sobs seeming to choke her as she whispered, "Please, please, please!"

She looked up through her hair and saw the smile of pleasure on his lips and the reflection of it in his eyes. The hand he put on her shoulder was almost that of a lover, so gentle was it.

"It is time to die." He was breathing hard now and she saw the bulge lift in his tight black breeches.

"I am so afraid." She wailed softly under her breath, the

27

terror of a hurt thing which feared more pain. "Don't hurt me, please!"

The hand moved along the contours of her throat, touched the trailing hair and brushed by her ear. Out of the corner of her eye she saw him holding the thick pieces of cloth torn for the noose that would receive her neck. His other hand moved purposefully behind her head. She could feel the eagerness of his sex as it brushed against her leg. He meant to take her and kill her at the same time! How she knew this Carlotta did not know, but it was reality. The horror of it shook her to the bone. He felt her tremor and laughed that soft laughter of death and satisfaction.

Carlotta swayed toward him and sobbed. He pulled her closer and in that instant she drove her knee up into his crotch as hard as she could. The loose robe did not impede her and the full force of the bone struck his most vulnerable area. He cried out in agony and fell to the floor. Carlotta lifted both hands so that they formed a striking edge and slammed into the side of his neck. He groaned and lay still. She stood over him for a second and then set to work.

Soon she stood ready, a country boy garbed in pieces of finery and his own clothes as well. The dark breeches were ill-fitting but they covered her adequately. The ruffled shirt was covered by a piece of the bodice from the dress she had worn, this in the interests of both disguise and warmth. The breeches hung down over her old slippers, which had to suffice. She bound her hair tightly down and wound part of the cloak over it in rough semblance of a cap. If she moved at night, it was likely that she had a chance.

The bound man on the floor groaned slightly through his gag and the dark eyes flickered open. He gave her an incredulous look as he struggled briefly, then ceased. Carlotta caught up the dagger and held it before her as the words spewed out.

"Carrion! Your vanity made you think I walked in fear of you so that I could do nothing. You gloated in my fear! Murderer! Taste now the fate you would have brought to me!"

She brought the blade down only inches from his face and drove it into the floor. He jerked back instinctively and, mingled with the fear in his eyes, she saw the insouciant smile that never seemed to leave them. Murderer he might be, but there was courage in him.

"I ought to kill you but I'll not have that stain on my soul." Her anger faded as she felt the pressure of passing time. She bound another strip of cloth over his eyes and pulled the bed around so that his body was hidden from view. Then she balled up her wet clothes and thrust them under the covers so that it would seem she slept. It was not a device that would fool anyone coming close, but it would have to do.

She took Michael's pouch, which held only a few silver coins and some pennies, and fastened it inside her clothes. Her stomach twisted with fear of what was to come, but she had gained her life for the time being and that was what was most important. Now she moved closer to the door, then paused and gave one final look around. The bound man was not visible, and he could make no sound so securely had she fastened him. They would certainly bring food and drink, but that would not be until late in the morning, if she knew this house. Any inspection before that time would likely be cursory; she hoped that a brief glance through a crack she had noticed in the wood might suffice until such time as they confronted her with the physician from London.

She swung the door gently open and looked out into the empty hall, where the one candle had long since guttered out. There was no sign of the guard, and the silence of night lay over everything. The moment must be taken. She moved out of the room and pulled the door shut behind her, then slipped carefully along the wall until the narrow staircase was reached. She saw no other person, not even a late-moving servant, as she emerged on the lower level and darted into a closet that she knew from experience contained only a vast amount of cleaning materials. Only two corridors away was one of the little-used exits from the house, and she did not think that on such a wet night as this one had promised to be there would be many watchers.

Carlotta started to open the closet door to begin the next part of her journey, but a sudden chink of metal close by made her pause and draw back into the dark safety. It was well that she did so, for the tramp of feet came almost instantly into her hearing.

One male voice said, "There's those that'll be sorry to see Sir Reginald dead. He was a good master, even if a bit peculiar with all those books and all."

A lighter voice, obviously that of a boy, said, "What do you think really happened, Martin? They're saying in the kitchens that the . . ." He broke off suddenly and gulped.

Carlotta froze in place, thinking herself to be discovered.

She put her hand to the dagger, for she knew that if she had to she would use it.

The older voice came hard now. "One thing you must learn if you mean to work for the rich. That is to keep your mouth shut and never repeat gossip. You never know who will overhear. Do you understand me, boy?"

There was a muffled sniff and they tramped away. Carlotta's heart felt as if it would hammer out of her ribs and her breath came in shallow gasps. The minutes seemed to drag by but she dared not venture out just yet. The air of the closet was growing dry and hot. She must take the chance soon.

She saw nothing as she moved from one doorway to another, from one tapestry to another pool of shadows. She took time to be thankful that the guests were housed in the more opulent wing of the house, well away from this older section. Her conception of time was one of an endless night as she went along. Darkness was her safety, light her danger; she felt that she had lived in a new nightmare since the time she had crept down the steps to look for water to cool her parched throat.

A scraping noise made Carlotta jump, and her hand flew to the dagger at her waist. She melted down into the darkness beside an enormous old chair which she had often seen piled with wraps the servants shed, supplies, or parcels of food to be taken home later. She waited for the sound to repeat itself, then a form darted across her feet and scuttled down the hall. It took all her control to hold back a scream, for this was one of the biggest rats she had ever seen here, and who knew if there were not others?

The chance must be taken. The time had come. Carlotta rose and ran for the door just visible in the gloom at the end of the short corridor. Her palms were wet, her throat dry with the fear that previously had come only in her nightmare, but her legs moved with the caution of the hunted.

Now she was at the barrier and her hand fumbled for the heavy handle, even as she prayed that it would not stick. It did not but yielded to her push with a massive creak that seemed to resound over the silent halls. She took the chance that the guard would not be stationed outside and pushed harder, so that the door yawned open into the chilly wetness beyond. Carlotta smelled the freshness of the air and it intoxicated her. She moved quickly outside, pushed the door back in place, cast a furtive look about, and then began to run with all the terror that had been building up inside her as impetus.

It was still very dark, but on the horizon there was a shade of gray that indicated daylight was not far away. The November weather was cold but not bitterly so; still it struck Carlotta to the bone, clad as she was in the thin clothes of Lady Leticia's lover. She drew deep breaths as she ran and they shivered in her lungs. Brambles slashed at her face and arms, drawing blood in places, but nothing mattered except freedom.

A stitch ripped up her side and almost bent her double, but she ran on until the world began to revolve slowly around her and her legs trembled with the strain. Carlotta sank down where she was and put her head between her legs as Uncle Arnold had taught her to do when she felt faint. Several minutes passed as she forced herself to concentrate on her breathing. When it was steady she lifted her head and looked around her.

The misty day was fully beginning, though the low hanging clouds made it seem darker than it might have been otherwise. She had come through the old parkland and up a series of little rises which were fringed with thickets; now she was near the top of one of the larger ones and thus had a good view of the way she had come.

The house swam up out of the fog as if thrown there in pieces of gray slate and dark stone. The massive wings spread out from the central area and looked from this distance to be preparing for flight. There was no light or appearance of movement from anything that she could see. She might have been alone in this section of England, a wraith left over from another time.

She heard the snort of a horse and the plopping sounds of carriage wheels as the coachman negotiated the often marshy path. It was some distance away but sounds carried easily in the stillness and they grew louder as the horses were encouraged. Carlotta rose but could see nothing. Panic caught at her. What if this were the physician summoned from London? If so, discovery was not far away.

She melted back against the tree and waited until the clucking sounds began again. Then she took a deep breath and began to run once more. This time she was more surefooted and paced herself. The cold and beginning rain did not matter. She was alive and free and her blood sang in her veins for life restored.

CHAPTER FIVE

Look to the Ending

CARLOTTA soon reached the top of the last rise and then started down the almost imperceptible little path that led into the wooded area and away from the village. Her sense of direction faltered in the fog and she had a horror of going in a circle, but the urgency drove her on. The elation that she had felt at the overlook did not fade and it was that which made the cold bearable. Her feet were frozen nubs and her body was shaking, but so long as she moved steadily along some of this was alleviated.

Her mind went back to her actions of the past hours and she remembered what Uncle Arnold had told her of the manner in which she had been found in France and how it had been obvious that she was a member of the gang of children fighting for survival in whatever means they could. She could still hear the soft old voice saying, "The hard survived in the Terror and the others, be they young or old, perished." It was obscurely comforting to Carlotta to think that even then she had been a survivor with a large amount of luck. Pray God it would still be so. Apparently she still had that ability, she thought, for she could hardly have foreseen the acting ability which had lulled the lover into giving way to his own sense of cruelty and thus making himself vulnerable.

"But what now? What of the future?" She spoke the words out loud and watched her warm breath hang on the air before her. Somehow she did not doubt that there would be one and that it would be of her own making. She quickened her pace as she moved deeper into the wood.

Despite her plan to travel by night, Carlotta knew that at this early stage it was important that she put as much distance between herself and the estate as possible. All that morning and into the short afternoon she forced her body to move faster even though all she wanted to do was lie down and rest. The rain began again and this added to her misery. Hunger cramped at her stomach and she was forced to remind herself that anything she endured now was better than death by hanging.

She was so deeply immersed in her own thoughts that the mournful lowing of a cow in the nearby thicket seemed at first to be counterpoint to them. Then she saw that the animal had a rope around its neck which had become entangled in some of the branches. The bag was full almost to the bursting point and this was apparently causing the anguished sounds. Carlotta had sometimes milked cows but always in the company of others and that long ago. This one looked harmless enough, brown-white with nubbed horns. She approached and put her hand on the smooth flank. There was no reaction so she touched one of the teats and saw the warm milk drip from it. Her mouth watered as she sank to her haunches and prepared to catch what she could in one hand.

A sudden blow to her head sent her sprawling on the leafy ground. The world spun in circles of red and black and nausea began in her stomach. She tried to get up but was stopped by the pressure on her back.

"Thief! What is this country coming to when a person can't even have a cow but what someone tries to steal it? Well, it'll be the magistrate for you, my lad. Just try anything and this stout club will tend to you! Thief!"

The voice was cracked and old and female. Several rich curses were added as the owner of it began to describe the possible parentage of so evil a person as this would-be thief and the penalties, law and otherwise, that should be invoked. Carlotta moved cautiously but the stick drove into her ribs again. The cow bellowed this time and was answered by a dog's yap.

Carlotta summoned the voice of a boy in his teens, changing and shaky. "I am no thief. I can explain. At least let me turn over. I am harmless." She thought savagely to herself that she spent a great deal of time in justification of why she should not be detained and murdered. There was a snuffling at her ear and then a long tongue began to wash it and her neck.

"Here, Boney, back. Don't get friendly with the likes of that. Back, I said!" The dog moved back and the stick was raised slightly. "You turn over on your back, but don't try to get up or I'll whack you again."

"I will do what you say." She roughened her tone and turned over very slowly, not wanting to risk another blow in her exhausted condition.

"Damn right you will." The voice snapped.

The sight that met Carlotta's eyes was not at all reassuring.

The woman might have been anywhere from fifty to seventy. Her face was seamed and battered; one eye was sunk far back in the socket and the other seemed almost opaque in the fading light. She wore cracked shoes and a collection of black garments in varying stages of age and disrepair. A black cloth was wrapped around her head but gray hair straggled out from it. The dog had gone to sit at her feet. It, too, was large and black except for a white streak across the back. Teeth gleamed white to match.

Witch and familiar! The old tales that she and Uncle Arnold had read in the evening firelight came back suddenly and her fingers started up instinctively in the sign against the evil eye.

The old woman laughed. "You're not from these parts, boy, but I see that you respect power. Old Bess is no witch to those who treat her right." The stick lifted from Carlotta's midsection as if for emphasis and then returned to a point at her side.

Carlotta raised a hand to balance herself and saw that the old woman did not catch the movement. The dog did, however, and a low growl began in its throat. She said, "Will you let me up? I am freezing."

Old Bess cackled again, the sound matching the bare tree branches. "Get up then if you must, but move carefully or Boney will attack."

Carlotta rose and watched the dog carefully. She saw how the old woman balanced on the stick and how one hand bent to touch the animal's fur. The words came inadvertently, "You can barely see!"

The crone's fingers moved rapidly and Boney rushed at Carlotta, his hackles raised. "I see well enough to know you for a thief!"

There had been an old man in the village of her childhood whom Uncle Arnold helped on occasion and of whom he had said, "He walks forever in an endless tunnel with only a flicker of light at the distance." Her foster aunt had said he was afflicted of God. Did it all come to the same thing, Carlotta wondered? She said now, "I swear to you that I was only hungry and thirsty for I have come a long way over the downs and have still a long journey in front of me. I have a few coins only. They are yours if you will believe me and shelter me for the night." Perhaps she was a fool to blurt things out this way but exhaustion was making her reel and her voice seemed to come from a long way off.

"Likely stolen!" Old Bess came closer and Carlotta caught

34

the rancid scent of her. "Where are you from, then, and where do you go? Speak up and be quick about it, my bones will take little of this air."

"I'm from Sutton, near the Avon River. My name is Wat. My father died recently of the fever, my mother a week later. My uncle apprenticed me to a tailor, even though I was over old for it. My father had been a tenant on a small farm, but there was no money and my uncle demanded that I learn a trade. I ran away and am on my way to Bristol to join the navy any way that they will have me." Carlotta thought of a dozen loopholes in this tale and could only hope that the old woman did not point them out. "I want to fight against the French before the wars are done."

"Always battles the men think about." She put her face close to Carlotta's and squinted, then slapped her on the back. "Puny for the navy, they'll likely make you a flunky of some sort. Best to go back and learn a trade as you were told."

The girl heard the relenting in the old woman's voice and felt the softness of Boney's tread on her almost bare feet. He seemed to have forgotten the menace she was supposed to be. She sought for a boy's blurting words. "I want to see something of the world. I want adventure, not the sweat and the needle." As she spoke them, Carlotta knew that they were true and that other such words had once been spoken in her hearing.

Old Bess said, "I believe you, boy. Boney hasn't bitten you and I let him loose. Anyway, I know what you mean. My grandmother, many greats ago, I forget how many, saw the Queen and never forgot her. She swore, they say, that the Queen waved just at her." She thrust the stick into the ground and started for the cow, the dog at her heels.

Carlotta stared at her bent back, suddenly bemused. In England after all these centuries there was still only one queen who was spoken of with that degree of reverence. "Queen Elizabeth! Did she truly?"

Hours later, they sat before the fire in Old Bess's hut and Carlotta listened while she talked of her ancestress who had seen the great queen on the way to Tilbury field and of the soldier she had met on that journey after the Spaniards were repelled. She had to do little more than listen for the old woman seemed starved for talk. It was enough for the girl to be partially warm as she drank warm milk and ate coarse barley bread.

The hut was very small and ill-furnished. It was built of

stones and mud with one thatched side. The floor was covered with straw and beaten hard. There was a separate section for the fire, which had to be kept tiny due to the dangers of smoke and conflagration. The smell of the place was that of grease and age. At this particular time in her life, however, Carlotta thought it a palace, for was she not full, protected from the elements, alive and free?

Old Bess drowsed off in the middle of a sentence and was soon snoring in the straw. The dog lay at her feet, his black eyes watchful, but his tail thumped as Carlotta moved to a pile of straw and pulled up the ragged remains of a cloak that Bess had given her earlier. Her clothes had dried on her for she had not wanted to give the old woman any idea of her sex. Her feet were bare, the torn slippers had given way completely, but there was a large stack of rags in one corner from which she could find something to bind up her feet and legs against the cold. Now she drew herself into a ball against the chill and gave herself up to the delicious release of sleep.

"Bess! Bess, wake up. You can sleep tomorrow on what I've brought for tonight. Open up!" The voice was almost gay as its owner hammered at the ill-hung door.

Carlotta sat upright, thinking that her nightmare had never taken this form. Then she knew this for reality and her blood iced. Was this pursuit? Had a reward been offered? Her hand went to the dagger in her belt as she checked the head covering to see that it had not slipped during that time of exhausted sleep.

Boney was barking, but the plumed tail waved madly in welcome. Old Bess was roused by the din and roared, "Who is it? Why do you disturb an old woman in the middle of the night?"

"You know very well who it is and it is barely twelve of the clock. Let me in before I freeze."

"Simon! By all the saints! Where have you been?" She scrambled up, a rag pile herself, and lurched toward the door on unsteady legs. She unbolted it and was immediately swept up in the arms of the tall man who bent his head at the low ceiling as he walked with her into the warmth of the hut.

Carlotta drew her hunched-up knees closer together at the blast of cold air that swept in. Then she stared over them at the man whose hood had fallen back in the excitement of greeting. He seemed well over six feet tall and in his early thirties, but it was his face that held her attention. His hair was silver-gilt that shone brilliantly in the faint light of the fire but his brows were arching black strokes above eyes greener than the depths of the forest on a summer day. His face was almost chiseled except for an off-center cleft in one cheek, which widened when he smiled, as he was now doing. He had looked at her briefly as he entered, then his gaze had gone round the room as if looking for danger. Carlotta shivered and the palms of her hands were suddenly moist.

"Who is this, Bess?" His voice was deep and sure, but Carlotta heard the undercurrent of watchfulness and thought that she would not care to be this man's enemy.

The old woman turned from him in a swirl of rags and dust. "This is Wat who is running away to sea. I have promised him shelter for a day or so in return for help with the cow and around here. He listens well, too."

The man stared at Carlotta for a second. "In such times every hand is welcome." A shadow crossed the mobile features. "You go to Bristol, then?"

"Aye, sir. I must not linger long here, though Mistress Bess has been so kind." Carlotta knew her face was pinched and thin, her voice reedy. Surely he would not suspect.

He dismissed her with a glance and turned back to Bess. "We are going to feast this night, or morning as it might be." He took a few steps to the door and brought back a large sack from which he removed several bottles, a large ham, roasted chickens, some wrapped pies, and cheeses. There were two heavy blue cloaks and a pair of sturdy shoes as well.

"Simon, you are too kind." Bess was eagerly breaking into the crust of one of the pies and reaching for one of the bottles at the same time.

Carlotta saw the intensity in the strange green eyes and the tenderness was almost palpable in his voice as he said, "It is not kindness, lady, I owe you a debt beyond all repayment." He took the bottle from Bess's hands and uncorked it with a deft movement of long fingers. "Drink in good health for it is Boney's best."

Hearing his name, the dog rose and came to nuzzle at Simon's knee. Simon laughed as Carlotta and Bess joined in. He said, "Half the dogs in England are named for Napoleon, I think."

The bottle was passed to Carlotta, and she drank deeply of the pungent brandy and then coughed explosively. Bess's eye rested adoringly on Simon as she said, "Business was good tonight?"

He looked warningly at Carlotta and said, "I would say so but some things are uncertain."

Bess drank deep once more and pulled one of the chickens apart as the brandy dripped down her chin. She was already affected and her words began to slur as she started some tale about the cow and a man who had tried to cheat her several days before. Simon ate and drank, smiling and attentive as he made comments, but Carlotta saw the tenseness of his shoulders under the brown worsted that accentuated his fairness. She ate hungrily, for she did not know when such food might come her way again. The brandy coiled warmly in her stomach and her eyelids drooped. Her last thought was that Bess's tale was uncommonly long and that Simon, whoever he was, must be a good friend to have. Then the tide of sleep took her.

When she woke it was full light, cold, and the hut was empty. Her mouth felt foul and her muscles were sore from the strains of the past days, but there was no indication that she had taken a chill. Carlotta felt the urgency rise in her; the sooner she left these parts the better it would be for her. She sat up and began to move her arms slowly. There was really no plan in her mind except that of flight, but now she thought that in her tale to Old Bess there had been a modicum of truth. Bristol was the largest city in this part of England and was perhaps two or three days travel by coach, longer by far on foot. There she might be able to lose herself until such time as any search might have died down. She would find some sort of work for bed and board—cook's helper, watcher of children, sitter with old people—there was always something for one who was young and strong. She would forge herself a good reference, speak of being robbed on the way, extoll her strength. Carlotta smiled to herself at the thought of the proficient liar she had become.

A few minutes later she went outside to wash her face in the bucket which was heavily rimmed with ice. The day was gray and cold, trees stood bare, their branches rattling in the little wind. She had put her feet into Bess's broken old shoes which were scant protection against the ground. The shock of the water went straight through her and she gasped. Enough was enough; Carlotta groped for the rag that she had brought out with her but could not find it. She dashed her hand against

38

her eyes in annoyance and opened them to see the hard green eyes of Simon inches from her.

"You startled me. Have you seen the cloth I laid down here only a minute ago?"

In the light his face was even more like a carving, and there was a faint bronze touch to his skin where the shirt opened on his chest. His face was darker than she had thought the night before. Evidently he spent much time in the sun.

"You were looking for this, Wat?" He held up the cloth. A mocking smile touched his lips.

"Yes." She stood still, feeling the drops cold on her face. Danger was very close.

He caught her shoulder so hard that she felt the bones crunch. "What is your game, wench? You make a poor boy, your masters should have known that. Speak, while you still can." His mouth twisted. "Chivalry was never one of my pleasures."

CHAPTER SIX

Stand and Deliver!

CARLOTTA was not prepared for the rush of rage that spread through her. Still less was she prepared for the excitement that his touch roused. Her skin burned where he touched it and yet she felt a curious languor. She saw that he was puzzled also, that there was another emotion behind the angry eyes.

"Is it a crime to dress as a boy so that one may travel the more swiftly and yet not be molested on the roads? I have no idea of what masters you speak. Release me." The words were cool, but her heart hammered and one part of her wanted him to hold her closer and in another way.

Simon said, "Who are you? What are you doing here at this time and how did you cozen Old Bess so easily?"

"The story I told her is true except for the fact that the apprenticeship of which I spoke was marriage to a lout whose father had hungry hands and to whom my uncle owed money. I took what clothes I could and fled. I will seek employment in Bristol, a maid, washerwoman. It matters not. I am free." She tossed her head and jerked her shoulder from his grip which had eased since she spoke so confidently. "As for Bess, I simply listened many times to the tale she tells of her ancestress and the soldier."

"You speak smoothly for a country maid. How will you obtain work in a city as large as Bristol? There are many hungry hands there and somehow I do not doubt that you could have ruled the ones in your village with competence."

"Forged references." Carlotta stared straight at him and saw the carved lips relax. "By me."

"A bold and articulate wench. But do you speak the truth?" He seemed to speak to himself.

"I do not understand what makes you think you have the right to question me or that I will stand here in the cold and listen to it." Carlotta started to go around him and he caught at her to pull her back. The cloth, loosened by sleep-tossing, fell from her head, and the auburn hair tumbled over her shoulders to make fire in the gray morning.

Simon whispered, "You light this day." He drew her to him and his lips melted down on hers as their bodies pressed together.

Carlotta felt the heat begin and suffuse her being as her arms rose to go around him from no seeming volition of her own. Her mouth opened to his delicate pressure and her tongue darted against his in scalding touches. She felt her nipples rise and thrust against the shirt she wore while his manhood touched her even through their layers of clothing. The world faded and she wanted only to be closer to this man and have him caress her more fully. One of his hands left her back and touched a nipple. She moved convulsively and moaned slightly.

He set her from him and the tanned face was hard. "How long do you think you will survive without a protector?" The bulge in his trousers was obvious, and his eyes were lit by her own passion.

Carlotta wondered fleetingly if he meant to offer her such, and her will recoiled even as her flesh longed. She was ever her own person, so now she said in a voice that shook, "I will survive. Of that I assure you." Oddly enough, she knew that this was true, and the pride rang in her words as it had not done in all the months on the Kilburton estate.

Simon smiled suddenly and his face was transformed by it. "What is your name?"

Carlotta stared. She could not tell him her true name nor anything close to it, for even now handbills might be circulating. "Call me Mara."

"For the Lord has dealt very bitterly with me and mine." He touched her face with a long brown finger. "It has been so with many of us. Very well, I will honor your wishes."

Carlotta had not thought he could see through her so easily nor yet that such as he could recognize and cap her quotation. Her cheeks bloomed pink as he smiled again.

"Let us go and have hot wine and ham. I count myself well frozen in this weather. We will not tell Bess of your secret; she tends to make much of nothing."

"Simon—" she hesitated, then blurted, "thank you."

"No, Mara, it is I who thank you." He did not elaborate but took her hand and drew her toward the hut.

Old Bess had gone out in search of the rags and scraps she hoarded. Simon departed on some errand of his own after

41

pointing out the place where she kept the better parts of her collection. "Let us say that your costume does not match." He had eaten and drunk standing, still looking at her with that curious expression in his eyes.

Now, as Carlotta hunted among the folded piles of old clothing for something that might come remotely close to fitting her, she tried to deal with the new and exciting feelings that this man had raised in her. There had been a stolen kiss or two in her days in the village but this was only part of growing up. Her heart had not been touched. One of the footmen at the estate had made advances to her, even tried to tumble her in one of the drafty halls, but her savage recoil had quickly driven him away. She had no experience of the perversion of Lady Leticia's lover who had taken joy in her terror and whose killing hands on her flesh had been sensual. But Simon's one kiss told her of pleasures beyond knowing, and now her body yearned for him even as her mind knew that this was madness.

Soon she was arrayed in a sober brown shirt and thick breeches of wool, which had only slight signs of wear. Wide bands secured them to her waist so that she appeared somewhat lumpy. Padding and cloth held Old Bess's shoes in place, and a warm but torn cloak went over all. She plaited her hair up around her head, then bound more cloth over it. All this would have to do. She was uneasy, however; if Simon had spotted her as a woman so might others.

Carlotta milked the cow, fed Boney, and tried to straighten up some of the clutter of the hut. The fire was built up and wood gathered for it by the time Bess returned, looking more like a walking pile of rags than she had the previous day. She came up very close to the girl and inspected her through the close vision of the remaining eye.

Carlotta said nervously, "Simon did not think you would mind if I found some other clothes. I washed those I had on out and can leave them..." Her words trailed off before the old woman's continued silence.

Bess had left the makeshift door open, and little flakes of snow began to blow in as the wind whistled around the corners. Carlotta backed away and almost stumbled over Boney, who had settled down near the fire with the remains of the ham bone.

Bess spoke. "It's all right, Wat. I just thought, with the snow coming and all, that you might stay a bit longer and help me. I like to have someone to talk to when the weather gets this way."

Carlotta gaped, for she had not known she was leaving so quickly. With the snow on the roads and paths, travel would be hard indeed. What was this?

A drawling voice came from the entrance. "Shut your mouth, boy. It is just that I have urgent business on the Bath road and have need of strong arms to help me. Afterward I will give you some coins and set you toward Bristol. No one will think of pursuing you in company with another, will they?"

Carlotta turned to see Simon smiling at her as he dropped one eyelid in a wink. He wore fine black wool with leather boots to match. A white scarf was knotted around his neck and his cloak was lined with white silk. His gilt hair was hidden by a black hat with a white plume. She felt her whole body shake with new hunger and knew that he, too, was not unaffected.

"I am grateful to both of you for your kindness to a stranger." She, too, could dissemble.

Simon went to Old Bess and put his arm around her as he spoke gently of business, of weather, and of how he would return soon with all manner of treasures, perhaps even a blackamoor to help her with the scavenging. Soon she was laughing and calling him "jackanapes."

Bess said, "Go tend to your business, but return soon, for you are sorely missed here." She patted him fondly, and he returned the pressure of her hand. Her good eye cocked toward Carlotta and she said, "God be with you, Wat. I hope you manage to give the Frenchies a fight."

They left her standing in the doorway of the hut, Boney at her feet and the snow already whirling thick around them. In the protection of the nearby thicket, two horses stood waiting. Simon unstrapped a heavy cloak and a feathered hat from a roll on one's back and handed them, along with leather gloves, to Carlotta.

"Put these on. I assume they taught you to ride there in the wilds of—what county was it? Somerset?"

She obeyed him but managed to ignore his question and pose one of her own. "Where are we going? I cannot think that you mean to escort a waif to Bristol in such weather."

He looked at her, his eyes brilliant against the gray afternoon, the black cloak swirling about his tall, lean body. "Mara,

43

will you come with me? To adventure? To that which was between us this morning? To an interlude?"

Carlotta swayed toward him, knowing well what he meant and not caring that all the precepts of pride and honor that she had been taught were fading before the lifting fire she felt toward a stranger who had kissed her on a winter's morning.

"I will come, Simon, for adventure—for all you name."

"No questions, now or ever?" His eyes bored into hers and the strange black brows drew down over his straight nose.

"No questions, now or ever. My hand on it!" She put it out and they touched, then clasped hands in the age old ritual of camaraderie.

"Then we ride." He boosted her into the saddle, mounted his own horse, and they moved away toward the little road that led eventually into the main one.

Carlotta rode slightly behind him, her hands careful on the reins, and was once again thankful that her foster uncle had seen to it that she had riding lessons. Excitement was a banner in her cheeks, and she felt as if she could sing to the leaden skies. Days ago she was in danger of her life wasted as a fourth-rate maid or being hung as a scapegoat. Now she was free and in the company of a mysterious, handsome man who found her desirable. It was as heady as the brandy of the night before. She would drink it to the lees and take what life might bring in the aftermath.

It was full dark when they halted in the shelter of a grove of trees. Simon took off one glove, drank deeply of the flask he carried, and passed it back to Carlotta. The liquid burned all the way down and heightened her feelings of anticipation.

Simon said, "Take this and grow used to the feel of it."

Carlotta took the pistol he handed her and noted the elegance of it and the high polish, even as she forced her voice to remain matter-of-fact. "What is this for? I have never used one."

Simon pushed back the edge of his hat with the barrel, his profile carved and sharp in the darkness. "You need not use it. You must remain in the background and be watchful. If there are any covert movements you must discourage them by meaningfully pointing the pistol and appearing menacing. If I give an order to you it must be immediately obeyed."

Carlotta remembered the watchfulness, the remark about "her masters," and the insistance on no questions. Her neck was already once jeopardized, could they hang her twice? She laughed, the sound pure in the wind-driven night. "You are a highwayman!"

He inclined his head. "Hermes. At your service, your Lord or Ladyship, after you have given me those flashing jewels and that fat purse."

Carlotta said lightly, "You have chosen your name well. The messenger of the gods and the watcher over travelers and thieves."

His hand was on her arm and steel grated in his voice. "I think that you are singularly well learned for a simple village maid." He might have said more, but in the distance they heard the sounds of horses approaching. They were moving slowly on the road, which was neither well travelled nor maintained. Simon looked up and his lips quirked with what might have been amusement.

Carlotta said, "I had aptitude for learning and the schoolmaster was fond of my family. Had I been a boy I might even now have been at Oxford."

He hooted softly. She felt her anger rise but yielded to the movement of his hand as he placed her behind him and drew up the reins on his horse. The pistol seemed to rise to his hand as his whole figure blended with the night and the white world.

The coach came into view now. There was one outrider going before it and only one coachman. It looked fragile enough, with the large wheels and raised body which appeared to be painted some bright color. There seemed barely room for two people inside.

"Come." The word was sibilant in the whirling snow as Simon touched his horse.

There was no time for thought. Carlotta felt her insides knot together, whether with fear or excitement she did not know. She urged her horse forward as they moved to the edge of the thicket. The coach was moving even more slowly up the small hill now, and she saw that the coachman had lit a taper, which he held slightly to the left as he drove. She wondered what this measure might mean and if he watched for slides in the road or for highwaymen.

Then they were beside the outrider and facing the coachman. Simon held the gleaming pistols in his hands as he called out, "It is Hermes! Stand and deliver!"

As the procession halted in dismay, Carlotta saw that his face was covered with a black mask and that the light of the taper shone full on her own.

CHAPTER SEVEN

Hermes and Hebe

THERE was no time for speculation as Carlotta held the pistol rock steady on the outrider while the coachman drew the carriage to a halt. Both were careful to move slowly, and she guessed that they had been in robberies before. Simon waved her forward and the light in his green eyes was one of pure devilment.

"Bid your passenger come out, Master Coachman. I would not keep you long on such a night."

The coachman was older, in his sixties, and his voice was quavery. "We carry nothing that would interest one such as yourself, Hermes. It is the London road that you seek."

"Aye, there is only the elderly gentleman taking his journey to his family in slow stages." The outrider was a country lad with goggling eyes and a fearful manner.

"Watch them. Shoot if they move." Simon strode to the coach and jerked the door open. "Come out, Lord Fenton, I will relieve you of what we know you carry, and then you may go in safety."

There was an angry shout from the interior, several curses, and then a high-pitched laugh that might have come from a woman. Simon snapped another command and this time the inhabitants emerged. One was a short, fat man in his late middle age with a red, angry face. He wore blue velvet and rings gleamed on his fingers. His clothes were in disarray and he struggled to set them right. Hovering at his side was a blond young man with thin features and delicate hands that shook.

"The devil with you, Hermes! I heard you'd left the country and good riddance! What do you want?" Lord Fenton was frightened and his bluster gave evidence of it. "It is as they said. I only travel to a friend's estate for a quiet week and have to go lightly."

The young man touched his protector's sleeve and laughed, the sound high in the chill air. Carlotta shivered, and not from cold, as she saw Lord Fenton's mouth go slack and hungry.

Simon said, "I will not play games and well you know it.

You carry the Fenton pearls and emeralds, as well as the famous matched rubies, to a safer place in the country. With the unsettled state of affairs in London, the King now mad and now sane, Napoleon on the move, you have considered all the possibilities and deployed your wealth. Do not bother to deny it. I will take them all."

Lord Fenton looked at the grim black figure. "How did you know? The secret was most carefully guarded." He put his arm out and the young man came eagerly to him.

"I have my sources. Hand them over."

Lord Fenton spoke craftily. "We could come to some agreement, Hermes. You have the reputation of a sensible man. If the worst should happen . . ." His little eyes peered through the snow and seemed to memorize Carlotta's face.

Simon thrust the pistol at the young man who gasped and moved back. "Get the jewels or I shoot him." He ground the barrel into the soft flesh before it.

There was no mistaking the determination in his voice and Carlotta, who knew him so little, knew that he meant his words. She swung her pistol toward the others who remained stiff and still, wanting only to escape with their lives. Pity touched her, for she knew what it was to want to live. Lord Fenton hesitated no longer but scrambled back in the coach and tossed out a velvet-wrapped bundle which fell to the snowy ground at Simon's feet.

"Open it." He nudged the young man who gasped again and seemed about to faint. It was Lord Fenton who cursed and bent to obey. The jewels tumbled out to glimmer in splendor in the taper's light. Necklaces, ropes, and rings, all the deckings of a queen.

Carlotta stared at all this beauty, and for a second her heart twisted with longing. What would Simon do with all this? She saw Lord Fenton's face at the loss of his wealth and paused to wonder which he valued more, the boy or the jewels. As she remembered the eagerness on his face when he looked at his young lover, she shivered to think that she might have looked so at Simon and only recently.

Simon poked one of the pistols in his belt and held the other ready as he took the parcel from its owner to stow it in his own pouch. Then he motioned to Carlotta to back away with him to the edge of the road, where the horses were lightly tethered.

"Mount up, lad." He bowed extravagantly to them. "I

leave you to the pursuits of love, your Lordship! Be assured that your jewels will have a setting worthy of them. Hermes thanks you!"

Simon swung into the saddle that now seemed part of him and they rode swiftly away, leaving the sound of curses rising richly on the air behind them. The blunderbuss carried by the outrider had been dropped in the snow when he saw Carlotta, and Lord Fenton's pistol had been confiscated by Simon at the outset. Now they were engaged in seeking the weapons and it might be long minutes before they would be able to proceed on along the road.

It seemed to Carlotta that she and Simon rode for hours through the whirling darkness. The wind had risen, and it cut sharply at her partially exposed face. Her entire body was numb, her lips were cracked and hard. Simon rode ahead, guiding the horse with an expertise that spoke of long years in the saddle. They had left the main road which had been, of itself, a trail and picked their way over hills, through thickets, and into meadows where the wind blew them along. She had tried to speak to Simon on several occasions, but her voice came only in a croak. The spirit of adventure had long since died. Now she thought only of warmth—the heat of fires on the hearth, the summer sun, a nest of blankets.

They came quite suddenly to a cottage, which lay between a dense growth of trees and a small hill on which rocks and snow mingled. The roof appeared to be of thatch, but it was so covered that she could not tell. Simon dismounted and gave a low whistle. The door swung open immediately and revealed a hooded man who moved to his side with jerky movements.

"Is all prepared?" Simon might have been querying a servant about the warmth of his bed, so casual did the question come.

"Aye, sir. You will find things more than adequate." He took Simon's horse aside and started for Carlotta, but his master waved him aside.

"Come, you will soon be warm." He pulled her from the saddle, tossed the reins to his man, and carried her into the warmth.

Carlotta was dumped unceremoniously on the fur rug by the hearth and another fur wrapped about her shoulders. He handed her a cup of some burning hot liquid and she gulped it down eagerly. As she began to thaw she looked about at her surroundings and was amazed at the luxury there in what had seemed at first a simple hovel.

Thick hangings kept out the cold and shone blue-green-gold in the light of the roaring fire on the stone hearth. Roasted meats, pies, and bread waited on a table close by. An assortment of cups and flagons held wine and brandy, the containers blazing with gold and jewels. Rugs in delicate patterns covered the floor and cushions were piled high on both sides of the fire. Sweet-scented candles blazed from another doorway. Carlotta stretched both hands to the fire and felt the brandy turn comfortably in her stomach.

"How does my lady like the hovel of the peasant?" Simon stood at the table pouring himself a drink. He wore a loose green silk shirt over the tight-fitting black breeches, and his eyes gleamed a darker green. His hair was brilliant in the shifting light. His teeth flashed white as he smiled at her with such intimacy as she had never known.

"It is fair." She could not say anything else. Her tongue seemed frozen to the roof of her mouth and she felt a veritable lump in her steaming clothes and bundled-up feet. Her eyes went to the long, supple fingers as they idly circled the cup. She thought of them on her flesh, at her breasts, tipping her chin to his mouth. Flame licked through her and she lowered her head so that she might not meet the intensity of his gaze.

"Mara." The softness of his voice made her look up. "There are other clothes in the next room. Go and make yourself comfortable, then we will eat. I vow, robbing is hungry work! That Lord Fenton is notorious for his taste in boys and jewels; we must inspect the haul."

Carlotta saw then that the sheen had gone from his eyes and he might be speaking to a comrade after a job of work had been done. She felt relief and regret wash over her as she retreated. The bottles clinked as he poured yet more brandy.

The bedroom was as opulent as the other area. Furs and cushions lay in profusion and green hangings masked the walls. Water for washing was ready on a stand, ointments and lotions were close by. Carlotta forgot her fears as she stripped off her clothes and let her hair flow freely. The water was tepid but wonderfully refreshing as she laved her slender body in it. She brushed her auburn hair until it crackled about her pointed face.

A furred robe of brown velvet with foamy lace pouring from the sleeves had been placed on the wide bed. Carlotta put it on and saw that the fit was good. Her small waist and pointed

49

breasts showed to advantage in the mirror. The full skirt swirled around her legs and bare feet. Her amber eyes were brilliant with excitement and her cheeks were pink from the fire. She paused for a moment and clenched her fists together in a strange mingling of emotions, the desire to laugh and weep rising alternately in her.

"I am eating all the food." Simon's laughing voice beckoned her.

"Then I must drink all the brandy, or have you finished that, too?" She caught her breath and went to stand in the door.

His reaction was all she could have hoped for. He bowed from the waist in the courtliness that sat so easily upon him. "By all the banished gods of Greece, you are fairer than those baubles." He waved a hand at the shimmering beauty laid out on the table, then picked up a long rope of pearls which he held out to her. "Let them draw beauty from you."

Carlotta knew that he wanted to place them around her neck but she was not ready for his touch. "I thank you, Simon, for the loan of this loveliness. Never have I seen such." Her own fingers shook as she took them and wound them around her neck, feeling the coolness drop into the warm hollow between her breasts.

The green eyes followed her hands, then went back to her face, and the black brows lifted in quizzical fashion, but he arranged the cushions for her and passed over a dish of meat and sweets. Carlotta's throat closed and she knew she would choke if she tried to eat. He nibbled at a pastry and poured clear red wine for her but never ceased to watch her.

Carlotta was in a sudden panic. Her hands were slippery from sweat as she said, "What news is there from France? You have been among people in these recent weeks far more than I. How goes the progress of the war? Is it as bad as last summer or the summer before when we were alone before Napoleon?" Her words seemed mere babble in the charged atmosphere of the room.

Simon laughed, the sound muted in the stillness. "You would prolong the honey, is that it? I like an inventive woman."

Carlotta smiled, and her tension was eased. She drank deeply and said, "Will you tell me of the political situation?"

It began as a bit of instruction, she thought, but the man's passion for his subject soon became a rallying cry as he spoke of Napoleon, chosen Emperor by will of the French, his plan to rule the face of Europe, and the possibility that, but for the

50

hated English, he might do so. He spoke of the genius of his generalship and of his power over men, of the terrifying danger this land faced and of the need to rouse the people from their complacency.

As he talked and paced, Carlotta saw the cottage fade and with it her bottled passion. The firelight became the red light of her nightmare and the rallying cry in Simon's voice, as he spoke of ships and blockades and maneuvers, became the cry of those who sought her in the dark. Her hands went to her face and her shriek of terror rang out.

Simon's hands were instantly on her shoulders as he pulled her shaking body to his. He murmured nonsense syllables in a soft voice. Carlotta was jarred back to reality and felt her face burn with shame.

"What is it? What frightened you who were not afraid on the highwayman's road?" He patted her back with gentle strokes.

From the depths of his shirt she found it easy to ask, "Why did you hide your face with a mask and leave mine bare for them to memorize? I but thought of hanging and it frightened me so that I cried out. Perhaps it was the drink."

He held her a little way from him even though she sought to hide her flushed face. "No offense, sweeting, but the face of one callow boy is like another and you were well muffled." He touched her neck where the pulse throbbed. "Come and sit with me."

She twisted free and rose to pour more wine for them both. As she handed Simon his, he looked full into her eyes and whispered, "Fair Hebe, cupbearer to Hermes." He set the untasted wine down and ran a questing finger up her arm as he pushed the lace aside.

Carlotta tried to pull away but his touch held her as it traced warmth up to her shoulder. He put the other hand on her neck and tilted her head to his, then the questing lips came down on hers. They touched, moved, and drank at first in gentleness. Then he swept her to him, her slenderness molded to his strength, his arms firm about her body. Carlotta melted to him as her mouth opened under his and their tongues met, retreated, and wound together. Her breath grew short as she felt the hard power of him against the thin material of her skirt. He opened her bodice with one hand and cupped the smooth breast, his fingers working the nipple so that spasms began to rise in her.

Carlotta was suddenly afraid of what she was feeling with

this stranger and she tried to pull back, but he held her easily, his mouth still questing and hard on hers. Her lips clung to his as she felt the burning begin in her loins, very like the pain-pleasure in her nipples. She felt a rising fear at her own hunger and lifted one hand to push him back. He captured it easily and held it behind her back as she struggled to free her mouth.

He looked down at her, sensing at last that her battle was real. The green eyes held something unfathomable in their depths. "What is this, Hebe? Your body curves to mine even as your lips, and yet you will not yield." His hand touched the bare, erect nipples. "You have nothing to fear."

"And yet I do, Simon. I did not mean to mislead you into thinking that I am other than I am." Her voice shook, and she turned her head away so that he could not see her tears. The throbbing began once more in her loins as she reacted to his nearness.

Simon sank down on the cushions and pulled her down with him so that she was partially in his lap. His muscular arms held her gently, and she was conscious of the fresh smell of his body. She leaned her head against his chest, the little golden hairs soft on her cheeks. He began to stroke her back, his fingers causing little ripples of her skin. She shivered as his hand drifted lower and moved into her secret depths. She put her arms around him and pressed closer; her fingers moved in the cornsilk of his hair.

"There is nothing to fear." He repeated the words so softly that she had to strain to hear them. "Little one, trust me."

Simon's fingers worked on the lacings of the gown while his mouth possessed her own. Flames licked through her and she melted in a liquid desire. She heard his clothes rustle to the floor, felt him toss her last covering away, and her defenses fell as her body arched upward.

His eyes were dark with passion and his mouth was set as he pushed her back against the cushions. His kiss stopped her protests but she began to writhe when she felt the length of him on her legs. Where his fingers had given the most intense pleasure, now it seemed that he would split her apart with the force and drive of his manhood as he took her, driving hard into regions unplumbed. He withdrew and plunged again and yet again, even as their tongues twined and drew on each other.

Pain mixed with pleasure for Carlotta as their mingled passion fed and, for her, retreated. She was conscious now of the sweaty body solidly on hers and the size of the organ that used her for a receptacle. Her thighs and the cushions were wet, whether with sweat or her own blood she could not know. His teeth ground against hers and she felt stifled. In the midst of such feelings, however, Carlotta felt again the sweet burning and the rising languor but could not reach any continuance of it. Simon gave a great thrust and she felt the very well of her being rise to meet it. Then he was outside her, his head on her heaving stomach, his gilt hair wet with sweat, passion spent and limp.

Carlotta felt a strange disappointment along with an absurd urge to cry. Was this all? She sighed and turned her head to gaze into Simon's face.

He smiled and one hand touched her lips. "No, little one, that is not all. Olympus itself awaits us both."

CHAPTER EIGHT

Shaft of Passion

CARLOTTA watched his hand as it trailed down her arm and over her rounded breasts and the slight lift of her stomach to the edge of her flank. Little chills chased up and down her naked body and her mouth grew dry. Simon bent his head and followed his fingers with small kisses that seemed to start slow-burning fires under her skin. He moved closer to her woman's mound with his lips as his fingertips stroked the soft auburn hair there.

Carlotta moaned softly and her legs seemed to part without her own will. Her nipples rose and shone in the firelight. Simon's body arched over hers now and he was tonguing her with expert abandon. One hand urged her back so that his whole concentration was on this part of her body. His tongue and hands were so feather-light that she longed for them to grow harder and deeper even as she reveled in the tantalizing delight that was given her. Her hips revolved, and so intense was the hunger in her flesh that she put both hands to her mouth as if in the biting down some of the excitement might find release.

"Simon! I can't bear this!" The words poured out, and she was fearful that he might stop to ask what she had said.

He did not, and the pressure grew stronger within in her. Now hands and mouth were one in her mound and clefts as the gilt hair spread over her white skin. Now the fire was leaping and she was poised to meet it. All around her was darkness as her feet and hands drummed on the cushions. He thrust deeply into her now with the moving fingers as his mouth drew her up. The light flared and then came down to envelop her in a blinding flame that pulled her being asunder.

She was only dimly conscious of Simon as he placed a soft cover over her sweating body and settled her into the crook of his arm. Her heart seemed as if it might hammer out of her chest and her breath came in gradually slowing gasps.

"You are learning of pleasure this night, I think?" The soft, drawling voice spoke in her ear and caused the chills to rise again.

"Aye, Simon." She had no breath for anything else. Weariness was a song in her veins, a cloud over her body, and she longed to give herself up to it even as she wanted the lighting to come again. Had it been so for him at first? Had he taught her to crave the sweet drug of the flesh that might never be satiated? The questions flickered through her mind which was ever prone to wonder about such things, and she tensed slightly.

"It is as close to death as we come and live." Her perception surprised her, and still it was oddly comforting.

"I am so weary." Her mind would move but not her body or her voice.

Simon pulled her close so that her body fitted into the curve of his. Her arms were wound with his arms, and the slow motion of his breath stirred the soft hair at the nape of her neck. The firelight lifted and moved on the ceiling as the logs crumbled and sleep took them.

Carlotta woke several times in the night. She was unused to sleeping with anyone. The warm scent of Simon's breath and the pressure of his body beside hers brought her back to reality as she curled more deeply into the warmth of their nest in the pillows. Once he spoke sharply, as if giving orders, and that jerked her from half sleep. She pulled up on one elbow and looked down at him as he spoke again.

"Dishonor or not, it is the only way. We get on with it!" His head rolled and his brow was furrowed but he slept on. He tossed now and tried to speak again but the words seemed frozen. The high, arched nose twisted as his hand sought for a sword.

Carlotta knew what nightmares were like. Clearly her lover walked in his own that had segments of terror or anger. She touched his hair, wondering again at the softness of it and the way the errant curls clung to her fingers. He turned his head but did not wake. She would have drawn back from the tenderness but for that fact. As it was, she bent to him and said softly, "We get on with it. Rest now and be ready for the morrow."

"Fair one. Foul fair one." The words were halting but hard. It was almost impossible to believe that he slept, and yet she knew that he did. He said them again and behind was a wall of pain.

Carlotta moved close to him and put both arms around as

much of him as she could reach. She breathed slowly and steadily as she murmured nonsense words of comfort that she had often waked to in her youth when the demons of France were upon her. His shuddering calmed and Carlotta snuggled up to the warm back and wondered what fair demon had come to haunt such a man.

The lips on hers were light and searching, the fingers tickling her chin also stroked the line of her throat. Carlotta woke from dreams of satin cushions and green-eyed lovers to find those selfsame eyes looking into hers with mischief.

"You sleep long, Mara. Can it be that you are weary for some reason of which I do not know?" He drew back slightly and offered her ale and warm biscuits wrapped around slivers of meat from the night before. "Eat, we must go out and see what gifts the gods have given while we dallied."

Carlotta saw that no dreams haunted him now. He was laughing down at her as she took the food from him. He wore peasant clothes now but the rough cloth could not disguise the bearing of a lord. She thought that he must be such, but their bond must be kept.

"Is it still snowing?" Again, the words sounded inane, but she knew he must sense the rising passion in her and she turned from it lest it overwhelm her.

"Aye. Hurry and dress." He touched her lips with his finger and she responded so quickly that he withdrew slightly. "I will await you outside."

Carlotta knew she must be careful. Something told her that this man was not to be tamed; she must follow his guide for now. She threw on the thick breeches and shirt he had given her and added the thick shoes, thinking wryly that the adventures of the night might have happened in another world. She opened the door and peered out into the drifting white world. The cold air burned her face and throat as she drew it in. Just then a shower of white exploded in her face and she threw up both hands to brush it away, only to encounter another one.

There was a shout of laughter and she opened both eyes to see Simon bent double as he cried, "Caught you fairly! Catch me if you can!" He hurled another but she ducked and it fell down the side of the cottage.

"No fair, you're three ahead!" She slipped to her knees as if she had something in her eye but in reality to gather up enough snow to make a mushy ball. She rose with a running step and threw it so that the force caught him full in the face.

He recovered and ran after her but she dodged and tripped him so that he fell full in the snow. Then she ran behind a tree and called taunts as he rose.

All morning they played in the snow like the children they had seen in the villages. They threw snowballs at each other, ran, shook the powdery stuff from tree branches, rubbed it in their faces, made giant steps in the virgin whiteness and amused themselves with trying to name what mythical monsters might produce such things, lay down in the steps and made variations of wings and horns for the monsters, walked far in the hushed quiet of the wood, then rushed back in the growing cold.

Simon caught her arm and twirled her to him. "Woman, I starve. Is not your place in the kitchen?"

She leaned back over his arms, her face covered with snow and laughter. "Summon the servants. I will eat from plates of gold and have the rarest of meats."

His eyes darkened suddenly as the gaiety left them and his fingers slackened. Carlotta knew that memory brushed him again as he said, "Aye, it is the way of your sex."

She caught his hand as if she had not heard and pulled him toward the warmth of the cottage. The sky was darker now and the wind keener. It seemed that a storm brewed.

Carlotta went into the bedroom to change out of the soggy clothes she wore. When she emerged wearing a loose tawny robe the color of her eyes, Simon was sitting at the small table already wolfing down the remains of the ham. Her place was prepared and clear wine bubbled in the golden cup. His manner was almost impersonal as he spoke of the weather, the health of the King, the new fashions in gowns and the ridiculousness of them. He quoted a Latin proverb and she responded with the next line.

"A learned lady from the provinces! You are not what you seem."

Carlotta smiled over the rim of her cup. "Nor you, Simon. But that is the game, is it not? No questions, remember?"

He reached across to take the cup from her hand. "I remember much." He set it down and rose. The green eyes shown down into hers, and the already familiar touch sent the sweet fire shooting up her arm. "Come and let us muse together on memory."

"Simon." She hesitated, the words slow in her mouth, but they must be said. All of love that she might ever know would come from this golden man with the shimmering eyes. Foreboding touched her as she remembered a woman in the old village who had been rumored to have the "sight." She would never tell Carlotta's fortune though she begged long and eagerly. "Show me of love. All of it."

He sighed, then smiled and pulled her to him as his mouth took hers. They swayed together for a timeless moment as his hand moved on the back of her head, then down into the small of her back and around to touch her swelling breasts. Her arms encircled him and strained to draw him closer as the drugging sweetness rose up.

The fire rose and ebbed for them both as it was prolonged and fed but never brought to full consummation. It seemed to Carlotta that all her senses expanded, so that she drew in the scent of his flesh along with the snapping flames of the hearth fire that still gave off the smell of summer. The tawny gown whispered about her body as Simon's fingers slid delicately over it and he smiled into her eyes. She leaned forward to kiss the lobe of his ear and let her lips trail down the firm length of his neck. The candle guttered on the table and their shadows stretched long on the wall. Outside the wind lifted in a long wail, carrying a wolf howl to them in their snug nest.

Simon pulled her closer and their lips met in a long kiss that held tenderness and leashed passion. Her body molded to his, and they moved steadily in the old rhythms. She saw that his face was dark with passion and took time to wonder if hers was the same. The cords on his neck stood out, and sweat beaded his forehead. Their hands moved on each other as they joined and drew apart. Carlotta whispered his name as she sought to become part of him and he of her. He swelled and drew inside her as the ecstasy grew.

He looked full at her, his mouth curved in a half smile that held both promise and lure. Her body arched to his as she held him by the shoulders, her senses even more excited by the long, powerful limbs dusted slightly with golden hair. She began to shiver with eagerness and drew him close. Her flesh was now one long burning, no longer banked. She and Simon were welded together, his mouth locked on hers, as they tossed in their own world of flame and thunder.

She thought that the beginning of life must be like this, the tearing and the plunging, the weight coming down inexorably. Then all ideas left her and what remained was the flood, the falling into light and the lifting up as they convulsed from anticipation postponed into gratification and glory.

They made love once more that night, after their first exhaustion had worn off. This time the flames were muted into warmth and tenderness as they moved slowly with each other in a mutual cherishing. His kisses seemed to draw the heart out of Carlotta and she clung to him even as she laved his face with her tongue. The light came for them again, and this time it shone so brightly that she wanted the piercing sweetness to continue forever. Simon lay very still in the aftermath, but the warmth of his fingers in their clasped hands told her all she needed to know. Tears burned in her eyes in love's sadness; it took no power of the sight to know that it would not be like this for her again.

Simon sighed and drew her closer in what was already ritual preparation for sleep as their bodies curved together. Carlotta knew that she would not sleep. She would lie here and savor this time out of time, the dregs of this sweet passion that had sundered her life so that she would never again be the same. The frightened girl had become a woman. She smiled a little as the sadness lifted. There was much she could tell the romancers!

"Simon?" Her voice was soft in the silence just before sleep.

He groaned slightly. "What is it, you insatiable woman?"

Carlotta did not know what prompted the question. Perhaps it was just that she could not sleep and wanted some part of his life to carry with her into the unknown. "What great service did Old Bess do for you that you hold her so highly?"

She felt him stiffen beside her. Surely he could not regard so small a question as the breaking of the bond to which they had sworn?

He said, lightly, "Women and their questions! I will answer that one and no more."

She twisted over so that her back was to him. "You need not."

The gesture might not have been made and she regretted the dishonesty of it. He took no notice but said, "She gave me shelter when the King's men pursued me once years ago. She did not know me and she took me in, risking hanging herself. I have watched over her ever since. The cry about highwaymen has risen so high lately that I may be forced to retire for a time. Bess knows that I care for my own. I pay my debts."

He moved apart from Carlotta and she knew that no more questions would be answered. She stretched and yawned

59

deeply, hoping that he would take her curiosity for idle talk after lovemaking.

"Forgive me that I pried." She put an arm tentatively in the small of his back. He did not push her away.

"Questions . . ." His voice trailed away and soon she knew that he slept.

The fire died and rose again as the new fuel put on it from time to time caught and blazed. Gradually the darkness in the room faded into the gray of day. She could hear the thump of a branch now and then as the trees close by succumbed to the weight of the snow. Simon lay on his side, and her eye traced the lines of his hard body in the dimness. His face was partially obscured but she could see the arrogant curve of it and the flickers of light on the high cheekbone. Her heart twisted in her as she thought of their passion. All her flesh was exhausted with lovemaking and yet she yearned to feel him large within her. Had Lady Leticia felt so for her feline young lover? She might have counted the risk of what she might lose well worth the cost. Carlotta thought she could understand something of the passions that drove people now, and that knowledge made her guilty for herself.

She turned her face away from her own visions and looked into the brilliant eyes of Simon. Wordlessly they joined once more in the hunger that drove them to the heights.

CHAPTER NINE

The Long Knowing

CARLOTTA stretched long and luxuriously and lifted her arms up over her head, letting the soap drip down them to the water below. A hot bath was still a marvelous thing for her after the dirt and grime forced upon her by the masquerade of the past few days. Simon had curtained off his alcove and brought the water for her, laughing as he did so.

"You will be the cleanest fair lady in all these parts. Old Bess would vow you had lost your mind."

"Perhaps I have." She laughed up at him and thrilled to the softness in the green eyes.

"Aye, it is an easy thing to do." He touched the spilling hair that was bound loosely on top of her head, and the gesture was oddly tender. "I must go and get wood for the fire now, but I will be close by."

Close by, Carlotta mused now, how safe that sounded. How secure. The water laved her loins, which were sore from the night before, and the chills rose on her arms at the thought of it. Her world seemed bounded by this golden man, met so strangely, and with whom she had chosen to dare much. She would never be the same, she knew that now.

"Dreaming?" The silken voice preceded him as his long fingers parted the cloaks and his wind-flushed face looked in.

Carlotta started and cool water splashed out. "Simon! I did not expect you to return so swiftly."

He held up a tawny robe. "It is freshly warmed."

She rose, cold stippling her nipples, and let him envelop her in it and bear her to the now roaring fire. He tilted her head back and their lips joined in a gentle kiss. Then they sat in companionable silence as they looked into the depths of the ever-changing flames.

It was the night of their fourth day together and Simon had said nothing about leaving. Carlotta hoped that the interlude would continue, but she feared the inevitable departure. She had schooled herself to enjoy the most and take it for what it was. They had walked again in the woods, spying once a buck

61

with huge antlers, another time a well fed wolf. They had talked, dreamed, eaten prodigiously, quoted the poets, wished many an evil fate on Napoleon, rolled and tumbled in snow and bed as if they were puppies. Much was held back by virtue of the agreement they had made, but Carlotta felt the communion between them and knew that Simon did also.

"Mara," Simon spoke reflectively, almost hesitantly, and she looked up in alarm. "You came to me virgin."

"Aye, Simon." She could think of nothing else to say as she watched the flicker of the firelight on his jaw. His swordsman's fingers moved absently on her arm and she felt the flesh lift to meet them.

"I am not usually a despoiler of virgins." His tone was rueful. "I thought that you were not, your clothes, the life in the village . . . now, truly, you will have little enough."

Carlotta pulled away from him and drew the robe closer about her body. "I have found great pleasure with you, Simon. I do not regret it."

He smiled and caught her hands in his. "Little one, I just do not want to hurt you." He pressed a kiss in the palm of her right hand and then trailed them up her bare arm, causing trickles of fire to begin. "I, too, take great delight in your body and mind. You are an enchanting woman."

Carlotta looked at his bent head with the springing curls of silver gilt and the brown hands that could be so gentle. Sudden tears misted her eyes for the happiness of this moment; somehow she knew that such words did not come easily to Simon. She put both arms around his neck as he touched soft kisses to her throat, where the pulses leaped. His hand dropped to her breasts and he caressed the swelling nipples. The world blurred for her as she called his name and they melted together.

It snowed heavily the next day and they did not venture out but stayed by the fire to eat, talk, and make love. They stumbled upon the game quite by accident. Carlotta and Uncle Arnold, with Aunt Rosa sometimes participating, had often quoted poetry in various languages to each other in the rainy or snowy winter evenings, pausing at a crucial place for the others to supply the next lines. Later they had acted them out, and Carlotta came to realize just how much she had learned under the guise of fun.

She told Simon of this now, being careful to make Uncle Arnold the schoolmaster who believed, far ahead of his time, that women should be versed in the classics. He lifted an inquiring eyebrow at her.

"Right gladly will I play but the forfeit shall be kisses . . . and other things."

They heard the hiss of the snow as it came more heavily against the walls of the cottage and the graying light of day sifted down. Carlotta smiled at Simon and accepted his condition, even as she felt the pang of knowledge that this could not last. His face was younger than she had ever seen it, and his green eyes were brilliant with laughter at the camaraderie that was between them. An inadvertent blast of cold air touched her as she moved a little away from the fire and drew the skirts of the tawny velvet gown more closely over her feet.

"'I know a bank whereon the wild thyme blows, where oxslips and the nodding violet grows . . .'" His words trailed off and the carved lips touched her fingers in the briefest of kisses.

"'There sleeps Titania some time of the night.'" For a second, winter faded as she saw them lying in the depth of the greenwood with flowers for their canopy, their bodies long and golden in the fading light of day.

He drew her to him, and his mouth slipped softly over her shoulders before pausing at the pulse in her throat. "You were right. The forfeit must be paid."

She laughed, the sound unsteady in the firelit room. "But I thought that was if one of us was wrong."

"Not so, sweeting. You will never make a gambler. The forfeit is the same, right or wrong."

She ruffled the soft hair at his temples. "I like your methods, sir, as well as your forfeits."

His mouth claimed hers then, and they drank of each other's warmth while desire coursed in their veins. Carlotta fitted in his arms as they melted together.

They played the game with lovers of the past: Dido and Aeneas, Admetus and Alcestis, Orpheus and Eurydice, their own version of Helen and Paris, those of the comedies of Shakespeare. The forfeits were many and each was taken lingeringly and long as the day faded and the fire burned low. Sentiment and laughter and lovemaking had had their completeness and the lovers lay in each other's arms, covered by a heavy silk and velvet robe, a little abashed by the heights to which their fancies had taken them.

Simon pushed at her gently as he whispered, "I am hungry once more. It is your turn to fetch food and wine."

She turned over to face him. "It is too cold in here. You must bring it and build up the fire as well."

"Do you seek to cajole me, woman?" He raised up on one elbow and his bare shoulders were instantly peppered with goose pimples.

"Not I, my lord, I simply point out that these are man things to be done by he who is the stronger." She cast her eyes down demurely.

"Your logic is faulty but your play-acting is scarcely better." He laughed softly and began to fumble for his own robe of green velvet which had been tossed hastily away in one of the wilder forfeits they both had paid earlier.

Carlotta looked up at his lithe, powerful body, where the muscles stood out, the flat line of his stomach, the wide shoulders and slim hips, and even as she warmed once more to him, she seemed to see something and the words rose to her lips though she fought to hold them back.

". . . bit by bit eaten and rotten, rent and shred, And we the bones grow dust and ash withal . . . we were slain by law . . ."

Simon turned to her incredulously and started to speak, then paused as he saw that her eyes stared through and beyond him to the gibbet that the poet had seen.

In that moment, Carlotta came back to herself. "Simon, forgive me. I cannot think what made me remember Villon . . . gods, my love, I am afraid for you, for us both!" Her voice cracked, and she put both hands to her face that he should not see her weep.

Simon pulled on the robe, then reached out and pulled her to him, his words tender in the chilling room. "Mara, do not weep. We have been happy together for these many days, and the human spirit is such that there must be sadness to balance it. Do not fear for me, I am a passing excellent highwayman. Your fear is understandable, and I am honored that you fear for me, but you need not."

She raised her wet face to his. "Simon, are you more than that? Surely there is another profession, an honorable one, to which you might return? I, too, am not all that you might think. . . ." Her words faded before the scowl on his face.

"We made a bargain, remember? I hold you to it." His eyes were hard and watchful as his hands put her from him.

"Forgive me," she said again as she forced herself to calmness. "I will not seek again to pry."

The laughter was gone from them both after that, and they did not try to find it again as they ate and drank before the now roaring fire. Their lovemaking was slow and sweet, with a lingering desperation about it that made Carlotta blink back the tears long after Simon lay apart in sleep.

She woke very early the next morning to find him gone from her side. Usually they wound together in the first light for kisses and murmurs before turning over to sleep again, but now her questing arm on the covers told her that he had risen long ago. She sat upright, pummeling the sleep from her eyes and shivering as she called his name. Nothing. There was no sound except the hiss of the snow and the crackle of the fire in the next room.

Carlotta jumped up and fastened the more voluminous of the robes about her body. Surely he would not have gone off and left her! It came to her with renewed force that she knew nothing about this man to whom she had given so much of herself, the first longing of her life. They had shared much and yet she knew suddenly that they knew little of the essence of each other. She knew his face, the way one dark brow lifted when he laughed, the angular cheekbones, the sun-bronzed flesh that crinkled near the brilliant eyes. She knew his long, muscular body with the flat stomach and firm thighs, the spread of his shoulders, and the long thrust of his manhood. She knew the sound of his laughter and passion, the way of his bravery and anger, but she was ignorant as to the manner of his nature. It did not matter, she thought, for she knew that she loved this man whose name she did not even know. The searing panic caught her and she fought back a sudden sob. She had endured much to find these few days of happiness; were they now to be taken away from her because of a few idle words? It seemed to Carlotta then that she looked down a long vista of years, barren because the one who held her heart was not there. The shivers began then despite the warmth of the robe and the blazing fire, as she looked at herself and knew that the chains had been forged.

Suddenly the door rattled and slammed back as the hooded figure entered. Carlotta raised her drawn face and looked into the sober green eyes of Simon as he stamped the snow from his feet and came across to her. He did not touch her, but his look was more eloquent than that as he said, "I had hoped that you would still be sleeping. Caleb, the man who keeps this lair and guards it for me in my absence, woke me while it was yet dark. The King's own troops have been called out to search for the highwayman, Hermes, and his young helper. There is a mighty price on my head, far more than usual, and he has heard dangerous talk in the village near here. We must go to ground, Mara."

She stared, unaware that her amber eyes and pale skin were lit with hope restored. Her slender hands clutched the brown velvet of the robe and worked convulsively. "I thought you had gone. That you were angered because of my words last night . . ."

He snorted and crossed the room to pour out some heady wine. "We leave this night. There is only today. Come and kiss me while we may, little one." He held out his arms and she ran into them, forgetful of tears as their lips met.

That day was filled with last things. Carlotta and Simon deliberately did not speak of the immediate future. Instead they lay curled in the cushions and watched the fire lift and crackle while they spoke idly of surface things or kissed gently in the warmth. Simon's fingers moved slowly on the nape of her neck and down her spine; Carlotta felt the chill lessening as tension uncoiled. The invisible servant, Caleb, had given Simon cold chicken and ham that morning, along with sweetcakes. This was their morning meal, well-washed down with thin wine.

Carlotta looked at Simon as he ate with gusto and felt her own stomach shrivel with loss. "This is likely the last meal we shall ever share. The last touch of his flesh on mine. The last laughter and the last . . ." She forced her mind to turn aside lest she weep before him.

There was a sound of heavy movement outside and several branches broke. Simon was instantly on his feet, the sword appearing in his hand as if it had been born there. He pointed with his other hand, and Carlotta slid over the floor until the gleaming pistol was in her grasp. The trampling came more heavily now. Simon moved closer to the door, sword at the ready. Carlotta thought that they could at least die together, then shame caught at her and she lifted her head in a desperate pride. Simon saw and his glance was a kiss across the room.

"Who . . . who's there? Speak!" His voice was low and quavery, old, perhaps sick.

Carlotta raised the pistol in both shaking hands and looked along the barrel. The movement was more pronounced now, a sort of trampling followed by banging sounds. Simon edged the door open slowly as an old person, alone and fearful, might be driven to do. Carlotta moved slowly to one side, the pistol suddenly steady. She would shoot to kill to save him, she knew that as surely as anything she had ever known.

There was a sudden whickering and a rush as the wind pushed against the door. Simon lowered the sword and burst into laughter. Carlotta rushed up to him and was in time to see the stately buck, tall-antlered, reddish hide spattered with snow, moving slowly off into the swirling whiteness. Reaction caught her and she leaned against Simon's warmth to give herself up to the healing laughter that banished fear.

"A fine old woman you make, Sir Highwayman! I would have thought you at least eighty-five and doddering!" She swung back from him, shivering in the icy air of the open door.

He shut it and reached her in a single movement. "Old woman, am I? You, of course, are the first guardsman of the King! That pistol could have taken the roof off!" He began to tickle her, laughing at her struggles to escape. She was hampered by the loose robe and could not free herself, turn and twist as she might. "My prisoner. Yield or I exact forfeit again."

Carlotta slowly relaxed in the warm hands that touched her softness. He pulled her closer and chuckled in his throat. She dug her fingers into his ribs and laughed as he jumped convulsively. She was free and the robe hung in his fingers. The air was still cold in the room and her flesh was stippled with bumps from it. "Forfeit, indeed, Simon!" She crossed both arms over her chest and edged closer to the fire, laughing as she did so.

"Mara." He held out both hands to her. "I yield to the fair."

"And I to the brave." She put both hands in his and they fused together as their shadows ran long on the walls in the firelight.

CHAPTER TEN

The Sunless Earth

THEY left their hiding place shortly after the early winter dusk had fallen. Both were clad in sober fustian and thick riding cloaks, gloves, and boots, and they rode mules which had seen better days. "Servants on the way to join their master, a merchant of Bristol, and delayed on the road by the storm." So had Simon explained to Carlotta as they dressed beside the fire. The silent Caleb had materialized once more with the mules, and they had left him dourly setting matters to rights, erasing all signs of habitation.

Specks of ice mixed with snow slapped Carlotta in the face as she rode slightly behind Simon over the rutted trail. He did not speak but rode hunched against the cold even as she did. Already the sweetness of the day seemed to fade against the reality in which they found themselves. Carlotta thought once again of the tenderness of that last lovemaking, his hands gentle on her breasts, his mouth warm and seeking as it cherished hers until they both trembled into flame. Afterward they lay deeply in each other, reluctant to move or to shatter the moment. Again and yet again her brain had whispered, "The last time." There had been no words, only their bodies speaking to each other in longing and affirmation. All too soon the discreet knock had come and their time was done.

Carlotta flexed her stiff fingers and wondered once again how far it might be to Bristol. It was a thought that was to occur over and over during that freezing night on the deserted road. They saw lights in the distance several times, and once a fast riding group of men disappeared over a rise and circled back to group themselves in a copse close by. Carlotta and Simon dismounted to lead the mules along the trail. Their footsteps were soon hidden by the drifting snow. By the time they dared mount again, Carlotta was wet and shaking with exhaustion. Simon's face was only a blur in the faint light and frost rimmed his cap, but she knew that he, too, must be as weary as she.

They came at dawn to a shell that had once been a hut of

the meanest sort before it had been blackened by fire and devastation. Only one sod wall was left and the remnant of a hearth was overgrown with brush now hung with ice. It would provide some shelter against the wind, however, and a small fire might not be noticed. "Sleep, and I will watch; then you can do the same for me." Simon's voice rasped in the hard air.

Carlotta was unable to argue, for she was dizzy from lack of sleep and all the excitement of the past few days. She took the heavy cloak and wrapped herself well in it as she huddled at the base of the wall. He handed her the small bottle of cheap wine such as minor servants might be expected to carry and watched while she drank. She gave it back and whispered, "Do not let me sleep long."

She soon found that she could not sleep at all. Her entire body was numb, and the piercing cold was damp as well. There was no comfortable position to be found though she tossed and twisted. Simon watched for a few minutes and finally came to her. "Here, Mara. Lie quietly in my arms and let your thoughts drift." She demurred but he lifted her to his lap and swayed back and forth, murmuring as to a child, the green eyes slitted against the gray day. Carlotta put her head on his shoulder and listened to the soft voice weave an enchantment all its own.

"The sea is both blue and green, very warm to the touch, and you can slip through the little waves as easily as a woman might wrap herself in softest silk. The sky is deepest blue and the sun hot on the skin as you lie on the white sand...God's own land, they call it, a land rich and promising...."

Carlotta seemed to feel the heat pressing into her bones and hear the lap of the distant sea as it lulled her. The cradling arms were sanctuary around her and she drifted free, the only sound the thump of Simon's heart and the hiss of the snow.

When Carlotta woke, the world was different. She had been placed at the base of the wall and wound in the cloak, but the howl of the wind penetrated to her ears along with the far-off yapping of dogs. Snow was falling still more heavily, covering the vague daylight. Simon stood at the mules, his whole body tense. As she struggled out of her cocoon, he turned to her quickly.

"We must go now. The storm will give us good cover. Yon barking may mean nothing or everything. Hurry."

She rubbed her eyes with gloved hands and yawned. The sleep had done her good. "Simon, did you sleep at all?"

He had retreated from her. The tenderness of the past might

69

never have been. "Aye, even as you did, Mara. Now we must press on."

The next night and day were one long frozen nightmare for Carlotta. Their pace was as rapid as the mules would bear, and they kept always to the lesser trails. Icicles rattled in the branches above them, the wind moaned and bit, the snow never stopped. Simon did not speak again and Carlotta could not bring herself to interrupt his imposed silence, for she knew that in some way he had exceeded his own limits with her. Instead, she remembered all that had passed between them and sought to warm herself with memory. The cold which had been a joyous plaything was now only an impediment; she remembered the warm land of which Simon had spoken and longed for it with an intensity that made her smile at her own fancies.

Late on the afternoon of the next day, a time when Carlotta was reeling with exhaustion and chill again, for they had paused only briefly in that time, they came out of the wooded area, crossed a small flatland, and came out onto a road which, though filled with iced ruts and deep ditches, seemed a broad avenue compared to the ones they had just left. An abandoned carriage, wheels askew, lay on one side in the mud and was already half covered by the snow. Simon, his face set in stern lines, lifted one hand and pointed to the top of the rise. Once there, they drew rein. Smoke was visible in the distance as were spires and several ship's masts. Dark smudges against the horizon indicated the presence of the city some thought second only to London.

"Yonder is Bristol town." Simon did not look at Carlotta as he spoke.

She pushed her stiffened foot into the mule's side and it ambled closer to Simon's. Her voice sounded high and shrill in the wind. "What happens now? Our adventure is done, I well know."

His eyes rested on her briefly and seemed to look beyond, into the snow drifts they mirrored. "Aye, Mara. It must be so. We both knew that." He waited for her nod before continuing. "I know a place of relative safety. We will discuss the future there. Come."

Carlotta was too glad to think that they were to have a future, even a short one, to regret that her feelings for him were palpable in her every word and gesture. An hour with Simon was worth years with anyone else, she thought as her flesh trembled with memory. Would he take her once again?

She smiled in anticipation and caught the green flicker of his glance as they rode.

The din in the streets seemed incredible to Carlotta after the measured quiet of the past days. Even in the fierce night cold tradesmen called their wares, carriages and wagons clattered by, street criers and scavengers mingled with the richly clad gentlefolk as bold women shouted from upper windows. Wild music poured out of several tavern doors as Carlotta and Simon walked along, leading the mules. Mud was splashed up on them both but they did not hasten for they did not wish to attract undue attention, even in these low surroundings which were quite near the wharves. Now and then Carlotta caught the fresh tang of sea and river air and her senses quickened.

They turned into the small inn yard at the end of one of the crooked streets. The tavern door opened off to one side and loud bellowing was much in evidence. On a faded red and gold sign which hung above the listing door and proclaimed this to be the Sea Lion, a once saucy mermaid touched a battered mane of a kneeling lion.

"Wait here." Simon strode off without a backward glance. She saw that the cautious tread he had used in the streets was gone; now he moved as he had at the hut and when they first met. What an enigma he was!

A howl rose from the interior of the tavern. "Emperor, is it? Who cares? He's still a bloody jumped-up Corsican and everybody knows it!" There were yells of assent. "Drink to it, lads, drink to his pratfall!"

Carlotta felt the cold of the yard fade and she saw a vaulted cathedral where voices were raised in thanksgiving and figures in cloth-of-gold moved slowly by as others knelt. The world swung, and she shook her head to clear it. An elbow hammered against her ribs just then and a drunken voice cried, "Not drinking, boy? Here, have some of mine. Got to drink to Boney's fall!"

The man was large and bearded with little mean eyes. Just now he was good humored but he looked as if he could turn belligerent at any time. He held the heavy tankard before her face and waved it. She recoiled before she could help it and heard his angry mutter. Suddenly a hand reached for her shoulder and twitched her back out of the man's path.

"The room is ready. Come." It was Simon, his face clear cut and sharp even in the flickering torch light. He turned to

71

the swaying drunk. "My brother is almost asleep on his feet, else he would drink to so worthy a cause even as I have done."

An instant later they were on the dark stairs, which seemed to go on forever before opening into a small room where a fire burned on the grate and food as well as wine was laid out. Steaming water stood in a container close by. There was one ramshackle bed but it was well laden with covers. Carlotta gave a small sigh of pleasure.

"Never was warmth so welcome. We shall surely sleep well this night." She snatched off the cap and ran her fingers through her hair so that it tumbled about her shoulders down to her waist. "Thank you for the rescue. He came on me so suddenly that I could not think."

Simon crossed the room with a quick impatient gesture and turned to warm his hands at the fire. "It would have been better had you drunk with him or appeared to do so. The city is afire with the news, though how it could have been unexpected I cannot fathom."

Carlotta stared, caught by the gravity of his tone.

"Napoleon has crowned himself Emperor of the French with his own hand, bypassing the Pope's authority that he sought and all that the Revolution once stood for. Is there no end to his power and ambition?" He slammed his hands together, his face weary and drawn in the light.

"Simon . . . ?" She longed to comfort him but did not know how. She had grown up with accounts of Napoleon and his exploits, the uneasy peace, the peril of war. Much of it had been remote to her, but of late a great pride had permeated her heart and she was again proud to call herself English. She opened her mouth to tell him of this and stopped abruptly. Simon was picking up his cloak and bending over to adjust his boots. Surely he could not be preparing to leave? "Where are you going? I thought we . . . I mean, I . . ." She stumbled to a halt before the last bit of pride should be bare.

He said, "Mara, I have business that will occupy much of the night. Lock the door securely and I will knock softly twice when I return. In the event that it takes longer than I expect, I will leave money for you." He held up one hand to still any expected protest. "Your share, let us call it, of the booty from Lord Fenton."

Carlotta saw that he was anxious to leave. The tender, considerate lover of the past days was gone and in his place stood a polite stranger. She tried to control her voice but it shook as she said, "I pray you, use your good offices to assist me in finding some sort of work here. I do not doubt that you know the city, it may even be that you know someone needing clerkly skills—I write a neat and careful hand, for the schoolmaster taught me well."

Simon's mouth quirked downward. "My dear, I am a highwayman, not one who can place young women in situations. Be well assured that I will help you."

Something in his voice caused her to look sharply at him. His mouth was smiling but there was a stillness about him that made her uneasy. Suddenly she was cold in spite of the warm room. "What do you mean?"

"Come, come, Mara. We have found pleasure in each other, have we not? Enjoyed much?" He frowned and the green eyes flickered over her body. "There is no need to upset yourself about the future or go into maidenly cries about what you are to do. After all, my dear, I have never cast aside a woman yet without making sure that she was provided for."

"Cast aside!"

Simon gave a sigh of exasperation. "Forgive me, my tongue is too blunt. I am tired and it will be long before I sleep. I only meant . . ."

Carlotta lost her temper then and she was thankful for it, because the tears of rage and shame were intermingled. "I take your meaning quite well without the interpretation! Get out! Get out!" She looked about for something to throw at him and reached for the wine bottle as the nearest thing. He caught her arm and shook it almost roughly.

"Behave yourself. There is nothing to be gained by acting like a fishwife in the market." He turned his back on her then and walked to the door. A moment later it clicked shut behind him.

Carlotta stared after him as desolation rolled over her. She put the mouth of the bottle to her lips and took a great gulp of wine which caused her to sputter. Tears came to her eyes and then she threw herself on the bed and gave herself up to them. She wept for the loss of innocence, but mostly she wept for the vision of love that had just been torn asunder. A romantic episode was one thing; surely Simon must have felt something for her. This casual supposition that she expected his money, expected him to treat her as his mistress for even a short time with the understanding that she would be soon cast from him and well compensated, all this stung her pride and tore her heart. She knew well enough that, had he asked it, she would gladly have ridden the high roads with him or waited to welcome him when he returned. This cold-blooded view of his, the total lack of caring in one who had been so tender, was unbearable. A romantic interlude, yes. Business, no. She cried the harder and did not know when sleep took her up.

It was very late when she woke and stretched, feeling herself again. There was a tiny window high in the little room, and she could see the grayness that was always daylight nowadays. Warmth permeated everything, for the fire was built high. She saw that a jug of liquid and some fresh cakes were placed on the table by the bed and a heap of clothes lay on the chair close by the fire. A folded paper lay on the covers close to her hand.

Carlotta sat up and pushed her hair back. All her thoughts and anger of the night before rushed back. Simon! Had he left her for good? Did anything matter besides this tall man who held her world? She snatched up the note and read it aloud, her voice growing soft in the silence.

"Mara, my dear. I am not the unfeeling cad you must think me. Please take this purse of gold and buy yourself some pretty things with it. We will speak of the future tonight when I return. You must hear me out and not unloose that temper. You gave me light these past days and I will always remember that."

His signature slashed bold and black across the page, as distinctive as the man himself. She touched her lips to it and felt the sensual shudder run through her body. He had reconsidered the effect of his words on her. She knew it. He must care for her. Carlotta felt her lips curve up in a smile. She would indeed hear his words this night, and later their bodies would drink deep of each other. The future could take care of itself. She would take now and make the most of it.

An hour later she was ready for the street. The brown dress, cloak, and shoes left by Simon fitted her reasonably well and would prove warm if not particularly becoming. She guessed that he must have obtained them hurriedly, perhaps at a pawn shop. How could she have slept through his coming into the room? Surely her senses would have told her of his presence but for her total weariness. No matter, she planned to be well rested for the night. She touched the purse of gold; it was heavy and would buy much. Now there was no compunction about taking it. She meant to fight for Simon and believed that he was more than half in love with her already. "I am shameless."

She spoke the words aloud and wondered again at the kind of person she had become in so short a time.

It was afternoon when she emerged from the inn. The proprietor had been dozing by the fire but she saw him twitch awake as she passed. Doubtless he would wonder where the woman had come from, but this was not the type of inn where many questions were asked. Outside a raw wind was blowing and the going was icy. People picked their way cautiously, even carriages went more slowly than usual. She walked for a time, breathing deeply of the cold air that bore the scent of water. She went past coffee houses where the fashionable would gather later in the day, taverns and inns of all descriptions, shops filled with the wealth of the world, into broad avenues holding the houses of the wealthy, and finally to a little hill from which she could see the river Avon. It was not thickly iced and she could see ships anchored, their masts bare and stark against the gray sky, while others moved slowly from the harbor, sails belling out before the same wind that buffeted her.

The cold finally drove Carlotta into a little shop several streets over from the hill. There was a display of fine lace in the bow window, and she could see several gowns hanging just beyond the thin curtains. The gold was weighting down her pockets, and this seemed a good place to start spending as Simon had ordered.

Inside it was warm and scented; she thought longingly of tea or chocolate but concentrated on the large, too-blonde woman who approached. She was clad in unrelieved black that accentuated the brilliant hair, and her eyes were a snapping brown.

"Are you looking for someone, girl? Your mistress, perhaps?"

Carlotta's chin rose and she heard the sharpness in her tone as she said, "You mistake me, madame. I had planned to buy. I need several gowns at once and can leave a commission for others. I should like to examine your wares, however." She extended one hand to wave at the gowns in the edge of the window and the gold chinked loudly.

· The woman smiled with her lips only. "Of course. Forgive me. I can show you several things now and then I have an appointment with a most important personage. We can set a time for you to return afterwards if you like. I am Madame Adelaide."

Carlotta drew the brown bonnet from her head and the candles of the shop lit the auburn hair with brilliance. She had bundled it up in her haste and now it tumbled around her shoulders. The woman's eyes lit up as she motioned to Carlotta to remove the cloak.

"You are fortunate that you are so small; there is a green gown here that will surely fit you and, if you wish, more can be made along that pattern. Will you wish to try it on?"

"Certainly." Carlotta was conscious of her muddy shoes on the carpet of soft gold and russet, but she did not falter as she followed in the wake of Madame.

A few minutes later Carlotta stood looking at herself in the curved mirror and knew beyond doubt that she was beautiful. It did not need Madame Adelaide's indrawn breath nor the gasp of the little maid who helped adjust the dress to tell her that. It was in the shimmer that the green silk gave to her skin, the slenderness of her waist in the soft folds which fell to the floor and drifted there, the deepness of her amber eyes which cast back the reflection of the rich color, and the tumbling hair that took flame from the light and shadow of the dress. The sleeves were long and trailing and they, too, shimmered and whispered as she moved. Her face was pointed, the brows dark wings above the curve of her cheek.

"I don't know myself." The words rose involuntarily to her lips.

"Aye, but your lover will." Madame Adelaide laughed richly, and Carlotta felt a chill go up her spine as if in fear for the future.

CHAPTER ELEVEN

The Double Heart

CARLOTTA, dressed once more in the brown clothes, the green dress and its accessories carefully packed in a bag under her arm, walked lightly over the mud-encrusted street which went to the general direction of the Sea Lion. It was growing colder and the gray afternoon was shading toward evening, but she might have moved along a flower-strewn path so oblivious was she. Thoughts of the time to come occupied her mind, and she imagined the light in Simon's eyes when he saw her. She had recklessly ordered other gowns as well; they came in colors to rival the spring—pink, gold, lavender, and soft white. Nothing she could have practical use for, she decided, but the excitement of knowing what she could really look like had carried her away. The future was far off just now. She was a woman going to a meeting with her lover, a woman who would risk much that she might gain all.

"In the bright May morning, Oh, the winsome maid sought her lover bold..." She sang the words of the old ballad half under her breath and then they rang out as her happiness increased. A middle-aged couple walked slowly past, drawing back as they heard her, and an urchin, poorly dressed against the cold, paused to gape. She did not notice. Her mind rang with his name and her breasts tingled against the rough fabric of her shift. "I never knew it was like this. The romances are pale copies." A snowflake touched her lips and she put out her tongue to catch it as she had done in her childhood, laughing as she did so.

Just then there was the sound of hoofbeats and an elegant carriage rolled by, the coachman muffled and arrogant on his high seat. Carlotta jumped aside as it missed her by only a foot or so. She landed in a puddle of icy water, and she had to fight to maintain her balance. Fear for the beautiful dress made her clutch it all the harder. The struggle left her a bit breathless, and she stepped back into the shadow of the nearby shop, one of many on this secluded side street. A wash of laughter, infectious and gurgling, came to her ears. It was repeated in the deeper tones of a man's amusement. Carlotta stiffened; she had heard that laugh in waking dreams for the past few days.

A man and woman were emerging from a shop several doors away, where the carriage had halted. The proprietor and several flunkies were following them, and a footman stood ready to assist. The woman was dressed in flowing white garments that accentuated her dark coloring and lustrous blue-black hair. Her gloved hands were tiny, the furred cloak fell back to show a waist of wasp size. Her face was a pure oval, her mouth soft and red. But it was the man who held Carlotta rigid. He wore highly polished black boots, breeches of bottle-green velvet, with frills of white at his throat. A cloak of paler green swung from his shoulders. The silver gilt head was bare to the cutting wind as he bent over the lady, a hand under her elbow, his face eager. It was Simon.

Carlotta's world shifted and narrowed before the intensity of her gaze. She could not have moved if the carriage had been launched at her. The girl laughed again, and now Carlotta could hear the tender amusement in Simon's voice.

"Faith, my lovely, you outshine all these creations you seem to find so fair."

"Flatterer!" Her words were low and breathy.

"Nay, only a truthteller." He lifted up her slight body toward the step, and his hands lingered on the small waist.

Carlotta's gaze seemed to have penetrated even the absorption of these two, for even as the girl swayed in the door of the carriage, Simon turned slightly and his eyes met those of Carlotta. His face hardened into dark planes and he made a swift dismissing gesture before swinging up into the interior and calling out, "Drive on, man! We are chilled."

The carriage had vanished completely by the time Carlotta felt her elbow jiggled and a sharp voice spoke in her ear. "Move, girl, you will discourage customers by gaping that way." The short, plump man had come from the leather shop to peer at the lowering sky, and now he viewed Carlotta with an annoyed eye.

She heard herself speak, the words coming slowly and heavily. "I am sorry, I just never saw so fair a lady as that one, just there in the carriage."

He laughed, momentarily distracted. "Aye. Lady Penshurst is the fairest lady in the realm and the richest. She graced my shop only the other day. My apprentices were struck dumb, I can tell you!"

Carlotta leaned toward him, one hand reaching out. "Did you see the gentleman with her today? Who is he? Her husband?"

The shopkeeper drew back before her urgency, his smile fading. "There is no Lord Penshurst! Why all this curiosity about your betters? Get along, girl." He whirled and marched into his shop, slamming the door behind him.

Carlotta began to walk aimlessly, splashing through more puddles, slipping on the cobbles and banging into other people several times. She tasted salt and knew that she wept, but it was as if she could feel nothing. Her legs continued to move, she breathed and shivered, but her mind seemed shut away. Her arms swung heavily at her sides and it came to her that she had once carried a package there, that her pocket had been weighty with gold. Now she had nothing. Nothing, how true that was. Something told her that this should be funny, a rich joke, but she could not laugh.

She went on and on as the night grew deeper. She had no idea where she was going or what was happening around her; she simply had to move. Once a ragged man stepped in front of her and moved with her as she tried to go around him. She stood still and waited for him to move; he laughed until he looked into her eyes. Then he stood aside and allowed her to plod on.

More endless streets, raucous yells and laughter, then a hand caught her arm and swung her savagely around. She stood docilely in the grip; sooner or later it would release her and she could walk on. Then she was shaken so hard that her hair fell back from her face and she looked into the familiar green eyes.

"What is the matter with you, you little fool? Why did you not go back to the inn? This is dangerous territory down here." Simon wore a black cloak now, the hood framing his face which was a mask of anger.

Carlotta stared at him, wondering at his tone. Then time seemed to turn back and she saw him again with the beautiful Lady Penshurst and remembered her own innocent delight in the night to come. Pain, bitterness, and fury swirled in her as the apathy left her. She was conscious of her freezing feet, shivering body, and twitching face. She cried, "Ah, from one doxy to another, is it? And what am I, Simon, that you dismiss me so casually in the street while simpering over your whore? Or is it the other way around?"

She saw his hand uplifted to strike and thought that she would welcome the blow if it would send her into oblivion, away from the pain that ate at her vitals. He pulled his hood a little lower, and the sharply planed face was very close to hers as his low voice mocked her strident one.

"I owe you no explanations, Mara. The bargain was struck, if you recall. Now, control yourself and return with me."

"I will see you in hell first." She jerked back and spat the words of her bitterness at him.

His laughter rang out. "I have been there."

Carlotta could bear no more; all she wanted was surcease from this. At the moment, it appeared the most desirable thing in the world that she not see and long for him. She turned and ran as fast as her chilled body could go. He started to follow her and collided with two drunken men ambling down the street singing bawdy songs. All three of them went down in a heap. Carlotta turned her head at their cries, then fled on, stumbling and gasping.

The stitch was raw fire in her side, her throat burned and ached from her struggle to breathe, and her feet were sodden clumps when she knew she could go no farther. She clung to an icy door for a moment before realizing that it was an inn of much the same nature as the Sea Lion. Here was the taproom, the bawdy conversation and songs, but on a much smaller scale. The warmth of unwashed bodies packed together and the scent of stale beer came over her as she edged inside and sank onto the corner of a bench where several drinkers snored unabashedly. She knew that she must try not to attract attention, thus she moved a little closer to one of them and huddled down. Fortunately, most of the other drinkers were engaged in disputing the charms of several women standing close to the roaring fire and thus paid no attention to the arrival of another waif.

The man next to Carlotta had not finished his tankard of ale before succumbing to drink. She felt the rising tide of faintness and knew that it must be offset. With a boldness she did not know she had, Carlotta reached across him and picked it up, draining it at one gulp. Instantly she regretted the action, for it was not ale or beer but surprisingly excellent brandy which hit her empty stomach hard. She felt the heat of it spread all over her numb body and her face flushed so that she put a hand to her forehead. As she did so, her eyes rested on a poster which was attached to the wall almost directly in front of her.

It was heavily lettered and boasted a crude drawing. She felt her vision blur, and the words were suddenly all too clear.

"Wanted for murder and robbery in the death of Lord Reginald Edmond, the servant girl, Carlotta Harmon. Three hundred pounds reward is offered. No questions will be asked." The information about contacting the solicitors of Lady Leticia was added. The features of the woman depicted were oddly like herself, thought Carlotta, for the pointed face and hollowed cheeks, the downdrawn brows, had shone from her mirror many times in unhappiness.

Carlotta felt true fear for the first time since she had met Simon. At the thought of his name she felt the tears press against her eyelids and knew that she could bear no more. These notices might be circulating throughout Bristol and certainly the countryside. Her time might be limited in all certainty.

One of the wenches gave a drinker a resounding slap and the others roared approval. It would not be long before they turned their attention to other matters. Carlotta slipped from the bench and was out the door in one brisk movement. She did not dare run now, for to do so would invite pursuit. Instead her pace was swift and purposeful, even though she had no idea where she was going.

The wind was even sharper now and it cut through the clothes that Simon had given her only that morning, which now seemed eons away. Carlotta remembered the laughing, fair face in the mirror at the dressmaker's and wondered if she would ever look that way again. Her hands were frozen, and she dug them deeper into the pockets of the dress for even the illusion of warmth. She encountered several gold pieces, then remembered that she had placed some there to balance the weight of the lost purse. Now she could only bless that impulse, for she was not totally penniless in this hostile world.

She heard cries, curses, and the thump of heavy materials being loaded close by and saw that she had come to the docks, where several ships were being prepared for departure, their masts stabbing the dark sky. This was no place for a lone woman; already she felt some assessing glances, and more than one ribald remark had come her way as she passed the local drinking houses. She turned to retrace her steps and knew that she was already too late.

The big, bearded man stood in front of her, both arms spread out, small eyes leering down at her body. "What's a little thing like you doing out in this cold? Looking for Old Abner to warm you up, I'm thinking." He laughed and reached for her.

Carlotta jerked back in a fury. Abner caught her chin in one huge hand and pulled her toward him. She caught the scent of stale sweat and old beer even as she saw a flea wind in and out of the thick beard. All her senses were alive now. The swirling snow, the cries from the nearest ship as stacks of cargo were shifted about, a laughing prostitute towing home her drunken catch, the howl of a beaten dog—all were sharply clear.

She aimed the toe of her heavy shoe at Abner's ankle and kicked with all her might. He let her go with a howl of fury and bent to his injured member. Carlotta backed away and saw that there was no place to run except in the direction of the loading ship or back the way she had come. But he now blocked the narrow street. Even as she hesitated, he straightened up, the good humor of drunkenness replaced by black anger. She turned and ran rapidly toward the ship. He pounded in pursuit.

Carlotta came up almost level with a tall man well wrapped in a heavy cloak as he directed the loading operations from a scrawled list in one hand. She caught his sleeve, jerking at it as she cried, "Sir, I am pursued by yonder man. Help me, I beg you!"

He swung around and she gasped at the vivid scar that went across his eye and nose down into his neck. "Take your waterfront quarrels elsewhere, girl! We sail for Boston at the dawn and I have no time for such foolishness." He moved backward, and she heard a guffaw from one of the loaders who was even now nudging his fellows. "Back to work, you louts!"

She looked around toward Abner and saw that he had stopped a short distance away and was now leaning against a wall, out of the cutting wind. He looked as if he were prepared to wait indefinitely for her. It was a thing out of a nightmare, Carlotta thought, hunted for her life, her lover gone, she homeless and possessed of nothing, almost certain rape waiting. Something flickered in her mind; she had felt this way before, known this same desperation, this same kind of impasse.

"You mistake me. I wish to buy passage on your ship. I wish to go to Boston. Will this take me there?" She held out the gold pieces in a hand that barely shook.

The man laughed. "This is not a passenger ship. We travel fast and light in these times. Go away, I said!"

"Is this enough?" She stood her ground firmly. "I know that most ships do take some passengers in addition to the cargo."

82

"Where is your baggage? Does no one travel with you? Are you a harlot who seeks amusement on our ship? Woman, you waste my time and I will have no more of it. Must I have you forcibly carried away?"

Carlotta knew that she could not go back into the dark waiting danger that was Bristol. In her heartsickness she felt that she must be free of England itself, free of any path that Simon had ever walked, free of the hanging that was a palpable danger. Here was some measure of safety, and she was being thwarted.

"I can work, scrub the decks, clean, wash clothes. I must get to Boston." She heard the pleading in her voice and knew it for a mistake.

He advanced on her and she saw the wolfish grin split his face again. "There are a couple of doxies for the crew. Would you join their ranks? You're a bit skinny for that and we have no time to fatten you up. There are several prisoners below who will be sold for servants, murderers they be, but likely a woman would be welcome." He spoke loudly now, and she saw that he did so for the entertainment of the men who still worked. Then he spoke the words that chilled her blood and terrified her beyond all reason. "Mayhap you've stolen that gold and are trying to avoid the watch. That's a hanging offense."

She knew that it was hopeless; it had been from the start. In the distance she saw Abner straighten up, this time he would be ready for her. In the folds of her cloak she carried a little dagger which might serve to buy her a bit of safety, for he would expect her to be frightened and tearful. Her head swam with exhaustion, and her legs shook under her. Was it worth this battle for survival? Survival without Simon whom she loved? She did not know. She knew only that she must fight on even to the very end of all life.

She heard her own voice speaking very quietly and steadily with no hint of the anger and fear she felt. "You seek to make sport of me. Forgive me that I have taken time from your preparations for departure." Her chin lifted and the light from several torches placed out of the wind shone on her face which had been in semi-darkness earlier. She turned then and started to move slowly away.

"Back to work, I said! Hurry up!" The scarred man's voice roared out once more as the work clatter began.

"Mistress. Wait." The voice came from the shadows at the

83

side. It was low and cultured, with the faintest trace of an accent.

Carlotta stopped and her hand went to her knife. "What is it? Who are you?"

The man stepped out into the light now, but she could tell nothing about him except that he was tall, lean, and dressed all in black. At the sight of him, the noise behind her ceased. His hood muffled his face from her vision.

"I travel on this ship and have certain influence on her master. Your gold pieces are fare enough, certainly, and I see no reason why you should not travel as a passenger."

Carlotta stared at him as if he were a visitation from heaven. "I am no doxy, sir."

He laughed and raised one hand in a quick gesture that brought one of the seamen running. "Frankly, I did not think so. I was bored this night, and then I watched your little exchange with Barney, the first mate. You did not flinch. I see, too, what waits for you back yonder." He waved a gloved hand at Abner. "I am bored no longer. I have, shall we say, a certain interest in courage."

Carlotta found it easy to believe the drawled words. "I seek only a passage to Boston and would be most grateful for your kind assistance."

He laughed again, and this time the sound sent little chills up and down her back. "Come then and sit while I speak to the master of the vessel. Oh, and you can let go of that knife, no one will touch you."

He walked imperiously toward the ship without waiting for her answer. Carlotta moved in his wake, conscious of a great relief even as she thought that he seemed the very lord of darkness himself, the shadow of her fate, whereas Simon had been all earthly light.

CHAPTER TWELVE

In the Name of the Compassionate

CARLOTTA lay on her stomach, her head pushed into the crook of her arm, and fought to avoid another trip to the bucket in the corner. Underneath her, the floor moved slowly up and down in the rolling motion to which the last two days and nights should have accustomed her body. She opened her eyes in the gloom that pervaded her little room at any hour and was once again thankful for the blessed privacy given her by the black-clad man. The ceiling was only slightly higher than her head; it held only the blanket-draped cot, a small chest, and a jug of water and a pan for washing, as well as the covered bucket for relieving oneself. The smells of the past occupant were noisome, but it had seemed all perfection to her that night.

She sighed and touched her matted hair with exploratory fingers. Was it too soon to think that the sickness might be abating? It had not come on her until the worst of her tears had been spent and the agony of thought burned through. She had been the wounded animal gone to cover; the shock of Simon's actions and her own expectations, the fury that had driven him back, the fear when she saw the poster, all her struggles to survive and the need to keep her wits keen, all these had faded when she collapsed on the cot to which the unspeaking seaman had shown her. The dark man had vanished but she had not cared. She had wept until her eyes were swollen almost shut, then she had tossed and twisted, slept a little, shivered greatly, and woke to weep again. Simon's name was on her lips, in her dreams, her thoughts. If only she had another chance, if things had gone differently, if she could be his mistress even with others; she tormented herself until her mind rebelled and the shaking nausea took over.

The ship pitched, righted herself, pitched again. Carlotta dug an elbow in her stomach, which seemed to have retreated into a hard knot somewhere under her ribs. For the first time it did not recoil. She sat up carefully but nothing happened.

85

It was the work of a few minutes to run her fingers through her hair and fasten it back under the rather battered bonnet she still retained. The cold water felt fresh to her still swollen face as she laved it thoroughly. Her arms and legs did not feel as if they could work properly, but she drew the cloak over her shoulders, opened the door, and went out in search of fresh air that now seemed the most important thing in the world.

The corridor outside was dank and forbidding, but faint trickles of light led her down its length, up some rough-cut stairs, along a lighter passageway to more stairs, and finally to another door which gave onto the deck. Carlotta made it to the rail in a few halting steps, then clung to it as if she could never let go. Her clothes whipped around her and the icy wind howled as the rain lashed the deck. She did not mind; it was enough to be able to breathe the freshness, to move without nausea, to be free of the racking pain of memory. She drew in the refreshing breaths hungrily, paying no attention to her hands freezing to the rail.

She looked about her with interest, knowing that rational thought must be postponed for yet a little while lest it become unbearable. There was no one in sight; she might have been alone on a ghost ship. Spreading square sails were directly above her. Off to the side were the banked oars, and down the deck, stairs rose to a small section which she assumed would house the captain and his officers. Ropes and equipment were tied down close by. But it was the sea that held her attention. She had traveled with her foster parents to the coasts and had seen the Channel, but that had been from the vantage point of land. Now she was part of this gray, swaying, moving, continually changing water. The waves were running high with white whirls of spume, the ship seemed to go from one crater to another, and the gray sky mingled with the water. The sun seemed a forgotten memory, all the world seemed wet and cold. As she watched, Carlotta felt something in her expand and lift past the burden of loss and pain. She was oddly exhilarated, at one with the stiff wind and lashing sails. The aches left her body, which seemed to be adjusting to the motion of the ship as she balanced herself from the drop to the lift and back again. She loosed the bonnet and let her hair toss free to wrap its auburn strings around her face and throat as she gave herself up to this new world.

"How do you fare, mistress?" The cool voice spoke almost at her shoulder.

She turned with a start and looked into the eyes of her benefactor who stood bare-headed, his black cloak flowing on the wind. He looked to be in his late forties, for his hair was snowy white and finely spun, his eyebrows black flecked with gray above brilliant black eyes. His skin was taut and firm, very white against the immaculate suit of gray silk with ruffles at throat and wrists. His boots were of highly polished black leather that shimmered in the faint light. His nose was high-arched, the nostrils slightly spread, and there were faint hollows under his cheekbones. A small whip was coiled at his waist. Now he returned her stare with a faint lift of his full mouth and sketched a polite bow.

She nearly lost her balance trying to give a curtsey on the bobbing deck, but his hand quickly righted her. It, too, was smooth and soft, far more so than her own. "I am better for the fresh air, thank you, sir."

"I gave orders that you were to be supplied with water and bread, otherwise to be left alone until you felt able to emerge." Again that curious accent mingling with the faint smile.

"Thank you." Carlotta could think of nothing to say to this elegant man who had very likely saved her from rape and hanging. She felt awkward and a little foolish as he continued to survey her.

"I am Austin Lenoir. As you may have guessed, I own this vessel."

"I am Carlotta Burton." It was the only last name she could think of in the second she had to think. She should have at least tried to change her first name to Charlotte to better protect herself, but she had resisted for so long losing the only small part of her past that she remembered that she could not now alter it. The chances of so elegant a gentleman reading posters were slim indeed, she told herself.

"Ah?" The dark brows lifted in an unspoken question. "Will you do me the extreme honor of dining with me this evening? I would hear your story; I am sure that it will be of great interest."

Carlotta wanted to refuse, but she was well aware that he had the right to command her if he chose. She hesitated, re-membering that she had not even given him the gold pieces she had offered the first mate in return for her passage. One hand went to her flying hair as the impaling eyes met hers.

He misread her intentions. "I know you have no baggage, nothing in very fact but those clothes you stand up in." His tone conveyed his distaste. "We carry gowns and the like for the ladies of Boston. I will furnish you with something suitable. Please, it is no favor to do this. I find the company of a fair woman most refreshing."

Carlotta said, "Sir, I will be honored to accept your kindness."

He looked hard at her then, and she saw the questioning look cross his face. She knew that possibly she should refuse the invitation, he very likely wanted her to pay for her passage with her body, but with a new spate of self-dislike she realized that she did not care. Simon had held her heart, mind, and body; she might as well be a shell. "Use this man," said her clear mind, "he may help you in Boston."

Austin Lenoir bowed over her hand and said unsmilingly, "My man will deliver the choices I make to your door along with hot water for a bath and some wine and cakes to soothe your stomach. Now I would suggest that you retire below. The weather is really quite rough."

It was a command, for all the silken tone, and she nodded obediently. As she moved away, she turned to look back and saw him watching her with that still, hard glance. Again the warning chills lifted on her spine.

It was not long after that several kegs of steaming water were brought to her cubicle by two straining seamen who assured her that more waited outside should she need them. There was barely enough room to accommodate everything, but Carlotta did not mind the squeeze in the delightful expectation of being clean. The men carefully averted their eyes from her face and body, speaking only when absolutely necessary. One brought a warm, soft robe of gray fur and slippers to match, as well as thick cloths to dry herself on and a rug that might have doubled as a blanket.

"We'll bring the other things later, mistress, after you've done with this. Do you just call if you want anything." The older seaman touched his forehead in a servile manner and backed away from her as if in fear.

Carlotta wondered what she might be going into. Was he simply cleaning her up before raping her? The harshness of the thought made her wonder what sort of person she was becoming, but she pushed it away. She would face him when she must and accept what she must. Was he not the sole authority on his own ship? If guile were needed she would apply it. Fear was not going to spoil her pleasure of the moment.

She took that pleasure in full as she washed and soaped her slender body, letting the water sluice down between her small rounded breasts, over her flat stomach, and between her smooth thighs. Her red-brown hair, separately washed and rinsed, was bound high on her head. She stayed in the half barrel of water until it was barely tepid, then stepped into the next which had been provided behind the hastily rigged screen. Carlotta had always been one for baths, a fact which Aunt Rosa had deplored, saying that no sensible person left himself open for pestilence in such a way. She filled her mind with such thoughts, knowing that she must not think of Simon and their time together or she would truly run mad.

The clothes sent by Austin Lenoir comforted her as to his intentions, for they were as circumspect as any great lady might possess. The slippers were soft, dark leather, the stockings a paler gossamer. The shift was white and edged with fine lace. The dress was a soft blue that verged on green, loosely fitted except in the waist, which was as narrow as her own, and it belled out into a full swirling skirt. The sleeves were full and tapered to points of lace over her slender hands; the neck was round and high. A soft shawl of paler blue matched it and felt warm about her shoulders. He had sent a small mirror, brushes, a soothing lotion for her skin. Carlotta could not but delight in these things that she had not really cared about since Aunt Rosa died. She wound her hair high on her head and let the curling tendrils fall around her face and at her earlobes. The mirror told her that once again she was fair, but she could see the marks of tears under her eyes and in her eyelids. Her face was thinner, too, and her naturally pink mouth was strained. She was far from being the radiant girl who had looked at herself in another mirror not too many days past.

"But I am not that girl." She knew that the words were true. Sorrow was a hard teacher. Resolutely she jerked her mind back; must her every thought revolve around a man who had made it plain that she was merely one of many and who had planned to discard her as soon as their passion—his passion—faded? There was a knock at the door just then; the man had come to fetch her. "I am ready." Pray God that she was.

They went through the bowels of the ship again in a roundabout way that left Carlotta confused. Eventually, however, they stood in front of a highly polished door with an attached knocker in the shape of a boar. The man sounded it once and melted into the background.

The door swung slowly open, and Austin called, "Enter, my dear. Let me see you." Then he was before her, taking in every detail of her appearance even as she stared with an awe that she could not conceal.

He was clad all in a white that matched his hair. His black eyes were the only darkness on him. A single thumb ring was set with a huge milky pearl which sent out pale shimmers of light as his hand moved in those curiously languid gestures. Another pearl of the same size was set adroitly in the folds of his exquisitely tied neckcloth. His cabin was so richly appointed that it might have done justice to a royal court. The walls were hung with tapestries in fading hues of rose and green. Slim white unicorns moved perpetually toward distant castles where thorn fences guarded the way to fair imprisoned maidens. She saw that this was the same in each of the tapestries and even in the rug. The bed, wide and strewn with white cushions, was apparently one of those which could be taken apart and reassembled, for such a one was never made for shipboard. It was curtained with milky white underlaid with rose; the entire draping was transparent. There were several paintings as well, all done in misty tones of green and blue, all depicting the sea. Books were stacked from the floor to the ceiling and held in place by straps going across their fine leather bindings. Candles flickered discreetly in low holders which were also anchored down. There was a faint, sharp odor in the air, a type of spice which mingled with the smell of the sea from the slightly open porthole. A table was laid for two in an alcove.

"Truly this is beautiful, Master Lenoir." Carlotta was glad that she could voice her admiration and mean it.

"You must call me Austin, my dear. Now we shall eat, for the food must not be allowed to grow cold. We will speak only of trivialities during the meal; exciting tales tend to upset the digestion, don't you agree?"

Carlotta could only nod in agreement, realizing as she did that she dared not do otherwise.

The dinner of fresh fish, cheese, dried and fresh fruits, some strange mixture of rice and rich sauce, several tart wines, and delicate sweetmeats could not be appreciated by Carlotta, for her stomach was too newly recovered. She ate a little fish and drank strong, hot tea and some of the tart wine. It gave her instant strength, and she could feel her spirits lift.

After they were finished and the dishes carried away by the silent servant, Austin said, "Now tell me how you came to this ship—her name is the *Indian Princess*, incidentally—and what you want to do in Boston." He leaned forward attentively, chin on his long, smooth fingers.

She knew she must go carefully, staying as near to the truth as possible while skirting dangerous particulars. "My mother was French, my father English. They died in my very early childhood and I was raised by his brother, a schoolmaster, and his wife. They died some months ago. I thought to remain in the village and perhaps teach the young children, but the war with France has so disrupted things that this could not earn me enough to live on. There was a man who made advances and did not offer marriage. I came to Bristol but could find no work of an acceptable nature. I have read much of the colonies and thought that Boston or New York would be a good place to go. Granted, it was an impulsive decision, but I do not think that I will regret it."

"But no baggage, nothing? How will you live? How did you so suddenly take this decision?" The black eyes bored into hers.

"I will be a maid, a governess, a minder of young children. I left the inn where I stayed to look for work. When I returned the few effects I had were gone. I protested and was told my bill was in arrears. They threatened to call the law. I fled and was pursued by that man you saw."

Austin laughed with real amusement. "Your knowledge of history is lacking. America has not regarded itself as the colonies for many years now. Still, a pretty woman should have no difficulties."

Carlotta half smiled. She had given in to the English predilection for seeing that land as the hub of the world. She lifted her head and tossed her hair back over her shoulders in one fluid movement as she started to make some small comment. Austin's eyes began to blaze suddenly in an emotion that might have been triumph, anger, or amazement. The hand with the huge pearl rose toward her face, then fell as quickly.

"What is the matter?" She heard her own voice tremble as she pulled back.

"Who are you really? Where do you come from?"

"I don't understand." She rose and he did the same. The smoothness of his face was contorted with anger. He still held a slender fluted glass of wine in his hand; now he lifted it and hurled it at the wall where the liquid drained down the lovely tapestries to drip on the floor. His eyes burned with savage black lights, and Carlotta felt that she looked for a moment into the very pits of hell. Involuntarily she crossed herself and the words rose out of her deepest consciousness. "God, the compassionate, the protector, and Mary, Holy Mother . . ." She had spoken in French without knowing it and now Austin was very calm once more.

His voice bore no trace of the spasm he had just undergone as he said, "That movement with your hair and your hand, I have seen it before, long ago. Only natives of France sound the way you just did. I abhor lies, and you have just finished telling me a pack of them."

His calmness was more terrifying than the anger; this was a man to fear. Carlotta whispered, "I do not know what you mean. My story is true." She tried to face his impaling gaze standing, but her legs began to tremble and she sank down into one of the delicate chairs.

He said, "You are overtired, I can see that. We have all the voyage to deal with these matters. I must ask your pardon for my outburst."

He was not a man who gave apologies. She felt the undercurrent of amusement and barely concealed fury in him and wondered if she had made an enemy. She said, "Yes, I do feel the need of rest." The words seemed inane. She thought with a sense of shock that she had not once thought of Simon since she entered this room, Simon whom she loved and from whose explanations she had fled and from whom she would ever be separated by an ocean. Regret hit her as with a hammer; her hands shook as she drew the shawl over her shoulders.

Austin did not miss her swift changes of feeling. A thin, cruel smile touched his lips as he lifted a tiny jeweled bell and rang it once. He reached into the pocket of a cloak tossed over the chair behind him and handed her a folded piece of paper. "I think you will find this interesting reading."

The seaman tapped at the door as she took the paper and unfolded it. It was the "wanted" poster with the crude drawing of her face.

"Sleep well, my dear Carlotta Harmon." Austin's laugh rang in her brain even as the rattle of the tumbrils of her nightmare rose up.

CHAPTER THIRTEEN

Vortex

THE nightmare came that night, as Carlotta had known it would. She fought off sleep as long as she could, but finally weariness took over and she woke shaking with the familiar terror. It now had added dimensions of waking reality. As she lay shivering in the aftermath, she remembered with a strange intensity how Sir Reginald and Austin had both seemed to recognize something in her voice or gestures and both had reacted violently to it. In this lowest ebb of her struggles she thought again of Simon, and this time nothing could stop the memories. She lived them again and again, along with her own actions, which now seemed the foolishness of a young, untutored girl. "I would take you any way that I could get you, Simon." She sobbed the words into the rough blanket and knew them for simple truth.

When the seaman came with strong tea and biscuits early the next morning, she demanded to be taken to Austin. She had determined to speak frankly with him, to try to find out what lay behind his having the poster and what use he intended to make of it. If he wanted a willing bed partner she would give him that gladly in return for his help.

The man said stolidly, "He's busy, can't be disturbed. Orders. I'm to take you up on deck and see that you're private, that you stay in the place he said for you to. No other speech with you."

She tried to get other information, but he would say nothing. He showed her to the small stretch of deck that was to be hers. It was roped off and two guards stood at either end with their backs to her. Austin was going to a great deal of trouble for one small girl, she thought wryly. In the several days to come she was grateful for this area, which gave her sanity and relief from the tiny cabin where she tossed and turned through the restless nights. She spent much of the time sitting on the cold deck wrapped in her old cloak, watching the ever-changing pattern of the waves, which were always as gray as the sky. Dread enveloped her, and her dreams were of hanging. The black eyes of Austin seemed to watch her constantly although she never saw him. She wept in the nights but during the days it helped to watch the sea.

It was in this time of fear and waiting that she was able to think of what she had felt for Simon, and truly still felt, in terms of the ballads of the first bittersweet love both tender and rare, destined never to actually flower. She knew this for simple thinking, but it helped when her mind probed the wound. Now, too, her thoughts turned toward America, where the power of King George no longer reached and where, it was said, opportunity was of one's own making. A new land, a new beginning, a chance to be free and her own person, dependent on none and responsible only to herself. Right gladly would she take the most menial of jobs in order to have such freedom. She found herself strengthened by this, and the nightmare came less often.

Five days passed in this manner, but on the afternoon of the sixth she rose from her seat on a coil of rope and turned to face Austin Lenoir, who stood, austere as always, immaculate in charcoal silk, just outside the band of rope where the guards had paced.

"How are you, Mistress Harmon? The voyage has given color to your face, and you look more rested." He might have been any casual acquaintance remarking on the health of one he had not seen for a time.

In her cabin of the endless nights, Carlotta had formulated questions and demands in a style ranging from reasonable to a flat avowal of her rights. But now she was face-to-face with that opaque gaze and her words faded into a stutter. She looked at the smooth face, the lowered lids, and cried, "What is it that you wish of me, Master Lenoir? Why have you made me a virtual prisoner on a ship when I have offered you the passage money which you indicated was sufficient? I can tell you the full story of how that poster came into being. I am no criminal!"

The glance with which he swept her was almost indifferent. His lips barely moved as he said, "Such stories do not interest me. I do not like lies, and you gave me many. No, I have another purpose in mind for you."

The tone stung her into anger. "You speak as if I were a toy or a piece of property set aside for your amusement. I am grateful that you gave me passage, but that does not entitle you to play such games as this."

He yawned, covering his mouth with one hand, which still

bore the milky pearl ring. The ship leaned a little to the side of the freshening wind, and the sails snapped above them. Salt spray leaped up, and the odor was rich in Carlotta's nostrils.

"You are wrong, my dear. A woman is nothing but a toy and a breeder. There is something about you that piques my interest and relieves my boredom, which is often monumental. There is a mystery . . . something. Doubtless it will be easily solved, and you will remain with me as my guest until I tire of the game, as you so correctly call it." He pulled a snowy piece of linen from his coat and touched his lips gently with the edge. The gesture might have belonged in a drawing-room. "You are favored, Carlotta, that is why I have been indulgent with you." His lips curved in a faint smile, and he stepped closer to her.

She backed away. "You speak of slavery! I am a free Englishwoman, beholden to no one. I will not tolerate it."

The cold voice followed her as she turned her back. "I can give you to the sailors, who will doubtless appreciate you more now that you are clean and fattened up. If you think of appealing to any on this ship, you had best know that I own it and many more. My word is law and I do not permit disobedience."

"A pestilence on you and your lordly aims!" She faced him now, her amber eyes flaming, the auburn hair whipping free in the wind. The days of reticence were done; it was all out in the open to be dealt with, and it was better so.

She was not prepared for what happened next. Austin's face was a set mask with no visible emotion and even his eyes were blank as he advanced upon her and picked her up bodily, holding her in so firm a grip that she could not wriggle free. She twisted and fought, but to no avail as he strode with her through the open door and down the corridor to their cabins. She could barely speak for her anger, but imprecations continued to come to her lips and she uttered them lustily.

Once in his cabin, he threw her on the bed so hard that she bounced. As she tried to jump up, he caught the flimsy velvet of her dress and ripped it from her so that even her shift was torn. His face was not expressionless now, for his eyes were holes of black fury and his fair skin was flushing red.

They fought in wordless silence on the bed as he stripped the rest of her clothes from her and she was naked before him. She did not try to shield herself but instead tried to rise and avoid him as he began to pull his own clothes off. His movement was pantherlike as he caught her by the shoulder and threw her down across the velvet cover of the bed. He caught her legs and forced them apart, then thrust his length into her so hard and deep that she thought she would burst. His whole body was beating against her now, and she could not breathe. The world swung dark as he fastened his mouth on hers and twisted her nipples with practiced fingers. She writhed in pain, and then they rolled over so that she was on top and he was thrusting into her, his eyes brilliant and hard on hers. She shut her eyes and felt him move more deeply into her warmth, which had opened so eagerly, so gladly, for Simon and which now protested this ravaging.

Austin pulled away from her now and again, only to return and thrust yet again. It seemed to Carlotta that this went on forever, she the beaten receptacle, he the destroyer. Her loathing must have shown in her eyes, for she was past words. He laughed eagerly and muttered something in a language which sounded as if it were French and yet was not, and his tongue found her ear. She pulled her head away, and in that moment his body convulsed and his release came.

They lay in mutual exhaustion for a time, though Carlotta rolled as far away from him as she could. Her hair was tumbled over her face but she could see him, lean and muscular with no signs of age as he lay on his back with his eyes closed. He moved slightly as she watched, and she jerked back with a gasp of fear. The heavy-lidded eyes opened and glittered into hers. She pulled the coverlet over her nakedness as she glared at him.

"I suppose you will rape me again now?"

He rose and reached for his clothes in easy gestures. The silence grew long between them before he said, "The cabin next to mine will be readied for you. You will conduct yourself as a lady should or you will not like the consequences. I will make my wishes known to you, and you will hasten to obey."

"And if I do not?" She was afraid of this man, more so than anyone she had ever feared in her life, even in the nightmare.

Austin bent over her in a swift movement, his face inches from hers. "Then, my dear, you will most bitterly regret it."

She could bear no more. "Let me go. Set me ashore in Boston. What do you want of me?"

He smiled as he walked slowly to the door. "Be thankful that I do not know the answer to that question as yet."

Shortly thereafter the men came to move Carlotta into the designated cabin, spacious and well furnished in the blues and greens Austin favored. A sea chest of gowns in varying colors was brought, and some of the books from his own cabin were carefully placed on a table. Wine and biscuits were furnished also. The door by the comfortable bed opened into the other cabin as she had known it would. It appeared that her role was set. When she was alone, Carlotta slammed her fists against the bed in hopeless rage. The man must be depraved to behave so! Her flesh ached with the force of his assault; under the cool manner smouldered a rage so fierce that the observer must tremble before it. She knew that he could kill and smile all the while. If she would live she must dissemble and bide her time. Sooner or later the chance for escape would present itself. So her fighting spirit rallied as she planned her strategy.

It was late when the knock came at her door and Austin entered, cool and elegant. He bowed politely. "Will you take a turn on the deck with me before I retire? Doubtless you will wish to stay up late and read. The fresh air will help us both."

Carlotta gaped at him. Was this punctilious gentleman the rapist of a few hours ago? Very well, she could play at this game for her life and sanity. She inclined her head graciously. "How kind of you to suggest it. I should be delighted."

"Excellent." He picked up her cloak and placed it gently over her shoulders, then held out his arm for her to take, smiling as he did so.

The sense of half realized danger remained with Carlotta for the next week and more. Austin did not touch her again; no man could have been more proper or less interested in her body. That questing look of half recognition did not reappear, although she often saw it in her dreams. Oddly enough, the nightmare did not surface during this time of fearful anticipation. She thought that she had prepared for the eventualities but was rapidly coming to realize that Austin was far ahead of her in deviousness. He remained polite and cordial, giving her books to read out of the excellent collection he carried, and she was impressed by the wide range of his interests in art, history, science, and politics, as well as the fiction and poetry that she loved. Her days took on a routine as she read, walked the deck regularly on Austin's arm, tried on the gowns in several chests, dined with him in the evenings and listened to his tales of London and Paris in the days before the world twisted awry. He would see her to her door, lift her hand to his lips, and bid her a correct good night.

People could get used to anything, Carlotta often thought

as she lay stiff and frightened in the bed, listening to the soft movements only a wall away. Such a situation would have seemed bizarre only a short while ago, and now she could sleep reasonably and chat and laugh with a man who held her prisoner and threatened her with untold evil. At such times, she summoned Simon's laughing face, the clear green gaze, before her, willed herself to hear him say, "'I know a place where the wild thyme grows. . . .'" If this were to be all of love, she could at least count herself blessed.

She lost track of time during these days, knowing only that the ship skimmed before the wind, which was always blasting and cold, laced with rain spears which thrust deep into the gray sea. The world seemed narrowed down to the little contained area dominated by the man she feared. England, the war with Napoleon, the new land of America, all faded before the unknown future.

Carlotta woke with the sense of lateness that told her it was afternoon. She turned her head on the pillow and felt her temples pulsate with a headache. Her neck was sore and stiff, her mouth dry. Her first thought was that the nightmare had come again, but there was no memory of it and those were always horrifyingly real. There were no marks on her skin; Austin had not touched her. She felt as she had when recovering from an illness, when Aunt Rosa had dosed her liberally with pain killer. When she rose and found her robe, it seemed that the floor swayed under her feet. The usual pitching motion was not present; it seemed that the ship rocked gently.

She rushed to the door and jerked at it but it would not open. She hammered both fists on it and called as loudly as she could, "Open this door! What is happening? Open it now!"

A bolt rattled from outside, and the door creaked as the burly seaman looked in, his bearded face incurious. "Rest you quiet, lady, the master will return soon."

"Return? Where are we?" She knew the answer as soon as she asked the question, and her heart began to hammer.

"Boston Harbor. Been here off shore all day. We sail tonight." He started to shut the door, then leaned back in to ask, "Will you be wanting your tea now?"

She nodded, for she was too choked with anger to speak. Austin had drugged her the night before so that she would sleep while his business was undertaken in Boston. He must have thought she would try to escape or make a great fuss. "Oh, that I would have!" Her clenched teeth ground together as she thought of the opportunity missed. She had learned to swim in her early days; had it been warm weather she might have plunged into the sea and taken her chances. How precious freedom was and how little she had thought of it until she lost it.

The door rattled again and her tea was presented without comment. She took the hot container but did not drink. Who knew what it might contain? Rebellion swept her; this was not a thing to be endured. She felt the beginnings of tears and dashed them aside with her fingers. Something must be done or she would go mad with waiting. Her cloak swirled about her feet as she moved back and forth. She went past the closed door of the adjoining room and, impulsively, tried the knob, which turned easily in her hand.

The room where they dined each night was as immaculate as its owner. She went to the little recessed area where the wine stood in several delicate bottles. The headache had not abated; the surging anger made it worse. Now she poured a portion of wine into a cup that stood near and felt the heady tartness lift the heaviness over her skull. Just then the ship swayed a little on the waves and the bottles tilted. She grabbed at them and, in so doing, bumped one of the chests stacked along the wall just behind. It fell with a great clatter, spilling the contents at her feet.

Carlotta bent to them. What if Austin returned and found her so? There was a jumble of papers, several ornate coats of velvet, and a lady's green silk gown made in the style famous before the French Revolution. There was an elaborate wig of the same period, the powdered waves and curls crushed and browning yet still evoking that distant time that was really only a few years ago.

She picked up one of the packets of letters and the closely written words jumped out at her. "Leave my dearest, my very dearest, while you can. Come to me. Leave that maelstrom. Nothing is worth your life. Nothing." The letter just below that one was very short. "They will kill you. I am coming to fetch you. Await me at our place." The next letter was so passionate and longing that Carlotta felt her cheeks burn. They were signed with Austin's name.

She felt the tears prickle as she put the letters back. She could read no more of a man's deep sorrow. Her hand brushed across another in German, which was apparently of a much later date. Uncle Arnold had taught her a little of that language but this was written with elaborate curlicues and elegant twists. Addressed to the Estimable Austin Lenoir in the city of New Orleans in the Spanish Territory, the first sentence said starkly. "There is no trace of the lady; it is as though she had been obliterated."

The door swung open and shut behind Carlotta, and she half rose to see Austin standing there, unbuttoning his gloves, his black eyes opaque in the fading light.

CHAPTER FOURTEEN

The Warm Winds of Life

"ARE you quite done scavenging, my dear?" He crossed to the wine and poured himself a small drink.

"It fell, I did not mean . . ." Her words came to a stop and she faced him directly. There was nothing else to say, and she would not give voice to the fear that he aroused in her. The memory of those hands on her body, the hard thrusting meant to be demeaning, the casual utilization of her as a receptacle for his relief, all these burned in her anew and triumphed. It was no shivering waif who stood before Austin now.

He saw and his mouth lifted in that smile that was no smile. He seemed to pad as he walked closer to her. "Had I thought you 'meant' as you put it, the streets of Boston would now be enriched by a new whore. Instead, we will sail within the hour."

Carlotta felt the sickness swing free in her stomach and fought it back with all the determination she possessed. Did he mean to keep her prisoner forever? "Set me ashore, I will make my own way. What pleasure does this game give you?"

"That is just it, Carlotta, my dear. I do not know, and that enhances the delightfulness of it." He lifted his hand as if to forestall her furious words. "Your temper will avail you nothing. Spare me that or I will have you taken below."

She turned her back and headed for the connecting door, which she managed to slam with a good thud. He did not follow, and for that she was grateful. She snatched up a book at random and forced herself to concentrate on the words if not the sense. As it was a complicated treatise on mathematics, this did not help very much. Soon afterward the familiar rolling motion began as the ship moved out to sea.

Her knowledge of the American continent was vague and she had no idea where they might be going. None of the books gave any geographical information. When she tried to go up on deck later, she found that the door was barred, and she would not demean herself by screaming in Austin's hearing. Once again she must wait. Time spun out as food and drink were left at her door by the silent man who served Austin. She forced herself to eat, for her strength had to be maintained at all costs if an escape attempt were ever to be made. She could hear Austin moving about at night, and sometimes the doors moved as if they were about to be opened, although they never were. Her sleep was fitful as the nightmare returned and mingled with her dread of what might happen next. If he touched her again, Carlotta thought, it would be unbearable. She tested the door onto the deck at odd intervals but never found it open. It was in this time of enforced seclusion that she found herself in desperate need of exercise and began to do the fencing motions and techniques that an émigré friend of Uncle Arnold's had once taught her in exchange for their hospitality.

Once she tried the door and it was unbarred. She did not go out since Austin might well have been trying to trick her. The basic routine did not alter, however, and she grew bolder. Her cabin had only a tiny porthole, and she had never been able to see anything but gray sea outside it. It was at least a way to tell night from day. In the time when darkness seemed complete outside, she tested the door and found that it swung easily to her touch. Austin had come in earlier and, it seemed from the total silence next door, gone immediately to bed. Carlotta slipped into a loose black gown and lifted it around her ankles so that she could move more freely. In a moment she was in the corridor and heading toward the deck that was her customary place to walk, or had been before Austin's anger took the form of retaliation.

There was no one about in all the long expanse of the deck. She went down from the high area where their cabins were and came onto the work area where rope and equipment lay about in stacks. The sails billowed above her head as the ship floated in darkness. The wind had a touch of warmth in it, and she recalled that the night chill had been much less of late, even in her solitary prison. The salt scent of the sea rose up and with it was the scent of earth and growing things. Carlotta breathed deeply, hungrily, before she started toward the section immediately forward where she thought she had once seen some small boats placed. She did not really know what she had in mind, but this opportunity to explore was not to be missed.

She was so intent on her goal that she did not notice when a dark figure detached itself from a nearby door and moved toward her. The scraping footfall alerted her, and she flung herself aside just as it reached for her.

"Austin!"

"Just so. Don't you know it is dangerous to wander around this way?" There was no anger in his voice, only a wry amusement.

"You left the door unbarred on purpose and followed me just as you have watched me when I thought I was alone." She recalled her restlessness and the fear she had often felt at such times.

He did not deny it. "We dock in Charleston, South Carolina, day after tomorrow. I have much business there. It is a fair city, warm even in this winter month." His hand circled her wrist and pulled her effortlessly to him. His mouth came down on hers, demanding at first and then soft as if he sought to kindle fires there.

Carlotta held herself rigid as she forced her mind back to Simon's face. Austin released her instantly and stepped back. "Come, we go below. There is a bargain that I wish to put to you."

"I will consider no bargain that does not include my freedom." High words, but she could say no less.

He gave a short bark of laughter as he pushed her ahead of him. "Your choices are quite limited, my dear."

They sat over fine wine in jeweled cups a few minutes later. Carlotta thought they seemed the very epitome of civilized people, and yet here was barbarism refined. Austin said, "Tell me of your life before now, Carlotta, and do not lie. If you do, I shall have to punish you, and I do not think you would like that. I can tell when people lie to me."

"Why would I lie?" She longed to scream out the revulsion she felt for him, to loose the anger that built steadily with each day, but she knew that the punishment he spoke of would be sexual, for the shrinking of her flesh was not a thing that could be hidden.

"Tell me." The words were soft, insistent. His face was in shadow as he leaned back in the chair and lifted his cup to take a tiny sip.

Carlotta began with the nightmare, her loss of memory, and the Harmons. As she spoke, she forgot that this man was her captor, her user, and felt only the presence of another listening person. It was a relief as always to speak in freedom. She told of Lady Leticia and her lover, omitting only his name. She left out the interlude with Simon; nothing could have made her mention him. Knowing Austin, she knew that she must furnish

103

some explanation of the fact that she had not been a virgin; thus she mentioned a footman at the Kilburton estate who had taken rough liberties on an occasion when the servants had been permitted to celebrate a holiday and all had been befuddled. She hoped that he would believe her; certainly she had struggled at his touch. He took her back through her childhood and the nightmare three times before she rebelled.

"I cannot remember anything else! Why do you torment me so?"

For the first time since she had known him Austin's face was lit with enthusiasm and the black eyes were no longer hard but brilliant. She saw then that he must have been radiantly handsome in the first glow of his youth.

"I knew there was something about you that stirred my imagination, that haunting familiarity, the way you speak! It is a fascinating little mystery. I think that you will do for my purposes."

Carlotta remembered the letters in his cabin and the passionate longing they contained. Once this man had known more than boredom. "Why do I seem familiar? Did you once know someone in France to whom I might be related? Tell me of it, please!"

He seemed to be speaking more to himself than to her. "A woman from the streets; the thing is amazing. One might suspect the irony of the Greek gods in this." The dark eyes swung to her as they assessed her yet again. "Carlotta, you are wanted for murder in England, there is a price on your head. You could be considered a stowaway on my ship and thus liable for return there. You have several gold pieces and only one old dress and cloak to your name in a new land. Lone women do not fare well here or in England."

"Let me go in this Charleston. I will gladly take my chances for freedom."

"You are well-spoken, and fair when properly dressed. Play a role for me, enact it to my satisfaction, and you shall have not only your freedom but enough gold to set yourself up comfortably as a young widow of good lineage who has suffered in Napoleon's new world of Europe and thus fled to the safety of America. I am sure that you could ensnare a suitable husband with no difficulty. Of course you could not remain in Charleston, but there is New Orleans, that rare and lovely city." His tone softened as he spoke this last.

"What is this bargain? What would you have me do?" She

did not protest his summing up of the situation. It was all too true from his viewpoint. She could not doubt that he had had this in mind from the very beginning and that all he had done to her had been with this set purpose.

"Only a bit of acting, a thing I have noticed you to be good at. Nothing difficult or painful. But essential to me. You will be my ward, lately come from France, who has suffered bereavement in family matters, and now on her way to New Orleans, to the Ursuline convent there. You are timid and retiring but will follow my lead."

It sounded harmless, and the price was her freedom. "You are of New Orleans. When the thing is done I do not wish to be in the same city with the likes of you."

His brows lifted as a flare of anger crossed his face and was as quickly stilled. "Then go to Boston or New York. It matters not."

There was one last thing that Carlotta intended to demand. "I do not trust you, Austin. Swear to me on the name of that woman to whom you wrote those letters that you will keep your bargain, as I will swear on the name of my foster parents."

Austin's face smoothed into a mask, the familiar expression he wore. "I should have had you whipped for prying into things that do not concern you. There are many ways to dispose of a recalcitrant woman and my thoughts are fertile on the subject. You will accept the bargain or bear the consequences."

"Or accept and bring you down in the middle of your negotiations, whatever they are." She kept her face impassive, her tone as cold as his. Inside, however, she quaked.

Austin slammed one hand on the table and his laughter rang clear in the room. "Damn, you are a bold one. Many men would not dare speak so to me. Very well, Carlotta. I swear on the name of Madeleine whom, as you know from your cursed snooping, I loved greatly, that I will hold and honor my bargain."

Black eyes met amber eyes and so the bargain was sealed.

The ship entered Charleston Harbor in the earliest dawn and dropped anchor some distance out. Carlotta stood on the deck and strained her eyes at the fog-shrouded land. She could see the shapes of buildings, church spires, and the bulk of many ships, some faintly lit. She turned to see a thrusting point of land, then looked to see what might have been the dark blurring of trees in the extreme distance. Even as she watched the world was growing faintly lighter and the chill was not as pronounced.

The smells of fish and mud mingled with morning freshness from the far woods. She caught her breath hungrily and wondered what the new land would be like.

Austin came toward her, snapping orders at the men, his black suit and hat rendering him a part of the lingering night. He paused for a moment to say, "Ah, my dear, you look the very lady. I chose well."

She nodded without speaking, wondering if he meant the clothes or this entire pact between them. She wore a tawny silk dress, softly fitted, with bands of silky fur in a lighter shade around the hem and sleeves. Her shoes were of supple leather, her gloves the same hue as her bonnet. Her hair was coiled demurely under it, and a little veil could be drawn down at the wearer's discretion. "You should be in mourning by all the rules of proper behavior, but I, as your guardian, have seen fit to command otherwise, since I do not believe youth and beauty should be wrapped in black." Austin had spoken sharply to her voiced comment on the subject.

They landed at the dock shortly afterward, and Austin helped Carlotta from the small boat while his man and another, whom she supposed to be a servant of lower rank, gathered their belongings together. Few people were abroad as yet but, just visible on the winding road to their left, was a dark spot that soon resolved into a carriage traveling at a good rate. Carlotta stood very still, feeling the ground lift and sway under her feet, as she drew the tangy air into her nostrils. The sky was faintly pink now, and she wondered if this was to be her first glimpse of the sun since her adventure had begun. She shivered with excitement and suspense.

The carriage came to a halt a short distance from them, and a very young man—really more a boy—of about fifteen stepped out. He had black hair that curled softly, and brilliant blue eyes, and he wore an elegant suit of paler blue. With a word to the driver, a tall black man, he came toward them.

"You are Master Austin Lenoir, sir?"

"I am." Austin held out a courteous hand.

"I am Charles Edward Windhope, sir, and my grandfather has come to welcome you to Charleston, even as I do." He smiled, but his eyes were on Carlotta, who lowered her lids demurely.

The older man now approached with the help of the servant and his cane. He looked to be in his seventies; his back bent with arthritis, his face seamed, his hands gnarled. His eyes were the faded blue that the boy's would be in age, but his hair was black shot with gray and his voice that of a young man. "Austin! I had thought you in Italy or still in England. Your messenger was doubly welcome this morning."

Austin stretched out a hand to him, and Carlotta saw that his eyes were as still and cold as black pools. "I sent the man even before we dropped anchor. There is much to speak of. May I introduce the lady?" He spoke the words he had told Carlotta he would say, and she smiled timidly at the gentlemen. He added, "And this is the old friend of my youth, Charles Windhope, with whom I traveled much in the days before the blight set in for all of Europe."

The older man put a hand on the boy's arm. "This is the light of my latter days, the son of my dead boy, named for him and for me."

"And for the Prince. May they all rest well." Austin's tone was the most reverent Carlotta had yet heard him use.

Charles Windhope looked at Carlotta with the eye of a connoisseur and his smile was warm. "Now you will grace our home with your presence, the both of you. The young lady need not be rushed to the convent, must she? A little experience of life, delicately obtained, in our beautiful city will be most useful in the years to come. How say you, my dear?"

Carlotta bent her head as though in an agony of shyness. "It is for my guardian to say, sir."

Austin said, "She is prone to attacks of the vapors and must rest often. Her mother died so suddenly after putting this responsibility upon me, then her personal maid took ill and could not travel, but my business was pressing. The voyage has not been easy. I fear that her activities must be curtailed for delicacy, since she is so recently bereaved and sickly withal. But we accept your kind offer of hospitality."

"Of course, I understand." Charles Windhope began to move toward the waiting equipage.

In a matter of minutes they were bundled into the carriage and began a stately passage through the streets, which were now drifting with fog even though the pale rays of the sun were beginning to shaft through. The carriage had tiny windows and these were partially curtained so that one could barely see out. Even so Carlotta was able to view shops, stately buildings, tantalizing little streets and wide ones, along with green vines

107

and trees of various kinds. She sighed with relief and caught Charles Edward's eye to smile at him. He blushed and looked away, but she was well content. It was a good omen, a good beginning.

CHAPTER FIFTEEN

If My Right Hand Forget

CARLOTTA moved slowly along the path as she tried to draw out this precious time of solitude. The black slave watched from far behind as she had been bidden, but this was much more tolerable than one at the door of her room and another in a curtained-off section of the very chamber itself. In addition, there was a very capable maidservant whose manner became soft and fluttery around the girl whom she tended. It all came to never being alone, she thought now, and it was all done under the guise of kindness and friendship. Charles and Sylvia Windhope opened their beautiful house to Austin and his bereaved young ward, offered them every luxury, and were unfailingly gracious. A few neighbors, fully as old as their hosts, came to visit now and then. Carlotta was introduced and as quickly hurried away to rest. Her protests were met with soft comments of "so brave," "mustn't tire yourself," "no excitement." Austin's dark eyes would glow into hers, and she knew that he had successfully foiled any attempts she might make at enlisting the help of the Windhopes or their friends.

Tanda, the black maidservant, had said guilelessly, "You's suffered a lot, Miss Carlotta, but no need to think about doing something to yourself; that's a sin. You young, long way to go."

"Who told you that?" Carlotta kept her voice cool and restrained.

"You has spells and they make you feel bad. Master Austin tell everybody."

She sank down on an old log suddenly and gave herself up to the beauty of this world. It was April now, and they had arrived in cold March. Spring had come delicately with soft rains and icy bursts. The trees were pale green above her head, and first flowering bushes waved golden arms at the border just beyond. Several stately trees surrounding the house had been green all winter, and now their leaves shone more richly in the pale morning sun. The sea was not far distant, for the salty tang pervaded the steadily softening air. This was very different from the chill of England; here the fog rolled smoothly in, rendering the world misty and cool, then faded in the day. The promise of even greater warmth lay over the land and Carlotta felt all her senses quicken.

She rose and smoothed down the skirt of the soft gray dress that had been ordered for her. She had many gowns in soft pastels now, girlish, drifting things that might have been made of the mist she loved. Eyebrows had been raised among the visitors at her lack of black, but she guessed that Austin's explanation sufficed.

A crackle in the brush let her know that the maid was close by and would soon come out with a soft query about her health if she did not move on. Many, she knew, would count themselves fortunate to live this way after the struggles of the past year and more. She was not one of them, for her whole spirit yearned for freedom. If she tried to leave now, however, she would be very kindly restrained, Austin would voice his regrets, and the local Bedlam would have another inmate. It was not a chance she wanted to take.

Her slippers moved soundlessly over the wet grass as she went toward the house. It shone pure white among the great trees. The several balconies seemed to drift in the mist, and the many white columns were almost translucent against the pink sky. Groves of huge oak trees stood off to the sides, their trunks so huge that they seemed to grip the ground to stand for a thousand years. Soft gray moss mingled with the leaves and hung low to the ground, as though the trees wept visibly.

She was so immersed in her fancies that she cried out when a figure stepped out from behind the nearest oak tree. Her face flushed as she realized that it was young Charles Edward, wrapped in a dark cloak, out for a morning stroll.

"Mistress Carlotta! Forgive me if I startled you. Are you quite well? Your face is so pink! Where is your maid? Shall I fetch her?"

The words rushed out as his own face grew pink. He looked about anxiously, made as if to take her arm, then drew back as if he might have offended her. Carlotta smiled inwardly. He was very much taken with her as an older woman, that much had been obvious from the start. She had sometimes lifted her eyes during the visits of the neighbors to catch his earnest blue gaze on her for a second or two before he turned quickly away. Now she saw an opportunity to help herself and knew that she must take it without bruising the delicate young sensibilities.

110

She stretched out a hand for his supporting one and felt the quiver of his flesh as he touched her.

"By the faith, Charles Edward, I am stifled by the servants who are with me constantly. Can you not dismiss this one and walk with me a little? I have so longed for the company of someone young, kind though everyone has been."

"I am honored, dear lady." He waved imperiously at the woman and she melted away in the direction of the house. "I am at your service."

"Tell me of yourself, sir, and of your life here in this beautiful city. I vow, I have yearned to see more, perhaps to go driving, but my guardian has not mentioned it, and I cannot ask as he, as all of your family, has been so kind to me."

Charles Edward smiled at her, and she caught the imp of mischief shining in the brilliant eyes. "But I have so wanted to talk with you! They said that you must rest, yet I have seen you walk many times with a swift stride." He drew back. "But I perhaps offend you that I speak so. My grandfather says I am too bold, that I must learn diplomacy before I go to the College of William and Mary in Williamsburg." He caught her blank look. "In our state of Virginia, the state of the American president, Mr. Thomas Jefferson, indeed, of all our presidents."

Carlotta stood up straight, her languid air gone. "A thought has come to me. Might it not be possible for us to drive about this plantation in a carriage sometimes. I do want to see more of it. Or do I ask too much?" She looked directly at him and saw him blush again.

"The wish of a guest is law. I am ashamed for us that you had to ask. They confer in the heat of the day. Would it pain you to go then?"

Carlotta saw that he wanted to grant her wish but feared or hesitated to ask his grandfather. The servants were another matter; there he would naturally, as the heir, have control. "On the contrary, I would be delighted."

They walked a little way together as Charles Edward talked of the beauties of Charleston and of the plantation, Windlea. Carlotta smiled and deferred to him as she asked artless questions. It was a time well spent, she thought later, for she found herself liking the young man for himself as well as for the information they provided.

The next afternoon, normally a resting time for everyone, they drove out in the small carriage that was Charles Edward's own. For propriety's sake a very young maid rode along, perched in the back, well away from them. They spoke in French, the language now being studied by Charles Edward in preparation for his studies and suggested by Carlotta because she was afraid of eavesdropping. They rode over the wide fields where cotton would be planted later and which now lay rich and black against the blue of the sky. Other crops were grown on another section of land which included the rice and tobacco yields. Flowers, both wild and cultivated, lined the well-kept roads of Windlea over which they traveled, and Carlotta saw that the hand of a wise master was evident in the care of land and slaves alike.

Sometimes they ventured out on the road which wound by the sea and would pause to watch the green-blue waves wash in while the gulls cried overhead and the spring sun shone warm on their backs. At such times Carlotta seemed to hear the deep voice of Simon speaking of just such a land as he held her against his body in the snow. Longing would sweep over her in heavy rushes, for time had not, nor would ever, dim his memory for her.

"Do you long for him so very much, Carlotta?" She turned to face the serious eyes of Charles Edward as they sat so one afternoon about ten days after their first ride. They had progressed to first names quite naturally, but he was still plagued with the blushes that came over his fair skin.

"Aye, all my life it will be so." It was a relief to tell the truth to the friend that he had become in just these few days. She knew that he chafed at the rule of his grandfather who still retained much of the strictness of his Scots youth and lived again the days of the Rebellion of '45, which he had been barely old enough to really remember. Charles Edward had been named for the Stuart prince for whom so many had died, fruitlessly, in the effort to place him on the throne of England. Scotland had been ravished and many of her nobles had fled abroad, Charles Windhope's family among them.

"Carlotta?"

She jerked back to reality as he bent toward her. He would go to the college in the fall and boast to his fellows of the sad lady he had comforted on a spring day, she thought.

"Do you enter the convent for love of him? Your guardian disapproves, of course?" It was the very stuff of the ballads they sang in the lengthening evenings at the select parties he was continually urged to attend.

"Aye, Charles Edward. May I speak freely? It would ease

112

my heart." She flinched away from what she was doing, but somehow she must be free of Austin's tentacles. He would never free her nor keep any bargain, she had always known that. There had been little alternative for her in his power on the ship, but now there was at least a chance of escape.

She spun the tale of the commoner attracted to the impoverished young noblewoman over the wish of her family, their untimely demise, and the guardianship of Austin who had whisked her away, the nunnery the only choice of a life now. "But my heart has returned to life, to the beauty of the world, the richness of friendship. Naturally, I shall never love again, but I do not think that I can go to be a bride of Christ feeling so."

Charles Edward said softly, "You are as brave as you are beautiful. We all believed you, forgive me, a little simple, dazed certainly, and subject to the falling sickness. And you are lovelorn." His feelings blazed from his eyes as he lifted her hand to his lips.

Carlotta looked down at the crisp black curls and envied the young girl he would eventually love. "There is a remote branch of my family living in the city of New York. If I could leave Charleston, go there, I would be able to find my own way, perhaps even return to England and seek Simon." Blood poured into her cheeks at the mention of his name. "My guardian would never agree. He is quite rigid, though surely kind."

Charles Edward clicked softly to the horses. "They are old, always fighting battles long done. How can they understand how the young feel? I wanted to go on the grand tour before going away to school. My grandfather says matters are too unsettled abroad. But there are always ways to travel. Now I must wait, perhaps for years." He was silent as they moved smoothly along through the spring air that had taken on a touch of chill. "I will help you, Carlotta. Give me time to arrange a plan."

She restrained her delight but her whisper was heartfelt. "I will thank you with all my heart for your kindness and gallantry."

He was boy enough to struggle for words. "It is nothing. You would do the same in my place."

That night Carlotta could not sleep. Plans and schemes of all sorts raced through her mind, each seeming more hopeless than the last. For the past several days she had not seen Austin or Charles Windhope, for they had remained closeted in the library. Sylvia Windhope was subject to exhausting headaches and, in her age, remained much in her room during the afternoon and night unless guests were expected. The servants were everywhere, but Carlotta had grown used to their silent movements. Their watchfulness would be hard to avoid.

The room was stuffy and the maids slept soundly. She rose and pulled on a dark green robe over her nightdress. She would go out in the cool air and hope that it would still the excitement she felt. Her bare feet moved noiselessly over the polished boards and soft rugs of the room as she eased the door open and slipped into the hall. There was no sound as she went along the corridor, down the wide staircase and along the central hall to the front of the house, and finally into the lifegiving air.

"I tell you, it is perfect. There's just enough resemblance to make anyone who's ever seen them or even a portrait, for that matter, stop and think. Royalty is always alluring, especially royalty in misfortune. It is a hook and that will be all we need. The disgruntled Americans will flock to us, too. Plenty of them do not care for Jefferson or his policies. I know many who feel Virginia has held sway too long in the government."

The voice was Austin's, cool, persuasive, a thread of eagerness in it that Carlotta had never known from him. She faded into the shadow of one of the columns, thankful that the night was moonless, her robe dark. He and Charles Windhope stood under one of the glossy-leaved trees with tankards in their hands.

"I have thought long on it, Austin. We have been friends so long and have both endured great misfortune, but I have been happier than you. Yet I remember the devastation England wrought on Scotland after the '45; we both know the horror of the Revolution and the misplaced ideals, the rising tyranny of Napoleon, and the war that this country has engaged in. My life here is good, but I would give it all up if Charles Edward might be spared the machinations of politics."

Austin said, "Power is the answer. It is sweeter than all else and as heady. The time and the territory are right; a figurehead is all that is needed. It is time to decide, Charles. Are you with me?"

"The girl. Will she obey?"

Carlotta felt the sweat come out on her forehead, although the night wind was chilly. She had thought this to be an abstract political discussion between gentlemen a little gone in their cups. Now it was bare reality.

A short, cold laugh. "She will. She has no choice. The gallows of America and England do not differ."

"Then I am with you. Heart and soul. To the death." Charles Windhope's voice was as strong as that of a younger man when he touched his tankard to Austin's. "Could it really be true, do you think?"

"Perhaps, perhaps not. But we shall use the supposition to create our own world, a separate world based on all the years of garnered experience. Power is the ultimate goal. I have truly learned that, Charles."

Austin was like some dark bird of prey as he stood there, the wind ruffling his white hair and blowing his black garments against his lean body. Carlotta shivered. What was the meaning of all this. How did he mean to use her? Once again she was blessedly thankful for the young man who had so chivalrously agreed to help her.

Austin was speaking again, the tone oddly ragged. "I have not forgotten, Charles, nor will I ever. Stephan is my dear flesh, the girl will bear the heir, but my youth and my life were blighted when they destroyed Madeleine. They, the world-changers. Now it will be my turn. Our turn."

It sounded like an ancient curse there in the blowing spring darkness. Carlotta's hand came up involuntarily in the age old sign against evil.

CHAPTER SIXTEEN

The Garlands Will Wither

CARLOTTA prepared the next afternoon for her ride with Charles Edward which had become a ritual. She meant to ask him the meaning of some of the things she had heard the night before, for certainly he must have some idea of them. The long afternoon waned and grew cool but he did not come. She asked the slave girl who usually went with them, but the question seemed to engender such fright that she was forced to stop.

When she went to her room there was a sheaf of spring flowers in a vase near her bedside. At first she thought that the maid had brought them of her own accord, but when she lifted the piercing sweetness of the bouquet to her face, a tiny folded piece of paper fell out. She covered it instantly with her skirt, then moved to the window and read it in the fading light.

"Carlotta, my lady, somehow we are found out. My grandfather has berated me, called me ingrate, and forbidden me to see or speak with you again. I am to be sent to our relatives in Richmond until it is time to enter the college. When you read this I will be gone. Forgive me that I have failed the trust you placed in me. The slave, Tanda, is intelligent and bold; she was the daughter of a chieftain in her native land. I have given her gold and she will seek to help. Think of me in time to come, my lady."

The tears rose unbidden to Carlotta's eyes. The slaves had told Austin and Charles Windhope, that was the only way they could have been found out. Now the boy must pay for her own indiscretions and his youthful worship of a new face. Yet matters were not totally lost; she had hope, and Charles Edward would flourish away from this air of decaying gentility.

She was drinking tea in the small enclosed patio that bordered on her room the next morning when the familiar cool voice bade the maidservant go, then remarked, "We leave Charleston in the morning, my dear. I fear that you have found things somewhat dull of late. I had meant to show you something of the city but business has kept me."

Carlotta shielded her eyes against the sun as he moved to

lounge against the wall which was hung with ivy and little flowers of a pale red hue. "Then you will keep your bargain and send me to one of the Northern cities."

Austin smiled urbanely as he adjusted a ruffled sleeve. "Do pour me some tea, these long nights are quite fatiguing." He paused until she had complied and he had tasted the brew. "I shall keep it in the same way that you kept yours, Carlotta. We sail for New Orleans, where I have plans for you."

She told herself to keep calm, that anger and temper would not alter this man or his ways. With him, the unexpected always had more power. But reason could not prevail against the frustrated fury. "You never meant to hold to your given word."

He came erect and leaned over her so that he shadowed the sun. His hands moved up and down her body as his lips took hers in a travesty of passion. His leg pushed between hers while he bent her backward. As swiftly as he had seized her, he pushed her back so that she almost fell.

"In New Orleans you will marry my son, Stephan, who is heir to wealth and a great tradition. When you are safely with child we will travel beyond the Mississippi River into other lands, and there the plans of twenty years will come to fruition."

Carlotta stared at him. "I will not. How can you force me? Moreover, you have lain with me yourself. It would be incest."

Austin viewed her with contempt. "They will make you ready." He turned and walked away.

Carlotta gave full vent to her anger as she picked up the teapot, still full almost to the brim, and hurled it at the wall where he had leaned. The crash was so satisfying that she followed it with both their cups. Then she stood in the midst of the debris and laughed, knowing that if she gave way to tears there would be no end to them. At that moment she saw Simon's face, the gilt hair, the brilliant green eyes, and it was so close that she could almost touch him. She seemed to feel his hand on her shoulder and his warm voice in her ear.

"Miss Carlotta!" It was the maid, Tanda. "Hold still, I'll bring you some brandy."

Carlotta took time to wonder that the faintly slurring, less than grammatical language that Tanda had always used to her was gone. The clipped accents had a British ring now. Then the cup was placed in her shaking hands while Tanda held it steady. The draught seemed to glide along her throat, smoothing it with richness, dulling the edge of her anger. The roaring

117

in her ears subsided, and she was able to take in the worried face of the other woman.

"Thank you, I'm fine now. I had a shock."

"I heard. I know." Tanda's slim, supple figure straightened, and the great dark eyes gazed into Carlotta's. She could not have been more than twenty-five but the wisdom there was ageless. Her face was delicately carved, the cheekbones high, her neck long. "Soon he will weep."

"Would God that were true! I would rejoice with all my heart. He is evil, that man!" Carlotta wrapped both arms around herself and began to pace. "Tanda, the young master spoke to me of you. . . ." She fell silent as the other girl held up a slender hand.

"There are powers greater than the Christian God, mistress. For now, you must follow the way that is ordained for us all. But the darkness already surrounds Austin Lenoir." She moved back, and a moment later Carlotta heard her footsteps running down the hall.

Carlotta was still in the grip of her anger as she bent over the teapot with some idea of recovering it for her hosts who, after all, had been kind. She gathered the tossed leaves in both hands, squeezed them together, and thought bitterly of her hatred for Austin. A bird settled raucously on the tip of a branch overlooking the wall, as wordlessly, she invoked that which had no name. Seconds later the warmth of the sun on her back and the cries of the bird brought reality rushing back; she felt a bit foolish as she released the soggy leaves and brushed her hands on the sides of her gown.

Austin did not come near Carlotta again, and she was grateful for that mercy. She thought of appealing to Charles Windhope but knew it was fruitless; he and Austin were comrades in whatever scheme was to be set up. Austin was almost a total mystery to her, the knowledge that he had a son came as a shock, the command that she marry him as an even greater one. She did know that he would deliver her up to the hangman without a qualm if she did not obey him, but that would only be after he had tormented her beyond all will or wish for life. These things came to her instinctively, and, though she recoiled, she knew them for truth.

That night Carlotta dressed in the old brown gown and went to bed early, before the slaves came to watch her. When the sound of slow, deep breathing resounded in the room and the light of the quarter moon was beginning to fade from the sky, she rose and tiptoed out, much the way she had come the night of her eavesdropping. This time, however, the door was securely locked and bolted. The great windows which usually opened onto the wide lawns were also locked. As she watched from the enveloping curtains she saw the shadows of several guards pacing back and forth, their weapons at the ready. Any attempt at escape would be hopeless. She sank down on the polished floor, uncaring that anyone might see. Was she doomed to remain a prisoner without control of her destiny for the remainder of her days or, far more likely, until Austin decided that she was useless as whatever pawn he intended to make of her?

Then the moonlit landscape receded from her vision and she saw again the narrow street, the running forms, the blood-drenched weapons, and the one person who sought her out to kill her. In a moment she would see his face, the face of the murderer. But this time she was not afraid; she was angry but ready for him. Her fingers sought a dagger, a pistol, anything. Then she was on her feet and staring out at the peaceful world.

"What does it mean?" She spoke the words softly to herself as she slipped back up the stairs, into her room, and out onto the patio, where she lifted her hot face to the cool night wind. One of the slaves half rose to come to her, but Carlotta waved her away with a gesture. The nightmare always brought the deadly, bone-chilling fear. That had been the pattern since earliest childhood. It rarely came in her waking moments or, if it did, was curiously fragmented. Never had she, as the grown-up Carlotta, recognized the danger and turned to face it, to face the murderer. Now she whispered the words out loud. "I must have seen my parents or relatives murdered, and whoever killed them came after me, too. It must have been personal, else why would I feel that I will see the face of the murderer at any time? It was no mob mindlessly after anyone who spoke a little differently or wore unusual clothes, anyone suspected, however foolishly, of being an aristocrat. It was personal." Chills ran up and down her back as she faced her knowledge and her fear.

She was still there when the dawn shimmered pinkly in the eastern sky. Her memory had been cudgeled unmercifully, a thing she rarely did since it made her feel so helpless, but nothing else could be unearthed. She could only think that something about the present situation paralleled that long-ago one, at least to her memory. If she could face that past terror, then the terror of now might be resolved as well. How she knew these things was beyond comprehension, but the fact of the knowledge was comforting.

"Mistress Carlotta! Come now and get dressed! Here's tea."

She barely heard the soft cry of the slave who usually brought her morning tea. The ivy fronds were tossing in the morning wind, which still had a bite to it. The sky had that far, remote look before the settling of day. Carlotta was in a remote place, the world of her inward self, a place where facts and supposition were welded together to alter her from one who is acted upon to one who acts. Austin knew, or suspected, something about her and her origins; enough, certainly, on which to base a scheme of great importance to him over a long period of years. That knowledge was vital to her now. "Learn what he knows. Bide your time. He cannot watch forever. New Orleans is a great city of this new land; there will be opportunities there that have not presented themselves in Charleston. Wait."

"Mistress." The girl, Tanda, touched Carlotta with gentle fingers. "It is time to come back."

Carlotta turned to her, conscious of the chill that pervaded every part of her body. Tanda wrapped the thick cloak around her and urged her to a comfortable chair before the hearth in her bedroom. Gradually, the shivering stopped and she felt the strong tea restoring vitality to her being. She had not slept the entire night but she felt curiously rested and ready to face what she must. A banging noise caught her attention; the slaves were taking down the belongings that had been obtained for her during the time here and preparing them for the voyage.

Tanda caught her glance. Her whisper was soft. "I travel with you as your maid, a gift of Mr. Windhope to his friend, Austin Lenoir. I will help you when I can, but we must be discreet."

"I trust you, Tanda." Carlotta's voice rasped a little and grew steady.

The other girl's eyes widened. "Mistress, what has happened?"

Carlotta did not pretend to misunderstand, but she knew that her own counsel must be kept. "I have thought long in the night. When the opportunity presents itself, I will be ready. Thank you for your help, Tanda."

"You will be strong, mistress. I sense it in you, and because of you the young master is free." She rose in one lithe movement and went from the room.

Carlotta permitted them to dress her in the dark green traveling gown which had panels of lighter green in the full skirt and a white bodice with ruffles spilling down the front and over her hands. The small hat was the same shade as her eyes and was bound with the same green as her dress. When she looked into the mirror she saw a fashionable woman whose eyes shone with excitement, whose cheeks were softly pink with it, and from whom the shadow of fear had, however momentarily, lifted.

She and Tanda walked slowly out into the morning sunlight where the large open carriage, already piled with baggage, waited. Charles Windhope and Austin stood chatting close by.

"My dear, you are ravishing this morning. I do so regret that you must leave us, but your guardian is anxious to press on." Charles clasped her hand in his frail one; the eyes on her were assessing, demanding.

"May I make my farewells to your wife, sir?"

"She is indisposed this morning. Our grandson has been ...indiscreet. Women worry too much. She sleeps now after a restless night. I will tell her of your kind thought."

Austin came close to them then. He was wearing the gray that so well suited him. The triumph in his black eyes was hardly veiled. "Ah, Carlotta, you look ready for the voyage. Are you quite reconciled to leaving this lovely, peaceful place?" His voice rang hard, and she saw Charles stiffen.

"Let us say instead that I look forward to the ocean voyage and our arrival in New Orleans."

They smiled at her as the tension relaxed. Austin helped her into the carriage and murmured, "You are sensible, after all. A woman must have her little tantrums."

She looked straight into his eyes, and this time they were the first to fall. "Aye, Austin, I am learning to be sensible."

They rode down the long curve of driveway as Carlotta turned to look back at Windlea. It sat, remote and dreaming, among the glossy trees, a white vision now repeated in their waxy, bittersweet flowers. She had learned much here and she was, indeed, regretful to be leaving. "Be happy, Charles Edward, dear friend." Her mind whispered the farewell as they turned into the Charleston road.

The drive to the port was leisurely, for as Charles Windhope said with his charming smile, "You have seen almost nothing of our city; you must remember her welcome and return one day." Carlotta noticed that the myth of the convent seemed to have been ignored.

So, with her new strength, she forced herself to ignore all contemplation of the future and gave herself up to the loveliness that would have made her heart glad in the cold English winter and now lifted it up. The sun was high now and very warm as it glistened off the leaves of the trees and shone on the white woodwork of the houses they passed. The shade was deep in places and mysteriously dark, very cool in the heat of the summer that would come. Live oaks and palmetto trees were everywhere, mingling with the soft plaster and wood of the houses, with their tracery of delicate-seeming ironwork and high walls. But it was the flowers and vines that drew exclamations of delight from Carlotta. They were everywhere in shades of red, pink, white, and yellow, spilling from walls, trellises, and balconies. She recognized roses, daffodils, the familiar forsythia, the oleanders, and honeysuckle of which Charles Edward had told her, the morning glories, and the great creamy magnolias.

The town itself was alive with people walking and driving or simply strolling. They went by the elegant shops, heard the peddlers and flower-sellers calling their wares, passed the first theater in the colonies, moved past a church whose steeple was so high that she wondered if it were the one she had seen from the ship that early morning only weeks ago, and came finally to the harbor where the rivers joined and the *Princess* stood at anchor.

Carlotta found herself wondering what it would be like to live in so beneficent a climate, to walk those alluring streets and have a garden of flowers such as she had seen. To be free. Her eye caught that of Tanda, and she had the strange feeling that the other girl knew her thoughts and shared them.

Austin was making their farewells now, calling to his men to bring the boat closer, urging the careful disposition of the luggage. She made her curtsey to Charles Windhope, heard his soft words that belied the glitter in his eyes, for he would not easily forgive her Charles Edward, and lifted her head to look at the distant *Princess* drifting with the sway of the winds.

"Austin, I will send messages by swift ship and courier if anything overt occurs. The others are as eager as we for the venture." Charles's voice carried to her over the sounds of the dock.

"So long as they know where the power lies." Austin's words were full of the self-assurance he carried as a mantle.

Carlotta looked at him there in the sparkling day, and suddenly she knew what Tanda had meant, for the darkness surrounded him, moving with him in the sun's clear light.

CHAPTER SEVENTEEN

My Son, My Son Absalom!

THE bright days ran together as the *Princess* went before the wind down the coast of the southern United States, which was sometimes in view, with great forests of trees lifting themselves on the horizon. The sun shone daily, the water changed from green to blue and back again in differing shades, gulls hovered above them, and the songs of the several slaves that Austin had purchased in Charleston rang out with their strange beat. Carlotta spent much of her time on deck under a shaded retreat that had been erected for her at Austin's command. Here she read, watched the sea, and dreamed in this quiet time that seemed a gift from the very gods.

She had the same room next to his, but this time Tanda shared it with her and saw to Carlotta's needs with brisk efficiency. She had thought to make a friend of the slave girl, but Tanda retreated from all such attempts by presenting a blank face and speaking only when spoken to, then in the combination of half English and slurring French that was often difficult to understand. Carlotta saw her speaking to one of the new slaves, a very tall man with massive shoulders whose back bore the mark of the lash, one early morning, and it appeared as if they argued. Then he lifted his hand to her shoulders in a gesture of tenderness which bore nothing of the sexual. Later in the day Tanda's usually impassive face was drawn, the skin paler than its normal glossiness.

Carlotta had discovered some volumes of history involving the United States among the books Austin had placed in her cabin, and now she read of the Revolutionary War and the founding of the new nation, and the documents of that nation and of its current president, Thomas Jefferson, with great interest. England was her country and had been since she could remember, but the concepts of this land fascinated her and removed her mind from her own predicament.

They had seen no other sail in all the days of their journey, but one afternoon Carlotta saw a ship approaching rapidly as if bent on attack. The men were assembling on the deck below as she watched, and Austin alternated between speaking to them and looking through his spyglass. He had not spoken to her except in the most correct terms since their departure, a thing for which she was very grateful. Now he looked up at her and waved his hand in the direction of her cabin. She nodded and withdrew from his line of vision but remained so that she could see what was happening.

Now he called to his mate, "She bears the personal emblem of Charles Windhope. Bid them slow the ship." His voice was calm; he was every inch the commander.

Carlotta remembered Charles's words, "if something overt occurs," and wondered what must have happened to whatever scheme he and Austin had in mind. If only she could ask Austin what all this was about! The opaque eyes would stare through her and he would turn away; during this voyage she had been thankful to drink in the peace of the sea.

The other ship drew alongside in a matter of minutes. She was far smaller than the *Princess* and well hung with sail, though her crew seemed much less. After the hails and presentation of captains, a walk was extended and three men came onto the deck. All wore black. Austin came to meet them, his face sober and correct. They entered a small area on an upper part of the deck, and a guard was posted at the door.

The silence was almost absolute. Only the creaking of the ships in the water and the flapping sails broke the stillness. Carlotta saw the men gathering in little groups to discuss what all this might mean, but they made no sound. The men of the other ship remained at their posts, making no effort to exchange cries or comments. Carlotta's first thought was that Charles Windhope was dead; after all, he bore the marks of his years, and she felt sorrow drift through her, for he had been kind.

Then the door opened and the men moved slowly out. Austin was walking slowly, painfully, not with his usual determined tread. Even in the distance that separated them she could see the graven lines on his formerly smooth face and the downward twist of his full mouth. His voice rose clearly to her. The arrogance was gone from it; a new raw emotion was there as he said, "Give my thanks to Master Windhope for bringing this news to me so swiftly. Express, too, my gratitude for his kind remembrances. Tell him that all goes as we planned and that nothing is altered. Nothing!"

"It shall be as you have commanded, sir." The older of the three men spoke, then all bowed and went to the crossing place.

125

Austin stood stiffly until they were aboard and the other ship had cast off before he walked to the stairs that led to his own cabin.

The *Princess* resumed her customary speed, but Carlotta was agog with curiosity. No one on the ship ever spoke to her; this was by Austin's order, she suspected. Tanda went everywhere and would likely know, but she was nowhere to be found. She decided to go to her own cabin and rest against the heat of the day, hoping that the girl would soon appear.

The voice was low and monotonous, repeating over and over the Biblical dirge, "Oh, my son, my son Absalom, would God I had died for thee!" The bitter cry of David the King as he wept for his dead son. "My son, my son!"

Carlotta stood in her own door and swayed with the motion of the ship as the full impact of what must have happened hit her. She had not known Austin capable of such powerful feeling, but then she knew nothing about him except his behavior toward her.

"He is bored no longer." Tanda uncoiled herself from Carlotta's bed in one sinuous movement. "His fate has come." The great black eyes blazed with delight.

Carlotta knew she should be glad. This could only mean that Austin's son was either maimed or dead, that she would not have to engage in a travesty of marriage to further some nefarious scheme. She could not help it; her heart was torn with pity for the arrogant man brought so low.

"You hate him! Why?"

"Aye, mistress. Do you not hate and ill-wish him as well? Did I not hear you vow this hatred in the walled garden? You waste your foolish girl's pity on such as he!" Tanda bounded past her and was gone.

There was silence from next door. He had heard them, of course; in his great pride this might mean that some cruelty would ensue. Carlotta tried to stir her own anger but she could only think of how bereft the world had been when Simon was gone from her. There was a rattling noise, and the bolt on his side of the door slid back. Austin stood, tall and austere, looking every year of his age, as his eyes met Carlotta's.

"Stephan is dead of the yellow fever in New Orleans. Rejoice, Carlotta, even as your maid, for your hatred has bloomed as the night flowers." His mouth twisted and was as quickly brought under control.

Carlotta said softly, "I will pray to the Blessed Virgin for the repose of his soul."

Austin's bitter laughter rang out as he lifted the tankard full of brandy and drank deeply. "Nothing has changed. We go on as before." He swayed a little and drank again. "Prayer, indeed!"

Carlotta saw that he must have drunk a great deal in a short time, for she had never seen him even slightly affected by drink before. "Would it ease you to speak of all this, Austin?" She meant to take advantage of his pain to find out as much as she could about what he planned for her. The new determination fostered by those resolutions in Charleston forced her on. "Tell me about Stephan."

He walked carefully over to her bed and sank down, drinking again as he did so. Carlotta brought the brandy bottle from her own cupboard and placed it within his reach. He said, "Devious little bitch! Women are all such. You want to know, do you?" He lowered his head into his hands and she saw his shoulders shake.

It should have been the supreme moment for Carlotta but she could not take delight in it. She who had lost love could understand the grief of another, just as she could now understand the forces which had driven Lady Leticia and her lover. Complete hatred was alien to her, and she could not now wish it otherwise.

When the dull, flat voice began to speak, she had to strain to hear it, but she did not dare move lest she distract him. These were things she must know. So she sank to the floor and listened with all her powers of concentration.

"I will try to explain it simply, but I realize that women have no real understanding of these matters." He regarded his pearl ring for an instant, then raised his eyes to her face. "In 1803, the President of the United States bought Louisiana from Napoleon and well-nigh doubled the size of his country. Many people there regard the Americans as upstarts and themselves as vastly civilized, since the French and Spanish have ruled for so long in Louisiana. There are those who think the city of New Orleans should be an independent city. Others feel that portions of the new territory should be separate entities or countries, that some of the western states should leave the Union. My friends in New Orleans tell me that the city is filled with those who have fled from Europe to find a new life and

127

who have no love for either the followers of Napoleon or the lovers of the monarchy."

He paused for breath, and Carlotta saw his pale skin begin to flush. She said, "But I do not see what all this has to do with me."

"Listen! The future can be shaped by men with determination in such times as these. The land beyond the Mississippi can be for the taking if one acts boldly. The government in Washington does not even know the extent of its purchase, much less the feelings of the people involved. I mean to take empire for my own; a strong hand, powerful friends, wealth— all these will make the difference. I have all these. Charles Windhope and I are in complete agreement and we are preparing troops for when they are needed. My contacts in New Orleans are ready."

He rose to pour a brandy, then paced back and forth, more excited than she had ever seen him. He seemed to have forgotten her, but his next words caused a thrill of excitement to go up and down her back.

"Americans are mad for royalty for all that they threw off mad George. Did New Orleans not welcome those royal brothers of France who managed to escape the guillotine with open arms and purse? They love color, pageantry, martial music, a cause. You, my dear, have a certain resemblance to some members of the French royal family. A gesture, a way of movement, an expression. Charles marked it almost immediately. A fair woman of royal blood, ill-used, now wed to a powerful man who could be a strong ruler, fruitful—the scheme has every chance to succeed. I would have wed you to Stéphan, but now my duty is clear."

She rose to face him. "Let me understand you, Austin. You truly think that people will follow some vague dream of empire and false royalty here in this land where they have so recently thrown off the rule of England? You are mad!" Here was another Napoleon, she thought, power-hungry and believing himself invulnerable.

He caught her shoulders and shook her. "Never say that to me again! The Revolution in France destroyed much for me and I have seen the rule of fools prosper. People are easily gulled; they follow where they are led. We can make a separate nation on the American continent! Now is the time to strike, before the Americans can prepare and while the territory is in ferment."

Carlotta said, "I thought that you sorrowed for your son. Instead you dream of an empire that cannot be. What manner of man are you, Austin Lenoir?"

"Empire that cannot be? Did Napoleon, ten years ago, dream of empire and fancy it only that?" He laughed harshly, his lips pulled taut against his teeth. "I can see that I have wasted time explaining matters to you. I see that I must demonstrate. We shall needs prove you fertile." He tossed her on the bed and pulled up her skirts as though she were any doxy. When she tried to break free he slapped her lightly but so expertly that the world blurred momentarily.

"No, don't!" She cried the words but it was useless for he was on her, thrusting into her tender parts, his hands grasping at her breasts even as the length of him hammered at her womanhood. She twisted and pulled but his strength held her down while he possessed her utterly. Even at the moment of his culmination he did not release her but held her captive until his power rejuvenated itself and it all began again. Carlotta finally ceased to struggle for it seemed to inflame him; she lay quiescent in his grasp and divorced herself from her body. Simon's face would not come in this time of trial, but the waves of the great sea rose up in their endless lashing and drowned out some of the groans and sighs that Austin made as he took her in anger and necessity.

Finally he was done and rose, fastening his breeches and sweeping the hair from his eyes as he looked down at her bare thighs. "Best pray that you quicken soon. I do not find you particularly appealing for all that you are not a virgin. A footman, I believe you said?"

Carlotta sat up and looked him straight in the eye. "You can force yourself on me, I cannot stop you, but what is it, an old wives' tale, which says that an aging man and an unwilling woman cannot achieve a child?"

Austin took her chin in his hand and she felt the impact of his words as though he had hit her. "It will not be for lack of trying. My first wife, Stephan's mother, was wed because we had adjoining plantations. She fancied herself unwilling. Eleven months after the nuptials, he lay in his cradle and she in the cemetery. My second had more sense for a time. I have been wifeless for some years. I suggest that you not try me too far. I will not kill you, you are my figurehead, nor will I mar you, but there are many ways to exact obedience."

He pushed her back on the bed and walked slowly out the

door, then turned and added, "Be ready for me this night. Wear something delicate and lacy. My duty must be done."

That night, part of the next day, and all the following night Austin spent with Carlotta, taking her each time with determination but without cruelty. He serviced himself at her while pausing only for brief naps and restoratives brought to him by his manservant. She was not allowed to see Tanda but performed her ablutions behind a screen, then returned to his grim embrace. Carlotta made her mind a blank, one with the rolling waves, and kept her body supple, as relaxed as she could. It did not matter to Austin; she was but a vessel. She forgot that she had ever pitied this savage man who might never have cried out against the death of his son. Now she sought only to find some means to free herself.

Early on the morning of the second day, Austin rose and dressed with his customary elegance. Then he bent over her and said, "Enough for now. We shall see what your monthly brings. All this may be to do over again. I will send your maid to you."

"If I am pregnant, the child will be a monster!" She propped herself up on one elbow and glared at him.

"My dear Carlotta, so long as it is a male, what does it matter? They have been known to rule, you know. And what do you think my only son was like, a paragon of all manly beauty?"

Carlotta turned her face into the pillow and this time she prayed for deliverance from this coil.

"Get up and we will walk on the deck. The fresh air will do you good." It was Tanda, brisk and forthright, her eyes neither allowing nor accepting the self-pity that Carlotta was beginning to feel.

On the deck in the soft wind, watching the waves—the blue-green water of which Simon had spoken—dance up and down, moving with the thrust of the *Princess,* Carlotta began to feel better. On impulse she turned to the dark girl and said, "I must speak or go mad with all this, yet you have retreated from me. Will you listen now?"

"Aye." The one word was enough. The dark eyes were suddenly fiercely interested, and Carlotta wondered if the restraint of the past time was but a pose.

The sun was slipping red-gold into the waters when Carlotta finished the tale which she had begun with her flight from England and ended with Austin's determination to have a child by her. Tanda listened with close attention, her pointed, high-nosed face alert. In the end Carlotta felt that same curious lifting of the spirit that she had experienced when she spoke of the nightmare in her youth, even to Austin.

The dark girl laughed softly, the sound eerie in the silence that had fallen. "He tries hard, that man. He sent an order that I was to prepare potions to make his body powerful, his seed strong."

"They worked," said Carlotta bitterly. "Whose side are you on, anyway? I thought that Charles Edward meant you would help me if you could."

Her teeth flashed in the light and Carlotta saw that the thin patina of this world had faded. "A slave learns to protect herself, mistress. You will learn that if you live. Your Austin carries darkness with him, as I have said. Your fate is intertwined with his and you cannot escape it. Cease to struggle. Bide and wait."

"How do you know these things? Can you see into the future?" Carlotta was a product of the rationalism taught her by Uncle Arnold, but she felt a chill go up her spine as the hairs on her arms rose. Tanda had spoken this way before and Austin's son lay dead.

"I can see. But it comes as it wills. My lessons were cut short."

"How?" Carlotta was conscious of a great weariness. She wanted only to go and sleep, to rest long now that her body was her own again.

Tanda laughed again but her eyes were savage. "The French! The French! I owe them much. I will tell you the tale in the days to come."

Carlotta sighed, "How far is it to New Orleans? I suppose that Austin will hurry even faster now that his son is dead."

It was not only the sun that caused the red lights to flame in Tanda's eyes as she turned to face the girl. "But we do not go to New Orleans yet. We go to the Mountainous Land, my homeland. We go to Haiti."

CHAPTER EIGHTEEN

The Perilous Mission

TANDA would say no more after that, but melted away as if she were a wraith in the darkness. Carlotta was too tired to think, but she woke in the reaches of the night to hear the low-voiced moans and King David's cry coming again through the walls. For all his cruelty and arrogance, it seemed that Austin was human enough to weep for his first-born, but she could feel no more pity. She would not, she decided then, openly defy him again. He had a peculiar kind of madness, and for her own safety she would walk carefully.

The next morning, as she walked on the deck, he joined her for a moment to say, "I have missed our dinners together. Will you join me this night?" He wore black again, and the unrelieved darkness was not kind to the deep circles under his eyes. She hesitated and he added, "You are quite safe from my attentions, my dear."

"Of course I will come." She stared challengingly into his face and saw the question enter his eyes before he bowed and stalked away.

Carlotta saw Tanda from a distance that day but the girl did not come to her. This was as much a mystery as any plan of Austin's, and Carlotta thought that if she played to his natural arrogance he would answer some of her questions.

She dressed that night in amber silk and wound her hair high, then used some of the sweet scent that he had furnished. The mirror showed that she was fair, yet regal. Austin's manner told her nothing, but now that she had experience of his body, she thought that he found her woman's flesh faintly distasteful for all that he had commented more than once on her growing attractiveness.

She said, "Tanda tells me that we are for Haiti. I know nothing of the place. You have revealed much of your plan, Austin, will you not tell me the rest?"

He leaned back in his chair, sipping the excellent after-dinner wine supplied by his manservant. "You begin to like the sound of a crown on that russet head of yours, is that it?"

She lowered her eyes and let a hesitant smile curve the corners of her mouth. "I have had much time for thought in all these days that I have known you. Your plans give me more. You have such . . . scope."

He stood up so quickly that the chair tilted back. "Do not seek to cozen me, madame. I am beyond it. I lie with you as I must, for it is my duty to the dynasty that will be founded. That slave should be whipped for telling you of our destination!"

Carlotta stood up and faced him. "She meant no harm, and what difference does it make? She has been invaluable to me," she said. "And to you, too," she thought, watching him pick up his chair from the carpet and settle into it again.

"Very well. We understand each other, I think. We go to Haiti on a rescue mission, a favor for Charles Windhope who is both my friend of all the years, as you know, and a man of powerful influence in South Carolina and Virginia. It means much to my cause that he is with us. Some say that he even has the ear of the Vice-President who was. The estimable Mr. Burr and his unfortunate duel." He caught himself up. "But I digress. Charles has kindly sent his foremost legal advisor to New Orleans to oversee matters there for me. Stephan was a recluse; my plantations and other enterprises were tended for me and are in good hands. He knew I would understand his request."

He paused to take a sip of wine, and Carlotta wondered again at his seeming calm which had come so quickly. Her innate caution warned her to say nothing, to betray no fear or emotion.

"I will be brief. Haiti is in a state of rebellion against Napoleon. The leader of it is dead but his works live on. White men and women have been murdered without cause, slaughtered as if they were animals. It is a bestial place. Charles has a younger sister, married to a wealthy man for some years, who lived in Haiti when all this broke out. We know that he is most horribly dead and thought that she, too, had perished. Word came by most devious means—it seems that she was well loved—that she lives and is hidden in the mountains with her young son. That was three months ago. He sent several experienced men to find her. Their entrails were returned to the ship. He was desperate. Slaves always know everything; his were no exception. It was not until after we sailed that he was told the slave Tanda and her brother, Louis, were from

133

Haiti and might be persuaded to assist him in exchange for gold and freedom. His letter told me of this. I have spoken to them and they are indeed agreeable. Of course the woman is dead and it is a useless journey, but I need Charles's help."

"She may be alive. What a fearful thing!" Carlotta's ready sympathies were engaged as she remembered the howling mob of her nightmare and the terror of the unknown. How much more awful to know that all you loved lay destroyed around you.

Austin sniffed. "We shall take no chances. Force is the only language these brutes understand. A hostage shall be kept and the other sent. I can, however, only applaud their zeal in sending the French forces running."

Carlotta thought of Tanda's quick intelligence and the powers she possessed. Austin was the brute, the despoiler.

He caught her thought and laughed. "Women are sentimentalists. Do not worry. I harm no one who is useful to me."

The days passed now in a long slow rhythm that engendered peace. Sometimes she dined with Austin, who was once again correct and proper, giving no sign that he had ever sought her body. She asked no more questions, and he volunteered no information. Much of her time was spent on the deck, watching the ever-changing waters and feeling the warmth of the sun on her skin, even through the thin garments that she wore. Her mind continued to dwell on Austin's impossible scheme, as she wondered what the circumstances were that could have driven so obviously intelligent a man to embark on such a thing. He was as he was, but what could have shaped him so? Simon came frequently to mind these days as they sailed under the brilliant skies and warm winds. Carlotta was thankful that they had shared what they had; it made the situation with Austin more bitter, but at the same time she could hope for the future, having once known love and passion.

They passed no other ships in these days; the entire ocean might have been theirs. The coastline of the United States and what Austin had told her was the territory of Florida, which belonged to Spain, had long since been left behind. The weather grew steadily hotter as they went always toward the south.

Tanda talked often with Carlotta now and they became friends, especially after Carlotta told her of the information that Austin had given her which explained their current journey. In the times that Carlotta was tempted to agonize over her own

134

fate, she thought of the story that Tanda told her in fits and spurts over the peaceful days.

Tanda and her brother were the only children of a hill chieftain deep in the mountains of Haiti. They were taken in slavery by a raiding party which killed those who resisted. The plantation owner who took them was not one of the cruel ones, and they learned much in the period of captivity. When the rebellion came, they and others helped their owner and his family to escape. Later they fought with Toussaint L'Ouverture in the struggle to free their country from the bonds of France, suffered the agony of his capture, and rejoiced when Haiti was proclaimed free, the first black republic anywhere. The ruler now had taken the title of Emperor and was said to desire the island purged of all whites. Tanda and Louis—"You could not pronounce our Haitian names," she had said—were taken captive with others who had ventured too near the coast, thus falling prey to slave traders who still frequented these waters. In Charleston they were sold almost immediately to Charles Windhope who, in his turn, had been kind.

Tanda said passionately, "This is our land and we will rule it as we see fit. Our blood drenches these mountains and beaches. Any who try to enslave us again will die as the others did."

Carlotta felt a pang of envy at such a sense of belonging. She loved England and cared for it, but would she risk her life, her all, the way this girl seemed ready to do? She said, "Is there a chance that the woman still lives? Austin will hold one of you as surety against betrayal, you know."

The other girl shrugged. "We have been gone a little less than a year. There is no way to know. I have a friend, a good friend, who knows much of warfare and government. I will find him and we shall see."

There were contemporary documents among the papers that Austin gave Carlotta to read, remarking that she needed to know all she could about the state of affairs in the world now. Here she read of the bloody battles waged over Haiti, of the bloodshed and destruction on both sides, and of the idealism which held to the Rights of Man, as opposed to the slavers and landowners who saw the rich island lost to France. She read of Toussaint's struggles for unification and his lonely death far from the land he fought for. She also read the warnings sent in letters from various officials and observers who now felt that to set foot on the island was death.

135

In this time Carlotta came to think that all she would ever want of this life was her freedom, the ability to earn some sort of living by tutoring, a quiet place to live, and her books. She knew, too, that she asked for the world in these few things and dared expect none of them. The thought of love she put aside. Simon held her heart and always would.

They came to the island of Haiti in the early morning, while the horizon was yet only faintly pearly and the dark tropical night still draped water and land alike. The bulk of the land seemed enormous to Carlotta, who was still rubbing her eyes. Tanda had roused her hurriedly and tossed her the first robe handy. "We are here; you must not miss the first sight of my country. Haiti." The word was a lover's name in her mouth.

The sails of the *Princess* were furled, and the oars were dipped slowly, rhythmically, in the warm water as she headed around the curve of land and toward the cove off which she would stand until the party could be landed. She would then go back out to sea until summoned by signal fires.

In the lifting light Carlotta could make out mountains hung with great forests that seemed to tumble down the sides. They appeared to rise into the clouds which were now turning pink. Gulls hovered around the ship for a short time and then flew away toward land. Far ahead the creamy waves broke on a small beach that looked to be only a dusting of sand.

Tanda sank to her knees on the deck and began to chant in the strange language that Carlotta had heard her use but rarely. Her eyes bloomed with that intense, fiery look, and her whole taut body was taller, more powerful. It took no imagination to know that she thanked whatever strange gods she worshipped for their safe arrival at the homeland.

There was a rush of movement now as the little boat was prepared and two of the other Haitians stood ready to go. Tanda touched Carlotta's hand. "I go with them. The gods will watch over you." She stood, erect and lithe, in the loose dress of dull green, her head wrapped in a matching turban that accentuated the brilliant eyes and high cheekbones. "I have said it."

Carlotta felt her throat constrict, for she knew that she might never see this girl again. "Your brother will be as safe as he has ever been. Austin will not harm him now."

Tanda smiled enigmatically and turned away to go down to the boat. Her brother, his arms chained, stood with several of the more brawny guards. Austin was close by. He called to

136

her, "Three days only. If you do not return in that time he will be sent to the shore in pieces. Small ones."

Louis did not turn his head from contemplation of the vast land bulk in front of them. The forests were now touched with the pink of the rising sun, which reflected off the green masses. Thin clouds floated in the tinged sky above. The *Princess* floated on the water with hardly a movement.

"We of Haiti keep our bargains." The quiet lilting voice of Tanda came to Carlotta's ears, and she saw Austin stiffen at the rebuke. Then the dark girl moved down into the boat and soon the slapping of the oars was the only sound in the morning air.

The ship went back out to sea and life went on as it had for all the many weeks of their voyage. It was very hot here, and Carlotta found it was all she could do to remain in the cabin long enough to change clothes and get out. The cool gowns that had been bought for her in Charleston now felt as if they were weighted wool; her flesh burned and itched under them. Austin gave her some white dresses that appeared to be only long shifts, remarking as he did so that she might soon need them for another reason, that of pregnancy. Whatever the purpose, she wore them gratefully.

Late in the afternoon of the third day, the fire rose high on the distant shore. The *Princess* had been drawing steadily closer for an hour or more before a boat was fetched to bring the others back. Carlotta was standing on the deck, watching with the rest of the crew. Austin, white hair lifting in the breeze, stood aloof, as befitted the master of the expedition. The returning boat bore only the two crewmen to man the oars and the armed sailors who had gone out. Carlotta could see their worried faces shine red in the glow of the fading sun that cast long shadows on the land just ahead.

"Where are they? What does this mean?" Austin beckoned angrily to the men as they stepped carefully off the ladder and came to face him. The slave, Louis, had been brought on deck and was watched, broad face impassive.

"Sir, we bring a message."

"Message be damned! Where is the sister of my friend? Or is there news of her?"

The man gulped and twisted his fingers. Austin had not raised his voice but it cut as if it were a lash. Carlotta felt the chills and sweat drip and move down her back. She did not doubt for an instant that he would make good his threat to kill the young slave in a horrible way. The sun sank into a bank of purple clouds just then and made a shining pathway across the water.

"Sir, the woman bade me say . . ." He stopped and mopped the sweat from his face.

"I am losing my patience."

"Bade me say that Damballah bids you welcome to Haiti, that news of the woman you seek lies in the highest mountain, and that you and your party, including the woman, Carlotta, must come there. You are given safe conduct; no harm will come to you."

Austin lifted a smooth white hand, and the sailor nearest Louis drew his knife. "Start with his finger, the first one on the right hand."

"Sir, please wait." The older of the men stepped in front of the one who had been speaking. "The slave woman, Tanda, says that she is a priestess of this Damballah and sees the future. That all you seek will be yours if you come, even the wide lands and the rule. Hold her brother as surety for her good faith only a while longer."

Austin laughed, the sound full in the dusk.

"I would as soon trust a rat as these people. You waste my time!"

Carlotta stepped up to him then, the soft wind blowing her white dress back against her slender figure, curling tendrils of hair escaping from the knot into which she had coiled it. "Austin, I would so like to go ashore. It would be an adventure, and I am sure that Tanda speaks truly when she invokes the name of her principal god. I understand that he is most powerful here in this land. Could we not?"

She felt his almost instinctive shudder away from her as she leaned close, then he controlled himself and smiled into her face. "Enter a land from which all whites have been banned on pain of a fearful death? I keep my word to my friend and have a tale to tell around the dinner tables of New Orleans. It is a thought."

His men backed away a little, and then it was that the drums began on the shore, the beat dull and slow at first, then taking on a curious lilt that fired the blood. Carlotta felt a strange familiarity, as if all this had happened before. The signal blazed up on the beach in the tropical night and was answered by another higher on the mountain. The drums tapped as if in acknowledgment and then started up the haunting beat again.

As the fire rose, Carlotta saw the flames of her nightmare before her eyes again.

The whisper seemed to come all around them as the men bunched together in physical fear. Even Austin put a hand to the dagger he always carried.

"Voodoo!"

"The secret religion! Voodoo!"

Louis had spoken first, his voice husky and frightening. One of the seamen picked up the word, and the others repeated it. Carlotta knew that they spoke of the native rites of this land, but she was at a loss to understand the fear evinced. She looked at Austin who said, "They are ignorant and know only what they see and feel. That is what these natives want. Well, Carlotta, my dear, I think you are right. It will be an adventure, and the woman will not want the blood of her brother spilled. I accept her challenge!" His eyes blazed with excitement, and she knew somehow that he found this more alluring than any temptations of the flesh. It was a thing to remember about him.

"I am so glad!" She let her own feelings rise, that curious combination of memory, repulsion, and enthusiasm. At last something would happen. She no longer waited, passive before her fate, but would go out to meet it boldly, taking whatever chances she might. Color flamed in her cheeks, and her hair streamed in the freshening wind. "I cannot wait until morning!"

Austin's laughter mingled with the beat of the drums as he bade his men carry the message. "Say to her that I await the meeting with Damballah. I and the woman I have chosen."

Carlotta felt the hammer of her blood and knew suddenly that the drums were meant to do just that, to stir and lure. Had she fallen into a trap? Had this been arranged to happen? She looked up at the dark land, the mountains flowing into each other, the little pinpoint of flame on the shore, and she folded her arms around herself in a shiver. So be it; the choice was made. Tomorrow, with the dawn, they would go into Haiti, dark land of rebellion and freedom, the land which had, alone of all others in the world, bested Napoleon, Emperor of the French.

CHAPTER NINETEEN

Lord of Light

"I BELIEVE you are enjoying this, my dear." Austin offered Carlotta some of the wine he had brought with him and smiled at her refusal. "The country has already won you. Remember, underneath all this beauty lies a savage menace."

Carlotta remembered the gravity of their errand and what had brought it about only too well. But she could not repress her pleasure at being away from the confines of the ship and on land, so green and flowering a land, that did not dip or sway. They had been traveling steadily upward since dawn, on paths so small that they seemed those made by small animals. The vegetation was so lush and thick that it appeared to grow by the minute. Palm trees, winding vines, exotic flowers, and soaring birds occupied her mind and vision. The sense of danger only added to the excitement of it all.

The party numbered ten of the brawny crew members, all well-armed and watchful, two of the black slaves obtained in Charleston, and Austin's personal servant who was reputed to have skill in medical matters, as well as Austin and Carlotta. Another contingent had been left at the little beach where they landed, and messages were to go back and forth to the waiting *Princess*. "At the first sign of treachery, kill the woman's brother, but be sure it is done slowly." This had been Austin's parting message, delivered in full hearing of Tanda's representatives, two unarmed men, tall with open faces and backs that bore the scourge marks, who met them in the dawn.

One had said, "You will find that which you seek before the darkness comes this night." Then they had turned into the lifting mountains.

Carlotta wore men's clothes for the trek, white for the heat, and a wide brown hat on her head. Even the boots fit relatively well and did not chafe her feet. She could not understand the strange feeling of happiness that pervaded her being, but, when she looked at Austin, she saw that he, too, seemed to share something of her feeling. That was bizarre enough, she thought, for she knew he suffered from what he called "exhausting boredom" and did not endure that state willingly.

They climbed higher and higher through the undergrowth, over rocks that seemed to have been tossed down by a giant hand, across the slippery bed of a small river, down into a ravine, and then upward again. Carlotta was breathing heavily; her shirt was clammy against her breasts. Austin was walking easily still, his hand never leaving his pistol. Suddenly the black leader who had met them stopped and held up his hand to say in accentless French, "Yonder is our dwelling place. Yonder is that place honored of the gods, and there you will find what you seek as foretold by our lady."

They parted the tracery of vines and looked down into a valley which surely had been thrown there by the capricious gods, for it was small and surrounded by walls of rock, themselves only partially covered by trees. A great waterfall fell from an immense height; the silence carried the roar of its waters, and the westering sun made leaping rainbows in the mist. A cluster of huts, just discernible at this height, stood nearby, sheltered by the forest.

"Eden." Carlotta caught her breath at the beauty, and again that strange familiarity tugged at her mind. She remembered what else had walked in Eden and her blood chilled. She turned her head and saw Austin looking, not at her face, but at the swell of her bosom. "Serpent" said her mind, for she knew that he waited for the first sign of pregnancy.

An hour later they stood on the floor of the canyon, having come down by a difficult and painful trail that required the use of every handhold and careful step that could be found. Then they walked through a screen of brush that was guarded by several men with spears at the ready. The leader spoke in the swift language they used and one ran quickly toward the huts.

"We must wait until she comes." He placed himself in the pathway so that they could not follow.

Austin started to protest, thought the better of it, and waved to his men to be silent. There was no sign of any habitation other than the remaining guard, who stared steadily into the distance. The waterfall was the only sound. The men tensed and kept their hands close by their weapons. The sun rays flared red against the dark background of trees. Then, almost as if blown there by the rising wind, a figure drifted out and onto the small pathway. A figure clothed all in red with a high turban intricately twisted, a figure whose hands seemed to be

141

writing in a dance all their own. The light struck the face and lingered there. Carlotta saw that it was Tanda. The proper and subservient mien was gone; in its place was an alien mask, the ruler come to greet the strangers in a new land.

"The woman whom you seek is here." She gestured toward a hut that was set apart. "Go to her."

Austin looked up warily. "We will all go. If you think to separate us by a ruse you had best remember that we are heavily armed."

Tanda's fingers never ceased to move in the patterns but her face was impassive. "Let it be as you will." She stood aside and the guard did likewise.

The smell hit them while they were yet yards from the hut. Several of the men drew back, and Carlotta put both hands over her nose. Austin did not flinch, but strode boldly up and drew the thatched screen from the door, then stepped inside. Carlotta would not show herself less brave than he, so she followed on his heels.

The stench was even more pronounced in the dim interior, although there was a wide hole in the top of the hut and another at the back so the wind might blow through freely. There was a pallet on the dirt floor in the far corner, and on it lay a skeletal figure. Long white hair trailed from its head and onto the floor. A low sighing sound came from the mouth that appeared only a gash in the semi-gloom.

Austin caught his breath in a swift reaction but did not alter his steady movement toward the pallet. Carlotta stayed behind at the door; she could not move for the terrible suspicion that had entered her mind. He knelt by the pallet and said softly, "Madame Bevenders? If you are she, nod as best you can. I am Austin Lenoir, sent by your brother to take you to safety."

Carlotta came nearer and could not suppress a gasp which earned her an angry glare from Austin. The woman's legs were bent at odd angles, and, though they were wrapped in bandages, still pus and blood stained not only the cloth but the pallet underneath. Her skin was ravaged and wrinkled, her eyes wild and rolling.

"Gillian? Charles has sent me. Can you understand me at all?"

She made a struggling sound, her mouth yawned wide, and Carlotta felt the ground shake with the intensity of her own emotion. Gillian Bevenders had only the stump of a tongue, for it had been cut out.

Austin murmured soothingly to her and then spoke to Carlotta in the casual tone of everyday. "Go out and bring the brandy flask to me. I think it long since she has tasted good spirits." He made no sign of recoil, he the fastidious, the elegant. As she watched, he took the tumbled straw mat which served Gillian as a pillow and refolded it so that she could lift her head slightly. His arm supported her all the while.

Carlotta backed out into the warm sun and the fresh air. She put one hand to her forehead and fought to steady herself, suddenly fiercely grateful for her young, strong body and unsullied mind.

"She will die soon, and it will be a blessing." Tanda's calm voice spoke from the shade of the nearest tree.

"What beasts are your people that they could do such a thing to a helpless woman? Better she were killed outright!" Carlotta felt the helpless, impotent fury rise.

Tanda rose and faced her accuser. Too late, Carlotta saw the tears in her black eyes. "The plantation owners did this and more for an evening's sport. Moreover, they did it for years. Madame Bevenders was protected by her slaves, and they died defending her and her son. She was taken off into the mountains where they lived for months before being found by the men of our Emperor Dessalines, who has vowed that no white shall live in Haiti, that all shall die. Her son was thrown into the ravine before her eyes, her legs broken, her arms twisted from their sockets, and her tongue cut as you see."

"It is unbearable!" Carlotta twisted her hands back and forth as if to remove the fearful vision from her mind.

Tanda continued in a flat, dull voice, "There are many who support the Emperor but do not agree with his cruelty, although for our country we will do anything, including killing the innocent. This camp is one such. Some of my people found her, and we have cared for her since that time. I sent messages to other camps by my friends when I was landed. It is strange that she should be here in my own, but so it has happened." She held out a hand to Carlotta, and after hesitation the girl took it. "Do not judge us, for who can know how they would behave in such circumstances?"

"I must get the brandy." She could not look Tanda in the face after such a recitation. Yet she must not make an enemy, for Tanda was their only link here with safety. Slowly she withdrew her hand and hurried to complete her errand.

When she returned, she saw that the woman's eyes were

calm now, and Austin was speaking blithely of how Napoleon would surely come to defeat against England and of how the thrones of Europe were even now shaking. His tone was light and gossipy, his eyes brilliant with amusement. Carlotta saw that his ruffled shirt was wet with sweat, however, and he looked paler than usual.

Now she said, "Why do you not go and bring fresh cloths, ointment if there is any, and I will give Madame Bevenders the brandy while I tell her of the new fashions in England. Men can only speak of war! Who is interested? Have you told her of Charleston and how it looks now?" Her voice did not shake but rose clear and bright, as though she herself stood in a drawing room of that city.

Austin's eyes met hers, and the salute there was as unmistakable as crossed swords in the light of morning. "You wrong me, my dear. I have spoken of Charles and all that we shall do when we return to his city. I go to do your bidding."

Gillian Bevenders had a fever in the night which produced alternate shaking chills and heavy sweats. As her delirium rose, so did her efforts to speak and move. Her torn and broken body writhed, and the cries of pain were grunts that continued to rise in intensity. Austin and Carlotta tended her as best they could with the help of two young girls who had been doing this before they arrived. There was no time in all that night and the next day when Gillian was free of pain or when she even rested.

The afternoon was drowsing away when Austin sent Carlotta out. "There is nothing you can do here now. There can be but one end to this."

She protested, but she was exhausted on her feet. Finally he rose and pushed her toward the door saying, "Go. You smell from your efforts." The harsh words belied the look in his eyes, which she knew was admiration. She went quickly before she gave way utterly.

Austin had not left Gillian's side since they arrived, and well she knew the strain that could produce. Once again she found it impossible to fathom this strange, cruel, oddly compassionate man. His voice carried to her as she walked down the path toward the waterfall. He was telling Gillian one of the bawdier tales about King George and the recurring madness. She quickened her steps until she stood under the very spray of the water which was a mist in the air.

Carlotta sank down on a huge rock which jutted out into the moving stream. She raised her face and let the water touch it softly, while the sun glinted through the drops. She was too tired to move; it was blessed relief to lie prone, letting her whole body relax in warmth and light. Thoughts moved sluggishly in her brain, drifted and faded. She took long breaths of the sweet air, perfumed as it was with sprays of red blossoms that hung directly overhead. One arm reached idly up as she stretched in the relief of muscles long cramped.

Then she lay still, frozen in position, flattened to the rock as if held there. High up on the face of the mountain down which they had come an eternity ago, was a ledge, probably one of many, that stood out as a lip might. A man stood there, looking down, his hat held in his hand. A black man was beside him, leaning over in an attitude of speech. Carlotta's sight was keen; she saw, as if it were a picture in front of her, the tall body, the gilt hair blowing in the wind, the brown face that was almost a blur at this distance. Almost.

"Simon!" She sat upright and put her face in her hands. What power of mind brought him to her so vividly across oceans and time at this moment when she was depleted in body and mind? She looked up again, and this time she saw the flicker of movement, the lithe stride that she remembered. Then the ledge was empty. "Simon." She spoke his name again, knowing it for foolishness but unable to resist the sound of it. Had she conjured him out of the mist and her own passionate longing? What would a white man be doing here in Haiti? But they themselves were here. Tanda and Austin must be warned.

Carlotta jumped up and the world rocked once more. It had done this several times in the past few days, and she had tried to ignore the possible meaning. Now she could not. Fancies and physical disturbances told their own tale. It was highly likely that she would bear Austin's child. She put her hands on her flat stomach and pushed. The thought was repugnant to her even as he himself was, but somehow the whole idea of his scheme was exciting, too. If she could not have love, then surely power, even as Austin's pawn, was next best. Slowly she began to walk toward the huts.

Tanda's people had begun to show themselves now, as they moved about their daily tasks with only covert glances at the newcomers. The men from the *Princess* had been given a separate area where they now lounged, weapons still close at hand. There was no sign of Tanda herself, but Carlotta knew that she was not far away. Not for the first time she wondered if they would ever leave this remote place.

Austin was standing outside the hut as she drew near. He was rumpled and sweat-stained, there were circles under his eyes, and he swayed from weariness, but his mouth curved up slightly. For once she could look at him without anger, remembering his tenderness toward the sister of his friend.

"How is she? Do you wish me to sit with her for a time? You must rest."

Austin looked at her, his gaze raking her body. "She is done with pain. We will leave it for a time, and then whoever is in charge of the dead here must be summoned."

Carlotta stared in her turn, knowing suddenly what he had done. "How did you do it?"

He lifted his hands and studied them in an eloquent gesture that chilled Carlotta, although she knew that this was the ultimate mercy for the agonized woman. "Charles shall hear that she was rescued only to die of the swift plague, even as did his nephew."

"You stand true friend to him and to her as well." She spoke the words with all her heart.

His mouth twisted down and the moment was gone. "Another to be avenged."

That night the drums spoke from the mountains and resounded in the valleys. Little fires burned high in the woods above their valley, and the moon rose almost full in the clear night. Carlotta sat in the doorway of the hut that had been assigned to her and listened to the pulsating rhythms. Sleep was beyond her. The body of Gillian Bevenders lay wrapped in the hut where she had died, and the door was guarded by two brawny watchers. The girl felt a fear she knew was foolish, but in these surroundings it was impossible not to be touched by feelings far older than the Christian God.

On the ship Tanda had talked casually of some of the customs of her people and how some of them, a very few, believed that those dead by violence walked in the light of the full moon to seek their murderers and exact full payment for what had been done. There were, of course, charms against such things, but one never knew. The conversation had ceased there, but Carlotta was not deceived. The warning had been given. Her fingers traced the sign of the cross as the drums rose and fell softly in the distance.

The camp was quiet, but underneath the silence there was an air of purpose and preparation. The guards by the hut where the body lay might have been carved out of ebony, so unmoving

146

were they. There was no movement anywhere, and only the sound of the waterfall and the drums remained constant. Carlotta shifted her position, wondering if she could possibly sleep now. She had bathed soon after the encounter with Austin, and the clean white shift felt soft against her skin. She brushed the newly washed hair from her eyes and tried to pull her mind away from speculation about the future.

A night bird cried raucously as if disturbed. The flicker of movement on the pathway caught her eye, and then the white blur resolved into the figure of a man, two men actually, but she had no thought for any but the first. Her lips shaped the words of the poet and turned them to a setting of which he never dreamed. "'It was no dream...I lay broad awaking, dear heart....'"

Walking toward her in the pouring moonlight which turned his gilt hair to shining silver was Simon, his tread steady as though he moved here often, one hand on the pistol at his belt.

"It is no dream." Carlotta said the words aloud and rose to meet him.

CHAPTER TWENTY

Road of the Undying

A LAST vestige of cloud scudded across the moon as the wind lifted so that the bushes near the door of Carlotta's hut swayed back and forth. She put out a hand to catch the skirt of her shift, and as she did so, Simon looked up and saw her. Her tongue was frozen to the roof of her mouth as she tried to speak and could not.

He stood very still, a statue in the light. The dark man with him did not move either, but she saw that his fingers hovered near the butt of a large knife. In the time that followed, Carlotta was to remember the incredulity and delight that swept Simon's face, the pleasure in his voice as he half-whispered, "Mara? Is it you? Are you real?"

"Aye, Simon, I am real." She walked toward him lightly, all else forgotten but the fact that by some boon of the capricious gods he was here in this dangerous land and not a world away. "I never thought to see you again in this life."

He had her shoulder in his grasp now; his touch sent fires down her spine, and she felt herself shivering with the intensity of her feeling for this man. He felt it too, and his other hand lifted toward her face. "I have seen you in the long nights and endless days, Mara. I feared you dead."

"As you shall be if you do not release her instantly." Austin's hard voice broke between them, and the cocking of a pistol sounded on the suddenly still air.

Simon stood very still but he did not release Carlotta. "They told me of a party of whites in this area but I could not believe it. Who are you?"

"You did not hear my command? Shall I repeat it?" Austin's voice was very cold; this was when he was at his most deadly.

Carlotta knew that he would shoot Simon without a qualm. She moved out from under his hand and tried to meet the green, puzzled gaze. Austin jerked the pistol in her direction and she stepped toward him.

"Carlotta, do you know this intruder?"

"I knew him once." Her voice was not yet entirely purged

of the joy that the sight of Simon had given her, and Austin's quick intuition caught it.

"Then perhaps you should explain to him that you are my mistress and my woman, that I do not relish another's hands on my property."

"Carlotta, is it?" Simon was smiling now, a rueful, slightly cruel smile. "You must forgive my presumption, sir, I knew the lady long ago and under another name. I do not trifle with another's . . . property knowingly. My apologies." He bowed correctly.

Carlotta forgot Austin, Haiti, the setting in which they stood, everything. She and Simon might have been the only people in the world. He must understand! "It is not as it seems, Simon, truly it is not! I will explain."

Austin smiled in his turn. "Women are so sentimental, don't you think? Always their lovers." He turned to Carlotta. "Go to my hut and await me there. We have unfinished business."

She ignored him. "Simon? I must talk to you."

He faced her then, and the moonlight revealed the coldness and scorn in the brilliant eyes that had been so tender only moments before. "I came seeking the leader of your expedition. I assume I have found him and must thus have immediate speech with him. It was long ago that we knew each other, Mara-Carlotta-Jane or-Mary. Let it be done with you as it has ever been done with me."

Pride came to Carlotta's rescue then, and she lifted her head proudly as she said, "You were ever arrogant. May I live to see you brought low!"

Austin burst into laughter that did not reach his eyes. "I am glad that you cajoled me into this journey, little one; it is most amusing."

He sobered and spoke to Simon. "You have found he whom you seek. Who are you and what do you want here, to come striding so boldly into a secret place?"

"I am Simon Mitchell and I once lived in Haiti. But, before I begin, might I not ask for a cooling drink and a seat? The journey was long this day." He did not look at Carlotta; she might not have existed for him.

"Go to the hut, I said." Austin did not raise his voice but she heard the whips in it.

"Aye, my lord." She retreated as gracefully as though she, no less than he, occupied a castle. As she went, she heard Austin offering hospitality and naming himself just as though

149

they two were well met and had not just narrowly averted battle over her.

She sat in Austin's hut until almost light. Her eyes were dry; there were no tears in her, neither was there hope. She did not know by what strange miracle Simon had come to this part of the world or how they had come to meet again, but she regretted their meeting with all her heart. He and their passion for each other had been a bright talisman to carry with her all her days. Now, however, she must remember that he thought her the plaything of an older man, that he doubtless thought she had had many lovers. She cringed with shame that she had pleaded with him. What manner of man as he to so humiliate her? She had no illusions as to what Austin would do now that he knew she had lied to him again. Her mouth hardened with determination; he would not best her this time.

The woven screen that served as the door rattled as Austin pushed it back and entered. He was expressionless as usual, his face smooth in the pink light of earliest dawn. Carlotta rose to her feet and faced him, strangely uncaring as to what he might say or do. He saw and interest flickered in his eyes. His fingers went to the little coiled whip he wore at his belt. He touched it in a manner that was almost sensual.

"How strange that you should find an ex-lover in this jungle, my dear. Have there been many?" The whip was long and black in the white hands. "You acted like a beggar maid. I think that when I am done with you the truth will emerge." One corner of his mouth lifted as he reached out to the neck of her shift.

"Touch me and it is all to do over again. Do you think your potency can endure another such concerted effort as the last? Will Tanda supply your needs now that she is in her own world and no longer your slave?" Carlotta's fists clenched together, and she lifted her chin so that she looked directly into the black eyes.

That strange look of recognition crossed Austin's face again as he lowered his hand. "You anger me at your peril. It is too soon. You cannot know."

"I was not raised in a small village for nothing. Aunt Rosa often helped at birthings, and I was taken with her to play with the other children and so divert their minds. I listened to talk and later saw for myself. I am with child. Your child. The heir you wanted for our scheme." Her voice rang hard and sure in the enclosed space. She had him now.

"Our scheme? If this is so, you have nothing to fear and everything to gain. If you lie again I will destroy your mind and use your body. There are those in these mountains who can concoct such potions."

"I know what I know," she said stubbornly. Then, because it had to be said and because he must believe her now, she added, "Let the past be done, Austin. The man, Simon, hurt my pride, that is all, and it was finished before it began. I was young and susceptible. It was the shock and surprise of seeing him again that made me behave so. I am with you. Willingly." All the sincerity she could muster was in her voice, and she half believed that she spoke the truth.

Austin coiled the whip up and put it in the corner as he began to remove his clothes. "I taxed him with you. He remembers you vaguely and says the same shock touched him to see a woman, much less one he knew, in this land at such a time." He tugged at his boots and yawned wearily. "Actually he is an interesting fellow. It seems his family once lived here and he was great friends with some of these who rule now. He is to be married in New York next winter, rather an heiress, I believe, and came here to see if any of the family jewels remained intact from the time they fled. Distant relatives, they were, and now reside in Napoleon's France. Enterprising gentleman."

Was Simon truly to be married? He had partially lied to Austin about his background, that much she knew. But why should he do so? Carlotta felt the punishing words hit her and reflected that Austin knew how to lash her. She said, "It seems singularly foolish to come here at such a time to look for treasure. Is he perhaps incapable of work?"

Austin stretched out full length and put his arms behind his head. "I fear you are a peasant, my dear. Work, indeed! His blood is good, I imagine. Go and rest now. Poor Gillian must be buried this day, and then we will return to the *Princess.*" He rose up on one elbow and fixed his dark gaze on her. "In another few weeks we should know for certain if you are to have a child. If so, we will marry."

It was the ultimate challenge and she knew it. Her blood still cried out for Simon even as she knew that there had been no choice but for him to repudiate her; Austin's intent had been clear. Her gaze met his and her voice was rock steady as she said, "I look forward to that day."

He gave her that same look that he had had when she came

to tend Gillian and had not flinched before the unbearable. It was measure for measure; admiration took the place of barely repressed anger. Carlotta found herself oddly shaken that his opinion of her mattered.

Gillian Bevenders was laid to rest at noon that day in a separate part of the valley, an open space against the bare mountain face in full light of the blazing sun. Simon was nowhere to be seen and Carlotta was passionately grateful, lest her new found resolution crumble. Tanda was there, her dark face inscrutable, and a gathering of her people. The crew members eyed them with barely concealed hatred, for they knew how the woman had died. Austin alone was cordial and smooth, his voice lifting effortlessly in the words of the burial service, both Latin and French. Listening to him, Carlotta found it easy to believe that light perpetual would indeed shine upon she who had suffered so greatly in this life. Gillian Bevenders had not been thirty-five years old at the time of her fearful maiming.

The grave was filled in then, and the Haitians began to pile great stones on top of it, ending with a final one that took four of them to lift. "So that her body will remain at rest and not walk in the mountains seeking revenge or be stolen by those who would render use of the undying." Austin whispered the explanation that was no explanation to Carlotta, then shrugged at her disbelieving look.

After the burial was done, Carlotta walked over by the waterfall and let the fine spray mist her face. Birds sang in the woods, and flower scents mingled with earth's lushness. The sky was barely visible through the interlacing branches. The emotion of the night and this morning had sapped Carlotta, and she was content to wander slowly along the path, a very faint one, which led around behind the waterfall and along the stream's edge. She reached out for an occasional flowering branch or sometimes imitated a bird's call, but thought had left her, the only reality was the welcome heat of the sun on her shoulders and the beauty around her.

Carlotta did not not know how far she wandered, for the path curved here and there while seeming to lead nowhere. Human relationships seemed far away, although she knew that sooner or later she must face what she felt about Simon. That time was not now. Just so did battle wounds encapsulate.

The earth was cool to her bare feet as she walked, and it seemed that the path was oddly level in this small valley. Now the trees were overlapping more, and the green darkness was almost that of twilight. She rounded a corner and almost screamed before she clapped a hand over her mouth. A small white chicken hung suspended in the crotch of a tree not a yard from her. Blood stained the feathers and dripped to the ground below. Carlotta lifted her gaze then and saw another, black this time, hanging higher in another tree just down the path. A long writhing sign in white curved from one tree to the other on the dark ground. Strange symbols were marked in red over the white.

Carlotta turned to go back, but now that the rustling of leaves was stilled, she heard the sound of dripping water and, over that, the sound of footsteps quite close by. She did not hesitate to think anything over but melted into the thick bushes which formed a barrier at one side. She had no sooner sheltered behind the bole of a large tree with drooping branches which fanned out than a tall young man came into view. He was wearing breeches only, and a curved sword was stuck into the waistband of these. He walked carefully, his eyes swinging from one side to the other. But it was those who followed him who took Carlotta's attention and riveted it.

There were ten of them, men in assorted sizes and shapes, carrying short swords stuck into their belts. Their skins had once been black but were now dull and dusty, almost gray. They followed their leader with slow pace that did not falter, and their eyes never left him or turned aside. There were no expressions on their faces, which were flat and dull. Each one bore a replica of the white and red sign she had seen on the ground on a type of necklace around his neck. One of the larger of the men passed very close to her, and she saw that his eyes had the turned-back look of the long dead, for there was neither light nor life there.

Carlotta watched as they disappeared out of sight on the path and did not move until the sound of their tread had vanished. Then she ran back toward the camp as quickly as she could move, not caring that she stepped on thorns or that the branches slapped her hot face. Once she slipped and almost fell in some red wax that had fallen by the trail. Some white and black feathers were mixed in with it, and the odor of blood lifted to her nostrils. Her terror increased, and she did not pause this time until she reached the welcome roar of the waterfall and saw the women pursuing their prosaic task of washing clothes there.

She saw their eyes follow her as she sank down near one

of the pools to catch her breath. The thought of what she had seen in the dimness filled her with fear and repugnance, for she remembered Austin's comment about potions which could destroy the mind and use the body. Had these been such evidence? She dipped a hand in the cool water and laved her face with it, noting almost impersonally that her hand shook. Up on the mountainside a drum spoke softly and was answered by another. There was a soft burst of sound around her, and the women began to gather up their washing swiftly.

Carlotta looked up but could see nothing in the high, hot afternoon to indicate what had stirred such activity. The drum spoke several more times and was silent. The woman nearest her was trying to gather the clothes together too hurriedly and several garments tumbled into the stream. She plunged in after them but the water was too swift. Carlotta waded in to help and caught the sleeves of two of them, managing to drag them to the shore and getting herself thoroughly wet in the process.

"Thank you." The woman, squat and dark, about thirty, caught up the dripping garments and dumped them in her woven basket. "Merci." She spoke the word again as if not sure what language Carlotta spoke. Her dark eyes were wide with fear as she backed away from the girl.

"What is the matter? Why do you fear me?" Carlotta said the words in slow careful French, spreading her hands in the universal gesture of peace.

The woman waved an expressive hand at the mountainside, brilliant with vegetation in the hot sun. "Angry! Angry!" Then she turned and ran just as Carlotta had done, her body stiff with fear.

Carlotta was suddenly very tired, so much so that her whole body ached with the need for rest, but she did not think she could move. In this state, the thought that she had tried to avoid came to her. It was said that in this land the dead walked, that there were those who could restore enough life to them to use the bodies for whatever unholy purposes might arise. And the word used was "zombie." Zombie! It sprang into her mind from the letter she had read among those that Austin had given her on board ship. The letter of a survivor who had escaped one of the massacres of the fall, writing to a friend in England, saying that those who killed his family were the undead, moving as machines might, untiring, relentless in pursuit. She had put such things aside, thinking in pity that the poor man was demented. Now she wondered.

The drums spoke on the mountain, and now the beat was faster and more intense but with a dull throb that set the nerves of the listeners on edge. As Carlotta walked to her own hut, she was glad to see Austin approaching, his face dark and angry. Whatever he was, at least he was of her own land and ways of thought.

"I was coming to tell you, Carlotta, to prepare for leave-taking, but they said you had gone into the woods earlier. Did you seek your lover?" His eyes glowed down into hers, and his fingers worked on the coiled whip.

"You shall not suspect every move I make, Austin Lenoir! I have told you how it is and was. That is enough!" She was angry, and her voice rang out in the sudden stillness between drumbeats. "If you are so suspicious then I will tell you what happened in truth." She lowered her voice and spoke swiftly, her terror rising again with each word.

Austin put his arm around her shoulders to support her, and they walked toward his hut. To the watchers it would seem a natural thing, a small lovers' spat and now the making-up. In spite of herself, Carlotta was grateful for his gesture.

He said now, "I suspected as much, Carlotta. I spoke carelessly to you, for my mind is much occupied. Tanda has forbidden us to depart until four days have passed. Of course she waited to tell me this until I had sent the messenger to the ship to say that all is well with us. The gods are angry and must be placated with ceremonial rites. All whites must attend. She would say no more but ordered me from her presence." His voice rose in the silken anger she knew so well and could only be thankful was not directed at her. "She shall pay for that before we leave Haiti. That I promise."

Carlotta's mind fastened on one sentence. "All whites?"

His voice was ugly. "Aye, even the free-wandering Simon Mitchell, who is far too arrogant for my taste."

Carlotta fought to still the joy that rose in her even as the drums beat ominously on the mountain. She would see him again. He had not gone. Common sense did no good; she longed for him still.

Austin's words penetrated now as he said, "Strange things happen in this land. I do not doubt what you saw. The wonder is that you saw and lived."

155

CHAPTER TWENTY-ONE

Damballah, Serpent, and Rainbow

"The gods are angered." What gods, how many, the degree of power, none of these questions had any hope of answer for the English and Americans who made up Austin's party and to whom he told all that had happened to Carlotta, as well as his own meeting with Tanda. "Do as they say, we have little option there, but have your guns at the ready and be watchful."

One of the men, tall and brawny with a wall-eye, who called himself Harry, said, "I've tracked Indians in their woods, scalped 'em, too. I can find the way back to the ship. Always did have a good sense of direction."

"You would be a fool to try." The cool voice fell across the gathering and stilled the hubbub of voices that rose. Simon came out from the trees on the edge of the clearing where the group was assembled, ostensibly for the evening meal. It was very dark outside their circle, and the brilliance of the flames highlighted his fairness.

Carlotta was sitting beside Austin, and she felt the excitement rise in her as Simon stood there in this hostile atmosphere, appearing very much at ease. His gaze swept over them impersonally and came to rest on Austin, who rose to face the challenger. The drums hammered softly in the distance.

Simon spoke as though to Austin alone, his voice low and compelling. "We are the aliens here. If we resist any part of what these people wish, they will kill us all. I have lived here and I know their mood now. The drums say that the gods are humiliated by the influx of strangers who have been permitted to come by one whom they counted as their own. Tanda, the priestess. Emperor Dessalines seeks blood and will have it. Here only is our safety. Go through the watching of the ceremony."

Harry bawled, "Heathens'll kill us all. I say fight! Take 'em by surprise!"

Simon laughed, "They know every move we make. Every word we say."

Carlotta stood up and put her hand on Austin's arm in a

familiar gesture that made his muscles tense. She felt again that strange involuntary wincing. She spoke to him, but her words carried as she meant them to do. "Tanda will hold to the bargain, Austin, I know it. She wept for Madame Bevenders." The wind blew her hair back as she felt the droplets of sweat form on her brow. "Remember all that is at stake."

"My authority is final here. We do as I have said and there will be no more discussion." Austin hooked his fingers in his belt and looked calmly at his men. Such was the force of his will that they murmured agreement and turned away.

Simon came closer to Austin and put out his hand. After a moment's hesitation the other man took it. Simon said, "My own ship waits even as yours does. My friend and I will join forces with you if we may, until we are free of this coil. It was unwise of any of us to come here at such a time." He did not look at Carlotta.

"We are allies. For now." Austin's black gaze was bland as he put his arm around Carlotta. "The lady will bear my child in the winter. She must suffer no upset."

Simon bowed politely. "My congratulations to you both. Now, if you will excuse me, I will hasten to tell the priestess of our willingness to do whatever is needed to assuage the anger of Damballah." He moved away, tall and lithe in the shifting shadows.

Carlotta wanted to weep when Austin smiled down at her and said, "I think he is a man of honor. He will not want you now."

"You disgust me!" She spat the words at him, then strode away, the shift twisting around her ankles. His laughter was demonic in the light of the rising moon.

Their trek began at dawn of the next day and continued all through it on the path that Carlotta had trodden. There were nearly fifty of the blacks from the camp, including women and children. Some few men were left behind to guard it. Tanda went before them all, remote and inaccessible, one set apart by the gods. The others kept together, differences forgotten in this unknown situation. Simon remained in the rear of the column with the silent black man who had come with him.

The visible signs of the ritual to which they were to go hung in the trees and were marked on the stones or in the dirt of the path—chickens, the sign of the snake, once a crude waterfall with an arch over it, entrails, a picked scavenger bird. Carlotta soon grew inured to it and did not turn her eyes away. The horrible details of the letters she had read continued to come into her mind, and she wondered once again at the motives that had brought them here.

They passed out of the valley in the afternoon and went through corridors of overhanging trees so closely grown together that the sunlight could not pierce them. The sound of water was continually in their ears as the path grew so steep that most of them were forced to use hands as well as feet to maintain balance. When they came to what appeared to be a tiny hole in the well nigh vertical side of the mountain, Tanda waved her people through and motioned to the whites to follow. Her gesture was somehow menacing and Austin rebelled.

"We go no farther. This is ridiculous."

Simon shouldered past him roughly and spoke swiftly to Tanda, whose high-arched nose quivered with disdain. Then he turned back to the rest of the party. "The time of the sacred rites is upon her and she can only speak in her own language. In the language of the Christians, this is holy ground where we stand and where we go. To demur now is to risk all; others come from camps in the hills, and each practices a different type of voodoo. I cannot interfere again."

Austin said, "So be it then. Our path is chosen. I walk with her to represent my own people." Tanda understood and moved aside on the path so that he could go abreast with her. "See to my woman."

It was the infuriating kind of courage and audacity that he had exhibited with his friend's sister. That and the off-hand way he could consign her to her lover made Carlotta want to both slap and cling to him. She could not wholly hate Austin and yet she could not understand what drove him, for now his eyes had a look of intense pleasure.

Simon inclined his head. "I will, on my honor."

"I do quite well by myself." Carlotta snapped the words out, feeling rather as if she were a package by their talk.

She had occasion to regret her hasty statement in the hours that followed, for they climbed into the small opening, went down a slope, and entered another world. A world of tiny winding paths which gave onto huge rooms with ceilings that reached up into blackness, small ledges which they had to creep along, holding each others' hands while underground cataracts roared below, around huge masses of stone which seemed poured from both floor and roof in lacy delicacy to which the hand of mortal could never have aspired. They carried torches which revealed paintings in red, black, and purple, drawn larger than even giant life, and bloomed out of the Stygian blackness with terrifying impact. Strange beasts, men with twisting faces, demons, and cowering humans were all represented. The light, when held high, also showed the convoluted stone in shimmering shades of rose pink, blue, and fluted lavender. It was beautiful and like nothing the imagination could conjure up. The footing was tricky. Carlotta often wished that she could spare time from negotiating her next movement to look around her more, but a misstep might send her plunging miles down into the stream that they seemed to be following, and life was yet sweet.

"You see the wonder of this world. Few are so privileged." Simon's voice spoke in her ear as they edged off a slippery length of rock and entered another wide cavern.

"If I live to remember it." Her tone was wry, but she was inordinately glad to hear a human voice in this immensity, for they had traveled in almost total silence since entering.

"I explored these as a youth with my fellows from neighboring plantations. They are dead now, killed either in the aftermath of the rebellion or by Dessalines." His tone was matter-of-fact, devoid of all self-pity or concern for those so savagely dead.

Carlotta felt the chills go up and down her spine. "Did you live in Haiti long?"

He said, "Four years only. Long enough, and that was another world."

She wanted to ask more questions but felt his withdrawal. He stepped back, and then the dark man was at her side. He and Simon exchanged no words but his hand was under her elbow as they stepped up the next incline. Simon took a torch from one of the men and walked ahead, holding it high. By that light Carlotta saw an impaled and skinned animal fastened to the far wall, blood dripping in a red wash to the floor, purple and black signs twisting all about on the wet stone. She made a little sound and the hand closed hard on her elbow. The man beside her shook his head warningly. She nodded and felt oddly reassured.

At the end of this cavern they filed through a passage so small that some of the larger men had to turn sideways to edge through. It was cool in the place, but Carlotta felt the back of her coarse cotton dress such as the native women wore sticking to her skin, and her hair was hot on her neck. She thought of

159

Austin's plan to use her as minor royalty and a smile curved her lips at the foolishness of it all. That smile froze when she saw the gorge directly in front of them and the narrow rope bridge spanning it, and heard the distant roar of the water far below.

Instinct told her that she must show no fear; these people had the courage of their faith. What did she have? The comfortable English God, the Virgin of her dreams—they were far from here. Then she saw the torch blaze on Simon's silver-gilt head, saw Austin standing boldly beside Tanda with the slightly mocking smile on his face, remembered all that Gillian Bevenders had endured, and her chin went up. She, too, could do no less.

The people walked slowly across the swaying, almost threadlike bridge. Two and three at a time spaced themselves out and, when the other side was reached, held the torches high for the others. Now, for the first time, a drum began to beat hollowly, resounding in the depths as if coming from the gorge itself.

"Don't look down." The man beside Carlotta spoke in sibilant French with the soft slurring sound she had come to like in Charleston.

"I will try not to." She paused, waiting for his name. "I am Carlotta."

"John." The name came uneasily to his tongue. "You are Spanish, then?"

She saw that he talked only to distract her from the swaying bridge in the red torchlight. Words would not come as the man in front of her neared the center and beckoned to her to follow. She stretched out both hands to hold the sides which were bound in cane, and, as she did so, the man ahead stepped heavily and the bridge tilted slightly. Carlotta jerked involuntarily and found herself staring down into the immensity of the gorge below, which was lit just enough by the several torches placed at the edge to enable her to see the jagged rocks melting into red points in the darkness. Panic froze her and the world spun. The one glance she gave the ceiling was no use, for that too had flickering shadows and hanging points touched by the light. The sensation was one of no footing anywhere. Her knees began to shake and she heard the muttering begin. She heard someone cry "Damballah" and knew that they might interpret this hesitation to mean that the god wanted her now. Still, she could not move.

The cry in Latin penetrated her fear and braced her even as she still trembled. "There sleeps Titania sometimes of the night . . ." Her eyes lifted, and her shaking hands loosened their grip on the sides of the bridge. Simon stood at the edge between the row of torches and the gorge, both hands on his hips, looking the very image of the highwayman she had helped so long ago. Everything else faded for her then, and she walked the bridge as though it were indeed the wild thyme. When she took the last step from it, Simon's hand took hers and his eyes smiled into her face.

"Thank you for the rescue." Her voice was trembly, and her legs felt as if they might collapse under her, but she would give him credit where it was due.

"We would all do as much for each other." He turned away and walked toward Austin, who still stood with Tanda, watching as the few remaining people crossed over, some almost as hesitant as Carlotta had been.

She expected Austin to say something but he ignored her, his face expressionless. Now they went single file again through several small passages, which seemed to lead gradually upward once more. Now and then Carlotta saw that Austin watched her, always with that mysterious, inward-turned gaze that never failed to make her uneasy. This time, however, the surroundings and the beating of the drum which grew ever louder made Austin Lenoir the least of her fears.

Fresh air, faintly tinged with rain, came to her nostrils now, and she breathed hungrily of the scent of growing things. They walked more slowly now, but still singly because of the close, damp walls of rock. Carlotta was not prepared for the sight that met her eyes when the passage curved sharply to the left and veered downward. Her whisper was sibilant in the hush between the softening sound of the drums.

"By all the saints, the beauty of it!"

Pine trees grew in profusion off to one side, and a small but perfect waterfall cascaded to stone steps just below her feet. Jagged crags lifted beyond, and the huge shells of ancient trees rose close to them, branches twisted like imploring arms in the torch-lit darkness. A tumble of red and pink flowers covered the rocks just ahead, and their sweetness was almost numbing to the senses. From where she stood Carlotta could see the overlapping mountains of Haiti going from height to height. Little fires blazed here and there in the green darkness, and over it all hung the full moon, appearing in this clearness to be a silver mountain, so close was it.

"Our beautiful torn land." It was the man, John, who spoke as he guided her down the crudely carved steps and into the partial shelter of one of the rock overhangs. "Remain here and watch. You will be safe."

She gave him her most brilliant smile and was rewarded by the slight lift of his melancholy mouth before he slipped softly away. She was grateful for his kindness and wondered if Simon had asked him to keep watch over her, then called herself foolish for entertaining such a thought.

The drums were beaten more softly now, and she saw them, large again as a small child, four in number, ranged against the cliff wall. A fire burned at the entrance to a cave, and beyond it figures moved as if in ritual dance, slowly, gracefully. It seemed to Carlotta that over a hundred people were present, with more coming. They were all silent, their faces very still. High on the rock face above the flickering fire she saw the red and white symbol of the serpent god, Damballah. It was as though he moved, so lifelike were the curves which drew the eye up to the great head, part rock and part drawing, that seemed reared to strike.

Now the tempo of the drums changed to a hard, clanging beat and the chanting began as the dancers moved from the interior of the cave out into full view of the gathering. There were ten of them, six male and four female, and they whirled together in a matchless smoothness that made each step seem an intricate part of the whole. They all wore white touched with red; their movements were slow at first as they used hands, heads, and arms to circle, invite, and lure. Then the tempo increased, they meshed, pulled apart, and went to kneel by the drums.

Now a white-robed priest came out and spread his arms wide. Four young girls cried out with one voice and began a low, entreating chant that was partly in French. Carlotta could make out some of the words because of this. "Open up . . . open the gate . . . pass. Legba, open . . ." Then water was poured out each time the name was mentioned. When this ceased, silence fell again. The priest, so thin that his skin barely covered his bones, began to move with delicate precision as he took a deep dish from one of the girls and dipped out the contents with the fingers of one hand to form the beginnings of a design on the ground. Carlotta strained to see what he was using but could

162

not tell. Whatever it was, the form of a snake in black, red, and white began to take shape, drawn with artistry and never a false movement, there on the beaten ground.

A young man, naked except for a loin cloth, approached with one flaming torch held high. The drums thundered on a different note as the priest finished and stood back. There was a rumble of actual thunder in the west, and the wind blew hot against Carlotta's face. Now machetes clashed in the background, and the chanting took on a martial note. Then there was absolute silence as all eyes rose to the top of the cliff wall where a torch suddenly illuminated the figure standing there, a figure in white skirt, breasts bare except for the twisting coils that curved around them and her neck, extending into her hands. A proud smile touched her lips as Tanda stood there accepting the homage of the people to the god whose instrument she was.

Another torch blazed up under the waterfall and caused the droplets to reflect a shimmering prism of colors. The snake lifted its head so that it was higher than Tanda's. The combined brilliance spread out and glowed as all cried with one voice, "Damballah is here! Praised be he!"

Then snake and woman were one as Damballah came down from the heights to his people.

CHAPTER TWENTY-TWO

The Red One

THE chant was long, interspersed with the spoken word and the divine frenzy, but there was no other sound or movement as the deep male voice continued, the head jerking back and forth, the torches writhing with it. The thunder came from the west again, and the heat pressed down, but nothing in this world or out of it concerned the people.

Carlotta folded both arms across her chest and felt the chills run up them. All very well to make out the features of Tanda among the shining black coils that undulated in the light, but what about the times when she was overshadowed by the larger shape of a great snake? She had been reared in rationalism, had memories of the Catholic church and its mysteries, knew of the gypsies and their "sight," but this was a thing beyond her imagination or comprehension. This was possession, and who was she to decry it?

The heavy voice paused, and several young boys began to sing in the high, sweet voices of children. The torch used to illuminate the cliff face was brought forth now, and the snake uncoiled itself from Tanda's slender body so that for the first time she stood alone. The heavy command came from her throat as the snake coiled around her feet and she thrust both bare arms into the torch and held them there. Her beautiful face was impassive, unmoving.

"Damballah! Damballah! Damballah!" Three times more the cry came from the people who rose as one person. The snake moved then, a swift, sinuous band of black that flowed into the rocks and was gone. Tanda moved out of the flame, held her arms aloft, and lifted her girl's voice in a song of praise as the white-robed dancers once more swirled and dipped over the snake design on the ground.

Carlotta stared at the smooth skin on Tanda's arms as she moved slowly around the circle, showing herself to all. Her brilliant eyes met those of Carlotta and saw the wonder there. In that moment, the girl feared for all their lives. This was a priestess incarnate, fresh from communion with her god and in accordance with her people. Surely there was no greater power. In the soft drumming that began now, she heard the whisper of her nightmare half a world away.

Clouds were drifting across the face of the moon, which was far down the sky. It was a little cooler, and Carlotta wiped the beads of sweat away from her eyes with a sigh of relief. She looked around for Simon or Austin but did not see them. John, too, had vanished. Tanda was at the waterfall and one of the maidens was sponging her back with a white cloth. Another held a long white robe ready. Carlotta stretched her cramped legs as others were doing and longed for a drink of cold water.

The cry of an angry woman cut across the drums, which were instantly stilled as she strode into the torchlight. The girl was young, no more than fifteen, if that, her eyes were wide, her features delicate. She wore a coarse brown robe and her feet were bare. But her voice was strident; fierce, the face contorted into a mask of fury, and her stance was martial as she caught a torch from one of the bearers and waved it with long sweeping strokes.

The people backed away, murmuring under their breaths. Carlotta saw that some of them walked closer to the girl as she moved and more joined them. Tanda turned from the waterfall and saw her advancing. She stepped back toward the cliff and cried, "Damballah, come again!"

The woman laughed a harsh, savage explosion of mirth and pulled a machete from her waistband. Those behind her howled in eagerness, and she turned to accept their homage. The light shone full into her glittering eyes, and Carlotta gave a whimper of horror. They were red as the pits of hell.

There was a movement by her side as Austin slipped down beside her. His forehead was wet with sweat but his eyes blazed with excitement. The esthete of the *Princess* was no longer visible. He whispered, "The gods challenge each other. The serpent god has left his priestess and the other challenges him to return."

Carlotta looked at the strutting woman superimposed on the body of the young girl, heard the cries that emerged from her throat, and saw the flaming eyes. She was amazed that her own voice was steady when she said, "Who is this? What does she want of Tanda?"

Austin shrugged. "I can understand only a very little of their talk. There is voodoo in New Orleans, of course, but it is different from this. The one there"——he nodded toward the girl——"is one of the war gods of Haiti, a drinker of blood. She has come, she says, to bring all these people to the true way. The land must be purged of all foreigners, and those who have been soft or kind to them must die. The usual cant, you know."

The red glance impaled Austin just then, and he stopped before the fury of it. Heads turned to follow her look, and those near them drew back. Carlotta stared in her turn and the gaze took them both in. The great drum beat ominously, slowly.

"Jérouge!" The voice was Tanda's and yet not hers, a female sound fading into the male that was gradually becoming dominant. "Jérouge!" Tanda stood, tall and fierce against the light of the fading moon. In one quick movement she came to confront the woman with the flaming eyes, her hands moving in the slithering movements of the snake, her head already appearing elongated.

Carlotta would have sworn that in that second of time when the torches leaped high and the drums beat a frenzied tatoo, the shadow of the great snake coiled around the red image which was woman and yet not woman to fight a battle not of this earth. The moon went behind a bank of clouds just then, and the thunder pealed. The women circled each other and waited as they spoke savage words that seemed to echo the beat of the drums. A hoarse chant began, one that had blood lust in it. The followers of the red one drew closer, machetes in their hands.

"Jérouge!" The angry male voice might have been that of several men, for it shook the streaming torches and stopped the men in their advance. Now the shadow of the snake was reality, for it was suddenly in Tanda's hands and around her slender body. It thrust out a blunt head toward the red one, and a long forked tongue flickered in the same instant as the lightning tore the sky.

Jérouge retreated, the coals of her eyes dimming. Then she whirled and pointed the fingers of both hands at the assembled whites, who had made themselves small in the outcroppings of rock close to where Carlotta and Austin sat. The coarse, vitriolic sounds of her voice were curses, the chopping gestures were eloquent of the fate she sought for them. Her followers cried aloud at the end of each sentence.

The great snake thrust out again, and this time it narrowly missed her head. The voice of Damballah seemed to split Tanda's throat, and the drums ceased to beat. In the deafening

166

silence, a white man, dressed all in white, strode up to Tanda-Damballah and bent respectfully before her. The voice spoke again, no longer harsh but still commanding. Jérouge hissed once and was still. Simon stretched out both hands and took the great snake from Tanda. It immediately coiled over his shoulders as he stood very quietly before them all.

"Dear God, keep him safe!" Carlotta did not know that she had spoken until Austin's hand closed on hers in a hard grip that made her wince.

The voice of Damballah sounded one final time, and the wind lifted slightly. The red light faded from the eyes of the young girl, and her body shivered spasmodically. Then she was limp on the ground, and those of her followers who had not retreated now began to return the machetes to their belts. Tanda waved a hand and the girl was gathered up by several of the women who bore her into the cave mouth. Carlotta was near enough to see the smoothing out of the young face and the shaking of her entire body.

Simon did not move as the snake slid down his body and moved toward the rocks. Tanda took his hand and led him toward the waterfall where she gently touched water to his face and hands. The people sighed and began to sway in a low chanting that had a note of triumph. Gourds were passed out now, the water dipped from the waterfall, and most of them drank eagerly.

Lightning burned along the top of the mountain in the west, and now the fresh scent of rain was carried on the wind. Tanda came toward the party with Simon in her wake. Her strong face seemed suddenly older; she still bore the marks of the god-battle. They rose to meet her in an involuntary gesture of respect.

She spoke in the cool, clipped accents of another world. "You must all leave here now. The gods are much inflamed and the people with them. Damballah has given you his protection but he will no longer look upon your faces. It was I who thought that some of the anger between our races might be mended, but it cannot be as yet. We have suffered too long." She turned to Simon. "Even you can no longer walk freely in these hills. Go to your ships and do not return to Haiti while you live. Split into several groups. A guide will go with each. There are many here who follow the paths of anger and Jérouge. They will seek you but they will not find you if you go immediately."

Simon said softly, "Will you go to Henry? There is yet time for you both."

The dark face relaxed but the line of her mouth was grim. "Henry Christophe fights. He has no time for me."

"He will make time. Already he is trying to turn Emperor Dessalines from his hunger for blood. You can help." Simon bent closer to her and the silver-gilt hair shone in the torchlight. "Such were his words."

She smiled and the strong planes of her face split into sudden brilliance. "Damballah will go your way and enter into you until you quit the shores of Haiti." Tanda swayed suddenly and the male voice of the god himself spoke. "Your woman will be fruitful with sons and your name great in your land. You both will walk the cleft of agony and treachery but triumph comes soon. The shadowed one will leave her and the jewels recede. Remember."

Simon stared at her, and Carlotta felt her heart wrench. This was the language of prophecy, elliptical and twisted but clear enough for all that. His heiress would be fruitful, would she! Let her have many girls first!

When Tanda spoke again in her own voice it was to command them to hurry. "The guides await beyond the rocks. There is no time to waste."

Carlotta rose to her feet. She had collapsed briefly on a nearby rock while Damballah spoke this last time. Austin glanced at her briefly and said, "Are you all right?" At her nod, he turned to Tanda. "Your brother will be set free as soon as we reach the ship. I thank you for your kindness to Madame Bevenders. She suffered much."

Tanda's nod was cold to him. She took Carlotta's hand in hers and said swiftly, "The path of blood is before you. Be strong, for you have walked that way before." She turned her back on them then, and her voice rose in a chant of praise that was joined by the assembled people as the torches were lifted high.

The party melted behind the rocks as they were bidden and divided into three groups. Thunder muttered briefly; the storm was not far distant. Austin accepted Simon's hand briefly, then watched as he gave Carlotta a quick bow without meeting her eyes. A moment later Simon and his branch of the party vanished down the narrow trail.

"A brave man, that." Austin started ahead, and the others fell in behind him at their guide's signal.

"Aye." Her voice choked up in spite of herself. That cool parting might be all she would ever know of Simon. She expected Austin to comment caustically but he said nothing.

The rain finally came, first in little spurts and then in drowning waves that made their footing treacherous and doubly dangerous. They dared not use a small torch and were forced to move down the mountain face by use of hands and knees, hanging onto each other and counting on blind luck. The rain beat in their faces, the rocks scraped their bodies raw, and Harry the seaman, who was in their party, kept up a stream of Portuguese curses which stirred Carlotta more than once into exhausted giggles. When the first gray light came, they saw that they were only at the foot of one mountain; countless others shone misty green under the rain. The slow thunder of the drums had begun once more.

Their guide, a small young man with ropy muscles, listened intently, and his face seemed to go gray as the morning. He spoke to Austin in a swift spatter of words, then motioned for them to hasten.

Austin said, "He says the gods war in the hills, that the red one's anger is kindled once more. We can expect pursuit, but we knew that. The drums speak of this to all."

"Hurry! Hurry!" The guide was frantic with impatience.

The rain slowed to softness during the day, and they could almost see the growth of the vegetation around them as they went along one endless trail and into another. There was no time for breath or speech, only for trudging. Rests were brief, sleep a snatched thing of minutes. The guide urged them forward anxiously, even as they looked behind with mounting uneasiness. The drums never stopped in all that long trek, but the tone altered subtly to become a fever in the blood, a warning of death that waited in many guises.

They crossed two gorges that day. The bridges were of rope and cane bound together and strung high across the empty expanses that fell to rocks and trees far below. Carlotta did not look down, she dared not think, but concentrated on Austin's back as he went before her and spoke ridiculously of the beauty that was Haiti's even at this time of danger. She was grateful for his concern, even though she knew it less for herself than for the symbol she was to be and the child she would have.

They came down a long incline of bare rock in the evening coolness, when the red sky of the west indicated a fair, hot tomorrow. A row of trees and low bushes grew to one side of the path, and a series of ledges gave way to a far valley beyond. Carlotta looked up, meaning to ask Austin how far away he thought the sea might be, but as she did so, she saw a wavering movement in the lush vegetation. Her gasp made him whirl to face her, and then the others were staring as well.

There was a scream of terror from the guide. "Jérouge!" He bent to the ground, chattering with fear.

Carlotta was rooted to the spot. Her heart hammered so that it matched the sound of the drums in her ears. The tall, dark men stood silently on the ridge in the last rays of the sun, their eyes gleaming like red coals, the eyes of Jérouge, red goddess of Haiti.

CHAPTER TWENTY-THREE

They Who Walk

THE guide screamed once more and groveled. Harry jerked out his sword, and the several other seamen did the same. Austin stood very still beside Carlotta, then he lifted his pistol and shot the largest of the dark men, who moved just as the ball struck.

It hit the shoulder, and Carlotta saw the flesh fly, but there was no blood, neither was there wound or movement. The guide lifted his head, and this time his wail was intelligible. "The undead! They have come for us! We are lost!"

As if they had waited for his words, the men or the dead, whatever they were, began to move slowly toward the party. There could be no mistaking their intent, for they, too, drew the machetes that gleamed in the light, and a low rumbling sound came from their throats. There were ten of them and they moved as one body. The guide jumped up and started to run but his fear was so great that he stumbled and fell. One detached himself from the others then, picked up the screaming man as if he were a chicken, slit his throat with the machete, and hurled him into the void.

Harry gave a bull cry of rage and called to his three fellows, "Come on, let's get 'em! Stick 'em!"

Austin thrust Carlotta behind him and raised his pistol to fire. It jammed and he threw it to the ground in disgust. She drew a small dagger, knowing it to be useless against the physical strength of these men. He pulled out his sword, the long blade glittering in the light. His men waited warily, their eyes on the others who now stood together as if waiting for a signal.

Austin turned to Carlotta. "Go down this path and do not deviate from it. It leads eventually to the sea; I do know that much from talk with Tanda." He took a chain from around his neck. A small box, flat and emblazoned with a crest, dangled from the end of it. "Take this. If they capture you, swallow the powder within. Death comes in seconds."

"I will not go!" She cried the words aloud. "I will not leave all of you to your certain deaths!"

He jerked her close to him and fairly hissed the words in her ear. "You saw what they did to Gillian. This is at least a chance. Take it, you fool!"

She stared at him, thinking how once she would have given everything for a chance at freedom. Now they were welded together in adversity. "Austin, I . . ."

That strange look flickered in his eyes and was gone. "It is very likely that I will join you with the others on the beach very soon. If not, bear my son and remember the royal house of France." He pushed her back and cried to his men, "Come, let us drive them over the gorge!"

It was pure instinct that made Carlotta slump to the ground as though he had tossed her aside, for one of the black men made as if to go to her though Austin's party stood with weapons ready. The hammering of the drums began to dwindle, to be replaced by a fast, skittering beat.

Harry bawled out a curse and charged, the others behind him. One of the men picked him up bodily and threw him back. Carlotta heard the crunch of his bones as he hit the ground. She did not wait for anything but ran down the path as hard as she could go. Behind her swords rang on machetes as the sun sank into a pool of purple clouds.

Carlotta had been tired and wrought up before but now all was forgotten as she went for her life, a life that might be taken from her by horrible means at any moment. Her bare feet slapped on rocks and dirt; they were torn and cut but she felt nothing. Her hair caught on vines and her hands were raw from using them to maintain her balance or to climb, yet nothing mattered. Her breath gave out, pain stitched down her side, but still she rushed on. Animals rustled in the depths of the bushes, and once she nearly fell over something long and slimy which moved as she did. There was no breath or strength to scream; she simply kept going.

The moon lifted in the sky, pale behind the cloud haze and half hidden by the lacing trees which rose high over her head. She took time to be thankful that the path was clearer and that it went downhill. She would not let herself think of what was happening to the others or what her own fate would be if she were captured. Her mouth was dry, her throat parched and aching. The sound of a stream lured her to stop for a mouthful of lifegiving water, even though she knew that just a minute's delay could bring lulling exhaustion and she might not be able to rise again.

Carlotta threw herself down on her stomach at the water's edge and drank in quick, hungry swallows. She buried her face in the cold freshness several times, hoping that it would revive her weary body. She lifted her head, more alert now, and then she heard the footsteps on the path.

They were clearly audible in the stillness, which was unbroken even by a sleepy bird, for the drums had suddenly ceased. The tread was slow, heavy, inexorable. She jumped to her feet and jerked the knife from her belt. The gesture was useless, she knew, but she had to try. Then she stepped over the stream, left the path, and plunged into the trackless woods, her every footfall seeming to thunder in the eerie silence.

She came to the top of a thickly wooded rise and sank down into the tumbling vines to catch her breath. Her body was slick with sweat, her mouth dry again. The moon gave off a wan light; by that light she saw the two hulking shapes moving slowly, steadily, on the rocky incline not far away. They seemed taller than ever, and her mind noted impersonally that they moved without fluidity, almost as if they had been set in position. She could only hope that they still followed the path. What were they, these fearful things who had men's faces and yet could withstand the blast of a pistol? Her blood chilled, for she knew that she must not consider other alternatives lest she run screaming through the wood and thereby hasten her already certain fate.

For what she reckoned to be the next hour, Carlotta slipped from bush to tree to rock, always following the general line of the path and going steadily downhill. She tried to move quietly in the times when the drums were silent; when they were not she crashed along, trying to make as much time as possible. She had lived with fear so long that it seemed natural to shrink back from a waving branch yet glance up and see those shadows against the rim of the mountain. It was a blessing, she thought, that she had watched the guide point out the trail and the general direction of the sea, otherwise she might have had no idea where she was going. She had little enough as it was.

Just then the drums began a slow, doomful bonging that seemed to reverberate through the hills. Carlotta put both hands to her ears but could not shut out the sound that pierced her head as though with an iron spike. She looked toward the trail, but the trees were brushing together in the warm wind and she could not see her pursuers. There was nothing for it but to go on, terrified as she was. The sound grew louder and louder until it seemed to permeate the entire mountain. Her breath came in quick sobs as she saw a fire glow large over on a distant ridge. It burned so high that the clouds appeared banked and dark. This could be seen for miles out to sea; perhaps it had been set for that very reason.

Carlotta almost lost hope then. She sank to the wet ground and put her head in her hands. As she did so, time rolled back and she saw her nightmare in all the customary scenes. This time, however, she saw a wide expanse of meadow, the turrets of a castle in the background, and a black-haired woman who wailed over a decapitated body at her feet. She heard laughter, self-satisfied and deep, saw a tall man walk easily toward the woman who pushed the child she had been shielding away, crying "Run!" and saw him bend over the woman with dagger held high. The voice of the mob and their lust to kill spoke through the drums as past and present melted together. In a moment she would see the face of the murderer.

She could not face that. All her fears rose; to look upon him would be death. She lifted her head, opened her eyes, and saw the apparition standing under the spreading branches of a tree no more than a hundred yards away. Her breath froze; she could not move, only stare at the grisly sight.

He was tall and very black, his clothes were unrelieved black, a very correct suit until the eye reached his bare feet. His face was painted white, and in one hand he held a white cross. He was grinning, the long mouth filled with shining white teeth. The other hand held what appeared to be a human skull, the fingers thrust through the eye sockets. As she watched, he waved the skull at her and the racking laughter rose.

The little control that she had had deserted her completely. Coming as it did on the heels of the expanding nightmare, this visitation was the end of things. She knew enough about Haiti's gods from Tanda to know that this was death himself, sometimes called Baron Samedi or simply Guédé. "Always good to know how and when you will die!" The mad thought rang through her head as she screamed, one piercing note after another, and turned to run. She had taken only a few steps before one of the hanging vines of white flowers wrapped itself around her upper body and entangled her.

The fearful figure came closer, a strange blur of black and white under the paling moon, half obscured by the clouds as it was, and the leaping fire in the distance made patterns on the black sky. Now she saw other movement on the ridge as the figures of her pursuers loomed up, attracted, perhaps, by her screams. They had not moved fast at any time but their size and lack of pause had eaten up what little time she had gained. Now time had come to an end.

"Carlotta! Carlotta!" The sepulchral voice rang in her ears as she jerked free of the vine, pulled out the little dagger, and held it high. She was conscious only of anger now, that she had endured much and was now caught between death and its very personification.

One of the men she could only think of as the undead dislodged a stone and sent it rolling. Samedi turned his head, then swung from Carlotta to face them, but arms lifted up, that high, crackling laughter ringing out in the silence between drumbeats. She thought to take the opportunity to run but, before she could do so, the men stopped in their tracks. Then five dark figures filed out from behind the trees to join Samedi. A white cross was marked across their chests, their steps were stumping and slow. But the clothes, the blacking of their skins, the wrapped turbans on their heads could not hide the fact of their essential whiteness. One man was taller than the others, his shoulders wider; a man such as no other in this world, Simon.

Carlotta stood dumbfounded once again this night as Simon turned slowly to her and his hands, held close to his chest, traced the ancient sign against evil. Was he alive or dead? What was she? Questions whirled in her brain but there was no time for thought. Simon walked to her as Samedi placed himself between the pursuers and what she could only think of as his new prey. She lifted the dagger again, knowing as she did so that she could not plunge it into that loved flesh, no matter what his state of being.

"Put that down! Stand quietly." The low voice with an edge of irritation was certainly Simon's.

She held it ready, but her movements were as jerky as those who sought her. "Are you alive?"

He took her wrist, twisted the dagger from her shaking hands, and lifted her in both arms. His flesh was warm and real against hers, and the green eyes burned down into her face. Insanely, his voice was brushed with laughter as he whispered,

"Under any other circumstances I would gladly show you how alive I am, foolish one."

He held her quietly as she clung to him. Samedi waved the skull and cried something in a voice that sounded as if it were tearing flesh from bones. The pursuers stood for a few seconds longer, then shambled away the same way they had come. In a moment there was the sound of heavy running and tearing brush. Then Samedi walked swiftly toward Simon and Carlotta, his minions behind him.

"Is she all right? Those will not come back but others may be looking for us all. Carlotta . . . ?" The soft voice trailed off. Baron Samedi, Lord of the Dead, was a very much alive John, Simon's own friend. His followers were those of Austin's crew who had left with Simon what seemed years ago.

Carlotta stared in total disbelief at the dark figures who were covered with mud and black paint and at John whose white face seemed to float in darkness. The skull he held was a white rock with painted eyeholes; it seemed to float in her vision and grow larger. She wanted to laugh at the ludicrous figure they all presented but could not. She turned her face into Simon's chest and began to cry in strangled sobs that shook her whole body.

He sat down with her and cradled her to him but made no attempt to give solace. "Cry, Carlotta, cry. You've seen too many demons and endured too much these past days. We are alive and will continue so. God wills it. Now cry, lady, for you are the bravest of us all."

She looked up, her face streaming with the tears of release, and saw the earnest face of John manifesting kind concern behind the fearful countenance of Samedi, saw Simon's tufted dark brows now thick with paint, and began to laugh in earnest.

"The court of Samedi meets! Hail, Lord of the Dead!" It was a feeble joke in very bad taste but she could not stop the words. Simon hugged her to him, and they all began to roar with laughter in the blessed release of tension.

It was altogether proper that Simon should turn Carlotta to him and stop her mouth with kisses that brought the blood back to her heart and renewed not only life but passion as well.

A few minutes later they rested from terror and laughter while John told Carlotta briefly what had happened since their parting. Simon still held her close, and none of them thought it odd that he should do so. The white face shone against the night as John said, "I think they followed us almost from the beginning but we managed to elude them long enough to find some of the plants that darken the skin when helped by mud. I carried some whitener with me by some strange fortune. All know the Lord of the Dead."

Carlotta whispered, for her voice was still rasped with her screams. "Why do they wish to kill us? Who are those terrible people?"

It was Simon who answered, "Haiti may be free and ruled by their chosen emperor but there are many factions still, and they serve differing gods. Voodoo is considered treason but it will not be stamped out. Tanda's followers are moderate in nature, those of the Red Goddess are savage and would kill all who disagree with them."

"But the undead...!" She shivered again at the memory of those staring eyes like peeled grapes, the torn flesh that did not bleed. "I will see them in my nightmares."

"Carlotta, listen well to what I say." Simon turned her face to his and it was as if they two were the only ones in the shifting light of the glade. "Haiti is filled with plants and trees which, if utilized by those who know the art, can produce states such as frenzy, a suspension very like death, loss of memory, somnambulism, and others. The mind can also simulate these things so that the flesh is not touched. Do you understand me?"

She looked into his eyes and tried to summon up the cold rationalism of which he spoke. Had Tanda's hand not felt the fire? Had she herself not seen the great shadow of the snake over the woman-face of the girl and had not the eyes of the red one gleamed in those of her followers? There was power there, savage and unleashed. Explanations could not alter that.

"Carlotta?" Simon was shaking her shoulder, his voice anxious.

"Aye, Simon. I understand. Thank you."

His eyes went soft and she felt the response of her eager flesh, too long denied. He saw, and she felt the withdrawal that was a blow. He said, "Send someone with her to the beach and set the fire so that our ships will come in." He waved a hand toward the signal fire still blazing against the clouds. "Both our signals will be in the shape of a cross, a little thing those others do not know."

"Where are you going?" Carlotta felt the return of the deadly fear.

"To find the others. To find Austin." Simon was looking straight at her now, and his voice was very level.

Carlotta wanted to cry out that by now he and his men were dead, destroyed by the undead, not to risk his dear life, to take her and their happiness and go from this beautiful, deadly land. What was Austin to her and she to him? She said, "We were attacked by those men, and he made me go while they fought. Pray God you will be successful, for his last thought was for me." As she said the words of renunciation, she knew that they were right. Austin had indeed saved her life, and she would bear his child.

There was warmth in Simon's face now as he smiled at her. No words were necessary.

It was John, every inch the dark god he impersonated, who took command as he rose, the others with him. "Simon, you and the others will go to the beach. I take only Tim with me. He is the largest of you all. No one will gainsay Samedi." Simon started to speak but John held up an emphatic hand. "Do as I say, Simon, you and your kind are alien here now. It is our land."

Anger crossed Simon's face, then he nodded. "You are right. I obey." He turned to Austin's men and waited for their nods, which came rapidly.

John beckoned to the thickly built Tim, who was grinning at the prospect of a fight. He said then to the others, "Wait for us until the moon rises tomorrow night. If we are not there by then we will not be coming."

"Go with God." Carlotta spoke the words softly in English, and Simon returned them in French.

John laughed shortly. "In Haiti it is best to specify the god you mean. This is the sort of undertaking that will amuse the real Baron Samedi." Then he was gone into the shadows of the wood.

Carlotta felt tears film her eyes, and Simon's hand squeezed hard on hers. Whatever time was left to them, at least it would be spent together.

CHAPTER TWENTY-FOUR

By the Blue-Green Waters

THEY came down to the sea in the faint light of earliest morning, when the mountains were still shrouded in black and only a line of gray showed in the east. The journey had been tiring, involving as it did the climbing of several sizable wooded ridges and the descent of their rocky faces by a nearly nonexistent trail. But Simon knew this country and he guided them easily. When the first glimpse of the sea appeared, all cheered as if they were fresh from school and rushed to dip their fingers in it.

While brush was being gathered to form the arms of the cross, Carlotta leaned against the bole of a large palm tree to rest before going to help. She watched Simon as he jerked at a dead branch tossed high up on the beach by a long-ended storm and, once again, wondered at the intensity of the feeling that shook her. Then the sound of the waves meshed with the warm wind and she knew no more.

She woke with a start, the sun hot on her skin, the end of a branch tickling her nose. She slapped with one hand in the irritation of broken slumber, but the tickling continued. Both eyes flew open and she stared straight into the brilliant eyes and laughing brown face of Simon. A Simon who seemed totally rested, the black gone from his skin, the white shirt and trousers now very gray. His feet were bare, long toes gripping the sand as he squatted beside her flicking the branch.

"Lazy wench! The sun is high. Will you sleep all day when there is exploring to be done?"

She looked at him sleepily, then reached out an arm and pushed him so that he toppled backward. In an instant she was on her feet and running toward the lapping water. He was beside her, picking her up again in his arms and ducking down in the salty spray so that they were both drenched in the space of three waves.

"We must investigate this beach. It curves back into the rocks over there, and someone must watch for a ship from that angle. One man watches here, the others rest." It was a challenge. Green points flickered in his eyes and his hands went to his hips as he stood boldly before her, dripping wet as they both were.

"We must indeed investigate this beach. I will watch with you." She looked down the expanse of sand to where a skeleton of the lighted cross had burned. If they came, Austin's and Simon's ships, there would be so little time. If they did not . . . that thought could not be finished. She put out her hand and Simon took it. Their bond was sealed.

They went around the indicated curve of the smooth, narrow beach, climbed up past more palm trees through an overhang of pink flowers, and came out at a small pool of fresh water made by a tinkling waterfall. Vines hung down to make a secret place, yet by parting them one might look out on the expanse of brilliant blue-green water that stretched to meet the limitless sky.

Carlotta went to the side of the pool and sat down to dangle her feet in the coolness. She felt grimy and suddenly shy. Simon turned his back and peered earnestly at the horizon, but his shoulders shook, and she guessed at his laughter. Quickly she took off the grimy shift which was already stiffening with sea water and tossed it aside. It was the work of a moment to spread her flowing red-brown hair out and allow herself to drift free on the water.

"Simon." She could say no more, but it had all her heart in it.

"Behold, my love, thou art fair." He was beside her, his warm breath on her cheek, as he held her slender body to his brown naked one. "Thou art fair."

They drifted in the water as he kissed her ears, throat, and face and lifted her fingers to his lips. Carlotta put both arms around him and fitted her mouth to his. Their tongues were liquid fire as they wound together. Her bare breasts thrust upward against his chest, and she felt his manhood firm on her loins. The drugging sweetness wrapped round them as they swayed, lost in passion.

Simon lifted Carlotta once more into his arms and placed her on the grass underneath the flowering vine. He sat back as if prolonging the intensity of the moment and savored her lissome body, the slenderness of her legs, the pink nipples, the hunger in the amber eyes. In her turn, Carlotta saw the bronzed skin, the hard muscled length of him, the shimmering silver-gilt of his hair, the tapering waist, and held out her arms. "Simon, it has been an eternity!"

"Aye, lady. That and more." He slipped down beside her, drawing her to him. His hand went around her waist and she shivered at his touch. Then gentleness was done, for they could wait no longer. Now he was thrusting deeply into her drawing warmth as his hands were hard on her breasts. Their mouths locked together while the hunger rose. Carlotta felt him driving more deeply into her and spread her legs wide that he might do so freely. Her hands clung to his broad shoulders as they blotted out the light of the sunlit day.

Now the fire was rising higher, stoked by the rhythm of his thrusting. She was his, he was hers; they were one flesh, one paean of desire and longing. His hands were moving over her in long strokes that burned and chilled at the same time. He was larger in her; she felt the contractions beginning as she gripped him the harder. She was flying in air, drowning in liquid warmth, falling, falling. Suddenly the burning was unbearable; her whole body tensed as she was suffused with flame. She arched, clung, and was still, floating on the waters of renewal.

They curled together, hands and bodies touching in drowsy contentment, while the warm winds brushed against them and the white flowers showered down.

"Carlotta. Is that truly your name?" His voice was low, musing, and his fingers caressed the nape of her neck, drifting through the curls there, making her tremble at the softness of it.

"Yes. Is yours Simon?"

He raised up on one elbow and put his hand on her chin. "It is. We must talk, little one. I do not know enough of you. But first..." He touched her lips with his, then pulled her closer so that the fire began once more.

Carlotta slipped her fingertips over his back, feeling the little chills lift as she did so. His heart was hammering wildly, hers answered it. He kissed the corner of her mouth lightly and she turned her face to his. Time hung suspended, and then they were in each other's arms as the consuming, licking flames rose once again.

Later they sat beside the little waterfall, letting the slow gurgle lull them into half-slumber. They touched and kissed, laughed at the soaring gulls, found faces in the clouds and rainbows in the mist from the water as the sun struck it. Simon rolled over on his stomach and sighed in lazy pleasure while Carlotta moved her fingers in delicate patterns on his back.

She said softly, "Simon?" At his lazy grunt, she continued, "I know almost nothing about you. Will you tell me now?"

He sat up and propped himself on both elbows, a wary gleam in his green eyes. "I asked you first, a while ago. Remember?" His hand touched the blowing tendrils of her hair and drew back.

"Aye, I remember." She hesitated, wondering how much to tell him. There were no illusions left in Carlotta despite the fierce passion they had shared. He could leave her easily and go to his heiress, but she did not want to spoil the loveliness of this time. "Ah, Simon, there is so much. What can I say?"

He leaned back again and his smile wrapped her round. "As much or as little as you wish, for it is times like this that I will recall."

In the end Carlotta told him much of the truth about herself and found it surprisingly easy to talk. The nightmare, her life with Uncle Arnold and Aunt Rosa, Sir Reginald and his murder, her flight and all that it brought about. She said, "I was angered when I saw you with the beautiful lady and even more so when you tried to pursue me. I was a girl then, with no knowledge of the worlds between."

Simon's eyebrows went up but he said nothing. She told him of how she met Austin but said nothing of the strange relationship between them nor of the plot he meant to implement with her. Her pride came to strengthen her as she said, "Austin's only son died of the yellow fever, and the news struck him hard. That night he came to me, and I could not turn him away. He spoke of another child and, because he saved my life, I yielded. He is a proud man and will protect his own. The rest you know, including the reason we are in Haiti."

Simon reached for his shirt and drew it around his shoulders. "I must ask your pardon, Carlotta, for the way I spoke to you when Austin found us. I saw his jealousy and thought to protect us both. Will you forgive me?"

"Right willingly." She reached out to touch his arm but he turned away under the pretext of adjusting the collar. Carlotta knew that she had been wise not to throw herself on him and beg for his help. How could a man such as he understand the mixture of cruelty and gallantry and deviousness that was Austin Lenoir? And because she was to have his child, she must follow his path if he still lived. If not, she would ask passage

182

of Simon to Boston and there try to fashion a life for herself. She loved Simon, indeed there would be no other for her so long as she lived, but she felt freer with Austin than she did with him, for Simon was a mystery to her even now.

Simon was saying, "You need not worry, the men will say nothing; they are grateful for their lives."

Carlotta looked at him, love and helpless anger warring in her. Why could he not take her and sail away into the lands beyond Haiti? She knew he cared for her, mouth and hands and voice told her that. The slanting sun turned his hair to living gold and glanced off his high cheekbones; her insides began to quiver with the force of her lifting passion.

Simon saw and rose to pace about. "Carlotta, Carlotta, I had been a scoundrel for much of my life—mercenary, robber, highwayman. I have had much in the way of jewels, sport, and women but I have not been one to wed. The lady you saw me **with** was one of several who proved herself most compliant in the way of information and, shall we say, other things. The King's men began to close in just after you ran away. I sold some of the richer jewels and outfitted my ship, then sailed to New York in the guise of a merchant captain seeking to settle down far from the turmoil of Europe, a thing essentially true. While there I met an old friend who introduced me to one of the city elders, a man of great property. His daughter, Beatrice, will be my wife in the new year. It is a good match, and I shall be a faithful husband."

He stared straight into Carlotta's eyes, and she gave him look for look. His path was set; he could be no clearer about it. Once again she gave silent thanks that she had not asked for that which he would not give. She said, "But you have said that you once lived here in Haiti. That you sought the remains of the family property or jewels."

"So I did. For four years when I was a boy growing to a young man. My mother, peace be upon her, was one who sought every advantage." His voice grew hard, and the green eyes flared angrily. "She taught me much of women, and I have not found it to be wrong, for experience has borne me out."

Carlotta had known too much of nightmare not to recognize it in another. Simon carried the shadows of an unhappy past, and bitterness marked him. It would be pointless to question him further. She spoke gently. "We do as we must, Simon.

How can we presume to judge each other or the past? Let it be."

He turned and walked to the edge of the pool where he stared down for a moment. Then he raised his hand to his eyes to shade them as he gazed at the horizon. Carlotta stepped up to follow his look and saw, on the limitless horizon, so faint as to seem part of clouds and sea, the mast of a ship.

"Austin's," he said in answer to her unspoken question. "Mine is the *Sea Wind*, smaller and swifter than many ships which ply these waters. Some have discovered that to their sorrow." He grinned and the laughter returned to the green eyes.

The constriction of the past minute was gone. Carlotta cried, "Simon! Have you taken up piracy, too?"

"Only in passing, my dear. I am going to be respectable, and that takes money."

"How I wish I could have been there!" She could see the poised ships, hear the ringing sword blades, touch the caskets of gold and fiery gems, feel the thrill of the chase as they closed in on the prey.

"Little highwayman, would you be a pirate as well? Good comrade, I think you would be an excellent addition to the brotherhood, but I have forsworn such pleasures." He drew her to him and kissed the corners of her mouth. "We have time for love, do we not?"

Carlotta felt the delicious languor building up as her loins began to tingle. She felt boneless as his mouth took hers and his hand began to touch the tautening nipple of her breast. Her hand dropped to his shaft and found it eager. He trembled as she touched it, for his hunger was rising even as her own.

"Simon." The name was endearment enough, for all her caring was in it at this unguarded moment. He tensed and read how it was with her in her face. He held her back from him, and Carlotta endured the scrutiny with a calm mask that belied the pain she felt.

"I did not know." He spoke softly, but there was no mistaking the baffled anger in his eyes. "I truly did not know. I have been a fool."

"No, I have been the fool." She moved back from him. How could he not have known that she loved him? He had known the love of many women, had he not said it? Had she really been no more than a comrade with whom one might relieve oneself of the passions or had he truly begun to care and thus was angry at himself for so doing? She would never know, for too much lay bare between them now.

"I have seen her look that way, too. Countless times, each with a different man, a different flirtation. Never knowing the meaning of honor. Not caring." He sounded distant, but there was a red flush under the bronze skin of his face.

"Who?"

"I was only a boy here but I knew. I knew. The foulness traveled with her. My lady mother who was no lady. Strumpet, they called her, and you can guess what they called me!" His voice held all the anger of a lifetime, and his mouth twisted with fury that should have been expended long ago.

Carlotta felt indignation stir as her frustrated passion cooled before the injustice of his actions. "You are a man grown now. What can it matter what your mother was called? You are the arbiter of your own actions. Besides, have you, too, not boasted to me of flirtations and fair ladies, of lies told and husbands cuckolded? Wherein lies the difference? You do not go pure to your heiress, yet you will expect her to come to you so. You say pridefully that you will be a faithful husband yet such as you would cast her out were she unfaithful, as you undoubtedly will be. You called me harlot in all but name when we met again, and I vow that you did mean it, for all your apologies!"

"No woman speaks to me so! Aye, I meant it! You stand here prating of knowledge and expectations, but you came eagerly, aye, hungrily to me, did you not? What do you know of understanding? I vow, you thought to cozen me as you did your rich lover. Well, he is welcome to you!" Simon whirled and walked away, slashing at the hanging flowers that had so lately hung over their bower of love.

Carlotta stood where he had left her. She was as cold as if the winter winds buffeted her. Was his anger simply due to the fact that he had seen she loved him? She regretted bitterly the words she had thrown at him. One more time of passion and sweetness to hold against all the endless years—surely she could have held her tongue instead of railing as if she were a fishwife.

The wind lifted her hair softly and she raised one hand to brush the tendrils back. Then she saw the two high-masted ships drifting like white petals on the shimmering water, heard the sound of running feet and a familiar voice, and Carlotta knew that the time of departure was at hand, for Austin had returned.

185

CHAPTER TWENTY-FIVE

Talisman

As Carlotta came round the curve of the beach, she saw Austin and five of the men who had been in the separate parties standing with John as they spoke to Simon and those who had accompanied him. Austin leaned on a cleft stick but his bearing was otherwise erect, and there was a jubilant note in his voice as he spoke with the others. She might be bare before Simon but would not show it. Carlotta ran toward Austin, her manner anxious as she cried. "Are you all right? What has happened?"

Up close she saw that there were several cuts on his face and dark circles under his black eyes, but curiously he seemed more alive than she had ever seen him. The sleeve was ripped away from his shirt on the left, and the arm there had a fresh wound. His foot was wrapped in a dirty cloth. He said, "Why, my dear, does my condition merit this concern? If so, I am grateful for it. Simon tells me that all is well with you."

She could not look at Simon or the others; she felt shamed for her own proud passion. "But you are well, not too seriously hurt?" Inane, she thought, to babble on. "I worried."

Austin smiled at her, and she caught the old mockery. "Those creatures attacked soon after you left. The men fought bravely but the odds were too great. They killed several of them, then started dragging the rest of us away. They tied us to trees and started one of those hellish fires. I passed out, and when I came to John here was there with his supposed corpses in tow. They were routed. And here we are. Those that are left."

John had wiped the white from his face and looked exhausted, the skin grayish in the sunlight. "Good men died, and all I could do was order those creatures away in the name of Baron Samedi."

Carlotta looked out to sea where she saw that two small boats were being paddled in toward the beach. The great ships themselves were anchored far off shore, possibly because of water depth and certainly to repel any invaders. Their gathering was so small that both rowboats would not be needed; this expedition had cost Austin dearly. She turned back and felt Austin's hand on her arm as he drew her apart.

"There has been no sign of your flux?"

"I told you, I know the symptoms. I am with child." She assessed the intensity in his eyes and prayed that she was right; otherwise he would have her body this night, and that would be unendurable.

"Your boat comes also." John spoke to Simon in a soft aside that Carlotta heard. "We may yet escape with our lives."

"Is there still danger?" Austin, too, had heard.

The surviving men clustered around them as John said, "I had no real power over those who sought to kill us. Their masters, or mistress I should say, will regroup them and . . ." He broke off suddenly and looked in the direction of the mountain down which they had come.

Carlotta followed his glance as did the others. In the far distance a small light was glowing in the rays of the sinking sun. As she watched it was joined by another and yet another. The first hesitant drum signal began and was answered emphatically by one which was much closer.

"They will be here soon, and this time no subterfuge can save us." John was fatalistic as he turned to gauge the distance between land and the approaching boats.

"There is plenty of time! Another fifteen minutes and we will be stepping into those boats." Austin looked out to sea as if to reassure himself and the others as well.

Simon cried, "When the drum is faintest it means that they are very close! Austin, take Carlotta and wade out as far as you can with one or two of your men. Call to the boats as soon as you can. The others can repel our pursuers here. My men will be armed, and I trust that yours arriving will be also. We can hold here."

The drums spoke more sharply this time and were answered by a softer note. Carlotta looked up and saw that the torches were moving more rapidly now, and that there were more of them. A high, angry chant came faintly to their ears. The deep green of the trees was fading into shadow as the sun dropped lower into the sea. A gull swooped by them, calling as it curved up into the light.

Austin caught her hand and pulled her to him as he turned to Simon. His smooth voice was rough with emotion as he said, "You have saved our lives twice over, you and your friend here. How can I leave you to fight our battles?"

Simon's teeth flashed white in the bronzed face, and the green eyes glowed as he answered, "A woman can do nothing and you are injured. Will you die needlessly to prove a point? Besides, it may never come to that. Already the boats are much closer."

They were, but so was the chanting. Carlotta felt the paralyzing fear encircle her, but this time she feared for Simon as well. The gaze he turned on her was mocking and she shivered. Could he read her mind even at this moment?

"Obey me!" It was a roar as he snatched up a machete from the ground.

Austin waved an imperious hand at two of his men, the nearest ones, and they came eagerly to stand beside him. "Simon, I owe you a great debt."

"Go or you will not live to repay it!" Simon turned from them and shouted a command at his friend in the language of the island.

The drums were more insistent now. Austin and Carlotta with the two crewmen waded out into the cool water, which rapidly came to their waists. They could hear the flip-flop of the oars as the others tried to hasten. There was an unearthly howl which was immediately picked up by what seemed a hundred throats, and Carlotta turned her head to see the dark men bursting from the woods onto the beaches. The tiny line of defenders looked ridiculously small against the horde.

"The guns! We must get to them. Do your men carry them?" Her voice rapped out, and one of the crewmen nodded. "Then swim to the boat and get them to shoot. Why don't they do that anyway?"

"I told them to await my orders always." Austin was pushing deeper into the water as he spoke.

"Mistress, neither of us can swim. Sailors don't, you know."

"Austin, I will swim to the boat. Will they obey me?" Carlotta twisted the shift around her body. It was no time for modesty. She was never more thankful for the time spent with certain of the village children in the days before Aunt Rosa decided that she was growing up and must forsake the company she frequented with such pleasure.

"They will obey. Be careful, Carlotta. If only I could go!" Austin waved his arms and shouted again. There was a burst of gunfire over his head and they all sank below the waves.

The water that had seemed so inviting only a few hours ago was now a heavy, tangible thing that pulled Carlotta down and impeded the strokes that had taken her easily through the mill ponds of her youth. She heard the hammering drums and the howls of rage even through the muffling depths, but the gunfire was the frightening thing. Who would have expected guns and voodoo together?

She surfaced to catch her breath and saw that the boat was very close. When she swung her head toward the shore, several fallen white bodies were lying on the sand. Thought left her, and she forced her lungs to a powerful effort as her bare legs kicked out. Then she was grasping the edge and calling, "Shoot, for the love of God, shoot! Drive them back or we will all die!" Willing hands were hauling her aboard, and others were picking up the guns to obey. "It is Austin's order."

The crewmen foolishly stood up to fire and one tumbled back into the water, his head a bloody flower of red and white. His gun fell to the floor of the boat and Carlotta caught it up. She knew little enough of pistols and less of the longer-range guns, but they were close enough now to Austin and the other men to pick them up, and she could at least repel any who tried to forestall that rescue.

There was a flashing form in the water, and a dark head surfaced just in front of them. The man held a knife and he was heading straight for Austin, who tried to raise his stick and fell, hampered as he was by his wounds and the water. Carlotta lifted the pistol, pointed it, screamed, "Duck, Austin," and fired. The man screamed in his turn for his shoulder was smashed.

Now the crewmen pulled Austin into the boat as best they could. He was bleeding again from his wounds, but he snatched up one of the guns only to have it fall from his shaking fingers which would not grip. Carlotta helped him up into the bow and bent down beside him. He kept a rich stream of curses going and Carlotta was almost shaken into laughter, but there was no time for it.

She looked toward the shore, which the sunlight now bathed in a red glow matched by the stream of torches borne down the mountain by the Haitians. It was a red river flowing to the sea as the drums kept up a wild, hungry beat. There was such a jumble of bodies and battle on the beach that she could not tell one person from another. She looked in vain for Simon. Surely that gilt head would have stood out, but there was nothing. Her hand went to her face, for her vision was oddly obscured; she had not known that she was crying.

The little boats were surrounded now by thrashing men all trying to drag the occupants out. Simon's men fought beside Austin's, but there was no hope of winning. Carlotta caught up the gun again but the fire was spent and she had no idea what to do with it. Austin grabbed her wrist and drew her down to him. He was weak from loss of blood and his voice shook but the hardness was there.

"Get down, you will be hit!"

"What does it matter? We are lost." She tried to pull free but his grip was too powerful.

"Do you still have the box, the powder?" His eyes blazed at her as she touched her neck where the strong chain still held it after all the struggles she had undergone since he gave it to her. "You ought to know the reason I . . ."

The world exploded around in a roar. The little boat sloshed with water and waves that shone red with blood. There were screams mingled with cries of pain and anger that rose to a crescendo as the powerful noise came again. Austin and Carlotta sat up together as they saw the sailing ship, her sails spread wide and gleaming in the red sunlight, the skull and crossbones rampant on the black flag streaming out, her guns blazing yet again. She would not be in time to save the fighters, however. The *Princess* was closer to Simon's ship.

The Haitians had few guns and could not stand against the broadside from such a ship in any case. They began to retreat in full scale demoralization. The drums slowed to silence, and the procession of torches in the hills paused visibly. Those in the water began to rush toward shore. The oarsmen sent Austin's little boat skimming toward the *Princess*, which was not, insofar as Carlotta knew, armed to such proportions.

"Simon, I cannot see any sign of him!" She cried the words to the wind, unheeding that Austin might be listening, blessedly thankful for her own life, yet despairing that Simon was dead. If he were would she not know it?

Austin whispered with the last of his strength, "I do not think that such as he die so easily." Then his head drooped and he fell forward into her lap.

She screamed at the men, "Hurry, hurry, he has lost too much blood." Once she would have longed for him to die, to set her free. Now, as she had thought previously, they were all bound together and the end was not yet.

The cries of the wounded gradually faded behind them as the *Princess* came as close to them as she dared in these unfamiliar waters. Austin was lifted up carefully and borne away to his cabin in gentle hands. A cloak was brought for Carlotta and she wrapped her shaking body in it as one of the men drew out a flask to give to her. She drank deeply of the burning liquid, feeling it bind up her shattered nerves and give her strength.

Simon's ship was still too far away for her men to tell where shots might be safely placed. The sun was a sinking red ball in the sea, the last light a path of flame leading to the incredible green mountains that rose and folded in on themselves. The beauty belied the horrors they had experienced there, and she shuddered with memory even as her whole being cried out to know what had happened to Simon.

A scream of mortal agony nearly split her eardrums and she jumped back. The slave Louis, Tanda's brother, hung suspended in chains on the lower deck, blood pouring from the stump of his leg at the hip. The rest of his limb lay on the deck floor, and one of the crewmen was staunching the blood with cloths while another began to lower the writhing man. While Carlotta watched in disbelieving horror, a section of what appeared to be sailcloth was brought and man and leg placed in it. Louis was still shrieking but shock was setting in, though he flailed about.

Carlotta found her voice, then. "What in God's name have you done to him and why? Are you fiends to behave so?"

The men gathered around Louis parted, and a thickset man in his thirties walked out to where he could look up at her. "Your pardon, mistress. I thought you had gone below."

"Answer me!" She clung to the railing and swayed with the motion of the *Princess*. "Who are you? You shall answer to Master Lenoir for this barbarity."

"I am Robert Nottingly, Mistress Harmon, placed in command of this ship by Master Lenoir who gave these orders that you have just unfortunately seen carried out." He turned to his men. "Put him in the boat and send it toward shore in our wake. No time is to be wasted."

Then the world did spin around Carlotta, for she knew that Austin considered Tanda's promise violated and this treatment of her brother was in full retaliation for that. Louis would not die, barring all complications, but a one-legged man in a land at war would be hard put to survive mentally if not physically. She remembered the pride with which Tanda had spoken of him, the way the dark girl had tried to protect them as best she could when killing the party would have been far the easier, and her stomach roiled in pain.

"How could Master Lenoir give such orders? You lie, for he was insensible when we came on board!"

"Your pardon, again, mistress. His wounds are being bound up, and the brandy restored him wonderfully. I think he is in no danger. These were the first orders he gave. Now, if you will excuse me, there is work to be done."

Carlotta looked out to sea as she fought her sickness and tried to shut out the moans of the unfortunate man. Then, for the first time, she became conscious of the movement of the ship. The land was already receding behind them, and Simon's ship seemed all the smaller. She gasped in horror, then ran swiftly toward Austin's cabin, her bare feet slapping on the rough boards of the deck.

One of the crew stood by the door and he stepped in her way as she reached for the handle. "No one may go in, mistress. Master Lenoir has been given a potion and soon he will sleep."

Carlotta raised her voice so that it might be heard clearly, not only in the cabin, but half over the ship. "I do not wonder that he needs a potion. Not only has he slaughtered a man who was totally at his mercy and never did him any harm, a man to whom his sworn word was given, but he has abandoned a man who saved not only my life but his and those of the crew twice over. Why are we leaving Haiti in this way?"

The sailor urged, "Mistress, you are overwrought. Please go and rest."

Then Carlotta lost all reason and temper as emotion swept her. The lack of knowledge as to whether Simon lived or died was the major part of her anguish, but her growing awareness of the degree of Austin's cruelty also contributed to her anguish. She rushed at the keeper of the sanctum, and he might have been Austin himself as she cried out, "Murderer, deserter, savage! I hope I lose your child! It would have been a monster!"

The door slammed back on its hinges and Austin, pale as his hair and leaning on a cane, was framed in it. His voice was husky with weariness but commanding still as he said, "She is overwrought after all she has endured. In such a state of mind she may do herself an injury. Put her in the little cabin, you know the one, until she comes to her senses."

"Aye, Master. Come, lady." He pulled at Carlotta's arm with a determined grip that drew her on.

Austin smiled maliciously. "Your concern for others is most

touching, my dear Carlotta. I suggest that you consider your own position, especially as regards handsome rescuers."

"Dreg." She spat the word at him and walked away with her captor, head high, the agony for her lost love only now just beginning.

CHAPTER TWENTY-SIX

City of the River

CARLOTTA slept, woke, and slept again. There were no nightmares in soft, velvet, peaceful darkness where the body stretched, relaxed, and turned over into cool sheets again. The nightmare was the waking to memory, remembering green mountains, valleys like slits below, friends betrayed, and a green-eyed man whispering "harlot" from a once tender mouth. She pulled the pillows about and willed herself into the long slide of oblivion as the swaying motion of the *Princess* sent her through the summer seas.

All too soon there came a time when her back ached and her head throbbed, when she turned and twisted in the haven of the bed and knew that it was haven no longer. She had a raging thirst and an even stronger hunger. Her active body yearned for exercise and the scent of the salt air in her nostrils. She sat up and inspected her skin closely. It was a faint golden color where the sun had burnished it; her arms and legs were scratched from the travels over rocks and in the woods, her feet were cut in places, but she seemed remarkably whole for all that she had undergone. She knew, too, that the child she carried was still safe.

Carlotta rose and went to the door of the cabin, the sheet wrapped well around her. The door gave easily to her touch but a sober, bearded man looked up from his seat beside it. She said, "I want food and drink and water for a bath. What day is this and where are we?" Her voice rasped from disuse as her head began to spin.

The man rose. "Instantly, mistress. We are three days out of Haiti and bound for New Orleans. You have rested long." He hurried away, leaving the door unguarded.

Carlotta went shakily back into the cabin and sank down in a soft chair near the bed. She examined her surroundings with the surprise that was becoming familiar to her where Austin was concerned. This was more in the manner of a sitting room than a ship's cabin. Three curtained portholes ranged along one side of the room. The bed was wide and soft, the

194

two chairs delicately made but still very comfortable. A carved table held books in French and Italian. An open trunk held brilliantly colored clothes, whether for male or female she could not tell. One of the strange misty tapestries Austin favored covered the other wall. The white curtains blew out a little, and fresh air filled the room. All in all, the arrangements for the master of the *Princess* bore the hand of a woman. Who, she speculated idly, could endure him? Or, like herself, had the woman no choice? She forced her mind away from the unbearable; in her present state of weakness it would only reduce her to tears.

The crewman returned with two others bringing all she had demanded. He handed her a note, then she was alone again. There was strong tea, bread, cheese, cold chicken, fresh melon of a sort that she did not know, and even a decanter of white wine. She did not unfold the paper until she had drunk long and deeply of the tea and devoured the wing and breast of the chicken. Then, while the steaming water cooled, she read Austin's brief words.

"I am glad to know that you are better after your ordeal. Rest and be at peace in these next weeks. We will talk when the mouth of the Mississippi River is reached. You will not be disturbed, I promise you that."

Relief surged over Carlotta as she realized just how much she had dreaded the confrontation with Austin. Weeks, he said. Nothing had to be faced now. She sank down in the water and made her mind a blank as she soaped her skin and hair, relaxing in the pleasure of being clean and in momentary freedom from fear.

As before when on the open sea, Carlotta found that a modicum of peace came to her in this special blue-green world where the sun was hot and fierce and the wind warm on her skin. The white sails of the ship bellied out before her as Carlotta sat for hours on end watching the ever-changing water. It seemed to her that if she did not mention Simon in her thoughts, if she pushed him far back in the recesses of her mind and did not permit him to enter, then by some strange charm he would still be alive in this world. Even if he did not love her he would still walk the earth with that arrogant tread, the green eyes brilliant with the delight he had taken in living. She wrenched her thoughts away as she felt the tears batter against closed eyelids. That way lay madness.

She lost count of the days as she paced the deck trying to

tire herself out so that she could sleep at night. Sometimes she was successful. When she was not she would practice the fencing exercises taught her in what now seemed another life. The stiffness left her body and she felt it grow supple again. The trunk had yielded several dresses which fit her closely enough, especially now that she could tell the narrow lines of her waist were beginning to shift. She tried to spell out some of the Italian in the books in the cabin and found that the discipline stilled her wandering mind.

One morning she went on deck to discover that the character of the water had changed. It was very green where the *Princess* floated but just beyond her it was brown. Curiously, the colors did not mingle but formed a definite line. Land was a dark smudge against the horizon on one side; on the other several sand bars lifted their humps into tiny islands. The ship moved very slowly but she crawled with activity, for all the crew were at their posts and watchful.

"It is the Mississippi, the great river of America. La Nouvelle Orleans lies in her curve." The quiet voice was full of pride as it spoke behind Carlotta.

She whirled to see the elegant figure of Austin, clad all in black, leaning on a black cane, the head of which was mother-of-pearl, his face shaded by a black hat with a curving white feather. He bowed politely before her. "I trust you are well this lovely morning? We must talk, you know."

Carlotta felt the familiar, frustrating fury rise in her at the sight of him. Betrayer, murderer, destroyer of friendship. All the words rose in her mind and she longed to fling them at him as she had done in those days just past. The frozen feeling, the strange detachment she had felt since they left Haiti, was gone just as the calm she had fought to instill in herself had vanished. Once more she was pulled and savaged by her emotions. The scenes in Haiti returned with renewed vigor, and Simon's laughing face now cold in death flashed before her. She clenched her fingers together hard and prepared to vent her anger. Release would be sweet indeed.

The wind blew up the side of Austin's hat just then, and she saw his eyes. They were glittering black holes that belied the smile on his lips. He had an air of waiting, a sick, anticipating hunger, that rose as a miasma. Carlotta knew then that he wanted her to lash out at him, that in some way such an act would free him to do as he truly wished with her and was somehow restrained from doing so long as a facade remained between them.

"Yes, my dear? You started to speak?" He leaned forward, those eager eyes blotting out the shimmering day, and in them Carlotta read the look of the hunter who has run his prey to earth and savors the moment, the long ecstasy of the kill.

She swayed a second and put a hand to her head. It took no effort to look white and exhausted for she felt that way. Her hand came away from her wet forehead where the blood seemed to hammer. It shook as she held it in front of her. She tried to speak but her mouth was dry and her voice rasped hard. Austin never took his eyes from her.

"Things get so hazy sometimes; they have done this ever since I went off by myself and the undead, or whatever they were, followed me. I was so frightened! I remember only a little of what happened just after we sailed away . . ." She let her words trail off and looked at Austin with worried eyes.

"But you will remember that you spoke savagely to me. You will recall your words, the names you called me." It was a flat statement, and the air between them thickened.

They were into the river proper now, the wide brown swath flowing around the *Princess* as she drove steadily upstream. Carlotta stared out at the swampy, rich earth now so plainly visible and tried to think what to say.

"I left your lover. I took vengeance for what he took from me and I punished the slave I bought. You are my property, too."

He meant to provoke her, that much was bitterly obvious. She stared at him and was horrified to see that the bulge of his tight breeches was now noticeably accentuated. He was enjoying himself with deadly intent.

Carlotta put a hand to her stomach and spoke as if he were not there. "The child remains with me but I have been nauseated of late and I do crave fresh things. That melon I had the first morning I could eat was so delicious. Where could it have been obtained?"

It was as if she had asked death for a glass of water. Austin drew back, and the sickening aura lifted a little. He moistened his full lips and said in a more normal tone, "We stopped at a tiny little island for an hour or so. One of my maps said there was a spring there, and we took on some of those melons that were growing wild along with the water. Are you all right?"

She turned a little from him and thought of some of the

things that she and Simon had done, what she would have liked for them to do had time permitted it, held her breath, and let the flush mount to her cheeks. "I am nauseated now but I need the fresh air. I fear that my attention strayed from what you were saying but I cannot hold back my illness any longer. Will you forgive me?"

She had reckoned truly. He was fastidious to a fault. He called to one of the men to fetch a basin and cloths as well as a warm cloak. She leaned limply against the rail and gave a heave or two, hoping as she did so that her stomach, always volatile, would not respond.

The sardonic voice floated above her, the tone normal for Austin as he said, "You may in truth carry my child; I must thank you for reminding me of my duty. I trust you will remember yours."

She turned back to him so that he might see her drawn face, watery eyes, and shaking hands, a condition not altogether feigned. The crewman was approaching with the necessary articles, which he set down a few feet away. "Fetch wine, man, and hurry." Austin snapped the words out, adjusted his hat, and hastened away.

Carlotta sat on the deck all that morning and into the afternoon and watched the marshes on both sides of the ship as she plied the muddy waters. Gulls cried above them and fish plopped close by. Sky and water seemed even closer here than they had on the sea. She breathed deeply of the air that seemed to teem with life—an odor of salt, draining earth, and fish— and gave thanks that she had been able to outwit Austin. He had wanted some excuse to savage her, perhaps even kill her; all her instincts told her that. Only her sudden pliant manner and the fact of the child had saved her. She would not make such a mistake again, for her life depended on her wits. Think of survival and consign Simon to memory, it was the only way. Carlotta was alive again now, the period of dullness and shock over. It was painful, but in fighting for her life she knew once more how dear living really was.

The *Princess* progressed slowly up the river, which, Carlotta learned not only from her readings about the American continent but from the day to day watching and listening to the shouts of the men, was placid and treacherous by turns. She never tired of the various sights that met her eyes, which were accustomed to the soft landscapes of England. The land rose as they progressed, strange birds flew low over the mud flats, huge warped trees hung with ghostly trails of gray were reflected back from the swamps in which they grew like sentinels. She often saw snakes sunning themselves on logs at the bank and, more than once, a dirty gray-black thing which appeared to be a log would open a toothy mouth and move ponderously toward the water. In the very early morning mist curled over water and land alike. At such times, Carlotta felt herself to be the only person in the world on board a ship of the lost.

Three mornings after her confrontation with Austin, she was wakened in the very early light by a tap on her door. One of the bearded crew members thrust a packet at her, mumbling as he did so, "Master wants you should wear these. Goin' to be to city by noon or before."

Carlotta unfolded the garments, noting that they were all unrelieved black—shoes, stockings, shift, petticoats, and dress. The bonnet had a long swathing veil of black, and her gloves were of fine leather. Now that she was roused, excitement took over and she dressed hurriedly. The mirror showed her face to be slightly rounded, color on her cheeks, amber eyes snapping. The dress might have been meant for proper mourning but it was finely made of lace and silk and rustled when she walked. It took little imagination to know that she would be presented to whatever part of New Orleans society she met as a bereaved victim of the new Napoleonic world.

She watched from the deck as they glided with the river past banks drifting in lush vegetation, flowering trees, and trees seemingly bent with the weight of their own leaves and moss, the branches rearing upward toward heaven itself. From time to time she caught glimpses at a distance of tall columns, templelike roofs, and crowned balconies. These, she assumed, were the great houses such as she had seen in Charleston; they would be the homes of the rich and powerful in this hot, damp land.

"I must ask that you go below, Carlotta. It would not be seemly for a young lady to be hanging about the deck when we arrive. The wharf is a rough place."

Austin wore black, even to his hat. She knew that he must wear it for his dead son, even were it not his personal preference. His manner was abstracted, with none of the baiting attitude of the days before. He looked her up and down and nodded with approval.

"You are growing fair. My choice was a wise one. Go into my cabin and draw one of the tapestries aside. You will be able to see our arrival in New Orleans from there. I trust I have your obedience in these things?"

The question was rhetorical but she answered, "I know that I have little choice, Austin, but I think it is time you took me fully into your confidence."

He laughed and turned away. "In time. In time." The mocking note was not lost on Carlotta as she went to obey him.

She stood at the wide porthole that must have been especially cut for Austin since it offered a view not only of the decks themselves but of the lower work area and was artfully concealed as well. Perhaps he had stood here many times and watched her as she paced or sat lost in reverie. The thought gave her chills.

The river spread wide now and barges, flatboats, small craft, and ocean going ships crowded it. The levee stretched along the waterfront, the barricade from the rising river, and it was crowded with ships, bustling with activity, men, and goods. Carlotta stared and wondered at such seeming confusion. Once Uncle Arnold had taken her to the Thames waterfront; it had offered much the same aura of excitement, but here the very hot air was permeated with it.

They rounded a final curve and she saw a cluster of buildings shining in the sun and stretching for what must have been miles. Even at this distance the twining pink flowers could be seen and smoke drifted on the late morning air. She heard the sounds of the river, the cries of the sailors, and felt the *Princess* slow into a drifting glide.

The door opened suddenly, and Austin strode in, fanning himself with his hat. "We dock in another half hour or so, then I will send for a carriage to take us to my city house." He crossed to the decanters and lifted one experimentally. "Will you drink a toast with me, my dear?"

Carlotta took her gaze from the crowded waterfront which now was a veritable river of boats in its own right. The *Princess* swayed back and forth as a large vessel so loaded with cotton that it almost sank in the water churned slowly by.

"I look forward to this city. I would be glad to drink with you." She came forward in a rustle of silken skirts to take the jeweled cup he offered her.

"To La Nouvelle Orleans! May our little venture prosper!"

"I drink to it!" Carlotta drank the smooth fluid that seemed to light her very being and give her a feeling of such elation as she had not had since Simon last touched her on the flowering beach in Haiti.

Too late she caught the familiar glitter in Austin's black eyes and threw the cup from her. The clatter as it hit the floor was the last thing she heard before darkness melted over her.

CHAPTER TWENTY-SEVEN

By the Seal of Holy Church

SHE swam in delicious languor, floated on rose petals, drifted in a blue-green sea, looked into green eyes that faded from her. Her mind was a thing apart from her body; it was trying to force the flesh to do something but it would not; there was danger but she could not move.

There was the sound of weeping, a man's deep voice, then someone was trying to pierce her body with a knife, several knives. Someone had some incense and was speaking sonorous Latin, no, it was heavily accented French. The blue-green sea was rolling in on a curving beach, and she heard her own voice crying "Simon, Simon!" Then mist rose up, drifted, and faded.

"The fever is leaving her. I swear she is cooler today!" The voice was soft with the hint of Ireland in it. "Try the broth, mistress. Open your mouth just a little."

Carlotta came back to the world that comprised at that moment an anxious wrinkled face in which brilliant blue eyes were set. Twigs of gray hair protruded from a lacy cap set awry. Her voice refused to work at first, then she forced the words past the constricture in her throat. "Who? Where?"

The blue eyes widened as the woman turned to someone in the background. "Tell the Master she is awake. Hurry."

"Who are you?" Carlotta twisted a little on the soft pillows, and the room spun before her eyes.

"Bettina, Lady. Your housekeeper and Master Austin's. Will you drink the broth for me? You have been most ill." She put a cup to Carlotta's lips and smiled with satisfaction as the girl drank. "There now, that's much better." She arranged the pillows and lifted her up on them.

Carlotta stared about with wondering eyes. The bed in which she lay was canopied in drifts of silk. Rose silk hangings were at the windows, and vases of that flower lent a subtle perfume to the room. Several delicate chairs and a finely polished table were a small distance away, and a gauzy rug lay on the polished floor.

"I have been ill?"

"Aye, Mistress Lenoir, these ten days. The strain of the voyage and your recent sorrow gave you the fever, not praised be God, the yellow fever. But you are better now and must look forward to the child. God's own blessing that is, for you and the Master both, what with his son so recently dead and all." The housekeeper tugged at her cap and eyed Carlotta carefully.

Carlotta heard only the first few words as the world swung once more before her dizzy eyes. Then, as the woman talked on, some semblance of calm came to her swirling brain. She put a hand to her head. "My memory is so distorted. I remember very little. This is New Orleans, is it not?" Surely the woman would talk on and reveal some of the gaps that she, Carlotta, could not fill.

"That will be all, Bettina. Go and fetch more broth for madame. She must not wear herself out with talking." Austin stood just inside the doorway. He was frowning slightly but his eyes were brilliant. His attire was impeccable as always. "My dear, you are truly better. I was so worried about you." His voice softened as he came to kneel at her side on the wide bed.

Carlotta wondered with a faint sickness just how many times in the past few months she had faced this man and waited for him to reveal the future to her. Once she would have railed out or tried to beat him at his own baiting but that was before she had known the perfidy of which he was capable.

"What did you put in the wine?" Her own voice was cool; the broth had given her strength.

He rose from the bed, paced twice around the room, and came back to stare down at her. "You have had a fever from which you are recovering. You are the frail young Mistress Lenoir in the early stages of pregnancy. We both have suffered great losses, your mother recently dead after fleeing from the armies of Napoleon and you consigned to my care. There was a swift romance, we were wed in England, and we decided to come here. My business in New Orleans will take about a month, after that we go up the river to my plantation at Natchez."

Carlotta remembered the Latin and the incense as her flesh crawled. She sat up suddenly. "Help me to the chair. I am no invalid." He picked up sheet, pillow, and herself, depositing them all in the most comfortable chair. "What about your scheme? What about your plan for power, that for which you long so eagerly and for which you will apparently do anything?"

He pulled aside one of the curtains and let the blazing day enter. She saw swaying flowers in a wash of red and gold as they mingled with green branches in the wind. His air of triumph was almost a smirk as he put both hands on his hips and faced her. "You will do as you are told. You will make yourself presentable to any guests we may have and will conduct yourself as my wife."

"But I am not!"

"I thought you might make difficulties, especially after your behavior in Haiti. The *Princess* and all her crew sailed for South America on the night tide; they could say nothing of our activities. The drugged wine made it possible to convey you here, have your pregnancy confirmed by a woman skilled in these matters, and yet make you act just a bit deranged." He held up an admonitory hand before the speechless girl. "Of course, we needed to have been wed earlier. I am passing rich, and Holy Church has her needs. The words were spoken, all perfectly binding unto death—whose is not spelled out—and my contribution was made to those who came to solace my dear wife in her hour of pain and loss."

Carlotta laughed, the sound light and silvery in the lovely room; her eyes met those of Austin squarely. He, for once, was taken for a loss, though his face was unmoving as he looked at her. "You went to a great deal of trouble; I was already acquiescent. I fail to see what has been gained by such subterfuge." She could only hope that her face did not reveal the disgust and horror that she felt. He had taken his own way to determine to his satisfaction that she was truly to have a child, and he had showed her that it was very easy to apply any type of drug or herb to her food or wine. She remembered the undead of Haiti and knew that he was not past rendering her so.

He smiled, a slow, cruel smile. "All that matters is that I considered it necessary. That is sufficient for your needs. Remember that wives are easily come by. My son will be born in wedlock. Guard yourself, Carlotta." He walked easily to the door and opened it before he turned casually back to her as if in afterthought. "One of my men saw your lover fall, while looking through his spyglass. His head was split by the blow of a club. Pity, he was quite handsome. Did you not find him so?"

It took all the courage Carlotta would possess in this life to look the archfiend in the face and smile vaguely as she said, "I have told you that so much of what happened is a blur. Perhaps I should rest and have no more upsets. We do not want your child to be born with no nose or arms, do we?"

His fair skin suffused with red, and the black eyes were pits of fury. "I remember long. Think on that when you are rid of your burden." The door slammed so hard that it reverberated on the hinges.

Carlotta knew then what it was to be beyond tears. As she had not wept on the ship for Simon so she did not weep now. She did not know whether or not Austin could be believed but she did know that he was coming to hate her. Dead or alive, Simon was beyond her now, and she had to think of her own survival.

The next few days passed in comparative calm. Austin did not come near her again but old Bettina was in near constant attendance, and Carlotta found that she was growing quite fond of her. At times the girl was conscious of a depression so profound that she thought it would not matter if she lived or died. She would waken in the bright mornings to find that her pillows were drenched, she limp and exhausted. Then she knew that if she did not weep for Simon in the light of day, she more than did so at night. Bettina grew worried and wanted to tell Austin but ceased her protestations at Carlotta's pleading that it was but her condition. Her condition, Carlotta found, was the true safeguard, and with it she began to lay the groundwork for her own safety.

She spent much of her time in the patio which lay to the back of the house. Here roses climbed in scented profusion, honeysuckle lifted in a trained tangle over the walls, other flowers were in ordered beds, and a fountain sparkled in the brilliant sun. A small stream ran through the patio on one side, and the banks were lined with moss. Purple flowers opened here morning and early evening. She was sitting on one of the benches conveniently scattered about when one of the young black maids came to her in the afternoon just before the universal nap.

"Your pardon, mistress. Master Lenoir asks that you attend him this evening after dinner in the long parlor. He says it will take very little time and hopes that you will feel well enough."

Carlotta pulled the skirts of her white dress back and rose. The command was clear. One way or another Austin would have her there. "I shall be happy to obey my husband in all things. Be sure that you repeat my words exactly."

The little maid's eyes grew big. Carlotta read awe in them and knew that Austin was greatly feared in this house.

At nine o'clock that evening she stood ready in a flowing gown of amber silk shot with green that moved when she did. The waist was high under her breasts and the sleeves were full, yet falling back to show her rounded arms. Her bosom was demurely draped in pale lace and a shawl of the same color lay over her shoulders. Her hair was gathered in curls high on her head, and little wisps drifted on her neck. Long green earrings were in her ears, and a pearl necklace glowed at her throat. The mirror told her that she was beautiful. The shadows under her eyes enhanced the delicacy of her face and made her dark brows appear winged.

Bettina cried, "Mistress Carlotta, you are lovely. The Master will be so pleased!" Her blue eyes were open with admiration as she patted the girl's shoulder.

Carlotta had tried in the past few days to get some information about the past and Austin from the old woman but her queries were brushed aside with the comment that she must not excite herself, thus she simply murmured, "Thank you," in a cool voice and walked on.

The room called the long parlor was both library and sitting area and ran the length of the downstairs house. It had floor-length windows which overlooked an expanse of lawn and trees. Candles flickered now over the polished furniture and leather-bound volumes, casting shadows on the rose carpet. A group of gentlemen in earnest conference with Austin looked up as she entered. He strode toward her, his smile welcoming even as his eyes warned.

"My dear, these are my closest friends." He named them so swiftly that she could not catch all the names, even though her ear was usually quick for such. There were some ten or twelve present; all were older than he by at least fifteen years. "Gentlemen, my wife, Carlotta."

"Carlotta? Carlotta? What sort of name is that for a good Frenchman's wife? For my part I shall call you Charlotte, as is proper!" The man who spoke had a shock of white hair and a small dumpy body. His hands were palsied with age and dotted with brown spots but his voice was resonant, his manner assured. He was easily eighty.

Carlotta remembered the days when her first name was all

that she had, now they wanted to take that away from her as well. Was she so far removed from the waif who had defended her accent in front of the village children? "Monsieur Rodane, I beg to correct you. My name is Carlotta and no other; I answer to that only. It is mine own, and I ask that you give me the courtesy that I would accord to you without thinking twice."

She heard Austin's indrawn breath as he stood beside her and felt his fingers burn on her arm as he squeezed it. She guessed then that the old man was important to his scheme but how could she know? He wore a simple brown suit, and his shoes were scuffed. She would not ask pardon for that small thing which was her right.

Monsieur Rodane glared at her over the tops of the spectacles that he ostentatiously withdrew from a capacious pocket. She met his gaze steadily, well aware by now that no one else dared to interfere. It was so quiet that she could hear a dog barking far away and the quickly shushed laugh of a slave on his way to the quarters at the back of the house. He sniffed loudly, peered at her again, and his manner changed abruptly.

"Come sit with me, Carlotta, and forgive an old man's rudeness that I not only wanted to rename you but now call you by your first name." He smiled at her, and she saw the ghost of long ago charm in the cratered face.

She, too, smiled, forcing all the brilliance into it that she could. A flicker of what might have been pain crossed his face and then was gone. "I am honored, sir." She held out her slender hand from which the brown had not yet faded and he took it. Austin relinquished her arm and the others relaxed almost palpably.

He bore her away to a secluded corner and began to ply her with questions about England and France, the mother for whom she was supposedly in mourning, the voyage, her thoughts about America. She was barely given time to formulate a polite answer to one before another took its place. Austin moved closer, and she knew that he could hear every word. It was not her answers the old man wanted, that much soon became obvious, for he watched her face as he slipped swiftly into Spanish at one point and then again into English rather than the French that was the language of New Orleans.

"I do not understand you, sir...." It was not true; she understood some few words even in his strange accent. Something about roads and travel. But in the quiet room another thing was happening. The nightmare was rising again, coming in the midst of the company and the prosaic candlelight.

Monsieur Rodane had taken a flashing jewel from his pocket and began to move it back and forth in slow movements. Carlotta found her gaze drawn to it and wrenched her eyes away, but they went immediately to the branched candlestick that a softly moving slave had just brought in. The movements of the nightmare flickered against the backdrop of her mind even as she sat very still, unaware that her hands had begun to shake and her lips to shape words.

"That will be quite enough! She has endured far more than she should be expected to for one so recently ill. Carlotta, it is all right." She felt Austin's hands on her shoulders and the relief from the intrusion of his body between the flickering lights and the rising fear of the nightmare. The longing for sleep burned her eyelids, and she wanted to tumble down into the release of oblivion.

"No. I want to know what he is doing and what is going on here." She pushed Austin away and rose to confront the old man who was smiling to himself as he fumbled for his spectacles. The voices and the tumult of the others rose in the background but faded as he lifted his head. Plainly this was a man used to command.

He said mildly, "Austin has said there is much you do not remember. I have found that we forget nothing, in reality. It is all there in the mind somewhere. My studies have borne this out. I have some small knowledge of medicine. Even more of history." He faced Austin, and the whole company seemed to feel the tension between the two men. "I have listened and I have observed as you requested. My advice is this: Take your young wife and rejoice in the new life you have the opportunity to make. New Orleans is large enough to accommodate French, Spanish, and the Americans whom you regard as upstart. Let be."

"You will not use your influence to assist us? But it is the chance to have our own land, to wield unlimited power." Austin's voice rose, and his neck cords jumped.

"That is correct. But I will not bespeak it either. Now I must go home. My granddaughter does not like for me to be out this late." He began to search about for the coat he already wore.

One of the other men, a portly gentleman in his late fifties, cast a despairing look at Austin and came forward to whisper

208

urgently in Monsieur Rodane's ear. The old man shook his head as a bull might and plowed toward the door. Carlotta saw her chance and took it.

Moving swiftly across the rug, she stepped to his side and said clearly. "Sir, you have intrigued me this night, and, while I appreciate your weariness, I would like to call upon you and your household within the next few days."

He looked at her out of shrewd brown eyes. "I am too old for subterfuge, madame. My decision is made. I will not espouse your husband's cause."

Carlotta felt Austin's anger as a palpable thing at her back, and the others whispered among themselves, but she said, "You know much of the things I would remember; it is for that that I ask. In my own right as a person."

His laughter was delighted. "I will expect you in three days time, dear lady, but you will be forbidden to speak of Austin's venture. Is that agreeable?"

"Entirely." She met Austin's eyes then, and the crossed steel rang between the adversaries.

CHAPTER TWENTY-EIGHT

The Blood of France

CARLOTTA smoothed the gray dress over her knees and lifted the fan to her flushed face. Bettina sat opposite her in the carriage, plying her own fan with vigor. They heard the cries of the street vendors as they extolled the value of their wares. The carriage lurched as one wheel went into a hole created by the downpour of yesterday, and the driver managed one lush epithet before remembering the ladies he carried.

Bettina kept a sharp eye on Carlotta, for she had protested this journey in the blazing afternoon heat, saying that no one called at such an hour and the mistress was not yet well enough to venture out. Now she said sharply, "Decent folk rest this time of day. What can Master Lenoir be thinking of, to let you go this way?"

Carlotta lifted an eyebrow but said nothing. She could have told Bettina that Austin had wanted to say a great deal; in fact he had started to do so when he faced her in the long parlor that night after the guests had taken hurried leave. Then the demons had glittered again in his eyes and the pulses in his temples hammered. He was more than a little mad, she suspected.

"How dare you speak so to my guest? This plan is for your benefit, too, you little . . ." He had paused to gulp a brandy.

"Austin, the man is old and needs only to be appealed to properly. I doubt he will be so adamant after my visit, and how can you blame me for wanting to unlock the doors of memory? He will think it strange if I do not come."

The strange light was in Austin's face again as he looked at her waistline, but he said merely, "I know, for you planned it thus. Do not push me too far, Carlotta, the world is full of women."

She had not seen him since and had been thankful for it. No obstacles had been put in her path, though Bettina did not cease to grumble. The nightmare had come with renewed intensity every night since then, leaving her pale and exhausted to face the day. She had learned from Bettina, who loved to gossip that Monsieur Rodane was fully as old as he looked; that he was legendary in New Orleans not only for his wealth but for the rumors of royal blood which he never denied, a strong knowledge of statecraft, and, some said, witchcraft; and that he had been friends with a succession of high-ranking Spanish officials as well as the French. A man of parts. His two sons had died within days of each other, one of fever, the other in a duel. His granddaughter, Zulina, was twenty-five, bookish, and strange. Suitors were not encouraged.

Carlotta thought of these things as she stood in the anteroom of the tall yellow house which was about forty minutes' rapid drive from Austin's own town house. She thought that his was grander, but here things melted together in a welcoming air that did not call attention to themselves. Flowers were everywhere, and she heard the sound of singing, an old French ballad, in the distance.

"Mistress Lenoir, welcome to our house." Monsieur Rodane, looking smaller and more frail than he had the night she met him, was advancing over the polished floor to greet her. He introduced the granddaughter, a pale young woman with black hair drawn tightly back in a knot, who smiled faintly and retreated with Bettina, murmuring about tea.

Monsieur Rodane led the way into his study, which was in incredible disorder with books and papers tossed everywhere. He sank into a chair and smiled at Carlotta. "Well, my dear? How can I help you?"

She sat down but almost immediately stood up and began to pace, her skirts whispering about her feet. "Sir, I do not know how to ask, so forgive me if I am rude. I had the feeling the other night that you knew things about me that I do not know myself, that you turned away from my husband's plans in part because of that. Am I correct?" She clasped her gloved hands together and looked at him, aghast at her own temerity.

He did not recoil from her bluntness nor did he refuse to hear more as she was half afraid he might. "Austin Lenoir is a secretive man who is little known in this city for all that he owns property. He lives here rarely and can command the attention of those Creoles who hate the American intrusion. I doubt not that his plan will find favor with them. Go back to him and say that. I do not admire the sort of mind that sends a man's wife to persuade and cozen an old man."

"You mistake me, sir." Her voice rang sharp in the room.

She longed to blurt out her feelings about Austin but did not dare. Right now all that mattered was the nightmare and her strange feeling that this man knew about it. "You have knowledge of memory and the things forgotten. Listen." She sank to the dusty floor before him and placed both hands on the arm of his chair. The brilliant sun threw her face into relief, and as he stared at her she saw the same look that had been on Sir Reginald's face and that of Austin. It was recognition. "Have you seen me before, Monsieur Rodane?" She spoke the words so slowly that they seemed to drag out.

"Not you, but one like you. Once long ago and then again only a few years previously. But that will wait. Tell me what you must."

So once again Carlotta relived the nightmare in the light of day as she spoke of the fresh knowledge that had come to her in Haiti and how she was almost certain that she could see the face of her pursuer, of her belief that it was no random thing bred of the Revolution's destruction of the aristocracy, but a planned murder. "Woman's fancy it may seem to you, and perhaps it is, but Austin has spoken of a resemblance that has been noted by others. Perhaps what happened has something to do with that. I saw that same look in your face just now."

Monsieur Rodane said, "It is recollections like yours that make me realize just how old I am. It seems only days ago that I visited friends in France in those years just before Louis began to concern himself less with his women and more with his soul. He would come among us, laughing, urging us to call him Louis and becoming savage when we tried to give him the respect due the King of France." He looked at her slyly. "I trust that you keep your maidenly sensibilities for the drawing room, my dear. I have no time for such pother."

She drew off her gloves, finding with surprise that they were soaking wet. It was a shock to realize that he meant not the king who had been guillotined in 1793, but his grandfather, Louis XV. The corridors of time yawned at her, and she shivered even in the heat.

"I have not always lived in drawing rooms." Her laugh was rueful, and she did not notice that he cocked his head as if listening to a familiar note.

He nodded and continued as if savoring the recollections of more lusty days. He chuckled a little, his voice suddenly reedy. "Everyone knows about the mistresses; the children, king's bastards, are something else. Male children have such great value in this strange world of ours. Louis found places for all his illegitimate issues and was fond of them, showing his paternity in gifts, estates, and appointments. I met one bright young lad who spoke boldly to me of the princess he would one day wed, saying that she would be very beautiful and rich. He was a handsome boy on whom his father doted. I remember thinking that it was a great pity such as he could not sit on the throne of France—history might have been so different."

Carlotta shifted restlessly as she wondered what a long ago visit to France had to do with reality now.

"I kept in touch with my friends there, and long years later I learned that that boyish wish was almost gratified. Our lad made a trip to Spain where he fell passionately in love with one of the obscure connections of the house of Bourbon-Spain. Good blood and no wealth. The girl was to be given to Parma or Sicily. You can imagine the fuss when they tried to run away together. The King of France himself, poor young Louis, intervened secretly, and they were allowed to live in the south of the kingdom and enjoined never to reveal their identities. There was much ill feeling over it at the time, and Spain was greatly insulted."

Carlotta began to get the drift of the conversation and stared at him with wonder in her eyes.

"Years later I welcomed some Frenchmen to New Orleans. One of them, a most noble lord, had a way of holding his head, casting a side glance, a certain movement of the fingertips, all done in a simultaneous gesture that had an air of assurance which was all the more remarkable for being unselfconscious. A small thing, you say. Possibly, but some things stand out in the memory."

"But, what . . . ?"

He held up his hand and savored the moment, the pleasure of the storyteller. Those gentlemen were the brothers of the dead King of France, the eldest of whom will one day, God willing, sit on that throne. You have that manner of which I spoke, and I have often seen the King, Louis XV, do the same."

"You are a monarchist!" She breathed the words out, thinking as soon as they were uttered that they were ridiculous, but the oppressive feeling in her chest was relieved by speech.

"Is that so strange? The greatest of the Greek thinkers thought little enough of democracy. The Americans have most of the continent now, but they do not practice that virtue overmuch. The rich and powerful gentlemen rule, do they not?"

Carlotta saw that he was about to wander off into speculation and spoke boldly. "Are you actually saying that on the basis of a few casually remembered gestures and a romantic tale there might be some connection to me?"

"It is a fascinating tale, is it not? I do know many things came out of the Revolution that are just as fantastic, many personal scores were settled. Who knows?" He shrugged, and she saw that he was losing interest after the manner of the very old. "You will feel better for all this, but I would advise you to dissuade Austin from his scheme if you can." He smiled faintly.

"I do not have the power." She rose and reached for her hat. A fruitless journey, after all, but what had she expected from him? She would tell Austin that she had not been totally unsuccessful; he probably would not press her, especially if she began to be ill from the child.

There was a heavy step in the doorway as the door was flung back to admit a huge black woman wearing a high turban and holding a laden tray in both hands. The slanting sun came through the windows to make dust-moted fire of the darkness beyond her. Zulina, a shadowy figure, stood just behind her, dwarfed and somehow shrunken.

Carlotta felt her throat close up and her legs begin to shake. Monsieur Rodane looked at her face quickly, then held up one hand to stay their entrance and was instantly obeyed.

Carlotta knew where she was and that there was no menace in a servant and granddaughter of the house, but she seemed to be caught in a stillness having nothing to do with time. The meadow and the castle of her nightmare's latest revelation spun out before her as it had done in the forest in Haiti. She saw the dark woman with the decapitated body of the man at her feet and heard the cries of "Run! Run!" She saw the child run, felt the pumping breath in the small struggling body, and knew the terror of years.

"Mistress Lenoir! Mistress!" Zulina rushed forward but was restrained by her grandfather.

Carlotta saw the two scenes simultaneously and felt with the emotions of both times, but her tongue was locked in her mouth and she could not move. Now the dark man walked slowly forward as he waved a hand to his followers in the background. The shivering woman faced him but her face was obscured. For the first time Carlotta saw the face of the murderer. He was tall with red hair, muscular shoulders, and a savage face. His long fingers gripped the dagger hungrily, and there was a relishing smile on his thin lips. Her scream split the air, shattering the past-present vision. She was suffocating; her fingers jerked at her throat.

"Get wine! Hurry!" Monsieur Rodane snapped out the order and the servant put down the tray to obey. Zulina, her own face flushed, came to Carlotta and urged her toward a chair.

The wine proved to be brandy but the fiery liquid gave throat and feelings back to her. She looked at the anxious faces around her and tried to smile. "I'm sorry. It just came on me. I felt so dizzy; I can't think what makes me feel this way sometimes." She began to shudder and could not stop, although the room was now quite hot in the afternoon sun.

"What did you see? Tell me." Monsieur Rodane edged closer to her, and she smelled the musty odor of him despite a faintly cloying scent of musk.

As she stared into the eager eyes, she knew what she should have known from the first. Sickness roared in her stomach and she shivered again. Zulina handed her a cloak and she wrapped it gratefully around her shoulders. She knew that she must dissemble and that she was becoming adept at it. "It was just the nightmare all over again. I am so weak from recalling it so much in one day. Do you think I might prevail upon your hospitality to lie down for just a bit?"

He ignored her request and fixed hard eyes on her. "You must have seen something different this time. Your face was bleached white, your eyes turned back. Surely it cannot affect you this way each time?" His veined hand, the ridges on it high, pushed at the edges of the chair.

She stood up, swayed, and counted on Zulina to come closer. Leaning on the other girl's shoulder, she said, "It was always the same. I remembered nothing more. I should not have asked for your help, kind though you were to give it. Perhaps when I am stronger things will be different."

Suspicion clouded his face but he spoke mildly. "You may rest in yonder sitting room. Take your ease, and when you are better I will order my most comfortable carriage to convey you safely home. Austin will not think kindly of me if you return in such a condition. Please feel free to come to me at any time. I can tell you many tales of France as she was." His mouth twisted in the smile she once would have thought gentle and now knew for the cynicism it was.

"You are most kind." She, too, could play the waiting game.

The house was very quiet as Carlotta lay on the comfortable, though ornate, bed and breathed deeply to restore calm to herself. Her dress lay across a chair, her petticoats on another. The restorative brandy was near at hand. She had refused to have anyone near her, saying that she must be alone at such times. Minutes passed and she could hear nothing. It was not safe, she knew that, but the chance had to be taken.

Clad only in her shift and light cloak, Carlotta crept to the door and peered down the dim hall. No one was in sight. A huge ornamental chair stood near the door of the study where Monsieur Rodane had welcomed her. It was but the movement of a second to dash behind it and sink down into the dusty shadows. She put a finger to her nose to keep from sneezing and thanked all the gods that the door remained open.

". . . friendly, Zulina. It is the next step. She remembers more than she says, I am certain of it. Cultivate her, get her to confide in you."

The assured voice which answered him was not Zulina as Carlotta had supposed her to be. This was a conspirator. "I will do as you wish, Grandfather, but how can it matter to our plans if she does or does not recall this event of her extreme youth?"

Monsieur Rodane sighed. "Napoleon will be unseated one day. Such as he do not last; history has shown that. When the King comes truly into his own, how will he take the fact that a member of the royal family, on whatever side of the blanket, was deliberately slain and for a profit, as appears likely? It would be well to have the particulars firmly in hand, especially if Austin's scheme succeeds and the wench is really of royal blood. France triumphant both here and in Europe! Austin and I work well together, though mine is the greater vision. The girl dislikes him, and we can use that." He laughed softly and Zulina joined him.

"Austin Lenoir is a man of great perception, Grandfather. I admire you both."

"Eh, you would not want to be wed to that one. He is dangerous but very clever. Each of us has the other's measure. But, look you, did the girl not respond well to my pose?"

"I drink to you, sir." They laughed together once more.

It was perhaps thirty minutes later when the slave who came to waken Carlotta found her staring at the ceiling where cherubs

216

romped. It was the same woman who had stared at her so when nightmare and day merged. Now she looked into the girl's face and recoiled in spite of herself.

"What is the matter? Have I suddenly grown two heads or three arms?" Carlotta spoke more sharply than she had intended because of the woman's actions.

"No'm. You breedin' and ought to be careful." She did not come close to Carlotta.

Carlotta pushed back irritation. Everyone knew her business and state of health. Dear God, if there were only one friend she could trust! Such feelings were what Austin was counting on, she knew.

The slave edged toward the door, then turned back to Carlotta and whispered, "The shadow's on you, mistress. Samedi's, beware."

The darkness of the Haitian night drifted in the sunny bedroom. "Why do you warn me?"

"You served Damballah's priestess. We know. Be careful." She slipped out, a large wraith in the dimness of the long hall.

Carlotta stood very still. Samedi was the god of death here as well as in Haiti. For whom did he come?

CHAPTER TWENTY-NINE

By All the Furies

"I WANT to go for a few days, a week or more. I am troubled, I do not sleep well, and when I do, I dream. You will know the sort." Carlotta paced up and down in the patio, Austin moving as she did.

He said, "What is this sudden impulse toward religion, my dear? What you need is to go about more. Shop, spend my money, buy jewels; it will look well. Zulina has called several times and you are always resting or indisposed. Make friends with her. I need her grandfather's support. Besides, it will do you good to have a woman to chat with, especially at such a time."

"My soul is troubled. Must I keep saying it? Let me go to the convent of the Ursulines. None will think it strange." She let her voice trail away as if in weariness. Her fingers lifted the trailing mass of hair, as yet undressed. "Is the tale told me by Monsieur Rodane true? Did I see my parents murdered as he suggests? Have you known all along?"

His aplomb was unshaken as he guided her into the shade of a flowering tree. Malice flickered briefly and was gone as he said, "The facts are basically true if one accepts the premise. The man who may have been your father was called Louis, surname Laurent. His wife was Carlotta. They were reported killed by an uprising against the nobility in the area where they lived. A son was stillborn earlier in that year. The daughter, a child of seven or eight, vanished at their deaths. It is this information that we will use to rally the cause of royalty. I knew almost for certain in Charleston, and Charles investigated as much as he could both then and after we left. It is a gamble, but the details of your nightmare are close enough, certainly. It may or may not be. The tale will gain us followers at any rate."

"But I would know the truth of my parentage! Of what happened and why!" Her palms were wet; she knew that she must not press him too far.

"What does it matter? We have a splendid coincidence." He

218

regarded the head of the cane he always carried now. His voice altered slightly and Carlotta knew that it did matter, that he and Monsieur Rodane had a strange bargain to try to get knowledge from her that she did not have but they thought she did. "Go to the convent if you must, but when you return I expect you to conduct yourself in a seemly manner with my friends. Is that understood?"

"Yes, of course." She fought to hide the singing elation in her heart. Getting out of the house, out of his view, was the first step.

The convent of the Ursulines reared old and sturdy against the brilliant sky as Carlotta, demure in gray bonnet and gown, stepped down from the carriage into the dusty street where Bettina waited. The girl breathed a sigh of relief as they walked into the walled garden where shrubs of all sorts were carefully tended. The steep tiled roof and cypress blinds melted into the plaster of the walls, and the atmosphere was one of peace.

In the coolness of the wide entrance an ageless nun was waiting, her habit mingling with the shadows. She lifted a slender hand in welcome and said, "Madame Lenoir, you are our honored guest for as long as you like."

"Thank you." Carlotta murmured the words and bent her head, suddenly in awe of this place.

It was her intention, as soon as she was settled, to seek out the Reverend Mother herself and confide the whole matter to her, asking the protection of the Holy Church. If persuasion were needed, she would tell of the voodoo rites and the peril of her soul. She had known as never before in these last days that Austin was more and more in the grip of his scheme and would stop at nothing to attain it. In some strange way, Carlotta felt as if she had come to a turning in her life and that only she could make the necessary choices now. But, as it had ever been, that kind of choice came down to marriage or the cloister and she was wed, however fearfully, to a man who gave nothing. She sighed inwardly as she bade Bettina farewell and followed the silent nun up the curving staircase, down a wide corridor, and into a tiny room that reminded her of the first cabin she had occupied on the *Princess*.

In the next two days she knelt in the church, walked in the enclosed garden, exchanged ritual words with the nuns who were well used to ladies seeking peace of soul here, and read of the first days of the convent with its long history of service as school, church, and cloister. At the end of that time, she put her request to Sister Matilda who had welcomed her, couching it in the terms that seemed best to fit this atmosphere.

"I am greatly troubled in matters both spiritual and temporal; there is no redress in prayer."

The nun spoke almost abstractedly. "I suggest yet more prayer and meditation, daughter. Our God comes not easily to some but the search is well worth the battle." Carlotta started to speak but the staying hand rose. "The Reverend Mother is much occupied these days for the world intrudes upon us. We have ever been part of this city, our hands of help and healing busy where needed, but now . . . go and pray as I will for you."

Carlotta reflected in the first flush of annoyance that it would take more than prayer to free herself from Austin Lenoir, but she smiled and thanked the sister. "I will ask again in several days, if this persists." She did not add that she knew it would.

That afternoon the peace of the convent was shattered by much rushing to and fro as flowers were gathered, food was prepared—with delicious scents curling out into the garden where Carlotta sat under a flowering bush with a book in her hand—the staircase was polished, and the floors were cleaned until they were satiny in the light. A passing nun told her that the Bishop of New Orleans was coming late that night for a conference of great import with Reverend Mother and several of those closest to her. The visit had come as a surprise, the message having only arrived that morning, and they were bidden to discretion.

That discretion was being observed, for when Carlotta went up to her room an hour later she found a message on her bed. It read simply, "Please remain in your room tonight. Food and drink will be brought to you. Our community meets and the presence of any of the laity would not be suitable." She was mildly curious; perhaps the Bishop did not visit often and was now bringing new pronouncements with him. She sank down on the narrow bed and began to thumb through the book she had brought up with her, an illuminating tome about martyrs, which had the salutory effect of putting her to sleep almost instantly.

She woke with a start. The face of the murderer had come before her in her half dream and then had faded just as quickly. The familiar terror had come and gone. Was it possible that that particular terror was fading from her life? She could only hope that this was true. She stirred uneasily as her stomach grew queasy. The little room was hot and stuffy; the tiny window was considered a luxury, but it was set high in the wall and offered no escape from the sultry afternoon. She debated. The message had stated night not daylight. What harm could a turn in the garden do now? She rose, smoothed down the white dress, one of several simple things she had brought to wear here, pulled her cloak, a pale gray cloth, very light, over her shoulders, and slipped quietly out into the hall, down the staircase, and out the side door. There was no other sound.

It was later than it had appeared in her room. Shadows were drifting long and the dusk had a smoky quality. She went to her favorite spot, a small bench near the corner of the wall where roses tumbled down in red and white profusion to mingle with the stand of oleanders. The scents mingled and drifted on the breeze. Carlotta was painfully reminded of the time that she and Simon had loved so passionately beside the waterfall in Haiti, and she wondered if she should pray for the soul that had passed. Then her soft lips curved up as the heretical thought came that perhaps her memory of their passion was enough; surely the poets would have it so.

A thin sliver of moon rose, and a little cloud moved across it. The branches over her head swayed in the wind as the odors of summer, cut grass, and roses, seemed to permeate her being. From the distance she heard the voices of the nuns raised in plainsong and knew that she should retire to her room as commanded but could not bring herself to trade this beauty for the stuffiness there. Decision made, she settled back on the bench and let her thoughts go where they would, to Simon and the happy days of their relationship and what might have been had they been other than they were. Would the girl in New York weep for him or would she shrug and seek another?

"My love, my fair one . . . him whom my soul loveth." She whispered Solomon's words with her own passion and half expected to see Simon striding over the grass toward her. She felt her breasts grow heavy, the nipples rise, and her palms dampen. Would it be this way all her days on a summer evening when roses bloomed and the wind grew soft? She shut her eyes against the picture of his face and saw him in her mind instead, silver-gilt hair lifting over his forehead, bronzed face alight with laughter. Tears dripped out from her lids and ran down her face. She pushed the hood of her cloak back, put her head in her hands, and let the pain come as it would.

The voice, warm and concerned, spoke from her left. "Lady,

lady, why do you weep in a walled garden amid such beauty? Are you real or fading dream or vision?"

"Simon!" She jerked her head up and stared blindly into the last vestiges of twilight at the caped figure standing near the largest of the oleanders.

"Ah, no, alas." The tone was now one of real alarm. "Forgive me that I have intruded on your privacy. I was bemused or I would not have spoken as I did."

Carlotta knew only that he was not Simon and that she had been discovered in disobedience to these sisters who had offered her relief from Austin. But what was a man doing in this secluded place? She said, "I fear that it is I who intrude for I am a guest in this house of God."

He said softly, "I am a guest in this city which was kind enough to welcome me with warmth. We share, then." He came into the full light of the rising moon and she saw that he was about Austin's age, lean and well built, simply clad in black and wearing a white shirt. His voice was deep and resonant, his hands long and slim. They two might have been the only persons in the world, so intently did he pay heed to her. The dark, direct gaze was disconcerting, however, and she averted her eyes.

A sleepy bird chirped near them and was answered by another. A carriage rattled in the distance and a dog howled, as if in protest. The sweet, pungent odor of crushed grass came to Carlotta again, and she heard the murmur of voices, one of them authoritative and male, coming from the door of the church proper.

The man said, "I will pray that our meeting has diverted you momentarily. As for me, I will remember your fair face, shimmering in the roses as though it were one of them."

Carlotta looked more closely at him then, as she thought the convent garden a strange place for a flirtation. "You are bold, sir." He was impressive, she thought, with his aquiline nose, high forehead, and firm mouth. His hair was dark and well-receding, but he had a quality that lured and held. "May I know to whom I speak, for I must go inside now?"

He bowed as the half smile left his face. "I am Aaron Burr, once of Washington City. Now . . . of everywhere."

Very faintly the memory of something touched Carlotta. She said, "I am Carlotta Lenoir, wife to Austin Lenoir of this city and Natchez."

She heard footsteps approaching and looked up to see a

black-clad priest coming toward them in swift strides. He called to Burr in a low voice, "All is prepared, sir, his Excellency and the others await your coming. The nuns are still at their devotions but Reverend Mother is ready."

"I will join you in a moment." It was the voice of authority, the word of one used to command. The priest hesitated, then drew back. "Madame Lenoir, I have heard of your husband even though I have only been in New Orleans for a few days and will not remain much longer. I understand that we share, let us say, certain views. Might I call, do you think?"

The flirtatious manner was gone but the admiration was still there; Carlotta felt her own response to it. "That matter must be taken up with my husband; I have come here for respite." Her voice trailed away as she felt herself trapped by the expressive, demanding eyes. Once again she heard Austin's words as he spoke almost in passing of the ambitions of one Aaron Burr and how his own actions had brought him low. "I have nothing to say with regard to his views, Mr. Vice-President."

His laughter floated out on the night air, and the priest stirred nervously as he glanced at them. "Simply a citizen, madame, but perhaps not that for long." He caught her hand and lifted it to his lips. "I have a fancy for greater things. Tell that to Austin Lenoir when you speak of me."

"How do you know that I will?" She could only wonder at the effrontery of this man even as she smiled at him.

"The nation speaks of Aaron Burr." He turned abruptly and walked away toward the dark figures now milling about in the shadows at the church door. The priest followed, his steps quick as he tried to keep up.

Carlotta waited until they were swallowed up and the garden was quiet again, then she ran for the privacy of her room. This time she passed several nuns who went by with heads bent, seemingly oblivious to all else. Once alone, she tried to sort out what she had learned but nothing fit. What was an ex-official of the United States government doing here at the convent of the Ursulines, and what did he know of Austin Lenoir and the grandiose plans her husband harbored? Her head hammered with the effort to concentrate. It was a relief to think that she had not mourned long for Simon; that way lay hopelessness.

* * *

223

"My daughter, I am told that you are troubled of spirit and wish counsel. I am Father Pierre. I often consult with the ladies who retire here to refresh themselves in this peace. You may feel free to tell me anything you desire."

Carlotta sat in the dim old parlor to which she had been summoned early the next afternoon. The priest, a dark man in his late fifties, eyed her benignly and waited with palms folded under his chin. She was restless during the night and found herself pacing about the garden and the halls this morning. The fear that she had felt at Austin's house had returned, and once again she felt herself helpless before it. She tightened her jaw in determination not to bend. It would be a relief to talk to someone with nothing to gain, but it would have been far more comfortable with another woman.

"My husband has a scheme with which he expects me to concur and of which I am afraid. He is both rich and powerful but he wants power, great power in the new land beyond the great river. He . . ." She looked up from the wide boards of the floor and into the eager black eyes of the priest. Eyes hungry as a predator's might be, a face that might have been reproduced in a hundred Spanish portraits. She shuddered and went silent.

"Yes, daughter? Speak freely. You must know that Holy Church commands wives to obey their husbands. You must do so. But tell me of this scheme?" The smooth voice went hard on the last word.

"And what nationality is Holy Church here, Father Pierre? French? Spanish? Italian?" She had the same feeling of warning here and now that she had had when speaking to Monsieur Rodane; a sudden panic came over her as she wondered if all the world plotted. Was she perhaps going mad?

"The Church is for all. So did Christ preach." The words were soft but the black eyes did not waver from hers.

Carlotta yielded to the instinct that had protected her in the past. "Father, there are things of which I cannot speak to a priest, only to a woman. I am not a Catholic and thus cannot confess. I do not mean to offend . . ."

He smiled with his lips only. "Then Reverend Mother will surely speak with you in several days." He stood and she with him. Then as they went toward the door, he spoke almost absently. "Our distinguished guest of last evening was very impressed with you. Mr. Burr is a great man."

Carlotta turned back a little but his face was expressionless. "That has nothing to do with me, Father."

"There you are wrong, my daughter. More wrong than you know."

Carlotta walked rapidly away, the drumming blood in her ears signaling danger, the fear she felt much like that she had known in Haiti at the shrine of another faith. The afternoon drowsed before her in the garden of peace that was that no longer. A drift of chanting praised the God of David's youth in passionate phrases, several bees droned in the pink roses, and the fresh smell of earth came to her as she knelt to smell a border of yellow flowers.

"I must go from this place. It is no more sanctuary." The words of another exile rose in her mind, and excitement licked at her.

CHAPTER THIRTY

Encounter

FOR most people in this hot climate it was the hour of rest, and the convent of the Ursulines was no exception. The slight figure in the gray dress of coarse cloth and bonnet of the same material who slipped out the side door, past flowering bushes, and through the iron gate at the back, might have been either servant or supplicant but certainly not a New Orleans lady. Carlotta had reason to be grateful that she had included these clothes in her hasty packing for the convent. She had no idea where she was going, only that she must get away and very quickly, for she felt that she was being trapped.

The world outside the convent and the seclusion of the Lenoir residence was a different one entirely. In her haste she had not stopped to think that it was a rough and tumble experience and one which might prove more difficult than the situation which she had just left. The air of freedom was sweeter to her now than the roses, and for a time she drifted, absorbing the sights and sounds of this city.

The walks here were narrow and close to the sides of the houses over which hung balconies fringed with wrought iron. These cast deep shadows and obscured the light. Ditches held water from waste and rain; beyond them the street area was roiled by the constant passage of carts, small carriages, and drays. Hawkers bawled out the virtues of their wares, a black woman in a brilliant red dress laughed with a darker man weighted down with bundles, several large women argued shrilly in Spanish, children jumped up and down in the deep street puddles, four tall, bearded men wearing fur caps stomped along roaring out a bawdy song, an elegant lady passing with her maid sniffed and drew her skirts disdainfully aside. Flowers rioted over a crumbling wall nearby, and their heavy odor mingled with the stench of the ditch as it curved with the street. An old man fumbled along with a cane, singing a Latin song as he went.

Carlotta moved with the flow of people as she went into narrow streets that held shops and houses alike; ventured up toward the market on the levee where fruit, vegetables, fish, baskets, and flowers were sold; went across the square in front of the cathedral and saw the very place where Louisiana became part of the United States less than two years ago. Then she saw a juggler balancing what seemed an improbable number of wooden pins and calling out in a strange patois that she half understood; the undercurrent seemed to be that of the Haitian drums. He was surrounded by children and curious adults who shifted back and forth with his own movements. Lured, she started to cross the street, which was wider here than at other places and thus had more room for the swifter-moving carriages.

There was a scream, the beat of hooves, a horse's whinny, and a man cursing explosively all at the same time as Carlotta looked up from her bemusement to see a gray carriage and two matched gray horses bearing down on her so rapidly that it seemed she would be crushed as if she were one of the melons she had just seen at the market. There was no time for thought as she threw herself to the side as hard as she could. In that same instant the driver of the carriage jerked on the reins in the other direction and the flying hooves missed her head by inches, the wheels by little more. She was flat on her side in the street mud, people were calling to each other, and hands were trying to lift her to her feet, but Carlotta was conscious only of life and the fact that she could so nearly have been killed. She was shaking and smiling all at the same time, even as the anxious voices demanded to know how she was and why she walked so blindly out into the street.

"You fool woman! You could have been killed and all your own fault! Now my horses will be skittish!" The angry voice penetrated the hubbub and rose in irritation.

She turned her head in the direction from which it came and spoke without seeing the man. "You were going too fast. The fault is yours."

"The devil you say! Why I . . . you!" The tone dropped and rose again in pure dismay. Boots rang on the cobbles and mud of the street as she looked into eyes that were terrifyingly familiar.

Carlotta cried, "What are you doing here?" Her vision blurred and ran together in the brilliant sunlight. The dark man before her was Michael Lanwardine, the lover of Lady Leticia, whose affair had begun part of this coil.

"Michael, who is this woman? Give her a bauble and let

us get out of this terrible heat." The speaker was tall and slender with a smooth face, a short brown beard, and glittering brown eyes that surveyed Carlotta in a superior manner.

The dark man put out a hand to his companion. "Tell the slave to see to the horses." The young servant was already speaking soothingly to the animals, however, and the other man stood his ground.

The crowd was now drifting away in search of other amusement, and several carts were trundled past as the juggler began his song again in a lower key that was no longer familiar. Carlotta felt the blood begin to move again in her veins, and this time she was swept by a strengthening anger which grew as she faced the man who had once tried to kill her. She opened her mouth to denounce him, to cry out for protection, and was dumbfounded when he began to laugh. His friend glared at her for a second and then joined him. She could only stare, thinking of the spectacle they must present, a young woman, muddy from head to toe, bonnet lost, hair tumbling over her shoulders in disarray, and two well-dressed young men whooping with laughter in front of her. She stamped her foot and the muddy water flew over them both.

"And she tries her laughter to regain, the shadowed lady of the mountains." The juggler sang now in perfect French as he tapped on the bottom of one of his pins. "He follows, the Baron follows, always." Carlotta whirled but he was moving slowly away, followed by some small boys who kept turning to stare at the young men now trying to shake themselves free of water.

Michael Lanwardine came to Carlotta and executed a perfect courtly bow in front of her as he held his plumed hat in front of his chest. "Mistress, I think that we are at least partly even. Will you drink a cooling drink with us in yon tavern? No harm will come to you here on the street, and I promise that we shall remain in full view of passersby. Carlotta, please."

To her own amazement, Carlotta felt the corners of her mouth quirk up in response to the unabashed smile he gave her. She said severely, "I would not feel safe with such a villain as yourself."

The other young man came closer, and she saw that the strange hostility in his eyes had faded a little. "Since he does not choose to introduce us, I will say that I am Antoine Masonet, late of France and now of New Orleans. I pledge that you will come to no harm in joining us for a few minutes. This has all the sound of a good adventure."

She told him her name, then said, "But for a short time only, though I am foolish to do it."

They walked across the street and into the covered patio of a small shop where fruits and flowers as well as drink were sold. A flowering tree with great roots twisting out of the earth offered shade over three tables set well apart yet still in full sight of the street. The elusive scent of roses drifted here, and Carlotta saw that a back wall was covered with tiny pink ones. Two children played there, voices shrill and high as they tossed a ball.

She sipped the white wine and looked at the two young men, both handsome and debonair, very at ease. In contrast, her hand shook and she could feel a fleck of mud drying on her cheek. "What are you doing in this city? Where is your lady for whom you would have killed me and did kill Sir Reginald?" Her words rapped out harshly in the stillness between them.

A flush mounted to Michael Lanwardine's dark cheek and he started to speak. Antoine leaned forward to touch his hand, and the look that passed between them excluded all the world. Carlotta caught her breath in dismay, for she knew then how it was with these two. She knew also with some strange instinct that Michael was no longer any danger to her; the hungry pleasure had left him, and he was not the same man who had tried to kill her in that garret in England. Her mind cried out warnings but this was beyond logic.

"Michael, tell me. I must know." Her voice was softer now, and her stomach was settling down. Even if her feelings were not correct, what possible danger could come to her here in this public place?

Michael shifted uneasily on his chair as he said, "Antoine knows all there is to know about me and this is another land, another time."

Acidly, she remarked, "Strange, I thought it was only last winter."

Michael's eyes sought Antoine's and seemed relieved by whatever answer they found there. "I do not deny what Lady Leticia and I did or what I did to you. I found you exciting and yet I knew I must silence you. When they found me there was a great hue and cry, a hunt mounted for you, and a reward offered. Leticia urged me to go away. At that time I was thought just one of many rather penniless gallants who admired her; we thought it better so. She promised me that when the estate was settled she would come to me and we would seek sunnier lands where war and Napoleon did not exist. Money was sent soon after I reached London, then I heard that when her decent mourning was over she would marry a member of the House of Lords, younger than Sir Reginald but of that ilk. I tried to see her but was rebuffed, and soon after there was an attempt on my life and then another."

"Good, then you know how it feels to flee before the murderer." Carlotta stared at him with angry eyes as she remembered her own days and nights of terror.

"He knows." Antoine's mobile mouth was tight now, and his fingers shredded a leaf that had drifted down to the table top.

"I took ship for America, thinking to find a new life, but I hated New York and the cold cities of the north. I had loved France and visited there in the days when we were at peace. New Orleans was reputed to be much like her so I decided to come here. Antoine was returning from a visit to an aging relative on the same ship. We became close, and here I am." He leaned back and took a quick drink of brandy.

"Yes, here we all are. Gods, it is like a farce!" Antoine's laughter was suddenly as shrill as that of the children at play.

Carlotta spoke quickly. "Lest you think to harm me, I will tell you that my husband is Austin Lenoir, a name now to be reckoned with in this city. Further, he is most protective and of a jealous nature. My maid awaits me at the Ursuline convent; I felt the need to get away for a little."

"Lenoir! God's bones and breath, lady. What harm could we, who seek only to be left alone, do you that you have not done to yourself by wedding him?" The young man looked at her with very real concern in his eyes and she flushed scarlet. "You have seen how it is with us; very well, that cannot be helped. Others have seen, as well. But this is an old society, and so long as one does as one is expected, marries properly and has the proper boy children, does nothing overt, many things are tolerated. But Lenoir!" He shook his head as his swarthy skin paled a little.

"I will not discuss my husband with such as the two of you!" She jumped to her feet, upsetting the goblet of wine, and ran toward the street.

No one paid any attention to the woman running through the streets, such sights were common enough in the city, after all, but Carlotta felt that all eyes were on her and, as she approached the convent, took care to smooth the wet hair back from her forehead and slow her breathing down to an occasional gasp. The gate swung back easily to her questing fingers, and she found herself once more in the comfortable walls. Her little room now seemed a haven indeed, but she knew that this was illusion. Intrigue was swirling around her, and survival was at stake.

She lay down on the narrow bed and gave herself up to speculation about Michael and his friend. How could she know if they meant her harm or not? Surely it would have been foolish to stay longer in their company. Austin at least meant to use her for his own ends; that guaranteed some measure of safety, did it not? A sudden bout of dizziness caught her and she turned on her side in the hopes that it would go away.

The door opened suddenly and Bettina, accompanied by a young nun, glided in. She said rapidly, "They didn't want to disturb you but I insisted. Mistress, you are bidden home. The Master has guests late this evening and wants you there to greet them. I'll get your things." The old eyes looked at her sharply, and Carlotta felt that every move she had made was known.

"But I am not ready. Who are these important people who cannot survive without meeting the obscure Madame Lenoir?" She sat up and was relieved to feel that the strange spell had passed.

"You must come." Bettina would say no more but began to twitch the few clothes that Carlotta had brought from their pegs.

Carlotta saw that she must yield, and in truth she was ready enough to leave. Reality had pursued her here in the person of a dark, enigmatic man and a worldly priest. Now she must go forth to meet the challenges offered. She turned to the little nun and said, "I am grateful for the peace of this place. Will you convey my gratitude to Reverend Mother?"

The nun lifted a smooth face and smiled faintly. "But you have already been most generous, madame. That purse of gold will feed many of the poor. Our God will bless you."

Carlotta looked at Bettina who pursed her lips and shook her head slightly. She wanted to tell the nun that Austin's money and life were tainted with evil but that was foolish thinking; she inclined her head modestly and so they passed from the room. As she and Bettina walked down the wide staircase the lovely chanting voices of the nuns rose up in praise, an innocent happiness of service that brought tears to Carlotta's eyes. The interlude of peace was over.

Bettina waited until Carlotta was settled in a copper tub of scalding water with more heating in the kitchens before demanding, "I came before and you were nowhere to be found. They thought you were either in the chapel or the garden but I went there and you were nowhere to be seen. Nowhere!" The repetition of the word seemed to give her satisfaction. "It is just a good thing that I was sent to fetch you and not someone else."

"You forget that I am mistress here, Bettina. Do not speak to me so." The cool words took them both by surprise. "Fetch the maid to do my hair and put out the new green gown. Then you may retire."

Old knowing eyes met the young ones, then fell to the swell of Carlotta's belly, just visible under the water. "Aye, mistress. It is as you say."

The dizziness came again as she was dressing, and she was forced to sit down while the world swung. "I am perfectly fine. I do not need tea." She forbade the maid to fetch anything but hastily daubed the beads of sweat from her upper lip when the girl turned away to proffer the mirror.

Her hair was gathered in a large knot at the nape of her neck. Half curls clustered at temples and ears. She wore no jewels but the brilliant light in her amber eyes was enough to heighten the translucent quality of her skin. The green dress was the color of sea foam, the color of the ocean at the beaches of Haiti. Simon. Simon. His name came unbidden to her lips, and she had to bite her tongue to keep from saying it out loud. Did he walk in some land of shades even now or did his bones bleach in that forbidden land of his youth? The time with him now seemed more real than the people she would meet tonight, than the husband she would greet.

She picked up the flashing emerald ring that had been brought to her to wear with the dress, knowing that it was Austin's own choice, and slipped it on her long ring finger. It picked up the color of the dress and reflected in the candlelight of her dressing table. The neck of the dress was cut low across her white bosom, and even the lace inset could not wholly disguise the swell of it. The skirt was long and wide and seemed to cream in wavelets behind her as she moved.

Carlotta slipped her feet into matching slippers and moved

to the mirror to check her hair once more. A stranger looked back at her, a person she did not know. Her eyes lifted and she saw the little maid staring at her, admiration mingling with wonder.

She came out onto the landing and stood looking down at the beautifully carpeted floors, the perfectly arranged and polished furniture, and felt once again that she was an actress in a play, a pretty figure who would recite her few lines and retire to wait upon the admiration of the audience. She half smiled at the foolishness of it, then grasped the banister to guide herself down. Had she run up these stairs only a few days ago? Strange that they seemed to waver, strange that her legs were suddenly so weak.

Then the world was full of lights and sea foam. She was drifting down into the depths, swirling about, and then the bottom rose to meet her. Was the bottom of the sea so hard? Her head was hammering, and her body felt as if it were parted in the middle.

The dream penetrated her fog. She was conscious of pain and nausea as faces bent over her, the serving maid's twisted with tears, Austin's a mask of rage barely concealed, two other men concerned; only Aaron Burr's was torn with pity.

CHAPTER THIRTY-ONE

The Dark Powers

"You did it deliberately. You lost my child deliberately." Austin sat in the rose-colored chair at her bedside, the solid black of shirt and breeches contrasting with his pale skin. His eyes were again the black holes where redemption could not reach. "Now it is all to do over again. Unbearable."

Carlotta was drained by her ordeal and very weak. Sweat matted her hair, and she trembled even as she lay against the pillows. It was mid-morning of the next day, and the hastily summoned doctor had said that there was no danger but that she must rest and eat well to regain her strength. Undoubtedly there had been too much activity, and all knew that breeding women were delicate. Carlotta had heard him talking to Austin in the anteroom and thought to herself that if he only knew all that she had done since the inception of this pregnancy he would never make such a statement again. "A misstep, probably a touch of the summer fever—certainly not yellow fever, rest easy there—rest and all will resolve itself." He had given her an evil-tasting potion and gone his way. Now she had waked to find Austin in a fury.

"Unbearable, is it? Do you think that I relish your touch or believe for one moment in your ridiculous scheme to set yourself up in power? I loathe you, Austin Lenoir, and have done all along." The fiery words belied her weak voice but she knew suddenly that she was in her right senses and only a fool would not fear such a one as he, yet she could not stop. "Let me go! My body will not quicken for you now."

"That is where you are wrong, madame. There are ways and it is time to employ them. I am done with patience." He rose to bend over her and smiled at her involuntary recoil. "It is passing strange, is it not, that you endure such experiences in Haiti as would have driven many a woman to miscarry if the child were ever to be dislodged, go through a pitched battle, then come here and tumble down the stairs? Beyond belief! A child is necessary! Necessary, do you hear?"

His nostrils flared and his reserve was dangerously breached, even as the odd pleasure that he took in the pain of another now showed itself. Carlotta clenched her hands under the sheet and forced her voice to calm.

"Why would I lose the child, my safeguard? That would be the height of foolishness and I have never been that, have I?"

"Perhaps you seek another's arms, thinking as you may that you carry the blood of royalty in your veins. How should I know what thoughts are in your mind? Be careful, Carlotta. I warned you once that I am knowledgeable in the matters of potions. Were it not for the fact that you have attracted the very genteel interest of Mr. Burr, the one-time Vice-President, and were it not for the fact that his plans march with mine, at least for now, I might even at this instant be sorrowing that my fair young wife has seen fit to retreat from the doings of this world, though she still shares my bed. Think on it when next you seek to leave here against my wishes."

He slipped out while the rose curtains lifted in the hot breeze and blew their lace against the chair he had vacated. Carlotta felt the cold sweat slip between her breasts and knew that he meant exactly what he had said.

Her body was young and strong and responded rapidly to the ministrations of Bettina and the maids. Rich foods, white wine, massages, warm baths, and short walks in the patio were begun the next day. She slept long and deeply each night but did not know if she were being drugged or not. It did not seem so but she dared not protest in her weakened condition, for she could do nothing until her body mended.

One morning the little maid brought a great bunch of white roses, their edges tinged with delicate pink, to her as she sat resting in a shaded corner of the patio. It was a brilliant day, though the high-piled clouds in the west gave promise of rain later, and the sun filtered down into the palm branches and glanced off her flushed face.

"How beautiful! I did not know we had such flowers here."

"Your pardon, madame. These were brought by one of Master Lenoir's friends who has come to call and says that he was asked by Mr. Burr to give them to you with his compliments. Mr. Burr has since left New Orleans. The flowers are specially grown on a plantation out of the city."

Carlotta felt a little chill. "Who is the gentleman who brought them?"

"I do not know. The Master himself greeted him at the door."

"Take these to my bedroom and put them in water." After the girl had gone to do her bidding, she rose and walked slowly into the house, making sure that she passed the long parlor on her way.

She heard the murmur of voices but could not see clearly because her eyes were still unused to the cool dimness. Candles blazed suddenly into flame as she moved by, however, and she caught a glimpse of an immensely tall man in a dark coat who was sitting intimately with Austin on the wide window seat. More of the lovely roses were placed on the desk near them. She dared not linger but went on, wondering as she did so what strangeness would make one blot out the light of day and use candles at such an hour. An echo of laughter drifted by her. There was a strange familiarity about it that was puzzling. She was in her room, parting the curtains to look at the expanse of lawn, before she realized why. That laughter of intimacy and sharing had been hers with Simon; she had heard the warmth between Michael and Antoine, now Austin. Was he as they? Again the chill smote her despite the rising heat of the day.

It was through Bettina that she learned they would soon go upriver to Natchez and Austin's plantation there. The summer heat in New Orleans was always great, and the danger of the yellow fever was never far from people's minds at this time of the year. The old woman was not directly unfriendly to Carlotta, but she seldom volunteered information and the sharp old eyes were constantly assessing the girl. She would say only, "It is time we left here. Past time. Cool there in Natchez." Then she would urge more rest or a soothing drink before departing to shake out more garments or supervise the slow packing.

Carlotta felt the well-being of her body and knew that this was due in part to the freedom she felt at being free of Austin's child. Had it been Simon's how very dear it would have been! She thought of how swiftly she had quickened with Austin's seed and how she and Simon had loved, yet nothing had come of it. She thought of him often now, and it never seemed that he was dead. "Would I not know if he were?" The question was voiced aloud and the answer was simple. She had only Austin's word for that, and he would lie for lying's sake. It was foolish to indulge in false hope, she knew, yet the world seemed a little less bleak because of that hope.

She was not permitted to go out at all. The one day she tried to leave the walled patio and go out into the lawn she was politely stopped and Bettina called. Then maids kept watch, and once she saw a slender black man watching her from a distance. It took little imagination to know that she was supposed to be suffering from the pangs of child loss and considered a little demented. The maids all spoke very softly and correctly to her as befitted her station in life, but she saw their care and the roll of their eyes. Austin had done his work well.

The sun-ripened days drifted slowly by until it was several weeks after her miscarriage. When Carlotta looked in the mirror now she saw that her body was still smooth and slim, her eyes a bit haunted, the hollows under her cheekbones a little more pronounced. Her hair had regained the old shimmer, and flecks of gold dappled it from her time in the patio. She read a great deal, cut flowers and arranged them, tried to talk to the cold Bettina, and walked as much as she could in house and garden. Austin she seldom saw and that only in passing. It was a waiting time; sooner or later the confrontation would come and he would seek her bed.

Very early one morning Carlotta was pacing in the patio as she looked out to the flowers which were still bent with dew. It was already very warm and she wore only a loose white robe. Her hair was bound up on her head but the few trailing tendrils made her neck hot. The sound of her name, "Madame Lenoir," took her by surprise, and she gave a faint gasp as she turned toward the sound.

A gray-habited nun stood by the first bench at the turn of the path, a figure very small and slight in the morning stillness. Carlotta saw the maid who had ushered her in moving respectfully away. Any visitor would be welcome, the girl thought, after the forced seclusion of these days, but this nun might be a messenger from the Reverend Mother of the Ursulines. Had she perhaps changed her mind and would she now be willing to listen to Carlotta's tale? She sped across the grass in anticipation.

"Welcome to this house, Sister. Have you been offered refreshment? I am indeed honored by your visit." She indicated the bench then realized that it was covered with dew. "I will have a cushion fetched. . . ."

"No, walk with me. Take this." The nun pushed a small Testament in French into Carlotta's hand. "I said that I must deliver this personally since you left it when you sojourned with us and that I was greatly grieved to hear of your misfortune

237

and loss." Her voice was soft; her small face seemed to fade into the gray she wore.

Carlotta was bewildered. "But I left nothing like this."

They were moving toward a large oleander bush that would screen them from the direct view of the house. The nun said, "There is no time, madame, so I will be blunt. I am no nun but a friend of Michael Lanwardine who asked me to play this role and give you a message."

Carlotta felt the flesh rise on her arms at the mention of that name. "Then I must ask you to go. He is nothing to me."

The other woman faced her then, and Carlotta saw the sincerity blazing from her eyes. "He bids me say that Austin Lenoir is a practicer of the dark arts and in league with the powers of evil. He uses you toward those ends. Beware."

"Your friend Michael once tried to kill me. Why should I believe him, and what exactly does this nebulous warning mean?" Carlotta remembered her own feelings that he now meant her no harm. "Why does he send thus to me?"

"I do not know of his past but I do know that he has recognized and accepted himself as he is, that he is happy now and wishes harm to none. Your husband's son, his nominal heir, was both a hunchback and raving mad at the time of the full moon. Few know this for he was kept far from New Orleans. He was made this way, it is said, because of experiments done upon his mother in order to render her with child the more rapidly. Lenoir's wealth buys silence on such subjects but it is said that the son did not die by the fever but by his own hand. You should escape while you can."

Carlotta watched the woman and knew that she did not lie. Nothing she told about Austin could surprise his wife, for had she not seen the dark pits of the nether regions look out of his face? "That you speak the truth as you see it, I cannot deny. Tell Michael that I am grateful."

The woman held out a purse filled with gold coins. "When the time comes that you realize your danger, these will help."

"Why does he do this if Austin is so powerful?" Carlotta knew that she should refuse the gift but she did not. One day she might stand in need of ready money, although she was certainly safe enough since Austin needed her for his scheme of power.

"Remember that Antoine and Michael are very close and know each other's hearts. Your husband once tried to wed the sister of Antoine and she refused. She was very verbal about

238

it. Now she who once was beautiful and gay lives apart, a decaying ruin. She has the Biblical disease, and she is no more than twenty-seven."

Carlotta folded both arms across her chest to forestall the shivers that were beginning. "I do not understand."

"She is a leper. The disease smote her within two months after she decried the old man who would take her youth. Lenoir looked older in those days. It is said, too, that he has given you the roses of death, those which bloom above the graves of the voodoo victims and their masters." She swung around and started to pace slowly back, Carlotta following. "He is what he is, and this is the most tolerant of cities. I am friend to both Michael and Antoine and know that all will be well for them. But Michael has said he owes you a debt. This is the payment."

Carlotta saw again the dark hills of Haiti and heard the drums, saw the rising head of Damballah and the red eyes of the servants of Jérouge. Austin? A follower of the voodoo cult. He of the smooth white skin and the rational mind? She thought of the potions he had mentioned and the twists of his mind but most of all she thought of a fair young girl whose flesh was slowly peeling from her bones with a fearful disease. Could he have caused such a thing? No matter, the girl had likely believed it and so it had come to pass.

"I thank you all. The debt is discharged." Carlotta's head rang with all that she had learned and with fears for the future.

"We are watched. It is the time of the sickle moon. Be cautious."

Bettina and one of the maids came across the grass as the nun lifted her hand and blessed Carlotta in swift flowing Latin that surrounded her with the promises of the Christian God.

After they had all departed, Carlotta went up to her room, which was mildly cool even as the heat of the day built up. She pondered all that she had heard and fought back the fear that it produced. Had she not endured much and still lived? The gold in her hands would buy her safety. She had counted it out cautiously and been amazed at what Michael had given her. His motives still puzzled her, but she could not afford to doubt them.

Her trailing skirts drifted across the polished floor as she moved back and forth, plotting. She must escape from here and seek passage on a ship going to Boston or New York; in the cities of the East she might set herself up in business, tutoring or book-selling, perhaps even for a short time that thing which was most dreadful to her, being a governess in a wealthy family. She did not know what ship passage cost, but surely there would be something left over. When she escaped from the house, however that was to be managed, she would find Michael and ask his help in getting on a ship of the type she sought.

She was conscious of a pang of loss at the thought of leaving this lush, hot land with the warm breezes and brilliant flowers. Something in her cleaved to this south country and would forever miss it. Then she smiled wryly. Freedom was the best after all, and it had been a long time since she was free.

Her glance went to the ghostly roses which still survived, and she knew that she could not do what she ought to if she truly believed what the false nun had told her; such beauty could not be destroyed. She put one hand to the pink edges and felt them as silky as the magnolias she had loved in Charleston. Then she knew the truth that had not occurred to her before—these were not the same roses that had been given to her under Burr's name, they were fresh ones. Again the far, faint drums of Haiti hammered in her mind.

She was abstemious during the next few days, saying that the heat pulled her down and made her weak. They must not begin the journey to Natchez until her plans were laid. Austin did not come near her, and for that she was grateful. She would use the old dress in which she had ventured out from the Ursuline convent and meant to obtain men's clothes at the first opportunity. She had taken a dagger from the display in the long parlor and kept it close to her now. It had been placed in the very back of an arrangement of swords and its absence was not likely to be noticed. Now it remained only to wait until the deepest night and hope that the slaves slept. Bettina had complained that the Master labored long in the library and that she, Carlotta, was not gaining weight as she should. The remark bore fruit now as Carlotta spent much of her time in bed in the afternoons. The watch was lessened by this, and she suspected that the old woman retired to her own room to take advantage of the lull.

The young moon waned in the night skies. Carlotta had assumed the messenger meant that this was the time of danger, but there had been no time to ask. She dared not risk waiting much longer, for soon they would either summon the doctor or begin to suspect her of malingering. Austin might well come to see how the empty vessel of his heir was doing. Even to herself in the dark reaches of the hot nights Carlotta could not think of what must have happened to the young woman who bore the hunchback son whom she was supposed to have wed.

The time of choice had come. She had wandered out the night before, fully prepared to rouse with a start from sleep-walking should anyone appear. The house was silent, and she had seen no one. The side door onto the lawn had remained ajar as it often did during the day. Beyond it lay freedom. She had been tempted then but had known she must wait.

Now she dressed in the old gown, pulled her hair back under the scratchy bonnet, put her shoes and the purse of gold in an old reticule, and slipped noiselessly down the staircase for what she devoutly hoped was the last time. The silence rang in her ears as she moved, a wraith in gray, toward the door. Then she stopped in dismay. It was bolted shut. The windows nearby were fastened and the shutters drawn. Carlotta moved rapidly toward the ornate front door and saw the shimmer of bolts over it as well. She shuddered. What could this mean? Had she been seen the night before? How long before she dared try again?

Her stomach contracted in very real pain at the thought of her failure as she turned to go back upstairs. She caught a flicker of light from the glass of the door and saw, through the upper panel, the sliver of the moon's pale light. It was then that she heard the low-voiced chanting and the slap of bare feet on wood.

CHAPTER THIRTY-TWO

The Sign and the Way

THEY came in files of three, seven lines of them, carrying black candles and wearing black hoods. Most of them were black, but there was an occasional glimmer of white skin. The chanting was in some type of French, but Carlotta could not understand it. She ducked back into an alcove and melted into the shadows there, blessedly thankful for the safety thus produced. They followed the curve of the hall and paused before the wide wall expanse which was covered with yet another of the misty tapestries Austin favored. One chanter's voice rose as the others were stilled, and the note in it was one of demand. Even as Carlotta watched, the wall slowly began to move and she could see the darkness beyond. They began to move into it, silent now.

She started to move out and then drew swiftly back, for she heard voices coming from the back room which led into one of the sitting rooms for guests. One was male and harsh, totally unfamiliar to her. It said, "Nobody can get in past those bolts. They never have. But I'll watch here with two of the men, just in case."

"See that you do. I'm going down with the others. The girl's asleep these hours ago. I put the potion in the water she drinks so much of." The laughter seemed to bloom in the quiet and then Bettina, draped in black, scuttled by her hiding place.

Carlotta breathed a sigh of pure relief. She had drunk little all this day so that nature's necessity might not come upon her in her plans for escape. She had arranged the covers in a tossed heap, the way she often slept, but without any real attempt at subterfuge. That had apparently been sufficient. What was she to do now? There was no way to get past the guards and the bolts. She could only go back up to bed and wait for another night, never really certain of what she faced. She hesitated and heard the chanting begin on a deeper note.

Enough! She would know what she dealt with; the passive role had been played for too long. Just beyond this alcove was another where the cloaks of guests sometimes hung. A black

242

one had hung there ever since they had been in this house, a legacy of some visitor long since gone, and it was the action of only a few moments to reach it and swing the folds about her slender body. The guard was pacing up and down in the other room and the hall was clear both as she darted into the alcove and when she crossed it to stand at the stone steps that led down into a red-tinged darkness.

The air of the passage was damp and fetid as it angled down and then went up again. The walls were of stone and moist to her questing fingers. The shadows just ahead of her were cast up on the low ceiling, then reflected back so that they drew long. Carlotta remained well behind so that she could run if they should turn and see her, but where would she run to? She put the thought out of her mind and followed, knowing that she was doing what she had to do.

They came into a large, circular chamber, built also of stone, with a hearth against one wall and a high, red-painted chair which looked to be gold-leafed placed on the top of a series of steps. Before it was a stone altar about which greenery was woven. The beautiful ghostly roses stood in masses to the sides, their silky white petals illuminated by the tall black candles which stood in groups of three at various intervals. Other worshippers—she could only think of them as such—entered from two other passageways as the chanting ceased and all sank to sitting positions. Carlotta did likewise, making herself into as small a bundle as she could at the section of wall closest to her own entranceway. No one paid any attention to his neighbor, for all looked straight ahead without moving.

The song began with a softly chanted chorus that built into a complexity of words and rhythm which rose and fell. The undertone was one of savagery, but there was a triumphant lilt to the words, which were in a language she did not understand. The drum started as punctuation and was soon dominant. One of the cowled figures rose to fetch a gourd cup which was passed from one person to another and filled again by the person at the end of the row from a vat in the corner. Some declined, and Carlotta shook her head as they had done when the cup approached her.

A fire blazed suddenly on the hearth and fell again to a low, steady flame that lit up the drawn pictures of a snake and a goat, both black, intertwined with human figures in a travesty of the act of love. There was a whirring sound through the air just then, and three bodies fell into the space before the altar.

They were black chickens from which the heads had been removed. A young girl rose and threw aside her concealing garment, baring her naked, lithe body to the flickering lights as she danced in a positive frenzy of ecstasy. A man caught her to him and rolled away with her into the shadows, but all the company could see that they tossed in the tides of passion. The chanting never ceased.

Three naked young girls now brought in a long, smooth chest, which they placed on the altar, and then stood back. A tall white man wearing only a loin cloth came to stand beside the altar. In his arms he held the largest black cat Carlotta had ever seen. The animal was drugged, she thought, because it moved only feebly now and then, yet the tip of its long tail twisted and thrashed.

"We are ready, great ones. Come forth! Let the servants and the seekers be at one!" The words were spoken in unaccented English, then were repeated again by the young man who bent low before the apparition which now approached.

The woman might have been as old as the flowing brown river or the dark ritual of which she was the pivot. Carlotta knew that she was being fanciful, but the strange ceremony held her spellbound and she forgot to be afraid. The woman's skin was the color of creamy coffee and as wrinkled as crumpled wet clay. She was tall and only slightly bent, but she carried a long red cane. Her robe was red also, and the turban on her head was black. She opened her mouth to chant and Carlotta saw with a shiver that her visible teeth were filed to fine points. Golden earrings reached to her shoulders, and a golden collar was looped around her neck.

"Madame. Madame. Madame." The toneless chant rose with the assembled people who stood as one. Carlotta felt her legs shake as she moved her lips without making a sound. "Madame. Madame."

Madame lifted a ringed hand and one of the girls removed the lid from the chest. The young man put the cat down on the altar and it stood stiffly as the light shone on the black fur. All eyes, including those of Carlotta, were riveted to the chest, and several people uttered low cries as the great black head lifted from within it.

The snake of Damballah had been large in the Haitian ceremony, but this one seemed to grow as the coils poured from confinement. It seemed strange that the slight girls had been able to lift so large a creature, but now they moved closer, their oiled bodies seeming part of a greater whole. The snake oozed upon the cat, which was now becoming aware of its danger and beginning to hiss while the hair rose on its spine. The drums began to beat, and the old woman was laughing soundlessly as the snake surrounded the cat, squeezed it, then opened its fanged mouth, and the living animal vanished within it. Another smooth movement and the coils were moving toward the dead chickens just below the altar. The company was very still now, and over the drums Carlotta could hear the rasp of the great body on the stone floor. It halted, then veered away toward one of the young girls who stood very still, her face a mask, but the protruding eyes showed her fear as the head lifted and twisted around her ankle.

There was a step in the corridor just then, and Carlotta, all her senses sharpened by fear, knew that Austin was in the room. She was barely able to keep from turning around, and, as it was, the glittering eyes of the old woman swung over her, paused, and returned to the young girl. The snake slithered part of the way up to her knee then began to retreat. This time it moved toward the chickens and Carlotta closed her eyes, thinking how nearly the victim had been the girl, who doubtless would have gone supinely to her death without any help from the others. The snake dealt with the rest of the sacrifice and slid away into the darkness.

Madame lifted her arms so that the sleeves of the gown fell away and cried in French, "He is pleased!"

This was the signal for pandemonium to break out. The first two lines of worshippers threw off their robes to reveal naked bodies and black and white men and women who immediately began to writhe in a sensual dance stimulated by the whisper of the drums. Minutes later they tumbled about on the floor in a massive outpouring of rubbings and thrusting from the heat of desire. The others watched, and this time Carlotta did also.

Madame gave a wave of her fingers and a black pot was brought forward and placed on the hearth, where it immediately began to hiss. She threw a small packet into it and a sickly-sweet odor began to rise. Several others followed that, and a green sheet of flame lifted into dark smoke that enveloped her. She threw back her head, and the pointed teeth gnashed as she cried out then began to laugh on a high, shrill note that hurt Carlotta's ears.

"Enough!" She pointed both hands downward toward the orgiastic revelers who melted away into the shadows. The long, nailed fingers lifted again and beckoned. "Come and make your request."

Footsteps sounded on stone as two other black-clad figures came toward her, pulling back their hoods as they did so. One was Austin, his whole body radiating excitement, his lips curved in a smile. The other was the tall, thin figure she had seen only in a glimpse. At first impression he seemed the living personification of the snake with his long head, jutting jaw, thick black hair, and sloping shoulders. He looked to be several years younger than Austin, whose eyes lingered over him as they faced Madame.

"What do the signs say? Will I have that which I have asked?"

"Say it before us all, Austin Lenoir, as you have said it in your heart. The Power will have nothing less than totality. You know that." Madame's voice had the lash of laughter in it.

Carlotta saw Austin's hands clenched, but he bent his head a little in the first submissive gesture she had ever seen him make. "A son, well in mind and body, to follow after me, the kingdom in the west, authority there, and to remain in full command of my body."

Carlotta knew that he meant potency, and the bitterness rose in her throat.

"And what do you give in return?" Again the half laughter.

"The woman who will bear the son shall belong to the Power, to the dark gods. Already, she has begun her journey, for the flowers have bloomed for her and she has accepted them." Austin's voice rang confidently in the hushed room as the green lights danced in the crackling flames on the hearth.

"It is not enough. The woman, your wife, is not within your caring, although the seal is already set on her. Your dearest possession will be required. Are you prepared to give it?"

Austin did not hesitate. His eyes fastened on the man at his side and the other's smile was suddenly swift as they communicated wordlessly. "I will and with all my heart."

"So it is done." Madame swung around in a swirl of red that mingled with the fire. "Send the woman living to us. The time is not yet; the hand of others is over her. Your own service has been long and your rewards great. Remember that in the time of testing."

Austin turned slowly around so that all could see him, and it seemed to Carlotta that his eyes must surely pierce her concealing cloak, but he faced Madame again and said, "I remember now. I will always remember."

In the breathy silence that fell after his words, they heard the rasp of the snake's body slithering on the floor. Soon the dark coils were settled in the darkest, coolest section of the wide room. Austin and his companion stood close to each other at one side of the altar as the drum began to sound softly. Madame made a quick movement and the contents of the pot spilled into the fire, quenching it, then flowed down into the floor area. A foul odor, similar to that of putrefaction, rose on the damp air.

Madame lifted her head and gazed around; the look on her face was that of the predator before his helpless prey. "Something is not right! I feel the struggle! I feel it!" She lifted up her arms and began to sway.

"No! No! Call the Power for us, Madame!" The people cried as one as they swayed in the opposite direction.

Austin and his companion sank to the floor, their bodies touching, but neither moved otherwise.

"Come upon us. Come. We are ready. What disturbs you?" Madame intoned the words as the evil smell increased. She began to gyrate slowly and lapsed into the unknown language these people used.

Carlotta rose when the others did and moved with them, sluggishly, as if bemused. The black candles were extinguished by the same young girls until only one remained. The snake was torpid in the corner, but the single flickering light gave evil emphasis to the shimmering coils.

"He is here. They are here. Welcome them with your bodies." Madame's French was guttural as she moved arms, hips, body, and head in a rapid shuffling dance that was swiftly imitated with glad cries by the others.

Some tore off their robes and began to flail about, some convulsed, one woman stood alone and naked as she began to shout, twisting her full nipples as she did so. Two men and a woman began to thrust at each other in passion as the candle burned still lower. Austin and his serpentine companion drifted back into the shadows now, their bodies close, their hands moving hungrily.

Carlotta clutched the robe closer to her as she realized that soon she would be the only completely clothed one there. A girl only a few feet from her pushed her sleeve up her arm and began to sway while her fingernails ripped the flesh open and blood ran down her arm. Madame was leaning over and bending backward as she called out in that hoarse voice that seemed the embodiment of evil. Her savage eyes raked the congregation even as she urged them on.

Carlotta's head was hammering, for she realized that the combination of whatever was in the pot and the liquid they had consumed, as well as the smoke, had combined to produce near frenzy in the people. They might well be capable of anything. She must escape when the candle flickered out and before they could find another. It would be her only chance. A red-haired woman settled in the arms of a fat, pale man who picked her up with effort and looked around for a place to settle. His eyes protruded, and his robe was almost gone from his body, but he leaned over with an effort and spoke. "Come join us. Man, woman, what's the difference to the gods?" His voice broke on a gasp of drunkenness that became lust as the woman began to fondle him. Carlotta moved even farther back in the shadows but knew that very soon she would be conspicuous by the very lack of participation.

A shriek shattered the moans and cries of the people. Carlotta saw Austin and his companion sit up languidly, then draw closer together. A drummer dressed in torn red breeches and red shirt carried his drum to the edge of the altar and began to beat it in hypnotic, dragging beats that gradually quickened. Madame shrieked again, this time oddly in tune with the beat. The frenzied whirls and dances did not cease but slowed as if to match. Carlotta dug her nails into the palm of her hand and kept one eye on the guttering candle.

She saw the huge head reflected in the fading light, the short snout gaping to reveal long teeth, and the rough body seeming to stretch back into the corridor. The impulse to scream until all her breath was gone was almost unbearable. Had she ever belonged to a world of quiet English villages and remote manors, where the most excitement offered was the coming of the lord on his quarterly visits? "Deliver me." The cry rang in her brain and this time it was not the Northmen from whom the ancient Christian cry begged salvation. "From the fury, deliver us!"

Then common sense reasserted itself and she saw that the advancing monster was but the skin of one of those water animals that she had seen lying on the banks of the river as they advanced toward New Orleans. It was a type of crocodile, she remembered that much. This one was huge and worn by a man who seemed weighted down by the burden but oddly agile for all that. The great head turned and she saw with a start that blazing green stones had been fitted to the eyeholes and now shone with an unearthly light that reminded her of the red-eyed followers of Jérouge of Haiti.

The drumming rose in volume and Madame cowered away from the advancing beast as the people swayed, making low moaning sounds. Carlotta had a sudden vivid sense of the river, mud-brown and inexorable, moving to a pre-determined destination. The dark creature came upon Madame now, emerald eyes burning and the teeth ready. She cried out again, the drum sounded a triumphal note, and then she spun so rapidly that she seemed but a circle of red. One hand flashed out in a gesture of reprisal and the young girls came up to join her. The beast fell back, the massive head dominating but somehow bending before the human it had menaced. The drumming rose now in a hammering sound, and Madame fell forward in a frenzy that shook her frail body. The beast bent before her, all but conquered. The people began to whirl and dance in unrestrained excitement as the black candle guttered one final time and went out.

Carlotta rose and backed away as quickly as she could until her foot brushed the corner of the wall. Then, holding one arm at the wall for balance, she let instinct take over and ran from that place of terror.

CHAPTER THIRTY-THREE

River of Life

AFTER the tension of the past hours and the horrors she had seen, Carlotta expected anything as she edged along the corridor and came to the wall where the tapestry covered the entrance back into the house and some semblance of normal life. She heard the muted cries of the orgy going on behind her and knew that she dared not linger, lest someone decide to wander after her, intentionally or otherwise.

Cautiously she pushed the soft material aside and looked out. The wide hall was empty, with no sign of the guard. She forced her leaden legs to move and felt the perspiration drip down her back, but she went from chair to chair, door to door, until she reached the staircase and scuttled upward. She touched the door of her room and felt the knob give way in a soft movement. Her bed was as she had left it; nothing had been disturbed. The first gray light of dawn was almost imperceptible in the open window, for she had left the curtains undrawn.

It was the work of a few seconds to roll the clothes up and thrust them into the corner of an old chest in the little dressing room which she had heard the maids threaten to clean out but which they never did. Then she slipped into the smooth whiteness of her bed and attempted to rest. She was safe enough, she thought, as she twisted and turned, her mind filling with the grotesque ceremonies she had seen this night, so long as they thought her indisposed and ignorant of their secrets. Should it ever become known that she had spied on them, her life would be in even more danger than it already was.

Tiredness beat in her pulses but she could not relax. She had thought Austin to be a cold, calculating man with periods of madness that he found pleasurable. His schemes for rule she had simply put down to the boredom of a rich man, but now she knew that were he not truly a worshipper of strange gods, then he used the voodoo of this land for darker purposes. There had been no mistaking the passion that he and the serpentine man felt for each other; now she understood the faint revulsion that he had seemed to feel toward her, even in the conjugal act.

She would go from this house the next evening no matter what came about. Surely they could not enact such rites again so quickly. It must be chanced, for she knew that she could no longer endure this life, continually being at the mercy of a man who was capable of anything. She would use the same method of escape and pray that it would be fruitful. Now she knew the validity of Michael's warning and knew, in some bone-deep, instinctive way, that Austin wanted her dead just as much as he wanted the child from her womb. Her flesh crawled at the thought of those white fingers on her smooth flesh, and she gritted her teeth against her fingers to keep from crying out.

The light was clearer now, the shapes in the room more distinct. A dog barked far in the distance and the sound carried. A sleepy bird twittered at the window where the climbing pink roses swayed. She twisted in the bed again as she tried to find a cool spot for her head and her gaze fell on the white roses of death. The urge to rise and slam them to the floor was almost irresistible, but she dared not so give herself away. "I can do nothing except react! Has my courage departed utterly?" She castigated herself, knowing that it was almost impossible to fight against this miasma in the air, this well-laid plan of Austin's to whatever end, but she was unable to think clearly for exhaustion and fear.

Carlotta was afterward to think of those morning hours as a time when the Biblical pestilence of spirit walked, when the brutal despair that was a palpable sin almost overcame her. It seemed that great leathery wings moved in her chest, that evil waited just beyond the flicker of an eyelid, and that there was nothing she could do about it except wait supinely for her role to be played out. Her whole body was stiff with waiting, her mind sore with anticipation. She knew that this was a thing beyond reason and rational thought. From somewhere in the intermeshing years, she remembered Uncle Arnold speaking of a feeling such as this, a feeling sometimes present in the monasteries, a great emptiness, a sense of the departure of God and the consequent flowing in of evil. He had not told her the remedy. She turned on her stomach and put her face in her arms as she called on the one sanity she knew, Simon and what they had shared. Whatever the outcome of their passion, it had been true while it endured. The dark face, the brilliant eyes, rose in front of her, and she saw the lips quirk in laughter, a laughter she suddenly felt would be there even in the direst moments, born not of foolish bravado, but of endurance.

"Mistress! Mistress! Wake up. Here's breakfast and you sleep so long!"

The voice pierced Carlotta's ears and jerked her upright. The little maid was not one she had ever seen before and surely bore no resemblance to any of those she had seen the night before. She could not have been over fifteen, and her dark eyes were liquid with eagerness to please. She held a tray of tea and sweetmeats which now bobbed dangerously in her hands as she backed away before the force of Carlotta's waking.

Her voice rasped in her throat as she tried to steady it. "What time is it? I slept so heavily." And she had thought she would never sleep again, even as she held the talisman of Simon's face before her.

"Almost noon, mistress. I must help get you ready." She set the tray down on the edge of the bed and gave a sigh of relief.

"Ready? For what?" Carlotta did not care at this moment if the tea were laden with potions. Her thirst was acute and so was her need for the hot, restoring liquid.

"Why, Natchez, mistress. The Master gave the order for the barges to be made ready and we go this afternoon. Oh! Let me . . ." She dabbled at the spilled tea that now dotted the white sheets, for the cup hung in Carlotta's suddenly nerveless fingers.

Carlotta did not even feel the heat of the tea. Her thoughts centered on the fact that her attempt at escape, feeble as it was, was now forestalled for certain. In Natchez, far up the Mississippi River, there would be no chance for anything except obedience to the will of Austin. She tried to gather her scattered wits but her face must have given her away more, for the girl ran to the door calling for Bettina.

The hard voice which answered her made Carlotta shiver. "Stop that shrieking, girl, unless you want to be left behind. Whatever is the matter?"

The little maid's babbling gave Carlotta time to settle back in the bed, one hand to her head, when the austere figure of Austin, his eyes weary, loomed over her. "I have sent the fool to fetch more tea. Are you all right? I regret any difficulty this sudden travel may cause you but it is a necessity." The latent savagery was gone from him; she might have been another man

252

or a casual acquaintance, not a woman upon whom he wished to beget a child.

"I am only weak, the heat, perhaps. I feel so drained. I do not think that I can travel, though. If you must, go on ahead. . . ." She sighed heavily and stretched her legs under the soft coverings. If only he would leave her in New Orleans!

"You have only undergone what countless other women do and they recover rapidly. I did not notice that you had any problem with the heat in Haiti. Ah, no, madame, you are essential to my plans and you shall not circumvent them. Burr has made contacts in Natchez and I have great power there. Prepare yourself."

She remembered his hands on his lover the night before and it took all her strength not to cry out the knowledge at him. Instead, she bent her head submissively and whispered, "I will try, Austin, for I, too, have all the reason in the world to want you to succeed, but must it be so swift? I am weary all the time."

His tone was less hard. "The river air will be good for you. I forget that you are lately come from another climate." She looked up through her long, dark lashes and saw that his expression was calculating. "Every concern will be taken for your welfare. You are the vessel of the future."

The maid tapped on the door just then and brought the tea to the bedside. Carlotta reached for it then let her fingers shake and fall to the covers. "I cannot."

Austin now looked worried. "We will have a litter for you. Rest now." He motioned to the maid who was holding the cup to Carlotta's lips. "Prepare her." He stalked out and Carlotta heard his usually cold voice raised as he commanded an unseen servant, "Fetch Bettina to me in the long parlor immediately."

The girl leaned against the maid's cushioning arm with a sigh of relief. If she had been at all adroit, it was likely that Bettina would earn a strong reprimand for overdosing her mistress and any further attempts at drugging her would be done carefully. A woman's weakness could take many forms, Carlotta thought, and she would have them all. Time gained was time won, even in the wilderness of Natchez.

Bettina came to Carlotta later, full of soft questions, her manner gentle. The girl was soft in her turn, speaking of the draining feeling she felt, the weariness. She had heard tales of the yellow fever and wished to remain as far from any thought of that as she might. It was a delicate path she had to walk, and her own turbulent nature had to be curbed if there were to be any chance for a life of her own.

Knowing this, she yielded docilely to their preparations and allowed herself to be bundled into a light carriage with the little maid, Sesa, in the early afternoon for the trip to the barges. It appeared that they were furnishing the house in Natchez and several others, to judge from all that was being taken. Delicately carved furniture, wrapped pictures, draperies, gold-mounted mirrors, tapestries, even a huge bed which could be broken down and put together again, two white horses, and a great stallion whose coat was the color of Carlotta's eyes, all these were to go besides the coterie of maids and a stern-faced housekeeper, Bettina, and all their luggage and Carlotta's. Austin's own baggage was arranged separately and she did not see it.

The carriage was curtained and Carlotta did not try to look out, but she heard the familiar cries of the peddlars and the chaffering of the women and their men, smelled the canals and the oleanders and the rising odor of mud, knowing as she did so that these would always call up New Orleans to her in the future. She thought of Michael Lanwardine again, how he had both sought her life and saved it, and spared a moment to wish him happiness. Lady Leticia had brought them both to a kind of ruin, yet from that had risen a new life. Her own time would come.

"The docks, mistress!" Sesa was bounding a little in her seat as she tried to maintain a sedate calm. She remembered her charge enough to say, "A chair will be there for you. You will suffer no waiting."

Carlotta smiled, trying to keep the pale and wan look that would serve her well, but did not speak.

The docks were crowded with ships, alive with people, and the merciless summer sun hammered down. The wide levee, the city's protection in time of flood, extended out, then sloped down. Wooden steps were fixed shakily to the bank at one point, and these were filled with watchers. Four bearers awaited the carriage with a large chair in which Carlotta was placed. A canopy shielded her head, and a summer bonnet helped also. They went off at a rapid pace, leaving Sesa to keep up as best she might.

They took Carlotta away from the public square and the market, past more boats and ships with foreign flags, down to a dock where three strange looking conveyances waited on the muddy river which seemed both wide and dangerous in the full light of day. The chair was set down beside the planks leading to the smallest of the boats, a bargelike affair with a mast and sails, oars, and a cabin stretching almost the length of it, yet enough space was left to provide a walkway in between, and long poles lay stacked to one side. The others were of the same make but far larger.

"Welcome, Madame Lenoir." The woman who waited in the door of the cabin was tall and spare, of indeterminate age, with a sharp-cut face and gray eyes. "I am Lena. My husband works on the lead boat, same as I do. Just wanted to make you comfortable." She looked at Carlotta's face, then at her flat stomach, which was all too plainly revealed under the gauzy white dress. "Come in and lie down."

Carlotta longed to stay out here and watch the river and the passage of the various craft, inhale the fishy air, and feel the beat of the sun on her skin, but she knew the price of safety. She smiled wanly and allowed the girl, Sesa, to lead her into the cabin.

Knowing Austin, Carlotta was not really surprised to see that the interior was well appointed with chairs, a writing desk, a long couch, and even a colorful rug on the floor. Adjoining doors led off to a small room where the maid could sleep and her own bedroom, to which she was now taken. It was white, with white curtains to be drawn against the heat and a wide bed, draped with more white curtains, which took up the rest of the area except for one chair and a tiny table. There was a chest for clothes and a rug of some animal skin.

Lena said briskly, "I'll just sit with you a while. The Master said you were real shaky. Scared of the trip upriver, are you?"

"Yes." The less said the better. She wanted to be alone to think about what this sudden journey meant and what means she could take to persevere. Not yet was she able to think about the attack of fear that morning and about the strange surcease that had come.

Lena pushed aside the skimpy skirts of the cotton dress she wore and sat down in the chair, which suddenly seemed too small for her. "We've been on this old river for years. Being scared is no good. The Miss'sippi's a woman, she knows. Respect, yes, fear, no." She scanned Carlotta's face again and something flitted across her own. "But it's more than that with you, I can tell."

Carlotta interposed hastily, "How long will it take us to get to Natchez? Is it uncivilized there?"

"Depends on the river currents, the wind, how fast they pole these barges. We're going upstream and that's hard work. That's why lots of people go up the Natchez Trace, the road from Natchez to Nashville, and use the trail from Natchez to New Orleans. But that's full of outlaws." She shrugged and her face was alive with amusement. "I'll take the river same as my man will. Anytime you want to talk, I can listen."

Carlotta noticed that she ignored the question about civilization. "I'll just rest, if I may."

"Suit yourself." Lena rose, a bit ruffled, and stalked out.

The boat shifted just then, swaying in the familiar pattern that she had become used to on the *Princess*. There was the sound of shuffling feet, men calling out to each other, Sesa giggling with someone, and then the slap of oars. She went to the window and looked out. They were floating freely in the river now, the swirling yellow-brown water bearing them aloft, past the levee she knew, past New Orleans proper and on into unknown territory.

Carlotta straightened up and went slowly into the main room. Sesa and two other girls were engaged in cleaning while an older woman watched. When the woman saw Carlotta, she said, "Are we disturbing you, madame?"

She wondered at this concern even as she saw the smooth hand of Austin in it. "No, of course not. Who are you?"

"Lula, madame. We are all slaves of the Master and here to serve you as best we can." She bent her head docilely.

"Who else is on board? Where is my husband?" The chilling thought had come to her that Austin might be planning to take advantage of the river trip to try to get her with child again, though it was far too soon.

"Master's on the big boat, seeing to all those things for the plantation and watching the river." If the woman wondered that Carlotta did not know the simplest things about Austin, she gave no indication, but the girl resolved to ask no more questions but to play her role as best she might.

The next few days were all of a piece, a time unique for Carlotta. She spent most of her time sitting by the largest window looking out at the river and the lands beyond. They went past the river plantations and the fertile grounds, the marshes, swamps, sandbars, and tangled woods. Sometimes, when the wind was right and the current suitable, their pace was swift. At other times it was laborious and painful, as the crewmen stood on the gangplanks that ran on the sides of the boat, pushed the long poles she had seen earlier into the marshy bottom of the river, and thrust the boat forward until the end was reached; then the poles were pulled up and the whole process began again. Very rarely it was necessary to tie long ropes around the trees on the bank and pull the boats. Austin's men were hardy and well paid, the boats converted to utilize the best of barge and keelboat along with sail and oars. This journey, difficult as it sometimes was, must be easy compared to some Carlotta heard the men discuss as they poled along.

They did not travel at night but tied up on the banks while the men watched with guns in hand for river pirates or outlaws. The heavily laden boats would make ideal prey for such predators. Sesa and the other maids discussed this in hushed voices, always ceasing when Carlotta ventured near. She found herself hoping they would attack; she might fare better at their hands than at Austin's. For the most part, however, she watched the muddy swath of the river as it faded into the misty distance and let its timelessness soothe her.

One night she was unable to sleep and went into the main room of the cabin to stretch her legs. The breeze from the window drew her and she went to it without thinking. She would have loved to walk outside but Lula had warned against this saying, "...Master wouldn't like it." From some of the unwitting talk of the men Carlotta thought she could understand that; some of the exploits of which they boasted would have upset the prowess of the Greek gods. Now she parted the curtains and looked out. The dark woods rose up close to their sandbar, and the swift rush of the river came over the night silence. She heard the tread of the guard as he walked back and forth. Uneasiness crawled along her spine and she swung her head to the side. There, standing on a sand spit only a few yards away from the barge, was the serpentine man she had seen with Austin at the ceremony. He lifted his head and his eyes met hers. She saw the flash of his teeth in the starlight, and the low savagery of his laughter came to her ears even as she jerked away from the sight of him.

CHAPTER THIRTY-FOUR

Stuart's Peace

THEY came to Natchez, the city on the bluff, on a blazing morning in midsummer when the clouds piled high in the west and the river seemed a flat, dark sheet in the distance as it curved through the land it made fertile. On the far side wooded flatlands stretched away as far as might be seen into somber green mistiness. The red-brown bluff, crowned with the city, now a jumble of roofs and great trees of oak and magnolia, drew the attention even from the Mississippi itself. A jumble of rivercraft of all types spread out from the foot of the bluff, and beyond these were the storehouses and docks. A thin thread of road seemed to wander up toward the city proper.

Carlotta was uncomfortably hot even in the thin blue dress which fit her loosely. The small straw bonnet she wore for propriety's sake weighed down her head, already heavy with the masses of coiled hair. She let the pretense of her weakness slip and stood with the others as they approached their destination. Austin's boat had already landed and she saw the glitter of his white head against his dark suit as he stood in the midst of a whirl of watchers and retainers to wait for her.

Lula and one of the boatmen handed her ashore with Sesa close at hand. The noise was deafening, for boats and ships were being unloaded, business was being conducted, baggage was jerked about, taunts and quips were exchanged with equal fervor by sailors, loungers, and townspeople. The place throbbed with life and excitement, just as the docks in New Orleans had done, and Carlotta responded to it.

"My dear, I am glad to see you looking so well. The river air must agree with you." Austin smiled silkily and offered his arm. "Allow me to conduct you to the carriage." He nodded at a black conveyance drawn by black horses which was waiting a short distance away.

Carlotta felt the blood pound into her face. She had no choice but to place her hand on his arm and walk with him. She had the shivering feeling that he had seen through her attempt at subterfuge, but she would continue the evasion as

258

long as possible. "I fear the dizziness has not left me as yet. I am really quite weak." Her eyes darted about but she saw no sign of the serpentine man who must surely account for at least part of Austin's good humor.

"Come. You will be better soon." The dark eyes were growing impatient.

The curtains were not drawn in the carriage and Carlotta was able to see the roaring life of the docks as they moved slowly away from them. Women in scanty dresses flirted with frontiersmen and sailors, filthy children chased each other up and down bawling obscenities as they did so, two men circled in the first stages of a fight to the glee of the onlookers, a bearded man turned up a jug and drank heavily, then ran toward the river, four well-dressed dandies sauntered along laughing, a young man and woman never stirred from a passionate embrace although the carriage passed with touching distance of them, drunken roistering came from the open doors of assorted taverns.

"Natchez-Under-the-Hill is a wild and dangerous place," remarked Austin, somewhat unnecessarily. "There are those who say that it rivals the very port of New Orleans."

Carlotta knew she must meet him with civility. "I remember reading in your books that England, France, and Spain have ruled here, that the Indians massacred settlers, and that this is almost the end of the civilized section of America."

"You are partly right, but this is a world contained in itself, one which acknowledges no overlord, and here, I am told, the estimable Mr. Burr found a goodly following. These people have no concern for a government far away in Washington City." His ambition flamed in his face and now he concealed his emotion less. "Aye, the time is right for this venture. A separate nation with an able ruler, ties of blood royal, an heir." He caught her hand and squeezed it convulsively.

She fought back her revulsion and sat quietly staring out the window. He fell silent, but she felt the force of his determination and knew that he would soon seek her bed.

The carriage rolled on into the city proper and paused at the summit of the hill before plunging down into the tree-shaded street. Carlotta caught her breath at the panorama of the great river swelling toward the north as it shone against the bluffs. The docks and boats were spread out below while on the other side the graceful city bloomed out. They clattered past elegant stores, churches, flowering walls, private homes with spacious

259

grounds, strolling citizens, and other carriages fully as elegant as their own. The street gave onto a smaller winding road which was thickly hung with vines dusted with red from the travel. Tall trees passed close to give thick shade. Then, suddenly, the road grew wider and the cotton fields spread out before them.

Carlotta gave a gasp, for the land shone faintly red-brown just as the cliffs had done and the green of the young plants mixed with the blue of the sky to form a riot of color. "How utterly beautiful!"

Austin's voice was for once devoid of mockery. "This Mississippi land is the loveliest anywhere. My capital shall be here, for these people are mine as no other could ever be. The very soil calls out. This shall be my nation!"

Carlotta sought to turn the conversation as she said, "You have extensive lands here then?" She wondered if he even thought of his dead son and what the true story of that was. Had he no fatherly feelings? Yet he had wept bitterly on hearing of Stephan's death. He did not answer and she turned to look at him. He waved an expressive hand at the flowing land on both sides of them as the carriage rushed along, the pace growing greater as the driver cracked his whip.

"Mine. All." The satisfaction in his voice was edged with greed.

They swung now into a long lane of trees which were tall oak and magnolia. These canopied over to make an archway which gradually widened out as the lane curved around. The wooded area beyond had little underbrush but twining vines and white flowers showed clearly. She saw a gleam of blue in the distance, and this grew brighter as they went uphill.

The carriage slowed in the next few minutes as Carlotta saw the great white bulk of the house swimming in green leaves, the columns lifting gracefully upward. Two pools were set to the sides and willows bent to them. There was an elevated porch and a cupola set back on the slanting roof. Flower gardens filled with roses, crepe myrtle, camellias, and many others that Carlotta did not know, stretched beyond the magnolias.

They stopped completely now and Austin helped her out. She saw the driver run to fetch the household, which must surely have been alerted for the coming of the Master, and then Austin was holding her hand, moving her to face him, as he said, "Welcome, my wife, my princess. Welcome to my house, to Stuart's Peace."

The slanting sun touched the brilliant facade of the house and flickered over Austin's hair. The pride in his voice was that of hubris, and his smile was complacent. Carlotta could understand his feelings, for here he did indeed rule supreme even as he had done in all the places she had known him, yet this was certain, this was his bedrock. It made him more vulnerable and that was good to know.

Over the cries of the running slaves being assembled to welcome the new mistress and the clatter of the great bell being rung to summon others from the fields, Carlotta said, "Beauty is too small a word, Austin. How came it by so strange a name?"

He turned that strange look of admiration and distaste on her. "Because a world ends here and a new one began. I will tell you." Then he took her hand and led her toward the great steps down which a tall, slender black woman was coming, her head bent in deference.

Carlotta's first impressions ran together in a jumble of sights and sounds—welcoming faces and curious looks, polished woods, priceless heirlooms, tapestries, and vistas of lawns. The house in New Orleans had been lovely but this one was that and more. She was taken to an equally elegant bedroom furnished in rose and white, which commanded an excellent view of the rolling lawns in the back, where more roses bloomed in ordered profusion.

A strangely quiet Sesa helped her bathe and dress in a soft yellow gown with slippers and shawl to match. Her hair was drawn back over her ears and wound in curls which tumbled down her back. The fan the young girl handed her was made in the shape of a yellow flower.

"Madame is beautiful this night. You are feeling better?"

Why all this concern with her health? Carlotta sighed, "The journey has wearied me. I am glad to reach Natchez at last." She started to open the door and heard the pattering footsteps behind her. Sesa was staring hard at her body but managed to avert her eyes. "What is the matter?"

"Madame, I . . . that is, if you need a potion or anything . . ." The little voice trailed away as Lula tapped at the door and pushed it open in the same moment. The young girl's eyes grew large and she backed away in confusion.

Carlotta did not miss the quelling look the older woman gave her helper, and her own voice was ice as she said, "Wait until I tell you to enter before doing so, Lula. Now, what is it?"

"Your pardon, madame, but Master Lenoir sent particularly to request your presence now." She stressed the last word faintly but her tone was respectful.

"Then I will go to him, but you must attend me down the stairs lest I grow weak." She would not leave Lula to castigate Sesa as she so obviously meant to do.

Austin was elegant in his usual black suit, but a white ruffled shirt softened the angularity of his features. There was a suppressed excitement about him and the hand that he extended to her was hot. He commanded Lula to bring chilled wine to the side garden. When she had gone he drew Carlotta out in the soft dusk where birds were uttering gentle night calls and the lush grass scents came headily to her nostrils.

"We will drink to the rising of our fortunes, my dear. This time next year will see us established as rulers of this territory and our son as heir. Yes, I will come to you tonight."

He caught her in his arms and his open mouth took hers in a deep, hungry kiss that probed and drew. His arms encircled her and crushed her against his chest so that she felt the hot urgency of him. The bar of his manhood did not rise, however, nor was there even a flicker of response. His tongue drove at hers, and one hand reached for her breast, the fingernail pushing on the nipple.

Carlotta knew that for her own safety she should simulate a kind of eagerness or at least obedience to his will but she could not. She went stiff in his arms and tried to pull her mouth free. It was a mistake; she saw that in the instant that he let her go. The fury that crossed his face for the space of a second was the same that she had seen in her nightmare, savage and evil. Words of explanation, of apology, of anger, stuck in her throat and she could only stare at him with wide eyes.

There was a step behind them and Lula said softly, "Master, the wine is ready."

His face smoothed out as he put a hand on Carlotta's arm. "Good, you may go now. Come, lady mine." He urged her along the well raked path to a bower of roses and heady yellow flowers where a bench overlooked the larger of the two ponds. The house rose white and secret behind them. Wine stood in chilled goblets on a small table over which a white linen cloth had been placed. The bottle rested in a silver bucket filled with what had to be spring water.

Carlotta sank down on the bench and took the goblet he extended to her. He was smiling and there was amusement in the black eyes. "To our fortunes, Carlotta." She sipped dutifully, then saw that he watched intently. Instinct came to her rescue for she knew, as surely as she knew that she loved Simon, that the wine was drugged.

"Tell me how the house came by its name, Austin. Stuart's Peace sounds somehow alien." Odd that the almost inane request should pull those fierce eyes from her and cause his lips to soften, but it seemed that she had said the right, the saving thing.

He twirled the golden goblet in his fingers and said, "When we were in Charleston, there was mention of Scotland by Charles Windhope. He comes from that unhappy land, and his grandson, as you know, bears the name of Charles Edward, that Stuart prince whom the romancers called Bonnie Prince Charlie. My own ancestors came from Scotland and from France. The '45 was long over before I was old enough to drink in the legends. We lived in France for years, and it was my father's one regret that he could not participate due to family struggles at the time. That happenstance saved us all, as Scotland still bears the marks of that fruitless attempt to restore the Stuarts to the throne. Every generation wanted to try. My parents died; I studied in France and went, as did many young people, to the sea to make my fortune."

The rapidly fading light showed the pulse pounding at his temple and the beads of perspiration on his upper lip although the wind was cool. He put the goblet down with a thud, and Carlotta took that moment to tip the wine in hers to the ground. He would not have noticed, she thought, if she had thrown it. He was in another time, another world, and she was about to learn something of the mystery of Austin Lenoir. He looked at her, through her, as his words came more swiftly.

"I prospered and bought land in New Orleans and outside it on the Mississippi. It seemed that I had but to want gold in order to make it. All that was lacking was a wife. I returned to France and there met one woman before whom all others palled. Her family was noble and wealthy; the bloodbath of the Revolution was beginning. I implored her to leave with me but she would not. I had to go to England on urgent business and when I returned she had vanished. I tried to trace her but was unable to do so. My name was on the proscribed list and I was forced to flee for my life. Years later I learned that she had been guillotined."

Carlotta drew an anguished breath as she remembered those letters she had glimpsed in his cabin so long ago. Loving Simon had taught her the ways of compassion; if Austin were twisted now, what might he have been had he been able to pursue the normal course of life? The hard voice was rushing on, the words rattling out as if they were pebbles.

"I wandered after that. Europe, the south countries, Asia. My golden touch remained constant but there was nothing I wanted. I married twice; you know the results of that. I was bored; I sought sensation. I learned to hate during those years, and I learned to use that hate. The rabble and those who use them, the despots and the power-seekers, those who flaunt a cause and profess to care passionately, the stupid and the foolish. Napoleon, the Stuart Kings, the battles in America for a freedom that is only a name—it is all the same. My kingdom will take advantage of all I have learned, for I know the uses of power and believe in nothing."

Carlotta said involuntarily, "I am sorry for you, Austin."

His raucous laughter set several hunting dogs to baying and caused the chills to trickle down her back. "You waste your sympathy. Take care that you do not bore me, as I have told you before." He sobered and swung round to face the rolling vistas of his estate. "Stuart's Peace was built several years ago and named for the peace that I have made with all lost causes. My son was one of those causes, but you will give me another."

The soft wind molded her thin dress against her body so that she felt naked before him. It carried the sound of laughter from the slave quarters that she had seen in the distance and for a second she wished bitterly that she had at least as much chance for happiness as they. Yet that, too, was false, for all belonged to this savage man in front of her.

She kept her voice soft. "You have told me much this night, Austin. I am grateful for the sharing."

"Sharing? Not so. You should know these things to make you more cognizant of your duty. I am not a man to be foiled. I trust your health will soon improve, madame." His fingers bit into the soft flesh of her forearm. "Have your maid make you ready. I will come to you within the half hour."

She did not know what effect the wine was supposed to have had but she knew that there was no redress from his determination. Softness must be her weapon and her ploy. She bent her head as if in obedience.

He walked beside her into the gleaming archway of the house. Candlelight cast drifting shadows on polished floors, and the scent of flowers was everywhere. Strange that such beauty was not enough. Still, would she not give all that she had ever wanted for the chance to be with Simon, to know that he still lived? Had he died because this man beside her would not turn aside to rescue him?

Austin bent over her and his lips were cruel on her unresisting mouth. His eyes looked deep into hers and she could not conceal the anger she felt. His teeth closed on her lower lip and his fingers touched her throat half in passion and half in a response to the distaste she could not help but convey.

"Master." Lula spoke from a few feet away, her voice unperturbed at the scene before her.

Austin gave Carlotta a small push. "Prepare her."

Carlotta stood still. There was no point in rebellion at this stage; he was capable of anything.

Lula ignored her and spoke directly to Austin. "Master, the news is good. Tomorrow you will see the results."

His voice was suddenly light, eager, as he said, "Is it so?"

Carlotta looked from one to the other and read in their inconsequential words the sealing of her fate.

CHAPTER THIRTY-FIVE

By Courage and Craft

His hands sought her breasts for what seemed the twentieth time, kneading their softness, twisting the nipples. His mouth roamed over her flesh without any pretense of eagerness or caring, only determination. Her skin burned with irritation from his nails and the stubble of his chin. The tenderness between her legs felt ripped and savaged, there were marks on her neck from his sucking lips, and her waist was raw from her jerking her to him.

He himself was exhausted. There were dark-ringed circles under his eyes, and his pale skin seemed to fold in on itself. His arms bore the marks of her scratches, and one hand had two sets of teeth marks set in it. His member lay pale and scrawny between his legs but it, too, ached with pain for all the struggle that had been lavished upon it.

The bright light of full morning streamed across their bodies and highlighted the purple bruises they had given each other in the course of the long night. It shimmered across the polished floors, the damask drapes, and the wide, soft bed, coming at last to dwell in the dark eyes of Austin Lenoir as he rose on one elbow to confront the woman who had witnessed that which was unforgiveable. He was impotent with her and had been so all the time that they turned and twisted in the paroxysms of darkness.

As he had accused her once of willing herself to lose the child, so did he now accuse her. "You made me this way by lying there as if you were made of stone. You rejected my body and have dried up my flesh."

Carlotta jerked the sheet up over her lacerated limbs and thought that now they had come to it. There was no pretense left. "You cannot believe such rot, you a rational man of this century! It is ridiculous!"

He rose and wrapped a black silk robe around himself. "I will have what I want from you, madame. Accustom yourself to my nightly visits until you quicken."

Reason and caution left Carlotta then. She jumped up to

face him, disregarding her nudity and the aches all over her body. There was a score to be paid and she would settle it. "Ah, is that it? You had to have potions on board the ship, did you not? Doubtless it takes that to whip your flesh into acceptance of a woman. You held me against my will, flouted all honor and decency, deserted the one man and his followers who tried to save your miserable life, and now seek to pollute the world by spreading your seed! You are not fit for life, Austin Lenoir, much less rule. I curse the day I ever laid eyes on your foulness!"

Her voice died away, for she saw her death in his eyes. His hands came up slowly as they reached for her throat. Strangely all she could think of was the brown age spots that had not been there a few days ago. His lips thinned to a long line and parted slightly so that the tip of his tongue showed. He would take more joy and pleasure in killing her than he had ever taken in the thought of her young body.

She had nothing to lose. She cried out her taunts in the intoxicating delight of freedom. "Old man, old man, you spew forth misshapen seed. Was not your son one such? And you blamed the mother as men always do. Was he mad as you are? As mad as you seek to drive others? You are capable only of cruelty and that will surely destroy you!"

His hand slammed toward her head and had she not dodged in the last second she would have been brained where she stood. As it was, she fell to the floor and the shock brought her to her senses. She had maligned the dead and torn the festering wounds of the brutal living. Too late she remembered Austin's anguished cries for his dead son and the quiet voice of Michael Lanwardine's friend suggesting that the young man had taken his own life. She tried to avoid the bare, hard foot that was swinging toward her but it caught her in the ribs and she cried out in pain. Austin began to laugh and she saw that the thin cover of civilization was completely gone from his face. A madman faced her.

The bellow of a baby held too tightly and left unfed cut across their mutual rage at the same time that Lula's urgent voice cried, "Master, Master, is all well? I have brought a thing to show to you." The bellow came again, and this time the slave laughed in reply to it.

"Go away! I will have you whipped!" His voice was guttural, hard, but the interruption served to give Carlotta time to regain her balance and twist the sheet around her naked flesh. She snatched up the ornate candleholder near her and vowed to give Austin Lenoir as good as she might get. She was no longer afraid; her blood sang in her veins and throbbed in her temples.

"It is a son, Master! A healthy son!"

Austin swung the door back and confronted the woman, her face alight with joy. She held a child who might have been anywhere from four to seven months old. His skin was the color of creamy coffee, the hair on his head was straight and dark, the set of the nose and face very much that of Austin Lenoir. He bellowed again and the features twisted into those of Austin in a rage.

"Give him here." He took the boy and unwrapped the clothes to reveal the smooth, straight limbs, the perfect hands and feet, the unbent back. The child wailed lustily and wept without tears. "He is mine. I see my face here."

"Even so, Master. Out of the slave Mintua whom you bedded once and swiftly on your last visit to New Orleans. She had known no other man and conceived that time to have this child."

The look that Austin gave Carlotta was one of triumph laced with vindication. Lula glanced at her and brushed her aside as unimportant. Carlotta knew then that it was this woman who supplied him with whatever potions he dosed himself and gave to her as well.

Lula was continuing, her voice low but clear. "And that is not all, Master. The other girl quickens."

"It is too soon." The thrill rang in his voice and he stood straighter, the marks of his battle with Carlotta already seeming to fade.

"Nay, say rather that you have been blessed." The woman was smiling at him as eagerly as though they shared a mutual prize. "I will claim the promise you gave me."

"All in due time. If she bears another son. If he is well formed and in his wits."

Carlotta's head swung round and she stared at Lula, who backed away before the anger in Austin's face. He appeared irritated at his slip of the tongue, and well she knew his propensity for blaming others. Lula knew it, too, for she bowed her head and scuttled away, her brief supremacy gone. Husband and wife faced each other again.

Carlotta moved to the attack. He should not find her supine before him in fear. "It seems that congratulations are in order. You have been busy."

He caught her arm in one hand, the supple fingers seeming to reach through her flesh. "You might as well know what this household and no other knows. What harm can it do? You will never reveal it. Stephan, my son, my first-born, my only heir, was not only a hunchback but a true idiot who could not put on his breeches without help. My manager governed in his name; the world thought that young Master Lenoir was frail and studious. I trusted my man with that life and secret; he never failed me. Would that others could have been so loyal!"

Carlotta knew then who the serpentine man was.

"I was anguished, bitterly so. I lay with other women. They quickened and miscarried of misshapen monsters. Twice this happened. I took potions and vowed that my seed was cursed. Then I despaired of having the son I needed for my empire. You rejected my body and lost my heir to be. But now the half-breed boy is perfect and an indentured girl with whom I lay briefly in New Orleans not long after we arrived has the signs of pregnancy. She is of good stock and my blood is of the best. The dynasty will come." He swayed back and forth, his pride restored, the edge of his anger blunted for the moment.

"Then set me free. Let me go to the north country. We have torn each other enough." She fought to keep the note of pleading from her voice but could not.

He smiled that smile of endless cruelty. "My dear, you are my wife. How can I let you go? You have been ill. Women who have lost children frequently behave as you have done. I bear you no ill will. You must rest and grow better."

"I will not endure another such night and morning as this, Austin." She pulled the sheet closer around her shoulders as if to protect herself.

"Have I demanded it? Ah, no, you have the name, almost certainly the royal blood of the Kings of France. My son will still be my son. The rallying points for my cause are diverse—they appeal to everyone. No, Carlotta, be at peace. Your flesh is quiescent after losing the child. That I know. I have been over-diligent."

He looked at her for a moment longer, then walked into the adjoining room and shut the door firmly behind him. Carlotta, shaken by the long ordeal, sank down in the closest chair and gave way to the shudders that racked her. It took no great intelligence to know Austin's plan, she thought wryly. She was considered a little daft, given to fancies and fears. No one would believe her if she tried to enlist aid in escaping Austin, and how could she do so anyway in this distant city? He would let her recover and, now that his belief in his manhood was assuaged, would choose his time in taking her. As he had said, the dynasty would come. She smiled mirthlessly to herself. Very well, it would be long before she regained her full strength and longer still before she ceased to tremble to the touch of Austin Lenoir. She did not delude herself that he would forgive those words of the morning, his revenge would be enacted sooner or later. The knowledge about Stephan was enough to make her his enemy. And, brute that he was, he would have mated her to this idiot.

Carlotta sat there by the window and watched the sunlight of summer pour down on the immaculate green lawns and flower beds. A swan drifted on one of the pools and was soon joined by another. A slave walked by with a long-legged, aristocratic dog on a leash. The sound of hammering rose in the distance. A climbing rose wound up the wall not far from where she sat, and several golden bees hummed in their sweetness. All was at peace except she herself.

When Sesa came to the door with the strong tea, she took it and drank gratefully, glad for the release it brought. It seemed to her that time drew out as she sat apart, watching the peaceful scene below and sipping the brew. She was not sleepy, only relaxed at last.

There was a movement off to the side and her eyes swung dreamily to the flash of white. Austin shone black against the swift moving horse as he headed down the lane of trees, a slave riding well to the rear. Strange that he should be rushing off after the rigors of the night. Was he not exhausted? Her legs felt heavy, her arms weighted her down, and she was forced to let the nearly empty cup drop to the floor. The sound of it rolling on the boards was oddly muted. She sighed and let the wind wash over her. Really, what had all the fuss been for? Let things take their course.

"Mistress, will you rest now? Let me take you to your room." Sesa was beside her, speaking softly, lips moving faster than the spoken word came.

Carlotta spoke but her lips seemed stiff and her tongue twisted around the words. She wanted to ask where Austin went in such haste but all that came was a croak. Sesa did not think it of any importance, for she came to help her walk. Carlotta tried to push her away and say that she could very well walk alone, but her legs crumpled and she was forced to cling to the other's arm for support.

Sesa helped her to the door, where another slave girl waited, and between them they assisted Carlotta to her room, where they placed her in the canopied bed. She lay, her body unresponsive, her mind sluggish but still knowing. Her voice would not work at all now. Her blood seemed to be draining from her veins as the weariness rose up.

The voices of the slaves came to her through layers of down. "Will she sleep now? Should we get more of the tea?" Sesa's voice trembled a little.

The other girl was more positive. "Miz Lula orders that. She's had a big dose, the mistress has. You get the fan and we'll keep her cool. Best wait until they tell us what else to do."

Presently the warm air was stirred by the big palmetto fan plied by Sesa who sat in the rocking chair at the foot of Carlotta's bed. Carlotta did not sleep but the potion that she had been given held her body in thrall and kept conscious thought down. She speculated vaguely over what Austin had done to her but fear was not truly present. It might have been a play or a waking dream. She knew that time passed, that broth was spooned into her mouth and her face washed, that Lula's sharp-featured face bent over her once or twice, that it grew dark outside and then light again, but it had no meaning for her. She might have slept but that did not matter. Nothing did.

Carlotta came to full awareness in the bright, hot light of another noon, when the thin sheet pressed down on her legs and thirst parched her mouth. She could move but not easily, and it seemed to take an unconscionable time to bring her hand to her mouth. When she turned her head she saw that the room was empty. Her mind cleared even more and she remembered anew that this was Austin's vengeance, his consummate cruelty.

As if she had conjured him up out of her waking nightmare, his voice rang in the hall. "Keep a watch on the mistress. She must recover her strength."

An unfamiliar voice said, "Aye, Master. She sleeps even now."

"She must be up when they arrive. See to it." His boots sounded on the boards and faded against the carpeted stairs.

Carlotta ducked her head against the pillows and pretended to sleep. The door creaked softly and then was as gently shut.

She opened her eyes and darted a quick glance around the room. No one was there. Who were the people who would be arriving? What would they do to her? Carlotta fought back the fear and began to work her muscles as well as her hands and feet in an effort to restore movement to them so that she could at least defend herself. She thought of an old woman in the village where she had grown up and how she moved with great care since every joint ached and throbbed with pain. That was the way she felt now. To make matters worse, her head began to pound like drumbeats in the temples.

Time faded again for her and when she next lifted to consciousness it was late in the evening by the slant of sunlight across the bed. This time a tray of food was on the table nearby and she saw that it looked to be meat with gravy and bread. A type of melon was sliced also, and there was a half bottle of wine. She felt the juices start in her mouth. Her hand went automatically out, and she felt the easy tears of sickness start. The slowness was less pronounced, her tongue was no longer a bar in her mouth, and her legs moved when she tried to shift them.

This time food and drink were untainted. She felt the power returning to her with each mouthful that the slave fed her. It was the ultimate foolishness to pretend this way, but she did not wholly trust her body, the body that had served her so well all her life and that she had never doubted before. She shook her head at the offered tea and asked shakily for the wine.

"I have been ill again?" She would never admit to the knowledge of what had been done to her lest it be redoubled.

The slave could not have been pretending. Carlotta thought that she saw treachery behind every smooth face. "Yes, mistress. You were taken quite suddenly. The Master was so worried! But you've been doctored and will surely be able to attend the party for a little while."

Carlotta wondered again at the curious blend of education and ignorance that Austin's slaves had. But Tanda had been the same. Was it a protective shield? She said, "What do you mean, party? I am very weak." Her voice wavered, shook, and righted itself.

"Tomorrow night. Big gentlemen from town and their ladies. Music and all. We'll fix a chair for you and you can watch." The girl's eyes were innocently clear.

Carlotta waved a hand at the tray, her appetite gone; the need to be alone was pressing. If she was to do anything about escape it must be in the next few days, while they did not know to what extent she had the power of movement and reasoning. She thought suddenly of the gold that Michael had given her, which she had packed away in the old chest. It had been kept with her, she was almost sure of that. There would be jewels, too; she might squirrel some away and hope that she could bribe someone with them. Then she shook her head impatiently. Her brain was fuzzy, of a certainty. All these people were Austin's not only in body but in the very soul of the ceremony she had witnessed. She needed someone not in his employ, someone sympathetic to her plight as she meant to show it. She thought suddenly of the tall, spare Lena who had spoken of the great river as if it were a woman and who had suggested that Carlotta talk if she felt like it. Was she in Austin's employ, she and her husband, the pilot of the lead boat? She had not sounded as if they worked for anyone regularly. And there was the girl, Sesa, who helped in what was being done to her but whose eyes had mirrored both admiration and concern.

Her resolve rose and with it the blood hammered again in her temples. She said, "Send Sesa to me!" Her battle had begun again, and this time she was armed.

CHAPTER THIRTY-SIX

Passion's Armor

CARLOTTA looked at the transformation of her face in the glass. The tenseness had left her mouth, it was pink as the roses blooming in the vase at her elbow, and the shadows under her eyes had faded in a faint darkness that lit up the amber flecks in them. Her brows curved upward, gleaming with the scented oil that had been touched to them to make them glossy. Excitement made her cheeks shine and the pulse in her throat hammer. Her red-brown hair was dressed high with ringlets cascading over her smooth shoulders. Waves at the sides of her head were deep and soft.

She stood up abruptly and the folds of the white gown drifted delicately down to be reflected back from the polished floor boards. Threads of blue ran through the skirt, and the long full sleeves were edged in the same color. The neckline was low, revealing the contours of her breasts, which were more full since the child. The waistline was loose and relaxed, and the gown flowed with her and made her seem a cloud of blue-white. Sapphires gleamed on her fingers and diamonds in her ears.

"Madame is fair this night." Sesa admired her from the periphery, then moved quickly in to twitch the skirt to a more favorable angle. "Will you have a dose before we go down?" She touched the pot which held the fresh tea.

Carlotta smiled at the young girl whose friendship she had sought in these past few hours and meant to cultivate even more. She had confided that she had not entirely wanted the child, that life in New Orleans had a lure she found it hard to forego, and that England was a gay place despite the war. Her longing for freedom had been evident, she knew, and was likely interpreted as the yearning of a flighty wife who might have a lover at the ready. Chatter it had been, the maunderings of a woman not yet fully recovered, but Carlotta was willing to gamble on the fact that few people in England had seen the servants as people and here, with slaves, it was less likely, for they were possessions only. She had talked as a woman might talk to another. It was a beginning.

Now she said, "No, I thank you. Will you be here when I come up tonight?" Surely Sesa did not know that the tea was a drug. Daring took her then and she stretched out a hand to the cup that had been placed earlier for her. "I'll just pour a bit out. The Master might be upset if he thought I hadn't taken it." She poured it into the water that had been used to wash her hands and lifted guileless eyes to the girl. Now let her betray herself if she were part of the plot.

Sesa smiled at her, the wide, conspiratorial smile of a child with a secret. "Yes, madame. I understand. Don't worry." She looked at Carlotta, clearly and openly. "I understand the tea is a special brew suggested by him. He would be worried if he thought you did not like it."

"We understand each other, then?" Confrontation had come sooner than Carlotta had intended and now she tried to project all her power of will into urging a young slave girl to go against the expressed wishes of the master of the house who had life and death power over her. Or, she amended wryly, over them both.

"I am Master Lenoir's slave. I am madame's servant in all things." The thin eager body quivered with sincerity, and the new dignity sat bravely on her.

Carlotta thought of Tanda and knew that she must trust another human being. She said, "I am grateful, Sesa. I will go down now." As the girl nodded and went to the door to call the downstairs servant who would help Carlotta to the seat of the mistress downstairs, music rose soft and hypnotic in the mournful English ballads of love and loss. The muted sounds of conversation came drifting up as Carlotta steadied herself.

The carved shutters of golden oak which formed part of the doors to the main drawing room were closed to leave one section secluded. A green-cushioned chair, itself upholstered in a paler green, stood near the fireplace, where logs would blaze in winter. The carpet was the green of young leaves in spring; the border was deeper green with yellow intertwined so that it seemed laced with gold. The golden motif was repeated in the curtains, which reflected against the misty green walls. Two of the tapestries Austin loved hung facing each other across the wide space of floor. Mirrors gave back the images upon each other, and the myriad flickering candles shimmered in their own golden light.

The maid settled Carlotta in the chair, fetched a glass of wine for her, then stood back where she could keep an observant eye on her mistress. The musicians in the recessed galleries launched into yet another plaintive lament, and Carlotta felt a chill go up her spine without knowing the reason. If she did not escape from Austin Lenoir soon, she thought she would go quite mad. How long would it take for Sesa to care enough for her to help her, to take risks for her? If ever? She tensed her muscles slightly and knew that the enforced lassitude had told on her usually strong supple body.

There was a rush of movement, the odor of lavender and rich wine, and a heavier scent of some exotic flower, and a babble of voices rose. A strong voice lifted above them all. "Madame Lenoir, let me present myself. I am Eugenia De Soucet, and this is my daughter, Alicia. My brother even now speaks with your husband. I hope that we do not intrude on your recent illness but I was assured that a brief few moments would not tire you."

The speaker was a large, capable-looking woman in her late sixties, gray hair built into an imposing edifice of rolls and curls, several folds of fat cascading into a shelf of bosom and stomach, the whole thrust into a lacy purple dress. Her daughter, perhaps sixteen, was a picture of what her mother had been at that age—fat, suet eyes, short, stubby fingers. Her smile, however, was singularly sweet in the round face.

Carlotta murmured, "Welcome to this house, ladies. You will forgive me if I do not rise to greet you properly?"

Madame De Soucet said firmly, "Certainly. Let me present Madame Tolino, late of France by five years, Mrs. James Linden, whose husband was one of the advisors to an important official in the government of President Adams, and our Spanish lady, Senora Hernandez, whose husband's voice spoke for Spain in this land until he was injured in an Indian battle and forced to retire from active toil."

Carlotta smiled as she looked at the curious ring of faces. The ladies were all middle-aged but well tended, with carefully powdered cheeks, jeweled hands and necks, and rich gowns. Their eyes were guarded; she could tell they wondered just how much of the plot she knew.

"Again, I bid you fully welcome to Stuart's Peace." She gestured to the slave behind her chair. "Bring wine and cakes for our guests."

In the ensuing exchange of pleasantries she had time to

observe the careful glances they gave her and was cautious in her own turn to note that their jewels were real, their clothes of the best. These must be the Natchez ringleaders in the women's circles even as their wealthy and powerful husbands, who, if Madame De Soucet was to be believed, had once been in the very centers of power. She passed one hand over her forehead but kept the smile firmly in place. They must report that Madame Lenoir was frail, weak, a little anxious, no danger to any plans being made.

Madame Tolino, bosomy and dark, said, "I fear we tire you, Madame Lenoir." Her voice dropped low as she leaned toward Carlotta, who caught the stale smell of unwashed hair. "I, too, felt so in your condition. I was delicate. My poor Edward suffered just as I did. Now we can laugh about it. But it is early on, yet. You will be better."

Carlotta stared at her in puzzlement which must have been reflected on her face, for Madame De Soucet snapped, "Let us walk out into the garden while our husbands confer. Isabel means nothing, madame, she does tend to natter on. With your permission?"

Carlotta made her face blank, her eyes soft before the heavy face thrust into her view. "Of course, of course. I know we will all be good friends when I am able to move about." It could not hurt if they thought her a little simple as well.

They moved slowly toward the door, the girl Alicia looked back with the frank curiosity that good manners forbade from her elders. Carlotta waved the slave back with a peremptory gesture and pretended to sip at the wine. A sickening feeling swept over her as she realized the significance of the Tolino woman's words. Was she supposed to be with child now? Rumor would have it so, it appeared. But to what end? What would happen when she did not grow larger? True, by then she hoped to be gone, but Austin would not permit anything such as this to be bruited about without reason. She shifted in the soft cushions and was suddenly aware that the loose gown she wore might very well be thought to conceal any phase of pregnancy. Austin thought himself potent now and perhaps he was. Perhaps he could impregnate others; well and good, she wanted no part of him. She must try to find out what was going on, however.

The music came liquid and golden to her ears as the doors opened and closed off the hallway. There was a rustle of notes, low humming, and an exploratory phrase or two. Footsteps rang on the boards where the rug ended, and she heard masculine voices raised in greetings to the ladies, who responded with soft laughter mixed with gushes of words.

"From here, from here, has he fetched me. He has taken me across the sea, the sea of dawn-light, and into a lightning-blasted land. His light is my light, his breath my breath, for all the length of life."

The voices rose pure and true in the song that was old out of conscious memory, the song that she had heard once at a village fair and again from Uncle Arnold in the cold nights of an English winter. The yearning in it had touched her even then, and now it threatened to bring the tears.

"And I walk with him in the mountains, the purple mountains, run with him to the rivers of my youth. All the days of my life. All the days of my life."

The front door opened inward, the draft sending the candle flames dancing in a wash of golden light that tossed back and forth. Two men stood in the glitter but only one held the eye. He was very tall with hair the color of early sunlight, his skin very brown against the bottle-green coat he wore.

"His light is my light." The singers exulted softly in the chorus, their voices mounting into a crescendo, then sliding into silence.

Carlotta sat up very straight in the chair and watched the man she loved walk toward her.

"Madame Lenoir. My greetings. I have come to speak with your husband. Do forgive me if I have disrupted the festivities in progress." His voice was the same, smooth and deep and assured. Now that he was closer, she saw the white scar at the edge of his hairline and the new lines on his forehead. The brilliant eyes had not changed; they regarded her now with skepticism and more than a little grimness.

Her mouth was dry. She tried to speak but no words would come. Her heart was hammering so hard that she could almost believe the poets when they said it might burst free. She lifted one hand and it fell numbly back. Simon. Alive. Not dead. Alive. "I would have known it for certain if he were dead." She knew the thought for very truth.

He stared at her strangely, and now the little man was whispering at his elbow, nodding his head toward the closed section of the room from which the low sounds of conversation still came. Simon swung his head to look, and Carlotta heard the rustle of skirts in the far doorway.

"...made every youth cry well a-day..." The piercing, tender voices came once again in love's lament for faithless Barbara Allen. Carlotta suddenly longed for a good rollicking dance or a spirited battle song. Her power of speech returned in full force and she forgot the languid invalid she was thought to be.

"Simon! What brings you to Natchez and to this house? I thought you were dead, although I could not truly believe it. How is it with you?" She stood up and the dress whispered softly about her body as the maid leaned nearer, fearing her mistress might faint. She saw that Madame De Soucet watched unashamedly from the door and did not care.

Simon came a step closer, the green eyes still scrutinizing her. "I still live, as you can see. It is kind of you to inquire as to my health but I do not wish to tire you. Monsieur Nichol reminds me that you have been ill. My apologies." The bow he swept her would have done credit at the mightiest court in Christendom. Others would see his courtesy to the wife of his host. Only she would know the irony behind it.

"...and the rose grew round the briar..." The song mourned to a close as the candle flames leapt in the wash of warm air caused by the door opening as Austin came in.

He was elegant in black and white, the dark eyes unfathomable, his bearing erect. Several portly men stood just beyond the threshold of the door from which he had entered. They were engaged in earnest conversation, their faces serious and almost anxious. Carlotta turned to watch Austin approach Simon and extend his hand, which the other took unhesitatingly.

"My dear Mr. Mitchell, so kind of you to join us. I fear we are a small party tonight." Carlotta heard the buried steel in his words.

Simon laughed, the sound rich and full in the room. "Now, Mr. Lenoir, you are kindness itself to my rudeness. I arrived suddenly from New Orleans and thrust myself upon good Monsieur Nichol here, whom I met in other circumstances. He was invited here and had no recourse, he said, but to bring me. I told him we had met some little time ago and that doubtless I might examine your library or exchange chats with the ladies. May I take the liberty?"

She watched as the politeness continued, the verbal passage-at-arms that no outsider could possibly have comprehended, and wondered again that Simon had come here in such a manner. Her own anger was building, the good healthy anger that brought a flush to her cheeks and lessened the lassitude that her longing for him had caused.

Her voice was gay and trivial as she spoke across their words. "I vow, my husband, that if Mr. Mitchell is to be left to his own devices, he must first pay his respects to his hostess. Later, if he continues polite, I may permit him to flirt with the young lady who is also our guest." She lifted limpid eyes to Austin, who scowled briefly. "I cannot bear to be away from the sounds of liveliness just yet."

Austin cast an uncertain glance at the others who waited for him, their faces grave. Monsieur Nichol looked urgently at him also and that seemed to decide him for he smiled at Carlotta, though his eyes were knife blades.

"As you wish, my dear. I am sure that Mr. Mitchell will bear in mind your recent illness and present weakness. A few minutes only." His glance flicked to Simon who nodded amiably, the impromptu guest who was a little embarrassed by all these references to health, a thing not done in polite society.

Seconds later the others were closeted again, the maid was waved back, and Madame De Soucet could be heard speaking bracingly to the young Alicia just beyond the entranceway. Simon stood a short distance from Carlotta's chair as was proper, his expression one of polite inquiry.

"You are looking well tonight, Madame Lenoir, if I may be so personal. The air of this country must agree with you."

She drew in her breath angrily. "You will not bandy words with me, Simon! Why are you here after what Austin did to you? After he sailed away without even attempting to rescue you? Or do you seek revenge? And what of the lady you had sworn to wed?"

He laughed again and any watcher might have thought that they spoke casually. His eyes belied any such assumption by Carlotta. "It is true that Austin did not try to help me; I was fortunate that the Haitians thought me dead and ran away under the guns of my own ship. My men came to bury me as they, too, thought that none could have survived such a blow to the skull. Fortunately, mine is singularly hard. I healed rapidly as you can see." His voice softened. "I am sorry about the child."

"Thank you. But why are you here?" Her breath quickened as he leaned closer and she caught the fresh scent of him, saw the broad shoulders move under the green coat. Her flesh remembered his.

"Let us say that I cannot return to my promised bride until

280

I have riches in my pockets. I thought to obtain those in Haiti; heaven knows there was enough when we lived there. I am now relatively poor." He shrugged.

The idea burst upon Carlotta so suddenly that she trembled with it. She had always known that any plan involving Sesa and Lena along with possible bribery of a ship's captain was risky enough but she had to break free. Now Simon was here and would surely help her. She said, "Simon, once we cared for each other. Do not deny it; I am wiser now. For the sake of what once was, will you help me to flee this city of Natchez and go to the north? I must be free of Austin Lenoir; he is evil and he means my destruction. He is mad for power and has the will to force it."

"My dear Carlotta, you have had a tiff with him. Do not be foolish. He is older and rich, you will be a queen on this plantation. I will not deny that I found you fair, but I will not antagonize a man so powerful and influential. I will not help you in foolishness." He started to move away from her as Madame De Soucet began to enter with Alicia.

"No, Mama!" The young girl jerked back and the clatter of her heels sounded in the hall. The harder ones of her mother rang in pursuit.

"I will pay. I have gold. There are jewels here and I naturally have access to them. They will pay for the passage to New Orleans and then a ship to Boston or New York. Help me and you will go rich to your richer bride." Her tone was hard, though she wanted to weep bitter tears.

"No." He walked across the room and paused to adjust his neckcloth at the golden mirror near the fireplace. "No."

Carlotta rose from her chair and walked over to him. She saw her reflection twist and distort in the mirror, her collar bones sharp against the drawn flesh, her eyes savage. "If you fear Austin, do not. He will be fiercely angry at first, but all he really cares about is his scheme of empire and when that is begun shortly he will think of nothing else. You owe me, Simon, and I call the debt. Is it not because of you that I am tormented by Austin Lenoir and his evil?" She had no honor, she thought, for she fought for survival itself.

His face changed and she saw that she had his full attention. "You are not the first who has spoken of him as scheming for empire as though it were serious. So did the ex-Vice-President, Mr. Burr, speak in his own behalf. What do you know of this?"

"I met Mr. Burr at the convent in New Orleans. A most

pleasant gentleman. Simon, I truly fear for my life. Will you let me explain?"

He might not have heard her. The green eyes were secretive, his brow knotted in concentration. "It fits. Damn, it does! And there is the link!" His eyes went to the door, and his carved lips drew wide in a smile. "Ah, madame, I must have the pleasure of an introduction."

The De Soucets now advanced fully across the carpet. There were tear stains on Alicia's cheeks and her mother was too angry at that to give much attention to Carlotta.

Simon said, "I will speak with you again. Wait for word." Then he advanced to meet them.

Carlotta waved for the maid to come and give her support. Her blood sang with hope but her heart ached, for she knew that he would just as easily abandon her.

CHAPTER THIRTY-SEVEN

I Will Go Up

CARLOTTA found herself thankful for the respite of the next four days. There was no sign of Austin, though she knew he was on the premises from the chatter of the maids who served him and those who came to confer with him. Something was in the wind and all felt it. Lula was absent from her service, and she was once again conscious of the relief this gave. She kept up the observance of her role as she sat in the gardens, reclined in the chair placed in the arbor at evening, rested late in her bed, and drooped in the afternoon heat. She was careful to eat just fruit, bread, and a little meat, and to drink only wine that was unstoppered in her presence. Sesa brought pots of tea and together they poured them out, the compact unspoken between them but nonetheless sure for all that. She tried to weld the young girl to her and thought that she was succeeding, for few could have treated Sesa as though she were a person in all her short life. Carlotta knew what that could do to a person, for had Austin not treated her thus? She tried not to think of Simon, but he walked debonair and smiling in her dreams. Bitterness rose in her when she thought that he had renounced her utterly yet shown great interest in Austin's plans. Did he perhaps plan to try to take part?

In the morning of the fifth day Carlotta was dressing when Sesa came to inform her of a visitor, Madame De Soucet. "She says she will stay only a short time, madame, that she fully understands your tiredness in this heat."

"Tell her that I will join her in the parlor in a few minutes." Carlotta hesitated. "Is she in her carriage?"

"Yes." Sesa's eyes looked their question but the warmth toward her mistress shone out and this decided Carlotta.

"I will ask her if you may ride back to Natchez with her and do some shopping for me. You are my personal maid and know best what I require. We will send someone to fetch you tomorrow but I do not like to disturb Austin at an inopportune moment. Will you carry a message for me?" She looked straight and hard at the girl. This was the time of decision for Sesa as well. "To Lena, wife of the boat captain who brought us from New Orleans. It will be in regard to a journey that I wish to make. A secret journey for two. Us, Sesa. At the end of it, if all goes well, there will be freedom."

"Freedom." Sesa breathed the word so softly that Carlotta felt the sting of tears under her eyelids. It meant so much for them both. "For that and for you, I would dare much. Will you write it out?"

The message when written was ambiguous, asking only that Lena come in the guise of a tradesperson to Stuart's Peace and ask for the mistress, who was said to be interested in new lotions for the skin. "Tell her what I have said, give her the note and this gold, say that this is a woman's difficulty and that I trust her."

"It will be done, madame." The formal words faded as Sesa whispered, "Thank you with all my heart, my lady."

Carlotta wondered once again at the strange diction possessed by all Austin's servants. He had once told her that he would have no dialect or untutored mumbling around him— all were trained to this and a fearful task it must have been. Her own plan seemed weak enough, based as it was on nuances and hopeful thinking, but she was a fighter and must take chances.

"My dear Madame Lenoir, I hope you are feeling rested this lovely morning. I will stay only a few minutes. Dear Alicia is being fitted with new dresses. I declare, seeing her with that handsome Mr. Mitchell makes me think of my own youth. Do you know they went driving twice in two days? I ought not to have permitted it, people will talk, but she's so hard to please. She didn't even want to meet him the other night, I had to insist, and now he is coming to dine next Sunday and may even take her to the ball at Merry Oaks...." Madame De Soucet paused for breath and a quick sip of tea while her eyes ran assessingly over Carlotta.

The girl felt the world sway at her mention of Simon, who seemed to be courting that lump of a girl. Was he seeking a Natchez heiress after all? Jealousy flickered redly at her as she adjusted the folds of the gray gown she had chosen. Her hair was caught back behind her ears with ruby-studded combs that served to point up the pale features. The woman was indeed a gossip and she might as well spread the news that Austin's wife was quite sickly, all the better for her scheme. She saw the little eyes settle on her stomach where the folds of her gown bunched and then move away with never a pause in her flood of speech. The little feeling of unease persisted. The rising inflection of excitement in Madame De Soucet's voice captured her.

". . . here just the other night! Urgent business in Nashville, they had, and time was precious so I understand, but they lost everything they carried and were lucky to escape with their lives . . ."

"What? Forgive me, I did not hear all that you said." Carlotta used her most limpid voice in the hope that the woman would simply think her woolgathering or foolish, at best. Something important had been said, her instinct told her that.

"Why, Monsieur Tolino and Monsieur Nichol, of course, madame. They were robbed on the Natchez Trace, that infamous place that is so full of outlaws! They traveled with a small party and were still taken. No one is safe these days. And it is said they carried a large sum of gold and jewels." Madame De Soucet's face was red with her excitement at the news and probably also from the tightness of her corset.

"Why did they not take precautions? Hire soldiers or go incognito?" She spoke carelessly but her blood was chilling for she knew that this trail that sliced through the country was the only way by land to reach any of the cities of the north. If passage could not be obtained by ship this would be her only choice and it was certain death.

"That is just it! They dressed as ordinary folk and mingled with the others of the party, yet were sought out and searched immediately. We live in dangerous times but it does seem that something could be done about those outlaws." She fanned herself and eyed Carlotta critically. "I have not upset you, Madame Lenoir, have I? I declare, I'm just such a gossip. Well, dear Alicia will be needing me; I'll just go along now."

"I wonder, Madame De Soucet, if you would be so kind as to do me a great favor?" Carlotta put her request in a soft, negligent voice, hoping that the woman did not read her apprehension in every syllable.

"Delighted! Delighted! I do hope you are better soon, dear Madame. You are really looking quite pale."

Carlotta suppressed an urge to scream at her, murmuring her thanks instead. When the large presence had departed she sighed with relief and went to stand at the window of the little parlor, an intimate chamber for the use of the mistress when

she wrote letters or planned the schedule of the household. She
stared past the overhanging branches and looked down to the
walk made of shells that led around to the back of the house.
The maid, Lula, was walking slowly beside a young girl whose
golden hair shimmered in the morning sun and whose body,
as the wind blew back the thin gown, showed the first slight
roundings of pregnancy. Another viewer might not have noticed
but Carlotta's body remembered. It must be the indentured girl
Austin had slept with so briefly. Her profile was framed briefly
against the background of leaves and sky; she was beautiful.
She and Lula laughed together, the sounds joyous in the warm
air. Carlotta shivered, for she had suddenly thought of the white
chickens hanging in the trees in Haiti. They had marked the
trail to the voodoo ceremony. Some meshing of fact and theory
confronted her but she could not put the pieces together. Now
she jerked the curtains together and started outside where the
cool shade just beyond the door might revive her.

If she had given conscious thought to what she did then,
she would never have taken the same path they had nor paused
to consider that she could be seen from the house or that the
slaves might look for her. Anger at her forced and very necessary passivity, pain at Simon's treatment, and an urge to do
something drove her to follow the women now. It was good
to stretch her legs and feel them respond. She had drooped for
so long that it had almost become a way of life.

The laughter drifted back again as they went around an arbor
of vines, along a path edged with orange and gold flowers, and
came to a little slope of hill where more roses had been set
out. There they paused and spoke together. Carlotta moved up
into the arbor and pretended to be inspecting the vines. The
leaves were thick and clustered tightly around her so as to
render her almost a part of them. She strained to hear and
wondered why she, the mistress in theory if not in actuality,
sneaked about to eavesdrop on slaves.

"It is taking so long. I grow impatient." The girl had a soft,
sighing voice with a tang of petulance. "He has promised that
if the child is a boy I shall have power even as she has."

Lula seemed to bulk against the slightness of the other figure
as she said, "All will come to pass as I have told you. She will
fall swiftly when the appointed time arrives. Her body may be
resistant to my potions but that cannot last."

"She may suspect. She may not even take enough food or
drink. Try other methods." There was the faintest ring of com-

mand in the young voice. "My child is impatient for his destiny."

"Remember your place, Walla. There may be something in what you say but the Master rules here and his power is absolute."

She tossed her head. "He is old and my child will be a boy. I alone will produce the heir."

She had gone too far. Lula caught her by the arm and shook her briefly as she spoke words Carlotta could not hear, but the sound of them was harsh in the morning softness. Walla nodded twice and moved lightly over the grass, her head still high. Lula glanced around and followed, still muttering to herself.

Carlotta walked on stiff legs to a bench some small distance away from the arbor. Roses grew here in abundance, spicing the air with their sweetness as they thrust up pink and yellow heads. It came as no shock to her to see that one bush grew apart and on it were four perfect blooms, white with the delicate pink edges. The flowers of death.

Her breath rattled in her nostrils as she placed both hands on the stone seat and gazed with unseeing eyes at the rearing white mass of Stuart's Peace, serene in beauty that should last for the ages and yet the scene of unspeakable evil. She knew now that Austin did not mean to have a child by her, that her time was even shorter than she had first supposed. He hated her even as she did him but she had believed herself necessary to him. Evidently the mind-sapping potions were in everything, and only Sesa's help had prevented her from being even more affected than she was. Carlotta knew, though she had tried to deny it to herself, that some of her lassitude was real.

"He has some fearful fate in store for me. If not death then perhaps to become as one of the zombies of Haiti!"

She breathed the words into the summer morning and shuddered with their impact. They were true; her instinct told her that, even as reason and logic militated against it. The very loose gowns made for her, Austin's determination to call her name as being of royal blood, his schemes of power and his grim intention to have a son—all these wound together. He would not care who supplied the son, his blood and name were all that mattered. A pair of dark eyes in the peace of a New Orleans convent garden rose before her then; they had burned with the same intensity as Austin's and the same force had been present. No wonder Austin felt that the cause of Aaron Burr was much like his own. Did each seek to use the other?

She rose and walked back toward the house. It must be something like drowning in honey, she thought. Surrounded, pulled down, enveloped, always with the taste of the heavy sweetness in one's mouth. If she confronted Austin he would only take that opportunity to convince others of her growing foolishness and she would be watched more closely. No, she must wait for Lena's reply and pray that such a slim chance would be enough.

The slave woman stirred in the corner as Carlotta entered the long hall and stood in the welcome cool. She might have been asleep but the girl had the feeling that she was not, nor had been. There was no other sound in all the great house.

"Where is my husband?" Her voice rang confidently.

"Gone riding, mistress. A gentleman came by and they went off together."

Carlotta's senses quickened. If only she could know what was going on! This might be an invaluable opportunity. She caught sight of herself in one of the long mirrors and was not surprised to see the flush in her cheeks or the disordered tumble of her hair. The girl would doubtless report that the mistress grew more daft each day. Was she playing into Austin's hands by acting so? It was a risk that must be taken.

"Leave me. I wish to be alone." She gave a disconsolate sigh and began to pace. "Later I will ring for tea." She watched the girl's lips curve a little as she bobbed and went away. It was the tea and everything else, of course. And they all knew.

When she was quite certain that no one was near, Carlotta crossed the hall and went into the green room where she had again met Simon. For all that had not been said between them, his aura lingered here, and she was obscurely grateful for the knowledge that he was again in her world. He was life and health and warmth after the scented, cruel world Austin dominated. To think of him gave her comfort.

Now she went to the shuttered doors and pushed them slightly back. Here the men had stood that other night. There was a tiny hall and there a door set in a recess at the end of it. A heavy lock was set in place but, as she drew closer, she saw that it had not closed all the way, though the casual observer would have been put off by the grim appearance. She pulled the doors closed again, returned, and twisted the lock free. The door gave under her hand and she looked into a small room which was cluttered with papers and maps and books. Several chairs stood about but they, too, were piled with more papers.

A scrap of red cloth lay across the desk close at hand. A sword and rose were crossed on it. The whole thing had the appearance of a miniature flag, the flag of Austin's new country?

Carlotta's fingers were slippery on the lock she still held in one hand. She extended the other to the pile of papers on the desk and flipped quickly through them. She had no idea what she was looking for, just something to arm her against Austin. One paper dropped from her fingers and fell to the uncarpeted floor. She bent and picked it up, noticing as she did so that the writing was in Spanish, the ink thick and black, the syllables oddly accented. Her Spanish was very little, gained as it had been through Uncle Arnold's fascination with languages of any kind. This letter seemed to be in reference to possible confiscation of property by the Mexican government and that monies would be sent to Austin by the bearer. The date was July, 1805. Last month.

Another spoke of deployment of men and recruitment of the soldiers last used to fight the Indians, the possibility of enlisting the English, occupied as they were with Napoleon, and ended with a list of strange names in a language Carlotta did not know. She unfolded a long sheet which listed names and what must be contributions. A map was attached to the back of it and there were little check marks in red at various places. She recognized the long curves of the Mississippi River and the sweep of territory that had been added by the Louisiana Purchase such a short time ago, as well as New Orleans, which was starred. Beyond that the cramped symbols written in black at the corners meant nothing.

She had been here long enough. She put the papers back, arranging them as best she could in the same disorder she had found them. The map and the list of names she kept as well as the letter in Spanish. Surely there were those who cared that someone as powerful and influential as Austin was attempting not only to set up his own empire west of the Mississippi but, if this could be believed from what she saw on the map, annex the port city of New Orleans as well. From all that he had said of Aaron Burr, this was what the former Vice-President intended, at least in part, and clash would be inevitable. Inevitable in a land where the war to sever the colonies from England was still sharply remembered and freedom a precious word. Carlotta slipped the papers in her bosom, thankful for once for the loose dress, and knew that she would get these bits of safety to Simon. He wanted money and she wanted passage to the north. Austin would likely pay much for their return and, if he did not, Simon would likely yield to the pressure of gold. It was a chance and a far better one than her own flimsy scheme. She would wait until Sesa returned and act accordingly.

It was the work of a few minutes to replace the lock, forcing it back with all her strength and trying to remember how it had been hanging. Then she moved to the doors and out of them as she caught her breath in a long-drawn sigh of blessed relief. It was too soon. There was a clatter of boots on smooth floors, the silence from carpeted steps, and then a voice spoke behind her back which she had instinctively turned so that she might be seen viewing the tapestry.

"Madame Lenoir, I have looked for you everywhere. A terrible thing has happened. I have taken the liberty of summoning your maids."

Carlotta swung to face the serpentine man whose face was almost eclipsed by the fierce, dark eyes. Here was the enemy, face-to-face.

CHAPTER THIRTY-EIGHT

The Shades Cry Out

SHE held her voice rock-steady as she said, "Who are you to come crying of misfortune? Do you not know that I have been ill?" Another few seconds and she would have been discovered. The consequences did not bear thought.

"I am Jeremy Doud, Mistress Lenoir. I have served your husband in various capacities for many years and count him as my closest friend as well as employer. I have been away on a journey and only now returned. It is my pleasure to meet you." He spoke smoothly with the right touch of gravity. His body was even more thin in his dark clothes than it had been at the ceremony she had watched only weeks before. "Will you sit down, lady?"

She sat, wondering at what game he played. "Well, what is it?"

She had touched him. Anger flickered as he said, "The slave, Sesa, to whom I understand you were much attached, is dead."

"God! How? I do not believe you!" The green walls of the room seemed to fade and swing before slowly righting themselves.

"Madame De Soucet set her down as she requested in the city. Her carriage was driving away when screams were heard and a runaway horse and carriage dashed by. Of course, she turned back and learned that the slave had stepped into the street without looking. She must have been killed instantly and without suffering. It was a less painful death than some. My condolences." He sketched a bow and stood watching her.

Carlotta would not weep before him, for she knew that that would please him. Sobs burned in her throat as she recalled the eager young face, the liquid eyes, the warmth of friendship that had only just begun to grow between them, the earnest way she had spoken of freedom. So young, so serious, now so destroyed. It was murder, there was no question of anything else.

"Brandy." The word came out harshly.

He crossed to the table and poured some out into a rounded glass which he pressed into her hand. Almost without thinking she wiped the place where he had touched it with the hanging sleeve of her gown. He drew in his breath but his expression of correct solicitude did not change. There was a scurry at the door just then and Lula came in accompanied by another slave whom Carlotta did not recognize.

"Mistress, what a terrible thing! We all liked her so much. You must come and lie down. The Master may be gone all day but he will comfort you when he returns." Lula's eyes met those of Jeremy Doud for a moment before returning to Carlotta. Her own face was expressionless.

Carlotta spared time to wonder if Sesa had delivered the message or if they even now held it. There was no more time and no other ally in the house. Simon must come to her but what would bring him? She said savagely, "I want to see Madame De Soucet. More care should have been taken. The girl was valuable. Send a message to her at once." The woman would come, she could scarcely do otherwise, and since Simon had escorted her daughter in the absence of a husband of either, it was highly likely that he would do so in a time of stress. In some way, Carlotta thought, Madame De Soucet was involved in Austin's schemes.

"But, mistress . . ."

"You must not overexcite yourself."

Jeremy Doud and Lula spoke with one voice, then fell silent before the command on Carlotta's face. She sat up very straight in the chair and allowed herself to tremble visibly. "Do as I say. In the absence of my husband I rule at Stuart's Peace. Have arrangements been made for burial?"

Lula said, "Late this afternoon, up on the hill, in our special place." Slaves were not interred with the quality. There was no resentment in her voice or manner; this was the way things were and probably always would be.

"I will be there." She knew people were buried quickly in this hot climate but it seemed somehow indecent, this hurrying away of the human flesh.

Lula opened and closed her mouth. The serpentine man moved his hand almost imperceptibly as he said, "As my lady wishes, but may I suggest that in the matter of Madame De Soucet . . ."

"You may not suggest. I do not permit it. Go." Carlotta sank down in the chair again and touched the brandy to her lips, noting as she did so the barest glitter in Lula's eyes. So the brandy was treated with the potion as well. If they did not leave her soon she knew that she would begin to cry disgracefully. "Go, both of you, I will remain here."

They withdrew before her gaze but Carlotta knew that she could not permit herself the luxury of tears for Sesa. That would be interpreted as weakness and retaliation would begin. Until Austin's return she would surely be safe. She stared dry-eyed into the distance and tried not to think of the young girl who had literally died for her.

A young house slave in her late twenties brought Carlotta a tray soon after, tea, chicken broth, a cup of custard. She chattered in a low voice as though she had been told to do so, the talk ranging from the possibility of rain to Austin's favorite hunting dog which was about to whelp to the latest robbery on the Natchez Trace which had happened only a few miles from Natchez itself.

"Leave me." Carlotta cut through the stream of words. "I am weary of chatter." She watched the girl scurry away to report and thought that her own time, just as Sesa's, was draining away. She swept the food and tea into a flower arrangement and hoped that it would go undiscovered or at least unrecognized. Then, alone at last, she gritted her teeth and held back the tears which would shake her apart. Truly, Austin had much to account for.

Thunderheads built in the afternoon sky and a hot little wind blew when Carlotta, still in the gray morning gown but with a black scarf around her shoulders, stood with some thirty of the slaves, Jeremy Doud, the white minister who must have been seventy if the estimate were taken, and a huge black man who muttered verses of Scripture under his breath. The grave yawned in the rich earth of the little burial place where stones and branches served as markers for other dead. The canvas-wrapped body lay to the side. The minister had spoken shaky words of comfort as he leaned on his stick, plainly anxious for the completion of his task. Carlotta felt vaguely sick; she knew she should pray but she had the feeling that a strange, alien god brooded over this place. Two men picked up the small body and lowered it into the darkness while the slaves swayed in a half song of ritual. The minister spoke again of dust, ashes, and the resurrection. The watchers started to turn away, duty done.

Then Carlotta forgot safety and wisdom in the swamping

bitterness she felt at the waste of this life, at this death that she, Carlotta, had inadvertently caused. She had picked a late magnolia, smaller than those of early summer, but its delicate whiteness was already bruised by the browning heat, the bittersweet smell pungent on the still air. She stepped to the edge of the grave and forced herself to look down on the container of death. The flower dropped in and she said, her voice hard, "She was ever a good handmaiden to me, a good and faithful servant, a friend in necessity. May she walk forever in the fields of our Lord. So cruel and senseless a death on this earth must offer all mercy in the hereafter. Blood cries out from the ground and her shade shall be answered. I swear it!"

The slaves looked at one another uneasily; even Lula drew back. The minister began to murmur a lengthy prayer but the serpentine man stared at Carlotta and she knew that she had given herself away this time if not before. It did not matter; the battle was joined for certain now.

He waved at the slaves and several of them began to throw dirt on the grave. Lula came to his side as he said, "The Mistress will soon be distraught as is natural. Escort her back to the house and put her to bed. I will deal with Madame De Soucet when she arrives."

Carlotta jerked back. "I remain here to pray for her soul."

Doud ignored her and Lula advanced. The slaves whispered, but she knew that if it came to confrontation they would obey the manager of the plantation to whom they had always answered. She knew she should back down but could not. Sesa should have one true mourner to bid her farewell. Doud walked toward her, the beginnings of a grin on his face. She glared back and then past him as she saw movement on the path near them. He followed her glance and even more confidence came into his bearing. It seemed that Austin was approaching and would bear him out.

But, no, it wasn't Austin. Carlotta felt time stop as it always did when she first saw that tall figure with the easy stride and the sun-burnished hair. The very air around her quivered, and the low mutter of thunder seemed entirely appropriate. He wore white this time, and a wide-brimmed hat was held easily in brown fingers. In a few moments he was topping the rise, calling out to them. Doud stood transfixed, a flicker of chagrin, now masked, in his eyes.

"Forgive my intrusion, Madame Lenoir, but I have been asked by Madame De Soucet to act as her very self in this most unfortunate matter. She understands the nature of your despair over this and sends her condolences. She would have come herself but was taken with fainting spells over the accident and what the loss may have done to your already delicate health. She will call soon."

Carlotta heard her voice, high and shrill, full of the emotion that she could not control. His brows lifted as he waited politely. "I wish to stay here and they are trying to force me away!" Her vision blurred, the tears were very close.

Simon said, "I will escort Madame Lenoir back in a few moments. All of you may go." His authority was easy, unquestionable. He glanced at Doud, saw the other man start to speak and think the better of it. "We will soon be down."

"Aye, sir." Doud walked away and the others trailed him. The grave was almost filled now but the diggers left, too. The rain was coming closer and it would have to be worked on again lest her spirit walk. Carlotta remembered the burial of another woman in Haiti and shivered.

When they were out of sight, Simon drew Carlotta into the sheltering circle of a nearby oak tree and said, "What is going on? What on earth possessed you to send such a command to Madame De Soucet? She is prostrate all right, but with anger. It must have been a terrible experience for her, and there you are talking about the money value of a human life! Have riches so hardened you, madame? And what was happening here? The atmosphere was savage."

"Sesa was murdered. I sent her to her death. I must avenge her." Carlotta fought the tears back again and made herself calm. "Simon, I must have your help."

"I told you, Carlotta, I will not be involved in helping a wife to escape her husband. My plans are working out quite well here."

"You are not thinking of wedding that little suet pudding!"

His laugh was low. "Of course not, but it suits me well that people should think so. Madame was most grateful when I offered to undertake this little errand for her." He looked up at the sky, noting that the blue cast of evening was returning despite the rattle of thunder. "It may rain soon and I do not wish to get wet. Shall we go and think of some tale to assuage my hopeful mother-in-law?"

It must be now or not at all. Carlotta held back and chose her words with care. "I will pay you well to help me. I have gold and jewelry as I said and I have other things—documents that my husband will pay well to recover. You can go your way and I mine afterward. I will make no demands. You are interested in his plans for expansion to the west, I know it, and were you not curious about Mr. Burr, as well? I have heard talk, I know that their plans will collide, and Austin is the very epitome of evil. I have the proof, I tell you!"

Simon's brow furrowed, his body grew taut and hard. "You seek to cozen me. Beware, lest I call the bluff."

"Call it. I have nothing to lose. Austin will pay for what I have but we must be far away with it." At least Simon was listening, listening so hard that he might have been part of the oddly still air itself.

"What do you have? By God, if you toy with me . . ." His face was suddenly that of the man who had loved her so passionately and briefly on the Haitian beach and then had cried strumpet.

They stood inches apart under the oak tree close by the raw grave, where birds were beginning to make sleepy calls, as Carlotta told Simon of Austin's plans, his ambition was outlined to her, the documents and her appropriation of them. It was only a sketchy outline, she could fill in the details later; the main thing was to catch his belief and hold him to a bargain.

"Where are these documents that were so conveniently to hand?" He had not relaxed a jot but continued to eye her narrowly.

"In a safe place at the house." She dared not give away her safety yet, not to this steely-faced man who might never have held and caressed her until her flesh burned with his.

"You cannot think I will take your word for this?"

"I had hoped you might." Ridiculous to feel the lump rising in her throat.

"Details! Tell me again of the plot." His eyes challenged her. "That is, if you can."

Twice more she repeated the few names she remembered, the information on the letter about Mexico, the territory involved, Austin's reiteration of the reasons his empire would be a reality. Simon asked several pointed questions in an attempt to trip her but the basic recital did not differ.

"Just so have I heard Mr. Burr speak, seemingly in jest or in speculation." Simon spoke as if to himself.

"Does that mean you believe me?" Carlotta snapped the words out, forgetting that he alone stood between her and Austin's revenge.

"Yes, so far as it goes." The words were almost wrung from him but the dark light was gone from his green eyes and they looked gently at her for the first time. "But, tell me, Austin Lenoir is an intelligent man. How can he think to produce a girl whose background is unknown and have people believe that she is an offshoot of the royal family of France? It reads like a fairy tale. And yet your other words are those of fact. Tell me all. This time I will listen, I promise it." He leaned back against the bole of the great tree as if they had all the time in the world.

Carlotta was uneasy without knowing why. She was a married woman, Simon almost betrothed by all the unwritten laws of this society, she thought to be ill, he come to do a favor. What could Austin make of such a situation? What if he returned suddenly with Madame De Soucet in tow? Then she looked at Simon who was both intrigued and interested, her only chance in the dangerous situation of the present.

"It is an incredible tale, Simon, and one not to be believed unless you have experienced it. Hear me with an open mind, I ask only that."

"I will listen, Carlotta. There is much at stake here. The times are perilous; each must look to himself." He folded his arms together and watched her. "Get on with it."

This time Carlotta spared nothing, tried no subterfuge or watered-down version, but told it all as it had happened. She showed the kind of man Austin was, all that he had done, the strange admiration that he could still stir in her, the voodoo, his machinations and trickery, her own pose of illness and the attempts that had been made to drug her, his assaults on her body and her fury. She told it all and in the telling the terrible burden lifted so that she could weep honestly and sincerely for the young life that had been.

She finished, "They counted the life of a slave nothing. I have told you the fate they plan for me. One of the living dead. I had to escape somehow. Now, will you help me?"

The recital had not, after all, taken very long. The summer twilight stretched out into cool shadows as the slight breeze turned back the leaves of their tree so that the undersides reflected a paler green. In the silence that was suddenly absolute, Carlotta saw a rabbit run between two swaying bushes, pause to scent the wind, and then bounce away. The insects rasped in the branches above their heads and were stilled by Simon's voice.

"A fairy tale, of course. But who can blame you? You are, after all, a woman and subject to fancies. Then, too, you have endured much. In the short time that I have known him, I have heard tales of Austin Lenoir and his treatment of women."

"Will you help me? That is the central question." He did not believe her, she knew it with a pang, but neither was his doubt total. If she knew anything about this man, she knew that he would not make her plight the butt of his own old hurts.

He straightened up and took her arm. "I must have the documents you took and as much more proof as you can get. It is essential that this be done. Now I am sure of conspiracy, and with documents the matter can be placed before the highest authority."

"What do you mean? Whose authority? I tell you, Austin will pay well to have those documents. Why risk more?"

He bent to her, so close that she caught the odor of shaving lotion and saw the flickering lights in his green eyes. "We will go up the Natchez Trace to Nashville and overland to the north. I will make sure that you do not suffer for what you have done, Carlotta. But we must have the papers and you alone can get them."

"You would not have offered had I not mentioned them." Her voice was flat.

"No." He smiled faintly. "We have come a long way, Carlotta. It is best to know what the other is capable of."

She put out her hand and he took it. "Then we are allies?"

"Allies. My word on it."

They shook hands gravely in the twilight as the night bird cried.

CHAPTER THIRTY-NINE

Damballah's Own

A TORCH shone in the distance and they heard shouts, then the drumming of hooves. Carlotta turned quickly to Simon, who had grown watchful in his turn.

"That will be Austin. What can we tell him?"

"You were distraught and needed quiet. Slaves talk, and I felt it best to try to calm you since I am supposed to think you are carrying. He will suspect us of being lovers but I do not think he will try to do anything about it since his plans are beginning to bear fruition, if what you say is basically true." Again the faint thread of doubt.

She ignored that and said, "When shall we leave, assuming that I am able to carry out your demand? He is capable of imprisoning me or administering a potion that will render my mind blank." She spoke no more than the simple truth but she knew Simon could not find it easy to accept.

"Alicia and I will call either tomorrow afternoon or early the next morning. We will make an appointment to go riding in the carriage, saying that you need the air. She will go her way, and we will go to the Trace. She will not be blamed but will be considered the victim of an experienced adventurer. Her slave will be her chaperone so that her reputation will be unmarred."

The white horse was closer now. Carlotta almost whispered, "He is a devil, that man. It will be a pleasure to bring him down." She knew, even as she spoke, that she and Austin had fed from each other, that she was no longer the fearful girl she had been. If he had grown in cruelty, she had grown in pride and courage. Some part of her must always thank Austin Lenoir for that.

Simon answered, "Courage, lady mine."

Once again they seemed to stand on the Haitian beach while the winds of passion lifted against their bodies. Now they were united in battle and, whatever had brought them to this time in their lives, they would face it together. Carlotta did not delude herself; this alliance was of the moment's necessity only, but she who had been alone in a hopeless endeavor was alone no longer.

Was it her imagination or did Austin's eyes glow redly in the twilight from an inner light—or was it merely the oncoming torches? He dismounted and came over to her, touched her face gently, and said, "You are well, my dear? They said you dismissed everyone and were like to do yourself an injury but for the intervention of Mr. Mitchell here. Mr. Doud was most distressed." He turned to Simon and held out his hand. "I owe you thanks. You did the right thing."

Simon smiled, taking the proffered hand. "I really did not know what else to do. The lady was distraught and Madame De Soucet had asked me to act in her stead."

Carlotta said, "I am tired and would like to go back now. You will call, will you not, you and Alicia?" She looked hard at Simon as she said it.

"Of course, madame. Tomorrow afternoon, I believe, would be a good time." He responded so swiftly to her lead that she felt ashamed of doubting his sincerity.

Three slaves arrived just then bearing a wicker chair. Austin guided Carlotta into it, his manners impeccable. Then he said, "I do appreciate the interest of yourself Mr. Mitchell, but I fear my wife must rest for several days in absolute quiet."

Carlotta started to protest but caught the drop of Simon's eyelid and leaned her head on her palm instead. He bent his head as if in obedience to a husband's wishes.

"Then I will send my man to inquire within the next fortnight, if that is suitable."

"Naturally." Austin gestured to the slaves, who hoisted up the chair and started down the hill with it. Carlotta saw him move closer to Simon and begin to speak with vigor while the younger man seemed all attention.

They took her to her room where she was bathed and robed in a white nightdress. She let them do as they wished, asking no questions, being calm in all things. In the one moment of privacy she was given to attend to her needs, she slipped the precious documents under the corner of the rug and pulled the corner of a chest over them. The obvious hiding place would have to suffice. She had no idea how she would get anything else from Austin's private room, but she was ready to lie to Simon if she had to.

The hovering slave girl brought wine which she rejected though her tongue was parched. Tea was also rejected, but she

300

rinsed her mouth out with water which was supposed to be straight from the well, or so the frightened girl said. What she would do when thirst became a real problem remained to be seen; hopefully by that time she and Simon would be on the Natchez Trace.

Sprigs of pink myrtle stood in a vase by her bed, the windows were opened to admit the fresh air as she always ordered, the curtains were pulled back, and the faint light of the sickle moon drifted in along with the scent of fresh-cut grass. A candelabra held tall white candles which cast reflections on the high ceiling. Carlotta was very tired and hoped that the confrontation with Austin which must certainly come might at least wait until morning. The day had been harrowing, all those to come would be more so. Light blurred behind her lids and she slept to dream of Simon's face smiling down into hers.

Something cold touched her body and moved her fingers with its passage. In her dream it seemed that Simon faded into darkness and was obscured by iron bars which crashed down to separate them. She opened her mouth to call to him and one of the bars came alive to glare malevolently at her. The call became a soundless scream as she opened her eyes and looked straight into the tiny ones of the great snake lying across her recumbent figure.

She tried to pull away and could not. She was frozen, her mind clear, but her will gone. Her blood hammered in her veins but there was no response to her fright. The snake was very long and very black; the triangular head moved back and forth while the forked tongue darted out. She was no longer in her bed but lay on a pallet on the floor of a chamber which was illuminated by flaring torches held by naked male slaves. Austin and the serpentine man, whom she could think of by no other name, stood before a leaping fire, their arms intertwined. Lula was there also, wearing wreaths of the pink-edged white roses and nothing else, her dark flesh shimmering in the light, her expression one of sheer pleasure.

"You are awake, my dear, I can tell by the terror in your eyes. I think that Damballah will take possession soon, don't you?" Austin ran an expert finger down his paramour's arm and the other's flesh trembled at the touch. Both wore white breeches and were barefoot. Snake medallions hung around their necks. Austin laughed and the note was high. In the distance a drum beat once, twice, and was stilled.

Lula began to sing a ritual song that might have come from

Haiti. The snake lifted a little on Carlotta as if to look around. The long coils slid cool and dry on her own naked flesh as her brain screamed orders to her unresponsive body. Austin detached himself and came over to look down at her. The pupils of his eyes were dilated, a nerve jumped in his cheek, and the little fans of wrinkles at the corners of his mouth were more pronounced. He touched her pink nipple, then took it firmly and called out to Doud who joined him in amusement.

"Little bitch, did you think to rut with your lover and I not respond? I can imagine the tale you told. He tells me you think I plot? That I plan to make a zombie out of you, to use you as a facade to lure men to my cause, that I will give out that you are crazed but fertile, that I practice voodoo, that art banned in Haiti. Yes, yes, my dear little bitch, your lover Simon told me all—he is, after all, a practical man with a strong love of money. I do have a great deal, you know."

Carlotta thought then that she truly wanted to die. He had betrayed her after all, this man whom she loved so passionately. Why? Had he not believed her at all? Why give her over to the power of this beast who had left him to die in battle? She knew that her eyes reflected the anguish of her spirit as well as the fear and that this delighted Austin beyond all measure.

"Ah, you will be wondering how you were taken since you were so careful not to drink anything and since the dead slave guarded you so well that the potions could not build up in your body. Powders on your pillows, in the flowers, on your night wear. I have learned much from my art, Carlotta."

The serpentine man ran his hands over the length of her legs and took her nipples into his hands. She saw the desire in him and wondered if Austin would resent it. He gave no sign of doing so but seemed to relish the sight of his lover's hunger. Now Austin put one hand on her head and let his fingers run down her rib cage until they met those of Doud. Then their hands clutched convulsively and came down to rest gently on the snake's back. It hissed and lifted once again.

A low chanting began and two of the house slaves that Carlotta vaguely remembered entered. They wore short skirts of pink around their loins and their bare young breasts gleamed in the torchlight. Lula began to sing a song of enticement which they acted out in movement and gesture. So real were their actions that they might have been performing the very actions themselves. Doud knelt before Austin then; the sheen of perspiration was on his face, his breeches bulged, and his mouth worked. Carlotta felt the palpable disgust rise in her even over the potion that held her in bondage. Potion or powder, what was the difference said her weary brain; she would spend her days as Austin's tool and finally as his useless plaything. He was bending over her again, ignoring the supplicant at his feet.

"You will find the time to come most interesting, my dear. A proper lady by day, speaking the correct responses, obedient, calm, and by night there will be this." He waved one hand around the chamber. "You will watch, participate, obey. Mine to control and destroy as I wish. You will think I hate you. Not true. You serve as my amusement, my vessel. That is enough to fulfill what remains to you of existence."

Carlotta felt the life-giving rage swell up in her, removing some of the fear that had threatened to swamp her. Her amber eyes blazed with it, and the blood roared in her ears. Austin saw, and his own eyes darkened with anger. She should have been weeping or fainting with terror. His hand lifted to strike the helpless girl but was arrested by Lula's cry of alarm.

The woman was whirling in a frenzy, her feet moving in the intricate steps of a dance known only to her and the god she worshipped. Her hands wove the same patterns but her face was that of a tribal mask. Now she cried. "Loose them! It is Damballah's will!" She shrieked again and the sound was that of a wild thing in pain.

Austin and Doud stood together, their faces pale in the flickering light. One of the young girls brought out a covered basket and the other came to cast the top aside and tip the contents to the floor. The brownish, spotted mass that tumbled out soon resolved itself into separate snakes which then began to slide over the floor. The huge one on Carlotta's body slithered slowly off her and toward them.

"Fire and death! Fire and death! Green flames in the tunnel of earth! It is split and rendered and the land goes on! I see it!" Lula's voice was guttural and deep as Carlotta had heard it in Haiti from another woman, another servitor of the dark god.

The snakes were coiled together in a mass now, and that was moving back and forth. Carlotta felt her flesh crawl and struggled with all her power of mind and body to be free of the drugging chains. From somewhere out of her childhood the slow cadence of the "Hail Mary" came to her and she repeated it in her mind endlessly. Her fingers twitched and her head moved as if in answer to the prayer, and she felt the cold stones under her flesh.

"Will it be mine, Damballah? Answer your most faithful servant." Austin spoke in a slow chant that had its own rhythm. "I have given you blood, sacrifices, offered your flowers, your ways, and will do so again. Tell me that all will be mine."

"Your lover. Give me your lover and I will answer. Not before." The heavy voice sprang from Lula so that she shivered with the force of it. "Hasten. I grow impatient."

Austin turned bemused eyes toward Carlotta who lay very still, even though her skin was beginning to itch and burn from the prolonged inactivity. She was very thirsty now; the inside of her mouth felt dry and crackly, her very tongue seemed heavy and hot.

"You shall have her. Is it to be slowly? A thing to be relished?" He might have been inquiring the price of a piece of goods for a gift.

The harsh laughter rang through the chamber as Lula whirled and pivoted to lift her hand at the serpentine man. Doud gaped at her and raised a stunned face to Austin, who did not move. Carlotta tensed, feeling the response of her muscles, and her eyes burned from the smoke of the torches.

"You mock me! Me! Damballah! Fire and blood, green flames! Your lover, Austin Lenoir!"

Doud backed away from Austin's sudden movement. "Austin, the woman does not know what she is saying. You cannot think to act on this!"

The guttural voice rose in a scream of laughter that rang off the ceiling and shivered around the dark walls of the chamber. The slaves stared straight ahead as did the young girls. Carlotta guessed that they had been drugged as heavily as they had hoped to have her and with more effect. Her eyes could not pierce the gloom beyond the dimming torches but one pool of darkness seemed less black than the rest; it might be a door or just a shift in the wall. She would try for this if she had to move. Any sort of plan was better than lying supine before the horror manifesting itself before her.

"Fire and death! Blood!"

"Jeremy." Austin's voice was slow and pained, more anguished than Carlotta had ever heard it since the time he wept for Stephan's death on board the *Princess* those months before.

"You'll not do anything, do you hear? I did what you wanted, didn't I? You wanted it done, that useless idiot could only hurt you. I just carried out your orders. I've always carried out your orders. You love me. I love you. You know it, Austin, you know it!" He screamed and ran backward.

The laughter rose until Carlotta fought not to clap her hands over her aching ears. Lula was shaking before the power that manifested itself in her. Her smooth body was wet and dripping as her head swayed heavily. Yet her mouth was open in that awful laughter that seemed to encompass all the darkness of the soul of man at his worst.

"No! No!" Doud screamed again and stepped to the side without looking. One foot plunged down into the mass of snakes which still writhed and hissed. Instantly they were upon the interloper, flat heads striking, bodies coiling and loosening to lift again. He screamed and screamed until the foam burst out from his lips and he fell among them. Then the snakes slithered over him until the body was nearly covered with their lengths.

Austin had stood staring, his skin paper-white, his face crumpled and twisted. Not one finger was lifted to help his lover and his friend who must have been dearer to him than any other had been. Carlotta was almost sick with the horror that she had seen and that must still be to come. She had no illusions about her fate now that Austin had lost his lover with whom he was to have taken such pleasure. Had the man no normal feelings of caring? "Dear God." The words forced themselves up through her stiff lips before she could restrain them.

"Jeremy. Jeremy." The words were an agonized whimper in the stillness of the death chamber.

Carlotta heard the squeak of hinges, the rattle of iron, and thought that more of Austin's henchmen were coming to join him. He stood now facing Lula, who was looking straight at him, her face impassive, her body still.

"What is Damballah's answer?" He was regaining control but his hands were still jerking nervously.

"Master?" Her voice was slow and painful as if she woke from a deep sleep. "What is it, Master?"

The laughter that rang out now was Austin's. It was bitter laughter, soul mutilating and crazed. "He has gone from you! He has taken his blood and gone! Well, I count myself answered!"

"Master?" Lula shivered as she wrapped a thin white robe around herself.

"Get out! Get out! Get those snakes gathered up and out of here. My friend shall have true burial on the morrow; he died in our mutual cause as surely as if he marched beside me. My son shall bear his name." He turned around to Carlotta and she saw the red anger that pervaded his very being. "As for you, I must have surcease and have ever found it in pain. You shall feel, I promise you that."

"Bloody swine! Miserable, weak swine!" Carlotta knew there was nothing to be gained by feigning immobility now. He would likely not kill her but better to fight now than be his endless victim.

"How . . ." He stared in amazement, then his eyes went from her to the little light area she had noticed earlier. "What are you doing here?" His voice was a blend of rage and stunned surprise.

Carlotta came up from the crouch she had been in and her gaze followed his. Simon stood in the shadows, two pistols gleaming in his hands.

CHAPTER FORTY

The Haunted Road

HE was all in black, the silver-gilt hair shining in contrast. One hand gestured with the pistol and the hard voice said, "One move, Austin Lenoir, and you die where you stand. I would not have the slightest compunction about it."

"How did you get in? My slaves..." Austin did not lose any of his aplomb but he was careful to remain still, even as his eyes assessed the situation. Lula had fallen to the floor in the weariness common after so exhausting a session with the god, and the others were in the depths of the potions they had been given.

"I said that I had an urgent message for you that would not wait. I said that I had further been bidden to the ceremony." He turned to Carlotta and his voice softened. "Are you all right? Has he harmed you in any way?"

Lassitude was sweeping over her and her legs were shaking but she replied, "I am not hurt." Not hurt, when her whole body ached and burned, her nipple throbbed with a life of its own, and her mind seemed full of colored lights! "I am not hurt."

There was the sound of footsteps then, and a figure brushed by Simon to come up to Carlotta. She tried to pull back and hide her nudity but the short red-bearded man tossed a cloak over her shoulders and held a flask to her teeth. The sharp odor of brandy made her stomach twist but she set her own hand to the flask and drank deep. The lights exploded into one coherent whole. The seamed face in front of her split into a smile and one empty eye cocked at her while a fierce black one beamed.

"Better?"

"Much, thank you." She pulled the cloak closer and was pleased to note that she no longer wobbled.

"Bind him and the slaves as well." Simon waved the pistol at Austin.

"May I ask what you intend to do? You have invaded the privacy of my household, looked upon my wife with lust, and now, I suppose, you plan robbery. I might remind you that any of these are grave offenses against honor as well as the law."

Carlotta said, "What do you know of honor, Austin Lenoir, or the virtues of a decent man? Your lover lies dead because of you, your own cruelty places you in the hands of the man you abandoned for dead in Haiti, and I owe you a great score myself. You are not worthy to be despised!"

Austin ignored her. "What are you going to do, Mr. Mitchell? Kill me?"

The red-bearded man jerked his arms behind him and bound them with savage thoroughness, then pushed him, so that he sat down abruptly, and began to bind his feet.

Simon said, "Come, Carlotta, we must find you clothes and those documents I need." He kept the pistols ready as his helper advanced on the slaves, who were already docile. Lula seemed to be in a faint. "Ah, no, I do not kill needlessly. Unlike yourself."

Austin twisted to a sitting position and his eyes were the fiery pits Carlotta knew so well. "Take jewels, anything, just go."

"As you command." Simon stepped over and slammed the butt of the pistol against his head. He slumped over with a cry, and a trickle of blood ran into the white hair. "Are you done, Ned? Then come."

A few minutes later they stood under the great winding staircase of the house proper. The chamber was almost directly under it but set deep in the ground. They had extinguished the torches and now locked the door and pulled a tapestry over it.

"Where is this room you mentioned, Carlotta? I must have proof as I told you." Simon paused and smiled down at her. "It is almost dawn. Can you get some sort of clothes? The slaves will wake soon, I think."

"Never mind the clothes. Let us get what we must and get out of here." She remembered that some old clothes had hung in one corner of Austin's private room. Surely something there would fit her. If not, what did it matter? She wanted nothing but to leave this place of death.

"Drink, lady, it will hearten you." Ned offered her the flask and she drank eagerly, welcoming the courage it gave.

They crept carefully across the floor, into the hall, across the drawing room, and through the oak doors. The lock was firmly in place but a blow from Simon's pistol dealt with that. Ned was left on guard while Simon lit the end of a candle and began to flip through the papers Carlotta indicated. She thought of those concealed in her room and knew that she dared not look for them.

"Simon." She explained quickly. "Will there be enough there for your purposes?"

He looked up from the contents of a velvet case that had been set to one side. His face was set and grim; the green eyes burned with purpose. "Your husband is not only villain but traitor by his own hand, and here are others linked not only to him but to those powerful in the government of the United States. Enough? Aye, and more!" He swept the pile of documents into a small bag and rose to check the drawers of the desk.

Carlotta went over to the corner she remembered. There were two pairs of breeches, a heavy shirt, and several vests. She wriggled into the first pair she picked up and tied the tassel of the cloak around her waist to anchor them in place. The shirt fell nearly to her knees, but she turned back the sleeves and rolled up the breeches. "I am ready."

Simon took one look and, despite their grave situation, roared with silent laughter. "Ragamuffin. Lady in distress." He doubled over again.

He had rescued her; did he have to laugh as though she were a comic article? Drink buzzed in her head and she forgot their danger as she opened her mouth to comment on his rudeness. Suddenly there was a hiss from the door, followed by the call of a whippoorwill.

"Simon, the signal!" Ned beckoned as the call came again, this time louder.

Simon slapped the bag shut and caught Carlotta by the arm. "Come, there is no more time!" The piece of candle guttered and almost went out as they rushed by.

It seemed an eternity before they were finally free of the house, even though they went out by one of the tall windows. They saw no other persons; house and grounds were completely silent. When they stepped down and moved into the shadow of one of the magnolia trees, Carlotta was conscious of a weakness that the brandy had momentarily thrust away. Lack of food and water as well as the fearful strain of the past few days had brought it on, but she dared not take another drink from the flask; her head hammered enough as it was.

A hand went under her arm and Simon's voice was warm

in her ear. "Only a little more effort and all will be well, I promise you."

She wanted to lean against him, to give way to the sweet, swooning sensation she felt, but she had had enough of falsity. She held herself erect and said, much as she had done in another life, "Lead. I follow."

He snorted in the dark and did not take his arm away as they melted with the shadows of the trees, not until the little hollow that hid the partial view of Stuart's Peace enveloped them. Here two men waited with horses while another crouched in the grass near them. It was he who had given the bird calls, for another came as he rose to meet them.

"You were gone too long. I saw someone going along the road yonder but they kept on and didn't turn in." His voice was low and thick.

Simon said, "Good man. All is accomplished. Now we ride." Excitement sang in his voice as he went toward the black horse tethered to a nearby pine. He swung into the saddle and lifted Carlotta up in front of him. She did not protest, though her prickly pride told her she should. She sat up stiffly, keeping her body away from his. His chuckle told her that he knew exactly what she was doing.

The others swung into place behind them as the horses picked their way toward the path that led away into what must be the trackless woods Carlotta had often seen from her window. The heavy darkness was suddenly brighter, and she heard an exclamation from one of the men. She and Simon turned together as he checked his horse.

The flames were almost self-contained as they licked up in the far corner where she knew Austin's document room was. The one window had been high up and curtained in some dark material; it would burn rapidly, just as the papers would. Even as they watched, the fire spread to another window and reached upward. Carlotta shivered as she thought of Austin and the others, bound in that chamber. Then memory turned back and she saw another scene of flames and an uplifted sword.

She scarcely heard Simon mutter, "I forgot to put out the candle. Damn, it will be murder."

The white bulk of Stuart's Peace gleamed in the reflected light, and the enclosing magnolias seemed to bend closer in the breeze of early morning. The house seemed a part of the little rise on which it stood, a part of this land so close to the green woodland that the smell of roses mingled with that of

310

earth. The tall white columns might have been made of cloud so insubstantial did they seem in the flame and darkness.

"No, no! Don't kill her, don't!" Carlotta saw the woman run and the child after her, hands flailing in panic. She clutched Simon's shirt and beat with one hand on his chest.

He bent to her and she heard his voice through the mists of the years. "This is now, Carlotta. You are safe."

"No." She sobbed the word again and again. She knew that she was in the world of the present but at the same time she was the child becoming aware of the dead body that was her father, the pale face of the woman, her mother, who sought to distract the murderer that her daughter might be safe. She was struck down and the man turned to seek the child. Carlotta saw his face again and knew in her adult perception why it was familiar. That look of blood-greed and pleasure in what he did had been in Lady Leticia's face, in the serpentine man's, and many times in that of Austin. It was the look that he had given her when his eyes were deep and savage, the look of Jérouge of Haiti and her followers, the call of Damballah in the night, this night.

She saw her small self run and heard the pounding feet, saw the red glow on buildings and in the meadow, saw the white walls of Stuart's Peace, and heard the crack of the pistol in Simon's hand. One of his men fired also, and then they began to gallop.

"You'll have them after us just that much quicker, Simon."

It was the red-bearded man, Ned, who spoke. His voice was sharp and real as Carlotta felt herself return with a visible jerk to the world of swiftly moving horses and the hammer of Simon's heart as she bounced against him.

Simon said, "Well enough. I am no murderer. Even traitors must live." He took one hand and tilted Carlotta's wet face up. "You are better, lady."

She smiled a little. "It was the nightmare come again for the first time in a very long time. I saw what happened and I saw the look . . ." Her voice trailed away as she looked for the familiar terror and saw only the light in the green eyes of the man she loved. "Aye, Simon, I am better." The words were pure truth.

"Good." His touch was impersonal now but his eyes were not.

"I am glad that you warned the house before the smoke

311

overcame them. Austin is a fiend but he does not deserve such a death."

He pulled her closer lest she slide off, so limp was her body becoming. She heard him as if from a far distance. "Rest if you can at the pace we must ride."

The first gray light of day was dawning as they skirted along a path just inside the woods. Carlotta saw the shadow of the great house and the smoke rising from it as they turned to go deeper into the thickets. Stuart's Peace and all that it meant to Austin would be damaged, perhaps he himself was dead. Gladness surged up in her and was quickly overcome in shame. She was alive and free and with Simon; what more could life hold?

When Carlotta woke completely she was lying under the shade of a pine tree with her head pillowed on a cloak. Sunlight filtered down onto her face, and she heard the gushing of a stream close by. She sat up abruptly as memory returned and, with it, hunger and thirst.

"You have slept long. It is well past midday." Simon sat on a rock to her left, watching her from eyes slitted against the sun. "There is water, bread, and cheese at your elbow. They will restore you. I know how one feels after potions such as you have been given."

"Where are we?" She thought that the best wines, the richest brandies, would never taste so delicious as that cold water to her parched throat. She crammed the food in her mouth, quite oblivious to what Simon might think of her attempts to act as if this were an ordinary situation. He was right; she could feel the strength coming into her sleep-refreshed body with every bite.

"About a mile off the road to Nashville and a good way from Natchez. We'll travel by night and early morning, rest by day, for a little while. One of the men will go back over the trail and watch for pursuit. If Austin lives, he may decide to try to regain his documents and his wife." Simon spoke lightly but Carlotta now noticed the watchful posture, the pistols stuck in his belt, and the knife loose on the stone.

"I thought there was only one way overland away from Natchez and that was full of outlaws." She recalled Madame De Soucet's excitement and the fact that two of those men who visited Austin the night Simon returned had been robbed within the next few days. "I thought one traveled with many others, that that was the only way of safety. We are, as I remember, few in number."

"There is nothing to fear. Be at ease." He leaned back on one arm as if to prove his own point.

Carlotta felt the flash of desire and stifled it. She would not be transparent before this man who had made it plain that he helped her only because it was expedient for him. "You never intended to go through with that plan you told me about, using Alicia and the like, did you? Why did you give away so much to Austin?" The memory made her voice rise, and Simon lifted an eyebrow in mild wonder.

"I needed to move swiftly. It seemed a good chance to provoke him into action, and I wanted a look at his papers. I did not think he would begin immediately, however. I certainly meant to rescue you, Carlotta."

"You provoked him for your own ends. You use people, Simon Mitchell, if that is even your name!" She stopped, aghast at the asperity in her voice. Why was she doing this to him? "I might have died there!"

His face went hard and he strode over to her. "If you were a man, I would strike you for such words. Knowing all that you have endured, I still have the urge to do so."

She stood up. "Do it then. At your peril."

They faced each other in the silence of the wood, their eyes wide with anger. Simon was the first to move. He put one hand on her arm and drew her closer to him. Her mouth trembled but she did not resist. She was sharply aware of the rushing water somewhere behind them, the shadow of a bird as it circled low, the bending back of a briar bush before the wind. Simon's sun bronzed face, the clustering gilt hair on his temples, the full curve of his lips—all these formed a mass of whirling impressions. She felt her nipples rise up full and turgid as the warmth began between her thighs; then she knew her anger for no anger at all.

He set his mouth on hers, hard at first and then more tenderly as she yielded to him. Her arms went around the wide shoulders, touched the hard muscles of his back, and held him close to her as if they would never separate. Her softness pressed against his chest and his fingers tangled in the mass of her hair that tumbled free. Carlotta felt the sweet ache stir into full blown hunger. His tongue sought hers and wound together with it, probing and thrusting. She felt the hard stalk of him and remembered the joy it had brought. His hand went to her breasts and massaged one of the nipples, touching the end with fire. She moaned and felt his response as his mouth locked more firmly on hers. The world drifted and faded; the only reality was this man and the passion that they felt for each other.

Suddenly he jerked away and the pistol materialized in his hand as if by some magician's trick. Carlotta was surprised at her own reaction for she placed her hand on the other at his belt and they stood, bereft of the hunger of seconds ago, staring at the shaking bushes and the small, red-bearded figure of Ned, backed by a huge black man, emerging from the shade of the path.

"Sorry to interrupt, but there's a party coming along, look to be well loaded with coin, and, from the sounds of 'em, can't wait to get to sinful Natchez." His eyes were bright with mischief.

Carlotta felt her cheeks burn. Simon's gaze was hot on her face, and there was laughter in it. Knowledge burst upon her then, and she felt the healing laughter come. "There is no need to fear the outlaws of the Trace, is there?"

Simon gave her a courtly bow. "Hermes, at your service, madame."

CHAPTER FORTY-ONE

River Blessing

THEY rode single file along the Natchez Trace in the early dawn of the next day. Besides Carlotta, Simon, and Ned, there were three others. The black man, Carl, who had run away from a savage master; Marty, thirty years old and a pickpocket since seven; the silent Joshua who spoke perhaps one sentence in twelve hours and had once, Simon told her, been wed to an Indian girl in strange circumstances. Ned was his lieutenant and watcher as well as friend; they had met in New Orleans in a tavern and after drinking deep decided to join forces. Of himself, Simon had said nothing, and Carlotta would not ask. In his own time he would tell her.

After that revelation of himself as outlaw, Simon had unpacked a saddle-bag and given her dark breeches, a loose white shirt, and a wide hat under which to tuck her hair. The fit was quite good and the boots he offered were most comfortable. She had said, "Do you outfit all ladies you rescue so well?"

The green eyes had changed to a more somber shade, that of the ocean before the storm. "Let us say that I remembered the shape and size of you, that I bought as for a younger brother." His voice lingered on the words as he watched her.

"As such, I thank you." She, too, could play at toss ball in this intoxicating new freedom from fear.

He said no more, but within the next few minutes they were mounted and riding toward the Trace where passage could be more swift. Ned was disappointed that there was to be no opportunity for plunder, but tales must not be carried back to Natchez. Carlotta gathered from their conversation that more of Simon's men waited at or around one of the "stands" or inns that infrequently dotted the dangerous Trace.

Carlotta had read of this road, the pathway of overland travelers through the wilderness; it alone connected Natchez, that outpost city, with the rest of the country. To travel down the river was easy; to travel up it difficult, but one risked death and murder on the Trace as it wound over swamp and bog and forest for hundreds of miles. People traveled in company with their weapons at the ready, but outlaws could swoop down at any time, and many of them killed all their victims rather than be identified.

Yet they rode along in peace now on this hard earthen track over which trees and bushes hung. One could see the woods stretching away on either side, the trunks of trees and the Spanish moss glistening in the soft mists of morning. Birds called, a squirrel ran down a hanging limb close as their heads, and a startled deer ran before them for a full minute before leaping up on the bank and rushing away. The fresh cool scent of earth and summer hung over all.

Simon touched her arm. "Come. I have something to show you." He waved a hand at his men and they melted into the woods; Ned went more slowly, his pistol very near his hand.

Carlotta wanted to protest that they should hurry. Austin could very well be pursuing them at this moment. It was folly to delay as they seemed to be doing. She opened her mouth to say as much and then shut it. Their time had come, hers and Simon's; she would have it, fear or no. The flame was in Simon's eyes, and she felt as though he already thrust deep into her warmth that had been so long without him.

He might have read her mind. "The men watch and they will warn us, Carlotta. We rest during the day for safety's sake. Those abroad on the Trace at night must know their business. I assure you that I do."

"I would expect no less of Hermes." She smiled up at him and then, because the strange tension between them had to be allayed in some way, asked, "Do you use that name when you rob here?"

He laughed and held back a flowering branch. "I use no name and I wear a mask in all the best traditions. Now, we must lead the horses from here. Come."

The morning was already hot and saved from being sweltering by a little wind that rustled the leaves and scattered the mist. They walked on for a few minutes, then Simon tethered the horses to a tree in a little hollow where they blended with the shadows. She followed up through some thick brush, past a screen of moss and tossing white flowers and low grass, to a rise which seemed to give onto the blue-gray sky of morning. There she stopped and stared, all thought suspended.

The great river was the color of the sky itself at this hour. It lay flat and placid, hung with curtains of mist through which birds shifted and darted. It curved around a bend of land in the distance and spread again to split a continent. On the far side the flatlands of green and brown stretched forever. She had traversed the river, watched it on mornings such as this, seen it from the bluffs of Natchez, speculated as to its nature and characteristics, but this was different. It was discovery and reality, a beauty undreamed of.

"What must it have been like to discover this?" The soft sounds came easily to her lips. "Mississippi. The Father of Waters. The river is a woman." Lena's own thought.

"They say the proud Spaniard is buried in it. A fitting end after such a discovery . . . Carlotta." Her name was sounded on a different note, but he stood waiting for her willingness.

Her face was answer enough and they were locked in each other's arms, mouths drinking hungrily, bodies straining to draw even closer. Carlotta never really knew when they sank to the ground, which was covered with soft grass. She knew only that the raging fire in her could not be put out except by this man whose fingers were twisted in her hair and who rained kisses on her face and neck. Her nipples were peaked and hard, her loins rose convulsively, and she heard her voice crying out for him to hurry. She was poised on the edge. She was floating and drowning. Then he was deep and long inside her, thrusting and withdrawing, only to go harder into her softness. The long burning was not assuaged as her flesh rose with him and fell again. He was murmuring between thrusts but she could hear only the roaring in her ears, could feel only her body impaled beneath him, subject and willing captive in this most passionate desire of her life.

Then the frenzy took them and they went before it into the storm that left them shaken and spent as if they had been flung down from a great height. Carlotta felt that she was melting and tearing into a golden fusion. Her cry came and with it the release. Simon pulled her into his arms and she felt the mingling of their perspiration. They turned as one and looked on the great river as they lay there, knowing that in some obscure way they had been blessed.

The cry of the whippoorwill came soft and insistent three times in succession. It was full light now, and the branches above them shimmered with diffused gold. The few clouds were pink that edged into white as they spread before the rising wind. A bird sang in the depths of the wood and was answered by another. The river flowed toward the sea as it had always done and would do when they and their troubles and passions were long done.

"We must go." Simon stood up and brushed the grass from him as he adjusted his clothes. "That was our signal. Ned knows a cave near here where we can hide during the day."

Carlotta gazed out at the Mississippi, that placid surface with the rushing current underneath, and felt the sadness that is the aftermath of passion. Why should she expect protestations of love? Had he not told her how he regarded women who cared for him? Was there not a darkness over his fairness where human love was concerned? Questions were foolish. She colored a little at her own thoughts; love came where it willed.

He came up beside her and took her in his arms, his warm mouth and urgent body saying all the things her heart wanted him to say. This time his hands held her as they might hold a chalice and his lips cherished hers until her being floated out to join his. Her eyes ached with unshed tears, and she held him in her turn as if they might truly be one flesh.

The call came again; this time with such urgency that it might have been a threatened bird before a predator. Simon pulled back and caught up the pistol that was never far from him. The brush crackled under the press of running feet and Ned burst upon them.

"Simon, are you mad to delay this way? There's word from Natchez. Lenoir's alive and he's given out word that you are one of the bandits who robbed his friends and that you get your information from the gentry of the city, then go out to act on it with your gang of evildoers." He paused for breath.

Simon laughed. "Well, I never wanted to kill him, and he certainly has the right of it as to my methods. I suppose he knows I was operating here before I ever came to his house, too. No matter, we'll be clear of all this soon."

"He's tripled the price on your head and will pay double that to the man who kills the unprincipled fiend who stole his dearly loved wife. So reads the proclamation. Not only his men but those in the city who have suffered from the other nests of outlaws on the Trace are banding together. Others come secretly but the hunt is up. Some of them passed us just a little while ago when we hid in the bushes up on the ridge, big fellows with a mean look, armed for a battle." His seamed face worked with worry but his eyes glittered with battle hunger.

Simon turned to Carlotta. "We must ride day and night now.

318

It will be hard but there is no choice. I feared this might happen."

"I am ready." She caught the air of excitement and knew that it was war. Austin had left them no alternative.

An hour later a party of four stained and dirty men rode up the Trace, hats pulled low, pistols and knives ready. A black slave and a slight boy with a reddened scar that crossed one cheek and went down into the filthy scarf at his neck rode well behind. Their pace was steady and relentless; they passed others several times but volunteered no information or greetings as they let Ned's drunken voice speak for all. The Trace was a good place to mind your own business, and they counted on this to help with the disguises. Joshua was expert with stains and herbs; this had come in very handy and might even save their lives.

The haunted road was redolent of every tale Carlotta had ever read, for when the clouds obscured the moon and the high walls of earth that formed the sides of the Trace at this point seemed to hem them in, she thought she saw men and ghosts lurking behind the huge boles of trees or lying in wait in the thick branches that covered the trail at some points. A pursuer could swing down before and after them and have them captive instantly, for the trail was hammered so deeply into the land by wheels, feet, and hooves and was so narrow that this was much of its danger.

"Carlotta, tell me again of Austin's plans. I must have every detail clear in my mind." Simon motioned her into their ranks as they rode as closely together as single file would permit.

They might have been comrades together only for no trace of the passion of the morning was permitted now. Carlotta knew that he sensed her unease and sought only to relieve it, but she began to tell the tale again in slow whispers that paused at the occasional scream of a wildcat or darting of an animal in the brush. Once they rounded a curve and huge eyes glowed like lanterns above them in the branches before the beast, whatever it was, bounded away.

"Aaron Burr and Austin Lenoir. How many others before this land is welded into one whole? What will it take to see that they do not succeed?" He spoke half to himself, so low that she could barely hear.

Carlotta's nervousness had begun to abate and now the trees were merely trees. The night air was sweet to her nostrils, and she saw the glimmer of stars in a break in the foliage over their heads. She said, "Will Hermes ride in other climes or does this end his activity?" The question was lightly put but she regretted his sober answer.

"When all this is done, Hermes will be only a memory. I have been sought for my life enough. Ah, no, Carlotta, I would be part of this country as she will be. As she can be when petty dreams of empire for gain are no more, when men realize that this country is bigger than the small colonies along the Atlantic, when the people of the West, here and beyond, realize that this is their country, too, when we all understand that this will be one nation to include all that our President has bought . . ." He paused and laughed unsteadily. "Forgive me, I did not mean to treat you to a lecture."

She had seen more of the eager, idealistic man in those swift sentences than she had known in all their relationship. "But you are English, Simon. Will you not long for our country to which you cannot return so long as Hermes is sought?"

He yawned hugely and shifted one of the pistols to a more comfortable place in his belt. "I shall live in America for the rest of my life. My little heiress has wealth, thanks to my activities along the Trace and certain profitable deals at sea that some call piracy; I do not go empty-handed to her. I rather think I might become a respected landowner and resurrect Hermes in tales for my grandchildren."

Carlotta felt as if she had been slapped. He had kissed her with love's own breath, saved her life, taken her with passion and longing. Now he spoke as if she had no place in his life at all. So be it. Pride spoke at first, but as she continued she knew her words to be simple truth.

"For my own part, I mean to go to one of the cities of the south country. Austin's books mentioned Virginia where this country began, the pleasant climate, the great men it breeds. I have money, a gift, and some jewels from Austin. Frugally applied that will be enough to set up a modest bookshop with perhaps some tutoring in Latin. I love this warm country and will remain here."

"Our futures seem settled. All we have to do is get off the Trace unscathed." He yawned again. "I mean to sleep a week when this is done."

All her life would be empty without him, Carlotta thought, but she would not thrust herself upon a man who wanted only her body. That would demean the new appreciation of freedom and self-renewal that she had learned during those bitter months with Austin. She was aware of Simon's voice and turned her head to him.

"I said, tell me the end of your dream, that nightmare. You had it again when we left the house." There was a new note in his voice that she could not identify.

She sketched it out quickly for him, wondering as she did so why the nightmare should seem part of another life when it had tormented her for so long. She told him this, adding, "I can see that face so clearly, and yet it fades before all that has happened in these past months."

His warm hand reached over to clasp hers. "Now that you have done so and recognized the horror for what it is, a part of the human condition against which we must eternally struggle, you may be free to live your own life." His voice was so gentle that she knew he spoke in part of himself.

She had vowed not to ask but the darkness wrapped around them, making a small private world despite the proximity to the others. "What of you, Simon? How did Hermes come into being?"

She felt his withdrawal. "That is long done. The future is my concern now. That and this mission." He stopped abruptly and said no more but drew his horse back as he leaned over to speak to Ned.

That movement may have saved his life for suddenly the pathway was lit up by blazing torches held high as two huge men stepped out from the tangle of roots in the earthen wall of the Trace. They held pistols in both hands and wicked knives shone at their belts. There was a high shriek over their heads and a small dark man swung to the ground.

His shrill voice pierced the night air. "The tall one there, that's Mitchell, and the little one's the woman. Do what you're paid to do!" As he spoke he lifted one hand almost negligently and the haft of the knife was buried in Ned's throat. Simon's head had been there only seconds before.

The little man fell to the ground, blood streaming from him, the life gone. Simon reached for his own weapon but it was too late. The men fired simultaneously and his own followers had no time to free their weapons before they were cut down. Joshua's leg was dragging after him in a welter of blood as he launched himself on the murderers, great hands swinging. The dark man who had shouted the orders snatched Carlotta's reins but she seized the little dagger that she always carried with her, which she had, damningly enough, left in Austin's document room the first time she was there and then taken up again in the rush to find some clothes when she returned with Simon. He was trying to help her but could not do that and aim at the other murderers who were now struggling with Joshua. Carlotta aimed the sharp little blade at the man's face but he threw up one hand and deflected it so that it rang on his collar bone, then went deep into his neck. He howled and fell back as he clamped both hands to the wound.

"Get back!" Simon shouted the words at her and fired the pistol point blank so that he jerked and lay still. Then Simon threw himself into the tangle of flailing bodies that was Joshua and the murderers. Carlotta caught up the long knife from one of the dead men's belts and waited for her chance. Behind her, the bodies of Simon's friends lay in violent death. Ahead, death waited to claim yet more victims on the Natchez Trace.

CHAPTER FORTY-TWO

Habitation of Dragons

CARLOTTA circled around the struggling men but there was no opportunity to use the knife that she told herself she would use with impunity. First one back and then another presented itself as they rolled and hammered at each other. She saw one of the torches still flickering on the hard-packed earth where it had been tossed. Possibly fire would help. As she started toward it she heard a crack, then a gurgle and silence. Jerking around, she saw Simon stand erect over one of the men, a bloody stone in his hand. Joshua had twisted the head of his own opponent completely around and now lay on the body as he laughed quietly to himself.

"They're all dead." Simon spoke very calmly, but his eyes blazed savagely in the faint light. "I should have been more watchful."

"How can you blame yourself?" Carlotta came close to him but he turned away.

"While we dallied on the bluff your husband was organizing and dispatching these men." His voice was bitter. "I was the leader of our group and should have known better. Joshua, Joshua, get up. It is over."

The dark man rose and they saw that his trouser leg was torn from powder burns but not bleeding. His face was twisted with rage, and his skin glistened with blood and sweat. His voice was thick and slurry. "Kill! I wait and kill others. You go, both of you."

Carlotta cried, "No! How can you know that they will be Austin's men? Don't let him, Simon!"

"Is this what you want, Joshua? You know it will be almost certain death." Simon looked at his fellow outlaw and ignored Carlotta.

"They come looking for bodies. I hide, be ready. A good fight." He was grinning, but the savagery of his expression did not alter.

Simon held out his hand and the other took it. "If it were otherwise I would never leave you, Joshua. You know that."

323

"Aye." He turned away and began to search the bodies for other weapons.

"Simon!" Carlotta cried out as he caught her up bodily and pulled her onto the nearest horse, which shied nervously. There was no sign of the rest of them.

"Hush." It was a command, his fingers dug fiercely into her arm. She obeyed as they went around the scene of carnage and up the trail of murder.

They rode for perhaps fifteen minutes in total silence. The path was even narrower now, the banks almost vertical, and vines hung down from trees overhead while gnarled roots thrust out at eye level. Menace hung over them in the darkness, which was lit only by the faint glimpse of the moon at intervals of a gap in the leaves above them. Carlotta felt sick to her very soul at what had ensued but she held herself erect, still clutching the knife, not daring to relax her guard for even an instant. The heat pressed down on them; there was no hint of a breeze anywhere. She felt the sweat trickle down her back and between her breasts but fear made her cold.

Simon drew rein suddenly and said, "We must go on foot now, there is nothing else to do."

"Will you leave me if I cannot?" She heard her words splinter against the iron of his control.

There was no hesitation as he dismounted and lifted her down. His face was a blur in the hot darkness, but she felt the convulsive reaction of his hands and knew that he longed to hit her. In her pain she would almost welcome it.

"I have no time for explanations, madame. Follow me or be left to the mercies of your husband's followers, who doubtless have their instructions as to what shall be done with you." He touched the horse on the flank and sent it on ahead, then he set his hands to a climbing vine which was as large around as his wrist. Using it and his feet, he was soon poised on a jutting piece of root high above her head. "Come on."

Carlotta scrambled up as best she could, thankful for all the tree climbing she had done in her youth. He pulled her the last few feet and then jerked his head toward a tiny trail in the brush which seemed to lead into a labyrinth of snakes and holes.

"Our only chance and a devilish slim one at that." He was creeping into the brush as he spoke and did not even look behind to see if she followed.

"I am quite ready." Her voice was level and cool. Carlotta

324

had realized in those desperate seconds that she wanted very much to live and be free. Much as she cared for Simon, the events of the past were crowding in on her and she wondered what manner of man he was. Was it only the lure of the flesh? That did not bear thinking about. She forced her mind to concentrate on moving as he moved, placing her feet in the same place as he did, and breathing quietly so as to give no sound to predators, whether human or animal.

They went this way until the night gave way to another dawn, until Carlotta's legs were numb and her whole body shivered with weariness. Simon's clothes were drenched, his gilt hair wet, and the stains of disguise faded. He held up a hand and pointed to a small patch of moss under a tree close by. They sank down in an exhausted heap, screened by some tall seedlings rising just at their feet.

"We'll rest here for a short time. I will watch while you sleep and then you can do the same." He looked gravely down at Carlotta, and she saw the lines from nose to mouth deepen.

"As you say." She did not even have the strength to protest his taking the first watch. Her whole body relaxed on the cool moss as she swept the heavy hair back from her hot face. He gave her a swift, quirking smile that faded almost instantly, but was none the less reassuring for all that, and went to stand a few yards away so that he seemed to blend in with the trees. A lone bird gave a trill in the distance, and a squirrel ran down the side of the tree directly across from her. Then sleep took Carlotta and she dreamed of the wide Mississippi, freedom, and Simon.

It seemed only seconds until he shook her awake and pointed wordlessly to the spot where he had been watching. Then he threw himself down on the moss with his face turned away from her and was asleep in almost the same movement. She looked as he had directed but her vision was still blurry from sleep and her entire body was wet with the perspiration of noon.

Nothing stirred in the woods; the only sound was that of the faint breeze as it rattled the leaves at her head. There was a great peace over everything; she could almost forget the deadly peril which surrounded them. "This time next year I shall doubtless be wishing for adventure." She spoke the words under her breath, wondering as she did what a world without Simon or the contemplation of him would be like. He groaned under his breath and she turned quickly, but he only dreamed, unpleasant ones from the look of his face as it twisted and shifted. He relaxed into slumber once more and she looked at the driven face again and wondered what his personal agonies were.

"I have slept long." Simon sat up and stretched, possibly two hours later. He appeared rested, certainly far more so than Carlotta herself did. "Do you think that you can go on along for another few hours?" He was already standing up, adjusting the pistol and powder, the knife, feeling for the case of papers which he carried now inside his shirt at his belt.

She nodded silently. She was hot, wet, and still tired. What right did he have to look refreshed and almost eager when his men lay dead and she, who ought to have some claim to concern from him, stood wan and hesitant at the thought of yet another trail. He looked at her for her answer and she knew his inward pain, for the green eyes were dark, the mobile mouth set. Somehow that was comforting to take into the miles that they must travel.

The sun was still high when they came to the little river set between low banks which gave onto small sandy beaches. A fallen log extended out into it and the water rushed by in white foam that gave way to lazy movement around the curve. Trees leaned over to trail their branches in it, and the long ropy vines twined down the trunks. A large bird rose flapping as they approached and sailed majestically away into the brilliant sky. It was cool here and Carlotta breathed a sigh of relief.

"Come swim and then we must talk. There are things you must know, Carlotta." Simon peeled the wet clothes from his lean body and waded out into the water, picking some up in his hands and pouring it over his head in delight at the refreshment.

Carlotta followed his action and shivered at the chill of it after the heat of the trek. She scrubbed her body with sand and washed her hair several times, then she ducked under to rinse it and let the current carry her along for a few yards before she rose and went over the clothes. Seeing what she meant to do, Simon came and rinsed out his own as she did, then they spread them out to dry on the hot sand.

He gathered up documents and weapons and carried them to a rock which was well shaded and low enough to the stream that one might sit comfortably with feet in it. Then he looked at Carlotta who gazed at his nude body, colored, and glanced away. Her hands went almost involuntarily to her breasts to cover them.

"Are we in Eden that you now view with shame that which you once found pleasing?" His voice was light, but she caught the undertone and straightened up instantly. He touched the surface of the rock. "Come, you must remember what I say to you in the event that we are parted."

Carlotta's lethargy left her then, and she looked at the long length of him sitting so casually in the shade, the silver-gilt hair shining in the reflected light, as he spoke of the fate that might await them. She was conscious of life as never before. Her bare feet dug into the sand of the river bottom, her hair tossed lightly on her shoulders, as she walked proudly toward Simon. A small insect skimmed the surface of the water and flew toward the sun.

"Where are your other men? Were they not expecting you to rendezvous with them? Why did you leave Joshua? What is this mission you have spoken of?" Questions tumbled from her as she made the effort not to be abashed before him, the man who had made such joyous love to her not so very long ago.

Simon sighed heavily as he separated the small packet of documents into two and handed one to her. "You had little enough, I know, and it was lost with the horses in the attack. These will identify you to a man who waits in the Chickasaw country, near a place called Pontotoc Ridge. He is my friend and will guide you to Nashville and beyond. Give the papers only to him who says, 'Eternal vigilance is the price of liberty.' Linger there, pretend to fish, look for work, say that you hanker to visit Richmond. Eventually you will be noticed." He felt about in his own packet and drew out something. "This is small compensation for what you have suffered but it will help establish you."

She did not look down but kept her eyes on his face. "How could I traverse this land alone? How would I know your man if I did survive? Simon, this is moonwash! Be frank with me!" She clenched her fingers and felt the roughness in them. She looked down and saw the diamond glittering there, a piece of perfection as large as her thumb, catching the sunlight and setting light to dancing in the water. "What?"

A tiny green lizard ran across the rock between them and paused to blow out a pink throat before darting away. Simon reached out as if to touch it, but drew back. "I can say only that Austin's plans are of great interest to certain people just as are those of Mr. Burr. The following both have received in New Orleans and Natchez may be an indication of the way matters are going in the next few years. News travels slowly and is often garbled. I have a relay chain that will carry it swiftly; that is all you must know for your own safety. As for the rest, you might be a young boy if you cut that hair and swagger a bit more. Wait along the Trace and try to fall in with a party moving together. It will be your best chance. But, for now, we go together."

"You could buy your heiress with this." She lifted the diamond to his view. "Do you think to buy me with it?"

His hand shot out to encircle her wrist and his eyes went dark as he fought to control himself. Chills shot up her back and arms at his touch; the familiar fire rose between them. She leaned toward him, her mouth dry, but he drew back.

"You have a deadly tongue, lady, but it is better than fear. I will answer your other questions while I can. First, my band was always small. Less than ten men, and those who are dead are the ones I truly trusted. The others will wait at one of the stands up the Trace for a few days; if I do not arrive they will seek the same employment. That was our bargain when I first began this outlawry. Let us say that it was quite profitable." His quick smile flashed and for a moment Carlotta saw the lover she had first known in England.

"Simon, I must know these things. It is my right." Her mouth was trembling, but she knew herself well enough to know that she must persist.

He looked past her as he said, "Joshua was a slave on one of the plantations near New Orleans, but he risked his life for the freedom he could not live without. He always intended to go beyond the Mississippi, but he loved a Chickasaw girl and married her. There was raiding party, men were drunk, the end of it was that the girl, his wife, was scalped. He attacked them, killed three, and the others escaped to Natchez to set a large price on his head. He became an outlaw on his own, and I met him when I sought men. He is my friend but he has sought death many times. He will have his wish now."

Simon lowered his chin into his hands and sighed. Carlotta touched his shoulder gently, then let her hand rest on it. The little lizard ran back between them, and there was a plop in the stream as a fish jumped. The wind lifted her hair and blew it so that the fragrant strands drifted into Simon's face. He caught one curl in his brown fingers and turned so that he faced her. His brows drew together in his serious look. She leaned toward him again and saw his eyes drop to her jutting breasts.

"Lady mine." His whisper stirred the curls at her temples.

"Ah, Simon." She sighed as he had done and half-smiled at her unconscious imitation.

He caught her in his arms, fitting her there as though she belonged. Their mouths met and clung, softening to deeper warmth and melting in tenderness. His hands found her breasts, fondled them slowly, then moved downward to the secret richness of her cleft where they moved slowly, tantalizingly. She shifted with him as her breath came harder. Their tongues wound together as they pressed ever closer to each other. Her own hands reached out to touch his maleness and found him hard. He twisted convulsively as she did so and withdrew his lips to put them to her swollen nipples. She put both hands in the silver-gilt hair for seconds, then returned them to his narrow waist and down over his smoothness to the thrusting eagerness of him.

Moments later they lay on the rock, joined together in the hunger that had never left them, as he thrust into her softness, withdrew, and thrust again. Her little cries came in his ear, then silenced as his mouth covered hers with kisses. His face was lit with happiness and pleasure when he lifted it to look into her eyes. They drew apart as her fingers teased his skin so that the chills ran down his sides. His long, lean legs shifted apart to clasp her between them, and then he was moving once again in her as she rose and came slowly down on his power.

Time faded for them both then. Carlotta was conscious only of her body and the delicious new sensations that came with each move Simon made. She saw that he, too, shivered and cried out as she set her mouth to him, touching her own hunger to him. Then the time came when they could wait no longer, the banked fires exploded, carrying them to the brink and beyond. Her flesh was melting, searing alive and returning. They were one whole, fused and bound by each other, one body and one flesh.

In the aftermath of passion and love, Carlotta could not hide the tears that filmed her eyes. She turned her face from Simon's questing gaze but he folded her to him and the often sardonic voice said softly, "I, also, lady mine. I know."

He kissed her gently as their passion rose again, this time to such heights of tenderness that she felt every inch of her body cherished by his lips and hands and shafting manhood. His mouth found her secret places, drawing her into the light of shared pleasure, showing her what delighted him and making it their own. When at last they lay together on the warm rock, the sun making dappled shadows on her white body and his tanned one, Simon and Carlotta knew that for them, whatever happened, the world would never be quite the same.

The sweet intensity was almost too much to bear. Carlotta shifted slightly in his encircling arm, and the scrabbling movement at her head made her jump so that he turned to see. The three little lizards scuttled quickly away, swarming up into the branches of the overhanging tree, changing color as they went.

"Dragons come to watch." Simon laughed softly while he watched her in his turn.

"To watch and flee." She met his laughter, and they clung together in the timeless moment that was its own sharing. Then they kissed and the world swung free for them.

CHAPTER FORTY-THREE

Cage of Honey

SIMON and Carlotta moved along the edge of the stream in the last glow of afternoon. It was cool now, for a breeze was driving the mugginess from the air. Their clothes had dried in the sun and felt fresh. The rich odor of earth and growing things rose up to stir the senses. She had never felt more alive or part of the world around her than she did in this time when she walked with her lover toward safety, leaving the danger behind that had threatened her for so long.

He smiled down at her. "We are going in the general direction of the meeting place but it is days away as yet. I do not think Austin, even with all the resources at his disposal, can track us through this wilderness."

She shook her hair back and tied it with a clinging piece of vine. "I wonder what it will be like to be safe. He has shadowed my life."

"You will build a new one in Virginia. This will seem as if it were a dream. Will you remember me kindly?"

The words came before she could stop them. "But I thought we would be together. Did you not mean it . . . back there?" The color poured into her face as she looked into the shuttered eyes and fought for control. "I see that you did not. I have been foolish, it seems."

He said, "I reacted violently once to your feelings on that subject, Carlotta. I am sorry if I cannot be what you expect. You are beautiful and brave and I honor that. I am as I am and have been made. Let it be. I have other battles to fight and can offer you nothing."

Pride held her steady before him. She remembered the anger he had shown on the beach in Haiti when she had been so foolish as to show her feelings for him. She was wiser now but it had done her no good. He had retreated from any feelings for her.

"I understand, Simon. There is no more to say."

"How can you understand? There is so much that is impossible to explain." He broke off and turned his back as if to start walking again.

"I do not ask you to do so." She drew abreast of him and saw, too late, that his face was white under the tan as if with pain.

"That is correct. I shall not attempt it. Come, we waste time." He strode out rapidly, leaving her to follow.

She walked numbly behind him after that, wondering as she did so how he could be so tender, murmur such words of sweetness in her ears, and yet be so cold when ardor had been assuaged. "Strumpet," he had called her once, and still the word betokened an old hurt, not a new one. Likely a woman had hurt him long ago and he resisted caring now. Always Simon had been a mystery to her, despite her knowing of his pain over his mother, of whom he had spoken so angrily in Haiti.

The moon rose to shimmer through the branches and reflect on the leaves as the wind rustled them. The early evening air was hushed before the coming night. They walked slowly but steadily; the ground here was growing comparatively free of underbrush; it was carpeted with grass and piled leaves or, where the trees were thick, was simply packed hard. Night flowers belled out in places and carried a sweet scent that reminded Carlotta of their afternoon love. She tried to remind herself that she must be thankful to be alive and rid of Austin, but her traitor heart told her otherwise.

Hours had passed when they came at last to a small bluff covered with trees which were, in turn, hung with vines in a solid mass of flowers. Their lushness assaulted the brain and drowned it with heaviness. Then the wind shifted and only the lightest odor remained to give an ephemeral memory. Simon went right up to the thickest of the vines and parted them with exploratory fingers, then held them aside.

"Thank heaven I remembered correctly. We can spend the night here. I stayed here once when pursued by the outlaw whose territory I invaded; I had reason to be grateful that Joshua was with me then." He spoke almost absently, but the reserve was still in his voice as they entered.

The little cave was partly open, and vines had grown down inside so that the flower scents still followed them. A tiny stream ran down a ledge off to the side and made a pleasant gurgling sound. In the back it appeared that a tumble of rocks led back into the bluff itself. She could see no more in the moonlight, for he had dropped the curtain of vines.

Inanely, she said, "What is that fragrance?"

"Honeysuckle. It grows wild and can overwhelm any building if left to do so." Simon settled himself near the doorway and placed the pistol at his hand. "You had best try to get all the sleep you can, Carlotta. Our pace will be swift tomorrow, for we go by day since we are getting out of country that I know very well."

The cool voice tormented her as she thought how good it would be to rest in his arms, to have him kiss and caress her eager flesh, to touch his and waken it to passion. She had been supplicant before him enough. She said, "You are quite right and I am very tired. Good night, Simon." She turned on her stomach, pillowed her head on her arms, and bit her lips to keep any sound back.

The soothing sounds of the spring and Simon's even breathing finally calmed Carlotta. Her body relaxed on the cool earth of the cave, and she drifted into sleep remembering that afternoon and all that they had done. At least she would have the memory, and that would have to be enough in time to come.

"You sleep so long. Surely it is time to wake." The voice was slow and soft as it spoke close to her.

Carlotta stretched a little and wondered at this new morning mood of Simon's. The words were delivered with almost an air of intimacy. She said, "But it is so peaceful here, Simon, and I slept so soundly. Are you ready to leave now?" She opened her eyes wider and looked around for him.

"Ah, my dear, I daresay your lover is quite ready to leave. It is just that he will soon embark on a far longer journey than the one he planned." Austin stood in the shadows but stepped forward into the pool of light made by the open roof of the cave over which the vines grew. He laughed at the expression on her face and that laughter was more fearful than all the rites of Haiti she had witnessed.

"What are you doing here? Where is Simon?" She jumped to her feet and looked anxiously around, anything to avoid that specter before her.

Austin still wore unrelieved black with a pistol and knife at his side. His white hair shone in the light, but his face was no longer smooth. It was scored by lines that had previously been almost unseen, and his mouth had a downward twist on the left side. There were pouches under his eyes and brown marks on his face. She had once thought him younger than he could possibly be; now a middle-aged man faced her. But the eyes gave him away; they had been impassive for nearly all the time she had known him except for rare occasions when he gave way to anger. They blazed with fury as he looked at her now, a fury barely leashed, and that spelled her death as surely as ever her nightmare had done.

"Where is Simon? Tell me, you fiend!" She moved toward him, fingers bent as if to rake him with sharp nails.

"He lives, for now. Whether he continues to do so depends on you, my dear." His soft words ceased and the demon looked out at her. "Slut, I owe you much. You would have been my empress, my lady, mother of the heir, honored and respected. Yet you refused to believe, to help, you abet this spy and run away with him. My beautiful house is partially burned and my records taken. Ah, there is much to be paid!"

There was a movement at the doorway and the vines were pushed aside as a tall man entered, forcing another ahead of him. It was Simon, his arms bound behind his back, another cord around his throat, the end of it held by a shorter man who had a drawn pistol in the other hand. Simon's face was bruised on one side and his hair hung over his forehead, his shirt was torn almost off him, but he held his head erect as his eyes went to Carlotta, and what she saw there made her body tremble. It was compassion and caring, fear for her, not himself.

"You are all right? He has not harmed you?"

"The swine has not touched me." Carlotta's voice rang with contempt, and Austin flushed despite himself.

Simon said, "I heard a noise and went out to check it. Then one of them hit me with a rock. When I woke I was as you see me. I am sorry that I failed to protect you, Carlotta."

"Oh, Simon!"

"This is all very touching, I'm sure, but I have not arranged this in order to listen to you two moon after each other. Carlotta, you will do exactly as I say or I will tie your lover down there in the swamp and stir the snakes up. I know a potion that can resist snake bite so that when the serpents strike again and again death is prolonged until the person is swollen in hideous pain and cries for death. The other choice is that I will simply deliver him to the hangman, who will indeed be glad to deal with one of the bandits from the Trace." Austin laughed and

334

nodded to his men, who pushed Simon down and bound him to a boulder near the entrance.

"He will kill me anyway, Carlotta. Make what terms you can." Simon might have been bargaining for a shirt in which he was not very interested.

Austin said casually, "These men are Samuel and Will, not very intelligent, but they obey my every wish and are bound to me by ceremony and law. They forget what they see. You, my dear, will return to Natchez with me and lead a life of seclusion from your ordeal. Well, what do you say?"

"I will do anything. Spare him." Carlotta did not look at Simon as she said the words. Anything could happen between now and Natchez. If she did not obey, Austin would take great pleasure in doing exactly what he had said and making her watch. She had no illusions as to her own fate; he would drug her and use her until he grew weary, then who knew? A wave of black hatred swamped her, and she shut her eyes against it. "Anything, Austin Lenoir. Anything."

"You love him." The statement was flat and savage.

"With all my heart. I always have. I always will." She looked him straight in the eye, then past him to Simon, whose face was carefully impassive. The men stood beside him as though carved there, their faces set stiffly. She knew then that here were those who had been treated with the potions he had mentioned and that she would be as they.

Austin laughed so that the sound rang around the area. He turned to Simon. "Well, my lord spy, you have had many a fair lady weep for love of you, they tell me. Does this declaration touch you?"

Simon did not reply but looked at Carlotta. It was impossible to tell what he was thinking. Austin picked up a saddlebag in easy reach and withdrew some filmy cloth and a case. He tossed the things at her and said, "Put these on, wash your face, comb your hair. You look the slut I have called you. Does it not disturb you that your lover does not echo your avowals of passion?"

"I love him but it is not necessary that he love me." She spoke to Austin but in reality she said the words for Simon and herself. If she lived, which she doubted, she would be the better for this consuming first love, the love that would be her last. One could not help where one loved nor could it be forced. Simon's way was his own, and that was as it must be. She looked at him then and saw that the tanned face was somehow

335

younger, the green eyes alight in a way that she had never seen.

"Kill me and leave her alone. She is young and does not know love from the imitation of it." Simon shrugged as best he could and stared at Austin.

"Obey me, Carlotta!" Little beads of sweat were standing out on Austin's face and the tight crotch of his breeches was bulging.

She dared not disobey, but nausea rose in her throat as she washed her face in the cool water and combed her hair into spun silk over her shoulders. She put the silky green gown on over her clothes and slipped quickly out of them before turning to face Austin's eager eyes. The gown was very low in the neck and the sleeves came to just below her elbows. The skirt was well above her ankles. It revealed much of her body and brought a flush to her face.

"Put these on." He indicated the pocket of the little case which had held the comb and, earlier, the gown.

She gasped as she withdrew the jewels. They were emeralds and pearls set in a curving bracelet that went up much of one arm, a tiara, several rings of matchless beauty, a high choker which spread in shimmering barbarism over her bare breasts, and several other necklaces, some of which also blazed with diamonds which caught the light from overhead and gave it back. She thought of the river and the shaded rock yesterday and their passion. How short and how bitter was the retribution.

"The jewels of a queen. I wanted you to wear them just this once. It is because of you that Jeremy is dead. I want you to know the feeling."

"Your partner in sodomy is dead because of you, Austin Lenoir. You cannot even face the consequences of your own actions yet you think to create an empire. How puerile!" Simon laughed in scorn.

"Swine of a spy!" Austin waved his hand and one of the men bent down to slam a heavy fist across Simon's face. He turned to Carlotta, and it took all her courage to stand still. "Let me tell you about this man you love. I warrant he has told you little."

"He has told me all I need to know!"

"Has he told you of his family? Mitchell, indeed." Austin smiled that evil smile as he looked from the rigid girl in all her jeweled splendor to the bound man whose face had been cut again by the force of the blow he had just been given. "Lord

336

Morancon of Cornwall, he of the fierce pride, would have disdained so common a name, would he not? Your ancestors had the wrong politics, my Lord. The German king was not disposed to look the other way when your father dueled with your mother's lover and lost, was he? That was against the law of England, as was that fondness for the Stuart cause. I could forgive you much for that, you know, but I am not an admirer of lost causes. Your mother was a strumpet and everyone knew it, only your father did not. Perhaps it was her French blood. The estates fell into the hands of King George on one pretext and another, but all knew. You traveled with her and saw for yourself, Haiti was not the only place you lived. The money was going, you were a pretty lad; did your mother and your many friends use you well?"

Carlotta was sickened but she kept it from her face. "What point does all this have, Austin? I have said I will do what you want. Do it and be done!"

"Ah, you are eager for the caresses of my men? They are not affected in the sex, if you follow me." He put his hands together in a steeple motion and watched her eagerly.

Simon was roused now. "Leave her alone! You are afraid to meet me in honest battle. Only a pervert and a coward would act as you do, and still you see yourself with blinded eyes!"

"You say that to me! You who have used your looks and body to gain entrance to the chambers of beautiful and rich women in England and America. Do you not think it amused the court at London to see the son of Lord Morancon calling himself by another name, gambling, dicing, wenching, giving of himself for money? Did you think they did not know?"

Carlotta cried, "If you think to disillusion me about him, forget it! I love him and always will."

Austin continued, "You were Hermes until it became an open secret who you really were. Did you bed at night and rob them by day? I doubt not the little heiress in New York will wonder what happened to her faithful lover. Unfortunate about the land in Haiti? Countess Annette, your dear mother, would have liked to know that you had something since she was so fond you. As fond as I of my own son." He laughed and the mad sound rang against the rocky walls. "The girl in Natchez will wonder about her mother's taste in men for years to come. Madame De Soucet thought you were a matrimonial prize! And now, not content with robbing on the Trace, you must come

337

and steal my documents. Did you think to find a buyer for them or to blackmail me for them?"

Simon spoke as if Austin did not exist. "Do you believe what he has said?"

"Does it matter?" Her eyes locked with his and they stood in their own world.

"Much of it is true. Too much."

"I cannot judge you, Simon. We do what we must." She thought of her own behavior over the past months with Austin. There was little blame she could attach to Simon or herself. "You know my feelings."

His voice dropped lower but it was passionate and eager, the voice of the man who had taught her how to love and what being a woman meant. "I know, Carlotta, and now that we stand in the presence of loathsome evil and certain death, I have no reason to dissemble. You have said that you love me. I have not loved before, not until now, not until I met a wench on a winter's morning."

Carlotta smiled at him as she remembered that all-consuming passion and the fruits of it. He had said the words and that was enough. Whether he meant them or not, he cared enough to say them. "Simon." The one word said it all and he knew it, for his lips quirked in the way they did before love's storm took them.

"Pretty. Pretty. Avowals of love before death. But nothing so delightful will happen for some little time. My dear, you look like a Byzantine princess in that flowing gown and those jewels with that sun and those vines shadowing you. It will be a pleasure to watch how you react now." He gestured and one of the men stepped forward to run his fingers down Carlotta's arm. She jerked back and was halted by the movement of Austin's pistol. "Willingly, I believe I said. You will act as if you enjoyed it. Perhaps you will. I know your newly professed lover will do so. I will not presume to touch you, of course; that has not been my interest."

The man reached for Carlotta's breasts and she forced herself to stand still while Austin smirked at them both. The cool words broke across his beginning laughter which he did not seem able to still. Carlotta saw only the green gaze mingling with the honeysuckle vines, and the drifting fragrance of the flowers wound around her as the sense of what Simon said came to her.

"Did you think that the likes of you and Burr and all those

who stand to benefit from your treasonous schemes could go unwatched? Do you not know that the American government is aware and that your activities have been reported? Why have I so consistently appeared where you go, Austin Lenoir? Think on it and know that I am one of several agents of President Thomas Jefferson in this Mississippi Territory. What you do to me will be avenged, and you will go down in destruction."

CHAPTER FORTY-FOUR

"Let Us Unite With One Heart and One Mind"
—Thomas Jefferson, Inaugural Address, 1801

AUSTIN faced Simon, his attention wholly caught by the bold words. Carlotta took that opportunity to edge away from the tall man with the dead eyes, who did not attempt to follow. He simply stood there, hands at his sides, as did his fellow.

"You think to save your live with a grandiose lie, my Lord Morancon. Do you actually think you can distract me from my purpose of revenge?"

Simon's teeth flashed white in the half gloom of the cave as a faint shadow fell over the sunlit place where Carlotta was. She glanced up, then back to the drama in front of her.

Simon said, "Did you truly think that the addition of all the territory gained from Napoleon would go unevaluated, that assessors of all types would not be sent out, that plots would go unseen? I have been in the service of Jefferson since before he took office and, you must admit, my pose has been good. You thought I sought my mother's revenues in Haiti? Not so. I was sent there to consider a situation which might prove dangerous to my country. A report has gone to Washington City on that and on you. Do you think we do not know that you sought English support for your schemes even as Burr has done? You are power-drunk and rich but you are not original."

"Whatever you are, whatever pose you maintain, I shall not be cheated. Both of you shall die. You, Simon Morancon, were the amusement of the many who knew your history and predilections; am I to believe that a womanizer, a gambler, a hot-tempered cheat, can be such as you say? As well to believe that this woman before us is a spy herself."

The veiled laughter in Simon's voice touched Austin's nerves. "I said you weren't original, didn't I?"

It was a mistake. Austin's white face went red and his eyes

bulged in their sockets. His voice rose to a faint scream, and he lifted the pistol. "Who cares what you are? I have carefully laid plans and the money to implement them. Mexico, the West, I have the names of those who will help. The outlaws took you. It happens all the time." He leveled the pistol at Carlotta. "Her face is fair, her body lush. I shall shoot her there but so that she does not die rapidly. Her cries will be the last you hear as my men castrate you."

As he spoke, the two men moved closer to Simon and one began to finger the blade of his broad knife.

"Perhaps we can strike a bargain for her life." Simon tried to wrestle free of the rock to which he was bound. Carlotta heard the agonized note in his words and knew that Austin would rejoice in it.

"No bargains. Only pleasure! Are you ready, killer of my dear Jeremy?" Austin raised the pistol and fired straight at Carlotta's bosom. She threw herself down on the floor in a last minute attempt at safety as the sound of the shot and the smell of burnt powder mingled together with shouts and curses.

"It is the sentence of Damballah! Die! Die! You who have misused his powers." Joshua stood in the entrance, torn vines at his feet, a smoking pistol on the ground where he had thrown it, two others in his hands, and a great black snake coiled around his neck. Austin's man lay silent and dead before him, the other knelt with upraised arms before Joshua as mumbles came from his shaking lips. Austin's own shot had gone awry and he stood staring at the useless pistol in his hand.

"The sentence of Damballah!" The long hissing cry rose from Joshua's lips as he and the great snake seemed to move together.

"I gave him what he wanted! I gave him much and would have given more!" Austin's cry was that of the supplicant before his angry god, a god of blood and savagery.

Carlotta saw that his attention was focused totally on Joshua. She slipped out of the light, around him, along the wall, and up behind Simon, who was very still. Her slippery fingers began to work at the knots that held him but it was of little use until she looked down at the rocks scattered about. Several had sharp edges and she jerked them up and down on the ropes until the strands began to part. It was no more than several minutes but it seemed an eternity. She dared not say anything to Simon, but the urgency in his eyes warned her.

While she struggled, Carlotta saw the remorseless movement of Joshua and the way the slick black body of the huge snake reached out ahead of the man who carried it. Austin retreated before it, pride forgotten.

"I will build you a new temple here. Aye, and you shall have sacrifices of blood. Have I not worshipped you long? Have I not given sacrifices in New Orleans and honored your name? I was preparing the woman for you and you have Jeremy, Jeremy, Jeremy . . ."

The repetition of the name seemed to bring him back from some netherland of terror and his eyes flickered toward Carlotta, then widened as he saw that Simon was nearly free. "You shall not escape!" He sought the other pistol in his belt and started toward them.

Simon stood up with a tearing of the cords that bound him. He swept Carlotta down to the floor and stepped in front of her. Austin aimed at his face but in that instant the great snake's head flashed toward him and the long flickering tongue darted out.

"Damballah! No!" The scream burst from his throat, rose, flattened out, and strangled as he fell to the floor as though knocked there. He thrashed about, his eyes rolled back in their sockets, his hands beat at each other. Another scream began and stopped. He whispered, "Madeleine, only you. Only you." Then the booted feet drummed one final time and the breath left him.

Joshua stood where he had been as he unwound the snake from his shoulders and looked at Simon, who had pulled Carlotta to her feet. "He was not touched. The snake was at least three feet away. He died of fright and his own evil."

"He is truly dead?" Carlotta heard the fierce joy in her voice and knew that she was free.

"Joshua is right. There is no mark." Simon bent to look at the crumpled body, then turned to the henchman who still sat gaping. He lifted a puzzled gaze to Joshua. "What is this?"

"It is the trance. I have seen it often in those who have taken much of a potion such as has been given to him. It will wear off and he will have no memory of his enslavement. He is harmless."

Carlotta caught at the jewels she wore and sent them scattering as delicate catches broke. Then she ran out into the fresh air of the hot afternoon. Thunder clouds built in the north and the honeysuckle scent was sweet to overpowering. All that mattered was that she lived, that the ground was hard under her bare feet, and that the sun beat on her unprotected skin. She had come from certain death into life, and nothing would ever be so fearful again.

Suddenly strong arms caught her to the wide chest she knew and a hard voice, roughened by emotion, said, "Carlotta, Carlotta. Thanks be to all the gods of man that you are unharmed. The swine meant to kill you and more." Simon's lips sought hers in the familiar drowning sweetness.

Carlotta pulled back. She would not be enslaved again, no matter how dear the chains. He stared at her in surprise, the lines on his brow deeper for all that he had undergone. He started to speak but just then Joshua came out. He walked with the suggestion of a limp, and the snake was nowhere in sight.

"Damballah—or his servant—has gone into the recesses of the cave. His will has been done."

Simon went out to him and clasped his hands. "You saved our lives and the mission, Joshua. What happened to you on the Trace and how did you find this place?"

"No others came after you left though I waited several hours. I decided then that Lenoir must have hired or obtained trackers, so I started out in the general direction that I knew you would take. I was never far behind you but I lost you when one of the zombie-men attacked me and I killed him. Apparently he had been left to watch. From then on it was a matter of caution. I was almost too late."

"Where did the snake come from?" Carlotta's teeth had begun to chatter in spite of the intense, muggy heat.

"There's a swamp down there." Joshua waved his hand. "Damballah was sunning himself and he came to me. Justice is done. He was an evil man who enslaved many of my people and killed others for his sacrifices that he thought kept him young and potent."

"We must bury them and make sure that poor wretch is safe." Simon turned to Carlotta. "I will get your clothes for you. You can wash in the residuals of the stream yonder." He pointed beyond the bluff where bushes glowed richly.

"Aye, my Lord." She had laid herself bare before him in the cave and now could not speak civilly to him. She took refuge in courtesy to Joshua. "There is no way that I can express my gratitude to you, but please accept my everlasting gratitude."

He smiled. "I, too, serve the American President, lady. I have done only my duty."

It was later than Carlotta had thought; many of the daylight hours had been spent in the struggle with Austin. His body and that of his man would lie in the cave, she supposed, but it did not matter, his evil would be purged from the earth. She sat in the tiny pool of fresh water and let it cool her body as she thought of Simon and all that she had learned of him from Austin. Much was explained—his reticence, his distrust of women, the look of brooding sorrow he sometimes wore. But the love she had sworn when they faced death and which he had reciprocated? How could she face him now that her heart was bare to him? But had it not always been? She was Carlotta and she could face the future, for it would be in freedom.

In the end the choice was hers to make. Simon came toward her, his face freshly washed, the livid bruise fading somewhat, his hand held out. She was wearing the shirt and breeches, her hair loose on her shoulders, her feet bare, as she rose to meet him.

"Walk with me, Carlotta." It was a command spoken in level tones.

She fell in beside him and they walked around the bluff, onto a winding path, and into the fading light of early evening. The silence was strained, something had to be said.

"What now, Simon? Do you still continue on with the documents? What will happen in Natchez when Austin does not return?" She was proud of her voice. It was very calm and did not shake at all.

"They will think the outlaws took him. The Natchez Trace is the most dangerous of roads. And, yes, the documents must be presented to the President. I doubt not that this will affect much of his policy toward these western territories."

She looked straight ahead. "What about Joshua? Did you tell his true story?"

"Certainly. He is a very fine actor in addition to all his other accomplishments, and I recruited him several years ago in New Orleans." He paused on the trail and turned to her. "It is true, you know, all that Austin said. I was all those things and more. Then, almost seven years ago, I came to America and, by virtue of some wild drinking parties, fell in with some men who were from Richmond in the state of Virginia. They invited me to their homes, and at one of them I met a man who changed my life. A tall, raw-boned fellow with an odd liking for a man, without thought of his background or antecedents. We talked about the French Revolution and ideals and practicalities. He

344

had proposals and asked if I'd like to try. I laughed but agreed. I obtained information for him, made several journeys, absorbed philosophy, and somehow came to believe in this country and what it might one day be. I am Jefferson's man and now my own man. I do not apologize for the past, Carlotta; you deserve the truth." The dark brows came together as he put one hand on her shoulder and watched her face.

"Why I should care about the truth and you is surely immaterial." She gave him look for look.

"You will exact full penalty then? You will make me say it, those words I have said so many times and never meant? I see that you will. Very well." He put his other hand on her shoulder and held her back from him. A slight red rose in his brown face and the green eyes shimmered at her. "Carlotta, will you be my wife? I love you and now I think I have from the first, though I fought it all the while for reasons that you know. I cannot offer you a noble name or wealth. The King of England has seen to that. My dear mother, dead of the fever one of her young lovers gave her, tarnished all honor. But here, in this land, anything is possible. I offer you love; I offer you Simon Mitchell, citizen."

Carlotta stood very still as the words she had never thought to hear from proud Simon rang in her ears and penetrated her mind. He had rebuffed her and rejected her enough so that she might still be dreaming. But this was no time for haughty pride. He was the man she loved, and for her there could be no other.

"'It was no dream. I lay broad awaking.'" The words of the Tudor poet rose to her lips as she remembered how she had spoken them on seeing Simon in Haiti. "Simon, I have ever loved you. Right gladly will I wed you." Chills went up and down her arms at the wonder of it.

His eyes flamed with green fire and he took her in his arms. Their lips joined in a kiss so tender, so gentle, that it might have been an act of mutual worship. He touched his mouth to her ears and hair, then brought it back to hers. Their arms went around each other and they clung for a long moment, lost in the glory of life restored and love found.

"Come." Simon put his arm around Carlotta and led her the few remaining yards of the trail. She drew in her breath at the panorama before them, then lifted her face up to smile at him.

"It is a gift, Simon."

"Aye, love."

Banks of sycamore, spruce, and oak tumbled away in layers

down to the mud flats and willows that gave onto the broad swath of the river men called the Mississippi. The evening was very still with sky the color of smoke and pewter. The sun hung on the edge of the horizon, a rounded red ball about to sink. A lone bird drifted on the soft air and through the faintly pink clouds. The hush of peace was everywhere.

Carlotta stirred in her lover's arms. This blessing had come only after great travail and pain. She could not yet wholly believe or trust it. She said, "Simon, the voodoo ceremonies, the things we both saw, the way Austin died . . . do you think there really is something to all that?"

His silver-gilt hair blew back before an erratic breeze. His mobile mouth softened as he gazed into her amber eyes. "Dear love, Carlotta, we are done with fear. People see as they are meant to see and as they will it. We are taught to think rationally and will yet admit to more than can be seen. So it must be with those who believe in any faith or cult or ideal. In the end, must it not all come down to the goodness of God and belief in ourselves and others?"

"We are done with fear." She repeated his words and felt the fires of her nightmare leave her in the warmth of this love that would now be free to grow.

He looked out at the great river and mused, "When all is quiet in Europe and the President no longer has need of me, would you like to journey to France and Spain and try to trace your parents? It is highly likely that the story the old man in New Orleans told you and that Austin believed is true. It is just unlikely enough."

Carlotta shook her head. "No, Simon. I do not want the falsity of it. Let it be. I want to live here, in this Mississippi land, beside the river there, and raise the children we will have in freedom with you. That is enough."

"That is everything." Simon bent his head to hers and took her in his arms as the sun sank slowly into the Mississippi.